OFFICIAL STATS

NAME: Royal Gaines

VITALS: Age: 38
Height: 6'0"
Eye Color: Green
Hair: Reddish-gold

OCCUPATION: Former cop

OBJECTIVE: To keep Elly Malloy's vengeful ex-husband from killing her.

ADDITIONAL INFO: Royal is a wicked charmer with a need to walk on the wild side. He's always just this side of the law even as he dedicated himself to it. His charisma and intelligence have always made everything come easily for him—until he's thrown into a situation that strips everything away from him he cares about.

DANGEROUS TO LOVE

DANGEROUS TO LOVE USA

LINDSAY LONGFORD
RENEGADE'S REDEMPTION

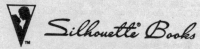

Silhouette® Books

Published by Silhouette Books

America's Publisher of Contemporary Romance

This book is dedicated with admiration and affection to Loyola Hospital's Home and Hospice nurses, especially Rita Veracruz and Sue Budd (and your tree-climbing Copper kitty!). You've become part of our family. Thank you.

SILHOUETTE BOOKS

ISBN 0-373-82307-X

RENEGADE'S REDEMPTION

This edition published by arrangement with Harlequin Books S.A.

® and TM are trademarks of Harlequin Books S.A., used under license. Trademarks indicated with ® are registered in the United States Patent and Trademark Office, the Canadian Trade Marks Office and in other countries.

Visit Silhouette at www.eHarlequin.com

Printed in U.S.A.

LINDSAY LONGFORD

is the award-winning, bestselling author of fifteen romance and romantic suspense novels for Silhouette.

A former high school English teacher with an M.A. in literature, she began writing romance because she wanted to create stories that touched readers' emotions by transporting them to a world where good things happened to good people and happily-ever-after is possible with a little work.

Her books have been nominated several times for the RITA®, RWA's recognition of excellence in the genre, and *Annie and the Wise Men* won for Best Traditional Romance in 1983.

In addition, *Romantic Times* has recognized her books with several Reviewer's Choice Awards and nominations and with nominations for Career Achievement in Series Romance and W.I.S.H. Awards for her heroes.

A native Floridian, she lives now in the Midwest, far from the Gulf Coast of her childhood that she revisits in her stories and shares with readers.

She enjoys hearing from her readers and may be contacted through her Web site:
http://www.ameritech.net/users/lindsaylongford/lindsaylongford.html.

Books by Lindsay Longford

Dear Reader,

I'm so pleased that *Renegade's Redemption* is being made available again. It's a favorite of mine because it has the elements that I love in stories, whether mine or someone else's. It has passion. It has a lush, Florida Gulf Coast setting. It has a loathsome villain out to destroy a vulnerable, single mother on the run, and a hero who can only save her and her child if he can find faith in himself.

And if he can make her trust him.

Royal Gaines is a character from an earlier book, *Sullivan's Miracle*, who demanded his own story. Charming, charismatic, he was a cop who walked a thin line and got away with it.

Until...he lost everything—the woman he loved, his reputation, his career.

I fell in love with Royal in the first book and couldn't bear his despair. How could I let him live forever in his self-imposed prison of self-destruction? Of course I couldn't! I believe in hope, in redemption, in the power of love to change lives. That's why I write romance.

And so Royal got his chance to find forgiveness and love.

I hope you, too, will fall a little in love with this rogue who likes his walk on the wild side—until a woman with courage and heart changes his life.

Lindsay Longford

Please address questions and book requests to:
Silhouette Reader Service
U.S.: 3010 Walden Ave., P.O. Box 1325, Buffalo, NY 14269
Canadian: P.O. Box 609, Fort Erie, Ont. L2A 5X3

Prologue

Tallahassee, December

Staring at the house and the empty driveway, Abby abruptly braked the car. Tires squealed against brick paving stones.

Home.

But not hers, never hers. *His,* always.

Looking at the house in the darkness, she couldn't draw a deep breath.

The engine idled, a low, comforting sound promising escape, freedom. But not yet. She had to do something first. Wet with sudden perspiration, her hands slipped over the steering wheel.

To the side of the brick house, arcing gracefully into heavy night, the driveway curved toward the garage.

"I'm tired, Mommy. I want to go home."

So did she. Abby couldn't look away from the house she'd lived in for ten years. She'd once called this place home, but she didn't have a home. Home meant safety, security. There was no safety for her in that elegant brick mansion.

Clambering half out of his car seat, her son grunted sleepily as he nuzzled her neck. "Want to go in. *Now.*"

"Shh, sugarplum. Just a minute." She curved her palm over the satin-smooth skin of his cheek. "Mommy's thinking."

"Don't think." He rubbed his nose against her ear. "Quit *thinking.* No more *thinking.*"

Abby sighed. He was more right than he could imagine.

"I'm tired and I have to go potty, Mommy. *Now.*"

She was tired, too. "All right, honey." Her eyes fixed on the velvet darkness, she kissed his cheek.

Branches of the oak trees standing sentinel on either side of the driveway stirred in the gusts of wind-driven rain.

Home.

Christmas lights sparkled in iridescent dots along the slope of the roof and outlined the windows where the yellow glow of electric candles gleamed. White lights twinkled thickly in the green-black of the wreath on the heavy front door. Rain dripped from the evergreen branches of the wreath and merged into silvery rivulets down its surface.

"C'mon, Mommy. *Please.*"

Eyes searching the darkness, she reached for the gearshift, hesitated.

Slapping back and forth, the windshield wipers blurred the scene in front of her. Gleaming in the fitful light of the Christmas decorations, the wet streaks shimmered and glittered.

Home.

In a sudden chill, she shivered, and the hair along her arms lifted. One hand on the wheel, she rubbed her arm. Everything looked the same. The automatic timers had switched the lights on.

She was being silly. Stupid. Of course she was. Blake wasn't expecting her. She'd been very careful not to let him find out what she'd discovered. She'd come back for insurance, for the tapes that would keep Blake out of her life, out of Thomas's life, from now on. Blake couldn't possibly know. He couldn't read her mind. He wasn't in there, waiting, like some malevolent spider spinning a web. Blake did not know, she repeated silently, reassuring herself.

But goose bumps tightened again, and she couldn't stop the shivers running over her skin.

"Mommy, I have to *pee*." Chubby fingers plucked at the neckline of her blouse.

"Shh, squirt. Sit down." Still watching the shadows of the trees shift across the driveway, Abby patted his hand, held it.

"I got to go inside. *Now*." He pulled free.

"In a second, sweetie, I promise."

Her four-year-old son draped himself urgently over the console separating them and rose up on his knees to her eye level. Resting his chin on her shoulder, he stuck his face around in front of her, yawned and fixed her with wide, sincere eyes. "I am *not* kidding, *Mommy*. I really am not."

"I know, sweetie. I know. Please, just a minute, and then we'll go in." She lifted her foot off the brake and edged the car forward toward the back of the house and the garage.

"A second is not as long as a minute." He frowned. "You said a *second*." His voice rose with temper and exhaustion. "Why we gotta wait a minute now?"

"Because." She scanned the shrubs growing close to the long, low windows.

He scowled at her. "I don't like *because*."

"I don't either, sweetie-pie." Her heart was pounding, and she didn't know why. She let the car roll slowly toward the end of the house, around and toward the wide loop that faced the garage doors.

"Well, I'm not gonna wait," he insisted, and plopped over to the passenger side, crawling out of the seat belt.

Hooking a finger in the back of his jeans, she held him in place as he turned to stare at her over his shoulder. Sticking out his bottom lip, he glared at her as his voice dipped into mournful. "You are ruining my very nice trip, Mommy. This is *not* a happy day for me *any*more."

"Thomas, sit down! Now!" Her voice rose in a slide of panic.

Arms folded, he sat while fat tears slid down his cheeks. "I am going to have an *accident*, Mommy, and I am way too big. And it is *not* my fault." Like the rain on the front door, tears wobbled, slipped into shiny paths down his face. "Daddy will yell at me." He hiccuped.

"I'm sorry, I'm sorry, sweetie. I'm sorry," she whispered, watching him, watching the darkness gather and press in close to the garage door. Slipping the gearshift into Park, she wrapped one arm around him and pulled him as close as she could, flipping the console back with her free hand as she settled him on her lap. "Daddy's not going to yell at you."

"He will. You know he will."

"I won't let him," she said, fierceness sweeping through her as she brushed back almost-baby-fine hair that stuck up in cowlicks and stubborn clumps.

"You can't stop him." Forlorn, unshakable truth shone in her son's blue eyes. "He will yell."

"No." Abby pressed her chin against the top of Thomas's head. "C'mon, sweetie, you drive." Anger licked through her, chasing away the edgy fear. Thomas stuck a finger inside the bottom loop of the wheel and held on to it as she added, "We'll go inside and you can hop out and use the bathroom off the kitchen. It's close. No problem, honey. No problem whatsoever," she said, and tried to soften the grimness.

"No problem," he echoed, unconvinced.

Then, tomorrow, they would leave and never come back to this house she'd come to loathe.

Thomas's small, sturdy body rested against her breasts as she slipped him beside her and engaged the gears, creeping forward as she tapped the garage-door opener. The doors remained closed. She pressed the black rectangular box again.

Thomas's head was damp with sweat and tears as he lay against her, and Abby was near tears herself, fury and fear mixing in a strong brew that gave her energy after the long drive back to Tallahassee from Naples. She ran her finger along his silky eyebrow. "Shh, sweetie, don't cry, you're not going to have an accident. Mommy will take care of everything. Don't worry," she crooned as the garage door finally rose creakily, lurching up to reveal the dark expanse of the garage.

A wink of the tiny red lights of the sensor that kept the door from crashing down onto anyone who interrupted the beam, and then they glowed again, steadily, familiarly.

But the overhead lights controlled by the remote remained off. She slapped her palm against the door opener again, and the door shuddered a quarter of the way down and stopped, blocking the entrance, but leaving plenty of room for the car. When she tapped the opener again, the door remained in position, some chip in the circuitry having a snit fit. "Damn," she whispered.

"Stupid electronics." With her palm still flat against the opener, Abby glanced down at the top of her son's head, where the brown strands puffed up with her words.

"The garage is dark. I don't like it dark." Thomas shifted closer.

"It's all right, honey. See, the headlights make it bright enough." She didn't like going into the dark garage, either, but she'd learned that turning into a mom seemed to require a certain level of bravado, and these ripples of unease were nothing more than the product of a tired brain and an overactive imagination. What kind of mother was she, anyway, to let her fear become Thomas's? "We'll pretend we're explorers, going into the cave of Rani Mani Spumoni in search of the lost jewels of the empire."

Thomas twisted to look at her. His hand rested on the steering wheel, and his eyebrows were stitched together in puzzlement.

She was talking too much.

She'd leave the car lights on. The battery wouldn't run down in five minutes. She was overreacting. If she didn't have to go into this house one last time, she wouldn't. She was prepared to walk away from everything.

Except what she'd returned for. Insurance.

Steering the car with one hand while she kept the other around Thomas, she drove forward. Against the far wall as she entered, the car's twin beams threw the darker shadows into prominence, increasing her vague sense of uneasiness as the shadows seemed to move and shift closer in spite of the headlights.

Edging the four-door sedan gingerly into the large, every-thing-in-its-place expanse, she disengaged the gears, punched the opener again and bent down to retrieve her purse, leaving the engine running. The heavy machinery of the door rumbled above her.

It happened so fast.

She reached to turn off the engine. Her finger brushed the smooth metal of the steering column as she reached.

Suddenly, the back doors of the car flew open, the car rocked with the weight of two enormous shapes and she shoved Thomas down, down, down, under the wide shelf of the dashboard and forced the gear lever into Reverse, slamming her foot on the accelerator. The transmission shook, whined, as the car careened toward the slowly closing garage doors.

"What the—?" The shape behind her bobbed forward, thrashed backward. His breath was a hot wash of garlic and beer against her as he snarled, "Get her, Markey! The crazy bitch's going to screw up—"

Flailing with one hand at the masked figures, Abby tried to steer the car through the door. Her purse slid off the seat and back under the dashboard, lodging under the brake pedal.

In wide, manic swings, the sedan crashed backward through the garage door, metal runners screeching out of their moorings as the weight of the door pulled them with it, the car roaring free of the garage and toward the oak tree she could see in the rearview mirror. She tried to control the wild whip of the wheel, tried to straighten the car, but she didn't have room, didn't have time, didn't have a chance.

"Damn! Now, Markey! Get her, I said. Damn!"

The car spun left, right, lurched sickeningly as she finally caught one of the spokes of the steering wheel and ducked.

A pop.

Nothing more.

Such a quiet sound.

The rear bumper of the car shrieked on the edge of the tree, slewed sideways, slamming the rear of the car into the raised wall of the patio.

She fell against the wheel, her hand dangling into the space where her son cowered.

There was no pain. She wanted to laugh, but she couldn't summon up the energy. No pain, only this warm trickle of blood into her eyes and this enormous lethargy.

But she had to move.

Thomas needed her.

From a distance, she heard the slow thump of her pulse in her ears.

From a distance, she sensed the movement of the car as the men lumbered out of it.

Close, close as her heartbeat, she heard Thomas's plaintive whimper. "Mommy?" His small fingers closed around her hand, and she clung to him with all her strength. "Mommy? Wake up, Mommy.'' He pulled at her hand. ''Wake up, Mommy, it's not all right.''

Thomas needed her. She had to get to Thomas. Thomas. She could hear her son calling as rain shivered around her, whispered against the expensive metal skin of the car.

''Mommy?''

He was so far away. She tightened her grasp around the tiny tickles against her palm. Hold on, Thomas, she thought she said. Mommy will take care of you. I promise. Hold on.

And then there was only silence and the far-off glitter of Christmas lights twinkling in a vast, empty blackness that swooped down on her.

Chapter 1

Palmaflora, June 30

He'd been watching her for five days. Until today, she'd always been alone. But today, she had the kid with her. That was what he'd been waiting for.

Hell of a job.

Sighing, Royal hoisted the brown-bag-enclosed bottle to his mouth and settled back on the hot sand. Allowing his gaze to drift, he let the burn of cheap whiskey slide down his throat. He could have bought a more expensive brand. He hadn't. He'd wanted the burn, the bite. Pain was real.

Settling the bottle back into the sand against his hip, he looked out across the slick-as-glass Gulf of Mexico. If he squinted, he could see a sailboat far out in the gulf, its sails glowing dark red in the setting sun. His chin itched and he scratched it, flaking sand and salt crystals into his lap. Somberly, he contemplated the sand caked on his wet jeans, the smear of grease down one pants leg.

How the mighty had fallen.

Smudging the grease stain, he glanced back toward the woman. A sliver of long, pale legs and silvery bathing suit gleaming in the sunset, she was moving aimlessly up by the pavilion in the distance, the kid tagging along beside her, darting away. A large, floppy straw hat with its crown wrapped in a purple-and-pink ribbon hid her face. Every now and then, she turned her head casually in the child's direction, keeping him in sight, the frivolous brim sagging and drooping with her movements.

Royal was surprised. He'd expected her to keep the boy glued to her. Her guard was down. No hurry. He had all the time in the world. The idea amused him at some basic, self-mocking level. He could see the humor in what he'd become.

A man with no place to go. No place to be.

Except he'd taken Blake Scanlon's job, so he might as well see it through, not that he gave a good damn either way it turned out. Wasn't his problem. Unless Scanlon decided to take the debt out of his hide. In spite of Armani-suited fastidiousness, Scanlon struck him as a man who'd take his pound of flesh if anyone cheated him.

Royal smiled. Maybe he'd just set a spell longer and watch the moon come up. Maybe go for a swim. Swim out as far as he could into the moonlight, past the sandbar and out to the mythic World War II submarine supposedly submerged offshore. To hell with the sharks. To hell with Scanlon and the three hundred thousand dollars he owed him. What could Scanlon do? Kill him?

Did he care anymore?

Apparently, Scanlon thought he cared. For three hundred thousand dollars, Scanlon thought he'd bought an expensive recovery agent. Well, shoot, why not? Three hundred thousand dollars was a lot of money to most people. Royal watched the woman and child in their slow movements through the aisles between the tables at the pavilion. That much money could make a man do almost anything. If he cared.

So, did he care? That, as the melancholy Dane had implied about life in general, was the question.

From the corner of his eye, he could see the kid's head vanish around a corner, the child following the silvery shape of his mother.

Tipping the bottle to his mouth again, Royal swiped the back of his hand across his lips, tasting sand and the coppery tang of blood. He probed the cut on the inside of his mouth with his tongue. "Damn!" He winced. The corner of his bottom lip was still swollen.

Gingerly, Royal touched the surface, where the skin at least remained intact. Pete, the old reprobate barkeep at Surf's End, had called the cops on him last night. The cops. There was a lovely bit of irony. And if Royal had had a moment of shame when one of his ex-buddies answered the call—well, what difference did that make, either?

He'd smiled and laughed as they'd hustled him out and driven him home, waving to them as they strode stiff backed to the squad car. "Thanks, boys. So glad to see you're ever ready to serve and protect. Sure would hate to see my tax dollars wasted."

"Shut up, Royal." Beau Bienvenue had placed one square palm flat against Royal's back and hustled him down the path, not speaking until they stood at the bottom of the stairs in front of Royal's house. There, dark eyes glittering with anger and disappointment, Beau glared at him and muttered through clenched teeth, "You gotta quit screwing up, man."

"Really?" Royal leaned against the wooden railing of the steps. "Nope, don't think so. No point to it, Beau. That's what *you* gotta understand. Screwing up's become my modus operandi." He felt his mouth stretch into a smile, the muscles aching with the effort, his lip stinging. "And I'm *so* good at what I do."

"This is stupid, man. It's a waste. I don't understand what in God's name is going on with you, but it's a damned shame." Beau slapped his hat against his leg. "Hell, Royal, I hate—"

"Ah, but *I* don't. And that, after all, is the whole point. *I* don't care." Giving his most brilliant smile, Royal turned and walked steadily up the stairs.

"You're not drunk, are you?" Beau's soft question was puzzled, a slide of sound in the still night broken only by the low throb of the squad car's engine. "You fooled me. I thought you were staggering-blind drunk."

"Not yet." Not turning around as he heard Sandor rev the

engine, Royal added, "But, Beau, the night's still young, and I'm a determined man. Hope springs eternal."

"Go to hell, then. See if I care." Beau stomped back down the steps, his back rigid with indignation.

With that, Royal swiveled on his booted heel to face the young cop who'd been his partner for a while, who'd idolized him until scandal had exploded in Palmaflora's police department, trapping Royal in the debris of rumor and fact. "Don't care, Beau. I don't. It's easier, not caring. Don't waste your time caring about me. Go make Palmaflora safe, Beau."

Beau looked over his shoulder. "Somebody's got to, Royal."

"But not me." Royal smiled gently. "Not me."

"Yeah. Guess not. But you were the best damned cop I ever saw, Royal, and that's God's own truth." Beau's smooth, dark face was sad, innocence lost. "I'll have one of the guys get your bike back to you. Take care, Royal. Not that you will." His voice was glum, his expression invisible in the darkness. "Call me. Any time." He stared at Royal for a long time. "But you won't, will you?"

Royal didn't answer. What, after all, could he say? Of course he wouldn't call Beau. Beau's reputation didn't need the burden of friendship with a disgraced former cop.

As soon as the red taillights disappeared into the moony darkness, Royal had climbed stone sober into his restored '68 Mustang and roared straight out at ninety miles an hour down the deserted old beach road, letting the wind and engine roar numb him.

He didn't have the nerve to wrap the car around a tree. Too easy an out. Besides, the way he was, as Beau had so bluntly put it, "screwing up," he might spend the rest of his life in a coma.

But he thought about it for that brief instant as the speedometer hovered toward one hundred.

An oncoming van came waddling out of the blackness. Royal blinked and lifted his foot off the accelerator as a skinny kid watched solemnly from a side window, his face pale and ghostly in the headlights before it vanished into the darkness.

Slowing down to forty-five, Royal kept the needle resolutely between forty-five and fifty, five miles under the speed limit as he headed back toward his house.

Now, sprawled on the gritty sand, thirsty, and with the remnants of last night's headache thumping inside his brain, he fingered the brown bag, tearing the opening into strips as he let his gaze drift in the direction of his quarry in her gauzy dress.

She'd changed out of her conservative, cover-everything-up silver suit that made her look like nothing so much as a small minnow flicking through the crowd, but he'd spotted her the minute she'd left the changing area. That hat made her easy to track.

She wasn't his type, but he'd liked the look of her in that smooth, sleek suit, the barely there curves shaping it as she'd strolled leisurely through the late afternoon with her son, the silver winking and drawing his attention to the swell of hip and fanny under the shiny fabric.

He took a deep breath.

Last night's brawl had probably been a mistake, but if a man couldn't satisfy a hankering for a little set-to in the midnight hours, hell, what was the world coming to, anyway?

Chugging another bitter swallow, he stared at the chop of the outgoing tide. He knew what his world had come to, all right.

The emptiness he'd danced with all his life, feared, had finally swallowed him up, leaving him on this hot beach watching some runaway wife while away the hours with her son. Royal wished he cared, but he couldn't find it in him to give a damn.

He'd skated too close to the edge too long, and now he was, as the cracker-barrel philosophers would say, "gettin' his comeuppance."

He was, after all, exactly what they expected him to be. Royal Gaines. Fast man on a fast track to nowhere.

Tipping the bottle once more, he frowned and shook it upside down. Empty. Hell. He checked out the woman, the flash of her loose dress catching his attention. Even from a distance, he could see the slightness of her small form. No, definitely not the kind of woman who appealed to him. He liked independent women. Strong women who could hold their own. Women who didn't need him, who wouldn't depend on him. Not fragile blossoms who couldn't thrive outside the greenhouse.

This fragile blossom was still near the pavilion and its parking area, the kid nowhere in sight. She was moving more quickly, stopping briefly to speak with passersby, who shook their heads.

And for three hundred thousand dollars, he was going to sell her out to her husband.

Crossing his legs at the ankle, Royal scowled into the sun and looked away from her. Damn, but he didn't want to be here. And he didn't want to go home. As for calling up his old buddy, his old partner, his former fiancée, Maggie Webster, well, she'd be happy to see him, but Sullivan wouldn't be.

Thinking about Sullivan Barnett's reaction if Royal dropped in, Royal almost laughed again. Might be worth it, just to see Barnett stiffen up and get that steely edge in his voice. Maggie and Sullivan.

Maggie and her bristly, wary Sullivan. Married. Cop and reporter.

Only Maggie wasn't a cop anymore.

She wasn't his partner. Not in any sense, not in any way.

Married, was his Maggie, that's what she was.

The Malloy woman he'd been tagging had moved to the far side of the pavilion, her hands moving in agitation. Royal shaded his eyes irritably.

At least Maggie hadn't asked him to give her away.

But he'd gone to the wedding. Oh, he'd had that much courage. He'd smiled pleasantly, courteously, at everyone whose glance skittered toward him and away, smiled until he wanted to slug someone.

Beautiful, luminous, her whole body curving toward the man with bleak, blue eyes, Maggie hadn't seen anyone in the church except Sullivan, the man who'd taken her away from Royal.

But Maggie had never been his for the keeping, not really, not since she'd died and come back to life. The Maggie he'd known, the woman he'd loved, had vanished after being shot in a convenience-store holdup. That Maggie was gone forever, almost as if someone else had come to live in that sturdy, sweet body he'd loved. She'd turned into a stranger, her warm eyes filled with secrets and confusion and a dark knowledge he didn't understand.

Elly Malloy's purple-and-pink dress floated like sunset as she headed onto the blinding white sand of the beach area, alone. Moving quickly across the sand in her brilliant colors, she reminded him of a hummingbird.

Maggie had always made him think of grass and earth, not fragile things of the air.

On the afternoon of her wedding, watching her as sunlight had spilled all around her in the old, shabby church, Royal could see that for Sullivan and Maggie there was no one else in the world, nothing else except the power of their feelings for each other as she lifted her face for Sullivan's brief, hard kiss, her eyes filled with Sullivan before they drifted shut.

In that sun-bright moment, Royal had been struck by the odd sense that Maggie and Sullivan were two halves of the same self, that the two of them had been places, seen things no one else had. Their world was each other. No, Maggie had never been his. She'd always been Sullivan's, and Sullivan? Well, he'd always been hers.

After the wedding as Maggie had walked back down the aisle, she'd seen Royal and drawn him toward her in a quick hug. He'd kissed her, teasing her in front of Sullivan. "Don't know what you see in this guy. A journalist, for heaven's sake, Maggie. Damn, I thought you had better taste."

Sullivan hadn't said anything. But he'd given Royal one of his back-off looks and stood there, his arm tight around Maggie's waist, a cold heat in his bright blue eyes.

Laughing, Maggie hadn't really seen Royal. Her whole attention was on the man beside her, and that was the day the emptiness finally flowed completely into Royal, settling deep and endless inside him, a sickness of the soul.

That night after Maggie's wedding, he'd gone to a notorious two-day, high-stakes poker game upstate. For two whole days, he couldn't lose. No matter how wildly he bet, he won. On the last hand, he'd held a pair of threes and gone for broke. When Scanlon had covered and raised, Royal grinned and, recklessly, knowing full well what he was doing, he covered with everything he owned.

Which, even at the time, he'd known wasn't all that much, not after he'd paid the legal fees for the lawyers who'd manfully striven to keep him out of jail. And after he'd paid them off, he'd plunged into heavy-duty poker playing.

Like they said, the devil made work for idle hands.

And his had been plenty idle.

He'd wound up in Scanlon's debt.

Three hundred thousand dollars. A lot of money, if you cared about anything. And because Royal had scraped up the money to salvage the Mustang and the old house, Scanlon was fool enough to think Royal did.

A seagull's shriek jerked Royal back toward the shore where a flock of gulls strutted and scolded before wheeling off. Watching their effortless soaring against the glowing horizon, Royal brushed his mouth again. Sand dry. God, he wanted a drink. Restlessly, he dug the heels of his boots into the sand.

In all the crowd of beachcombers, the small, dark dot way down at the end of the sugary stretch of white beach focused his attention.

If he'd had a hair more energy and a hair less hangover, he might have sat up. Instead, he shaded his eyes against the red glare and watched the dot shape itself into a kid, head down, trudging along the line of sand and water, heading toward the swoop of the island where the beach suddenly ran out, yielding to the slash of gulf and riptides.

Fumbling his sunglasses out of his shirt pocket, Royal wiped them desultorily with his shirttail. Sand and salt smeared, they weren't worth a hoot, but they shielded his stinging eyes from the still-bright sun.

Stooping, the kid picked up a shell or rock and tossed it from hand to hand awkwardly and then, like Royal, spotted the sailboat. He dropped the shell and waved, leaping up and down, chunky legs pumping as hard as they could.

Royal watched gloomily as the small figure waded ankle deep into the water. "Hell and damnation. The brat thinks he can walk on water."

Drawing his heels toward his butt, Royal rested his throbbing head on his knees.

Maybe the kid could swim.

The kid couldn't.

Slopping against him, waves swallowed up ankles, knees and droopy butt, splashed into the kid's face.

"Shoot." Reluctantly, Royal worked himself into a standing position, every bone in his body screaming. He didn't want to go within ten feet of this kid. Ambling down to the edge of the sand, he saw the top of the kid's head drop under the water, bob, disappear.

"Son of a bitch." Keeping his eyes on the kid, who fearlessly waved his arms underwater, moving ahead, Royal sighed and surrendered to the inevitable. Boots and all, he slogged through the water until, waist deep, he stooped and snagged the squirt under the arms, fishing him out.

Current and tide pulled against Royal's calves, his chest, tugged at his captive. With his dripping catch under one arm, Royal staggered back to shore, boot heels sinking into sand, jeans soggy with water.

"I wasn't drowning." Water streamed from the round, jug-eared face grinning happily up at him from under lank, dripping hair.

"Sure fooled me." Eyes narrowed behind sunglasses, Royal contemplated the unrepentant face turned up to him. "What were you doing, tiger?"

"I'm not a tiger, mister." The brat wiggled impatiently under Royal's arm. "I'm—Tommy Lee. And I wanted to go visit the boat." He waved his arm backward toward the gulf as Royal strolled back to dry sand.

"Underwater?"

"Diving. See?" Tommy Lee pulled up the water-filled mask dangling around his neck. "I can scuba real good and see 'zactly where I'm going. I was *not* drowning. And I was *not* lost."

"Huh." Extending his arm and its dripping burden, Royal examined the kid as he burped up saltwater. "You okay, Jacques?"

"Of course. But I'm Tommy Lee, *not* Zack." Tommy Lee wrinkled his face. "And I knowed what I was doing, mister." Arms and feet pumping, Tommy Lee swung in front of him. "See how good I swim?" Inquisitive eyes peered up at him. "So, what you doing, mister?"

"Fishing?"

"Where's your pole?"

"Where's your mom? Or dad?" Royal countered with what he thought was respectable cleverness. Under the circumstances.

Examining him from under brown eyebrows, Tommy Lee paused for a moment before answering carefully, "Over there." His arm waved north, south, east and west.

"You're a real big help, kid, I'll give you that." Scanning back toward the main beach area with its pavilion and refreshment areas, Royal waited hopefully for the kid's irate mother to appear magically, thus solving several problems.

Nothing. He'd lost sight of her when he'd snatched her son from the briny deep. "Uh, tiger, think you could narrow it down for me?"

The boy's sturdy body hummed with energy as he twisted and turned to see Royal. "Mommy went into the bathroom to change clothes. I was s'posed to wait by the counter and the mirror." The brat's eyes widened, and he clapped a hand over his down-turned mouth. "Oops."

"'Oops' isn't the half of it, kid." Royal sighed and tucked the soggy burden more tightly against him. He should have let the kid drown. Would have been simpler all around. With his wiggly catch tight in his grasp and imprisoned next to him, Royal sauntered toward the pavilion area. He wasn't about to turn the little hellion loose. Who knew where he would turn up next? Head down, Royal kicked a clump of dried seaweed in front of him as Tommy Lee squirmed against him. "Be still, kid."

"Thom—Tommy Lee!"

Slamming into Royal, a whirlwind of flowers under an enormous sun hat surrounded him with a scent of lemon and verbena, an old-fashioned fragrance that stirred memories within him as hands and feet and hat flailed at him.

"Turn my son loose!" Long, narrow hands plucked at Tommy Lee, who paddled happily in the air between Royal and the column of flowers.

"Hey, wait a minute, ma'am," he drawled, stepping back and breathing in her fragrance. Warmed by her skin, a lingering hint of sunscreen lotion drifted to him. Pineapple and coconut underneath the lemon. He inhaled that perfume of skin and sun, losing track of the moment in the rich warmth of her scent.

"Mommy, I dived!" Swinging back and forth, Tommy Lee chortled and waved at the flowers and sun hat. "Till this mean man stopped me." Tommy Lee kicked out, his sandy foot banging against Royal's crotch.

"Damn, kid! I told you to hold still!" Doubled over, Royal took a deep breath and straightened.

"Turn him loose, I said!"

Royal lurched to one side as the whirlwind pummeled his

chest and feet, sandals slapping against his boots. "Ouch!" Holding the brat out to one side, Royal caught the thrashing fists of Tommy Lee's mom. "Look, ma'am, slow down. Hold on a minute, will you?"

"Turn my son loose. Now. Let me go, too. Or I swear to God I'll make you sorry." From the shadows of the hat, soft brown eyes met his fiercely. The glint of a thin white scar showed at the edge of her forehead and disappeared into the shade of the hat and the cloud of brown hair curling onto her face.

"Believe me, I'm already sorry, ma'am. Your kid's a handful. You ought to keep a closer eye on him." He frowned at her, and the woman's face went utterly still. "Look." Royal studied her as he added, "He was two feet underwater when I found him."

"What?" Her face went sickly white, not a fragile, appealing paleness, but a green white, terrified white. She sagged, all the fury draining from her as she clung to her child's foot. "Tommy Lee? You went into the water?"

"Um…" Dangling from Royal's arm, Tommy Lee cast her a wide-eyed, limpid blue glance. "I wasn't drowning, Mommy. I *told* him I wanted to see the boat. I had to scuba to get there. Of course I was underwater." Indignant, he wiggled and glared at Royal. "I was *supposed* to be underwater."

The woman groaned, slid her arm under Royal's and pulled her child toward her. Gratefully, Royal released the terror. Despite the early-summer heat, her arm where it brushed his was cool, shock icing its softness.

"Thank you," she said, her eyes shifting away from his. "I thought—"

"I know what you thought." Royal took off his sunglasses, tucking them back into his pocket as he raked one hand through his sand-crusted hair.

"Not likely," she muttered, backing away from him and dragging Tommy Lee with her. Her floppy hat drooped down to her narrow shoulders, her shapeless, flowered sundress ended around her ankles and annoyance and leftover terror sparkled in her pansy brown eyes.

Stepping forward, Royal almost tripped over his brown bag.

Stooping to pick it up, he saw her gaze fasten on the bottle as the pulpy bag crumpled in his hand.

"And you're drunk—"

The brim of the straw hat flipped up, flopped back into place as she raised her cat face toward him with its narrow, pointed chin. With her movement, the neckline of the dress slid onto her shoulder, and Royal could see the tiny, delicate ridge of her collarbone.

"But not disorderly," he corrected mildly, watching the sunset dust her hothouse-pale skin with gold before he glanced back into her eyes.

There was a shadow deep in those brown eyes, an emotion that nudged what remained of his old self and prompted questions, but he ignored the impulse and smiled in the sheer enjoyment of the moment, a pleasure he hadn't felt in a long, long time flooding him. "Actually, I'm not drunk. Mellow, but definitely not snockered."

"I don't see the difference." She frowned. "But it's not my business."

"No, ma'am, it's not your business." He pitched his trash into the large metal drum nearby. "Not your business at all." Hearing the harshness in his response, he shrugged. "Not that I mean to be rude."

"You're right." Echoing his earlier thoughts, she added with chilly politeness, "It's not my concern." Like a recalcitrant puppy dog, her silent but wriggling son tugged at the end of her arm, moving her this way and that, purple and pink flowers on the thin fabric twisting and shaping to the curve of a rounded hip, the softness of breasts and small bumps of her nipples.

Royal felt his grin widen and lift the corners of his mouth as the loose, sheer fabric flowed and tightened like the stroke of a lover's mouth over the pale skin underneath.

Blinded by the power of his smile, Abigail Eleanor Malloy blinked and stepped back. Lifting the brim of the hat clear of her face, she stared at Tommy's savior.

His sandy, scarred snakeskin boots were rooted into the powdery sand, and his faded shirt hung open. Copper-tipped golden hair funneled to the small crescent of a navel, where a water-stained brown belt threaded through loops of sun-faded Levi's saved him from indecent exposure. All that sun- and hair-gilded skin blinded her, caught her unaware as fear and adrenaline mingled with a sudden heat, stabbing her with a longing to touch that golden triangle, to remember something besides terror, a longing that left her edgy and irritable.

She took a careful, raspy breath and stepped away.

His deep green eyes watched her carefully, observing her even as he grinned. There was intelligence and cleverness lurking in those sea green eyes. She suspected the gleaming humor. Intelligence she could handle. Tinged with darkness, his humor unnerved her. And that blaze of a smile was wild, reckless. Too cocky by half.

Never taking her eyes off his, she retreated slowly, watching him every moment as his smile widened and those green eyes cataloged her.

This was a very, very dangerous man.

With the sun blazing in his dark golden red hair and tipping his bristled cheeks and square chin with gold, he looked like a dissipated, fallen angel, an angel with wickedness bred in the bone.

A wickedness that called to her, tempted her. A wickedness that left her dry mouthed with a hunger she'd never known. This seductive heat spinning through her blood sang inside her veins, sang an old, old song and stunned her, leaving her unable to look away from his green, knowing eyes.

Backing up, her sandals clogging with sand, she muttered, "Thank you very much, Mr., uh—"

"Royal Gaines." He moved too fast, stepping forward more quickly than she'd believed he could in his state. His long fingers closed around her hand, stopping her. "And who are you, lady with the wonderful hat?"

Tugging, she stepped back and regarded him briefly. His unkempt state should have made him unappealing. It didn't.

Bristly, rumpled, his green eyes glinting with amusement and satisfaction, he made her think of unmade beds and crumpled sheets.

"Yes?" he encouraged.

She swallowed. "I'm a woman who doesn't give her name to strangers."

"Smart." His fingers stayed around her wrist as he stepped forward, the tips of his boots sending sand spurting up between them. "But I'm the man who just saved your kid from a one-way trip to Cuba." He tightened his grip. "Or wherever the tides would have carried him."

Her throat closed up, and she glared at him, not able to speak.

"They would have, you know." His voice was a soft wash of cream along her nerves, soothing and settling. As he turned his back to the water and the setting sun and followed her retreating steps, his long shadow fell over her, chilling her as he said, "The gulf is deceptive."

"People are, too," she said, grabbing the back of Tommy Lee's drooping swimsuit. "Let go, Mr. Gaines."

"No 'thank you'?" He released her and stepped forward, the toes of his boots nudging her sandals.

Taunting, teasing, his green eyes watched her, and, freed, she felt more captive than ever.

Deliberately, he tapped her bare toe. "For services rendered?"

The scrape of boot against her skin sent shivers down her spine even in the sultry heat. "I already said thank-you. But I appreciate your help. Believe me, I do," she said, wanting to spin away and run, yet afraid to turn deer to the hunter she glimpsed behind the smile. This was a man whose interest she didn't want to stir. "I have to go."

"You're welcome, Tommy Lee's mom." He stepped beside her, keeping an easy stride with her short, quick walk. He paused and then, his voice rippling over her nerve endings, he added, "How did you lose track of your baby SEAL?"

She took a shallow breath and made herself slow down as they neared a group of shell seekers, their heads down, their gazes fixed on the shining sand. "I didn't lose track. He slipped away before I could catch up with him." She'd warned Tommy Lee before about wandering off. She'd have to sit him down and impress the need for staying close again. She'd grown careless after all these quiet months. She tightened her mouth. Disaster had brushed by her on fluttering wings. She shuddered. "Only a minute," she murmured, angry with herself. "Sixty seconds."

"He's fast," the green-eyed stranger agreed, and touched her elbow, guiding her around a pile of seaweed clogged with glass shards worn smooth by tide and sand. Stooping, his palm cupping her elbow, the man, Royal Gaines, plucked the glass free of the seaweed and handed the pieces to Tommy Lee. "Here, tiger. A souvenir of your first dive."

Tommy Lee's hand swooped out, and she swung him away. "No, Tommy." The sparkling green bits fell to the white sand.

"It's only glass. Not candy." With a quick move, Gaines gathered the glass bits and stuffed them into his shirt pocket.

She sensed that he was mocking her fears, playing games with her, yet she couldn't think fast enough to erase the gleam from eyes as green as the glass with which he tempted her son.

"I'm not going to kidnap him, you know." His face had turned still, watchful.

"I don't know that. I don't know you. You could be anybody. You're a stranger." Her feet were skittering over the sand like tiny crabs as she neared the pavilion.

"I'm not a parent, but I can imagine what that would be like. Waking up and finding your child gone. A vicious trick. Brutal. Might make a person desperate, ready to do anything, I'd reckon."

Once again, that odd note in his voice sent shivers over her, as if there were a subtext to his question, a meaning she couldn't understand, didn't want to understand. "Yes." She lifted her palm to the top of her hat, anchoring it in an errant breeze. "The cruelest hand fate can deal. Unbearable, I think."

"But it happens, doesn't it?" Sibilant, blending with the sigh of the withdrawing tide, his voice whispered around her, disturbing her once again.

"Yes. But still, I don't think I could bear it. It would destroy me." The words slipped out, and as his glance sharpened on her with a quick interest, increasing her misgivings, she swallowed. She didn't want this man's attention, not in any sense, and especially not sharpened by curiosity. The urge to bolt was so strong that, nerves twanging, she stammered her thanks. Gathering her manners around her like armor and lifting her chin, she added politely, "I'm in your debt, Mr. Gaines."

"I'll remember," he replied, his drawl as polite as hers, its ironic tone unnerving. He studied her for a moment as if he were undecided about something before he said, "Look, I just happened to be at the right place at the right time." He looked down at the sand, drew a circle with the toe of his boot. "Anyone would have done the same."

"Of course." She walked quickly toward the pavilion, Royal Gaines trailing close behind.

As they neared the outdoor-shower pole, Tommy Lee tugged at her hand. "I'm thirsty, Mommy." Tommy Lee pulled at her hand again and let himself drop to the sand, bending her forward. "I want a drink."

Distracted, she stooped to confront the insistent face of her stubborn, damned-if-he'd-give-an-inch son. "All right, Tommy." She shoved the sagging brim of her hat back from her face. She knew when a battle was unwinnable. "We'll get a lemonade."

As she lifted Tommy and spun away, taking a deep, relieved breath, feeling as though she'd narrowly escaped...*something,* Royal Gaines's hard palm clasped her shoulder, stopping her. "I'm sorry. I'm scaring you, aren't I?"

"Of course not." Lying, she stretched her mouth in a smile as he turned her to face him.

"Of course I am. And I *am* sorry," he said, almost as if to himself. "Terrifying women and little children. Hell." Dropping his hands, he shoved them into the back pockets of his sun-faded jeans. He shifted uncomfortably, his boot heels sinking with his weight into sand wet from the shower runoff as she leaned away and Tommy Lee slid down her leg, landing in a heap at her feet.

Releasing her, Royal Gaines made it difficult for her to walk away. Fumbling for words, she frowned, curiously reluctant to hurt him. "You saved my son. I'm grateful to you. But it's late. Tommy's tired. I'm tired. I'm in a hurry. And you—" she surveyed the grubby length of him "—you must have your own plans, too."

"Nope." He shook his head, and the fading sunset lingered, trapped in its dark gold red strands. "Not a single, solitary plan, truth to tell." He looked out over the gulf to the dying flash of red sun. "Nothing."

"I'm sorry." She shrugged. She didn't necessarily believe him. Royal Gaines seemed to say one thing and mean another. He was a man whose easygoing manner was deceptive. Like the gulf with its hidden depths and bright, clear surface, Royal Gaines could drown the unwary. But the unexpected melancholy on his lean profile made her hesitate. If he'd joked, turned the

moment into flirtation, she would never have hesitated. But she
did. Even knowing better, she lingered that crucial second and
reached out to him, the loneliness she sensed in him echoing her
own.

But at the last instant, as her hand fluttered over his arm, she
let hers drop to her side. Twisting her fingers in the light cotton
of her dress, she repeated, "I don't know what to say."

"I get ice cream at my preschool, mister," Tommy Lee volunteered, bouncing into her side and grabbing her hand. "And
cookies." He pulled his legs up and swung from her arm, his
solid weight forcing her to hold on with both hands. "Sunshine
Center Preschool."

Royal watched the woman's face tighten as she went very,
very still. Her mouth thinned, the soft plum turning white as she
looked down at her son. Her reaction seemed more frightened
than guilty, but he ignored it, seizing the opening her son had
offered.

"Yeah?" Hunkering in front of Tommy, Royal nodded. "I'll
bet you know my friend Alicia, then, don't you?"

Tommy nodded. "Yep. And Miz Maggie and Lala and lots
of people," he summed up with a last, lunging swing from his
mother's arm.

"Oh?"

"Tommy, come on. We have to go." Desperation skimmed
over the woman's words as she hoisted her wriggling child into
her slender arms and settled him on her hip, the sundress riding
up with Tommy Lee's movements. A length of pale thigh shone
in the dusk.

"Tell you what, Tommy's mom. Next time you take this water boy to the center, check with Alicia or Maggie. They know
me. They'll tell you I'm harmless."

"Maybe," she said, throwing him a quick glance over her
shoulder as she hurried toward the lights and crowd. "Maybe."

Later that night, phone receiver in hand, tumbler of bourbon
in front of him, Royal thought once more about the wary, fragile
woman calling herself Elly Malloy. He scratched his chin with
the receiver and smoothed out the scrap of paper with Scanlon's
phone number.

That quicksilver woman hiding under the sun hat wasn't what
he'd expected. She wasn't the woman Scanlon had described.

Spoiled? Selfish? Not Elly Malloy. Royal scowled at the amber brown of the bourbon as he took a long swallow. Every cop instinct remaining in him supported that reading of her character. A runaway? Possibly.

And Scanlon wanted her back. To the tune of three hundred thousand dollars. Her and the kid. Interesting. That much money could make a person suspicious.

Hell of a lot of money.

He punched out the first digit.

A man might do anything for three hundred thousand dollars. If he cared.

Chapter 2

Downstairs, a floorboard creaked.

"What?" Elly frowned and stared uneasily at the empty hall-way. In the middle of squirting glass cleaner onto the shower doors of the empty rental unit, she paused. Cleaning liquid dripped onto the shower floor, down her wrist and arm as she listened.

But she didn't call out.

She *listened,* every nerve in her body straining toward that faint sound she'd heard. A trick of wind? A cat landing on the deck outside? A foot shifting on the uncarpeted floor?

Stale, hot air and the sound of quiet plops of cleaning fluid landing on the shower floor. Sweat pooled against the waistband of her shorts.

Nothing.

She walked to the smoky glass window of the bathroom and stood to one side, checking the street below. Heat shimmered and danced along the concrete sidewalks, radiated from the asphalt street surface. Parked in the driveway of the unit, her beater was the only car on the block.

The rapid tattoo of her heart left her breathless, waiting. Waiting for *something*.

Ever since the encounter at the beach three days earlier with Royal Gaines, she'd had the feeling she was being watched. Her nerves jumping like grease in a skillet, she flinched at any chance movement.

She hadn't seen him again, but she hadn't been able to get him out of her mind, either. Even in that frantic moment, she'd recognized the man's aura of wildness, the dangerous sexuality that shimmered like heat waves around him.

Later, annoyed, she'd decided that it was the reckless, don't-give-a-damn glitter in his brilliant green eyes that had drawn her.

Or maybe not.

He was so damned *physical*.

He made her feel anxious and itchy, and she'd wanted to step right up to him and see if his skin burned as hot as his glittering eyes.

Stunned, she'd stepped back, frightened by the other danger he represented. The danger to her and Thomas. *Tommy*.

Fretfully, she rubbed the scar along her forehead as she stared at the empty street. She'd been careless. She'd relaxed into the lazy rhythms of Palmaflora's small-town friendliness. She'd messed up.

But how? Royal Gaines had saved her son. Appearance aside, the man hadn't threatened her. He *couldn't* know anything about her. He was a man who'd fortunately been on the scene when Tommy needed someone. Nothing else was involved. She was foolish, seeing plots and conspiracies in ordinary events. Sometimes, a cigar was a cigar, and not a symbol.

But—

Royal Gaines was an enigma. One way or another, he was a threat to her.

She pressed her face to the edge of the glass and forced herself to breathe slowly, slowly.

If she didn't get herself under control, Tommy would start having night terrors again. One finger lingering on the thin white line that disappeared into her bangs, she waited a moment longer, enveloped by the heavy heat of an empty house.

She heard only the normal sounds of a house settling, the creaks and sighs of a closed-up house.

She was alone.

A line of perspiration dripped down her spine, settled into her waistband. Lifting her blouse, she dried the sweat and, shaking, covered her damp face with the tail end of her blouse. That creaking floorboard had terrified her more than she'd realized.

Returning to her job, she squirted purple cleaner on the glass again, hurriedly scraping at a stubborn soap deposit before wiping paper towels over both sides of the shower doors. "C'mon, c'mon," she muttered to the spot of soap scum. "No big deal. Keep moving. Don't let your imagination take over. It's broad daylight, for pete's sake." She scraped the soap spot with her thumbnail. "Stupid spot."

She *hated* working the vacant rental houses. In occupied homes, whether the owner was there or not, she didn't feel quite so—vulnerable. But the rental units paid more, and she needed every nickel she could find.

Cleaning houses was honest work, it paid well and she didn't have to answer many questions. Show up. Do the work. Take the money.

Elly prided herself on giving value for the dollar. Like now, with this confounded spot she couldn't walk away from. She groaned with relief and stood up, giving a final swipe to the frosted glass as the clot finally floated down the drain.

"Five more minutes. C'mon, Elly, *move*." Her voice was intrusive in the silence, but she needed *sound*. She squirted a mixture of lemon juice, peroxide and cola against the rust around the faucet handle and scrubbed. "Good enough. Almost done," she encouraged herself. "Then, out of here. Pick up Tommy. Home. Iced tea." Squatting down beside the toilet, she sprayed disinfectant and wiped, her movements jerky and rushed.

Throwing her cleaning supplies into the compartmentalized tote, she surveyed the bland, furnished rooms as she quick-stepped through the hall. "Hallelujah. Another day. Another dollar." Running her finger over the hall table, she checked for dust. "Okay, Mrs. Doone, you get your rent money this week." The upright vac was in the car, she'd completed everything on the cleaning list and she was out of here. She'd done a good job. She'd be paid.

Hurriedly pulling the front door behind her, she saw the clump of drying dirt on the walkway by the door first. Washed by the afternoon downpour, the walkway had been clean when she'd started work. In the flowerpot, the brown stub of a cigarette poked up from the gray-white dirt.

Once upon a time, in a better world, she wouldn't have noticed that brown stub.

Now, though, she noticed.

The tote trembled in Elly's hand as she stood there, her other hand on the door, and then, not even thinking, she slammed the door shut and ran for her car, her fingers scrambling in her shorts pocket for keys that kept slipping through her frantic fingers. Running, eyes darting left, right, she couldn't hear anything except the pounding of blood in her ears. Holding the bucket of cleaning supplies like a shield, like a weapon in front of her, she finally jabbed the key into the lock and opened the car door, collapsing inside as bottles of disinfectant and cans of furniture polish tumbled around her feet.

Locked inside the oven of her car, she sorted out the supplies with shaking hands and started the engine, backing carefully out the driveway as she scrutinized the road in front and in back of her. "Okay. Okay. Get a grip, Elly," she muttered in a monotone. "All right. Imagination didn't leave that dirt. It's real. Someone was there. Watching." She shuddered.

Knowing she was inside but not ringing the doorbell, someone had watched her. "All right. You have a problem, but slow down. Don't rush into anything until you're sure. One step at a time. *Think,* Elly," she admonished as she slammed on the brakes before she barreled through a red light. "You need to think this through. Could have been a potential renter. Anybody."

How could she pack Tommy up and move again? Was no place safe for them? Would no place, *ever,* be safe again for her and her son? She needed a safe place. She needed a way out of this unending nightmare. Where else could she run? "Oh, God, please, please." A tiny sob escaped her, but then she clamped her lips together, shoving the fear down deep. She drove carefully through the intersection.

She'd do what she had to. She always had.

By the time she pulled into the curving driveway of the Sunshine Center Preschool and turned off the engine, she'd regained her composure. She'd quit talking to herself. She had a plan. She wasn't unprepared this time.

Scanning the shrieking crowd of kids at the front entrance, she wasn't all that surprised to see the rangy silhouette of Royal Gaines leaning against the wall near the door. It had been that kind of afternoon, and he'd said he knew Alicia and Maggie. Swearing under her breath, Elly climbed out of the car and yanked at the edges of her shorts, vainly trying to cover as much of herself as she could. Plopping her sun hat on her head, she headed grimly for the porch. Around a man like Royal Gaines, she thought glumly, she needed all the armor she could scrounge up.

Opening the gate of the cyclone fence, she caught the flicker of his tiny, satisfied smile when he turned his head toward her.

As if he were waiting for her.

Was he waiting?

Was he the person who'd stood out on the front walk, strolled around the condo to the wooden deck in back?

Elly rubbed her forehead. She was crossing the line between caution and paranoia. She had to remember her plan. One step at a time. She repeated her mantra silently as Royal Gaines stared at her. She and Tommy would be okay as long as she didn't panic.

Tommy barreled into her. "MommyMommyMommy! Bye!" Giving her a lemon-scented smack, he spun away from her hug and bolted back toward the porch, leaving Elly's empty arms outstretched toward him. She yearned for the feel of his hot, baby-damp self against her.

His earthy boy-scent remained in her nostrils, the richest perfume in the world. Tommy was happy. Tommy was safe.

She'd done something right.

Alicia's sculpted dark head swung in Elly's direction. "Hey there, Ms. Malloy. Royal's making mischief. Otherwise, the kids would be lined up and ready to go. Sorry."

"Not my fault, Ms. Malloy, ma'am. Don't blame me." Royal's low drawl was teasing. He tapped Alicia's arm with one long finger. "You need to get better organized, Leesha, that's all."

"Ignore him, Ms. Malloy."

"Right, Ms. Malloy." Repeating her name, Royal Gaines's voice dropped a notch, the teasing taking on a darker note. "Ignore me."

"Certainly." Elly threw him a cool, blind glance and gave all her attention to Alicia, the co-owner of the Sunshine Center.

Removing her hat, Elly fanned herself with its brim. "I don't mind waiting, Ms. Williams. Actually, I'm a little early."

"Oh?" Alicia squinted at her oversize wristwatch. "That's unusual."

"The job went faster than I expected."

"Lucky you," murmured Royal. "Lady of leisure."

"Be quiet, Royal. Pretend you're invisible," Alicia said.

His laugh was rough. "Too much truth in that idea, Leesha."

Alicia stared at him for a second before turning to Elly. "Do you want to take Tommy right now? It would only take a second to pack up his stuff if you'd like."

"Please don't worry about me. Tommy would be disappointed if he missed the afternoon story. He looks forward to it."

"Anyway, we'll hurry, Ms. Malloy." Alicia shook her head, the tight, asymmetrical wedge of her haircut a sleek helmet to her elegant presence. Like Royal Gaines, she had an inborn elegance that translated into movement and presence and owed nothing to clothes. "That's to say, we'll speed up as much as we can, kids being notoriously resistant to being rushed."

Instead of wailing in frustrated exhaustion and fear, Elly leaned against the rail running horizontally along the porch. She wanted to go home. She didn't want to run the gauntlet of Alicia's and Royal's scrutiny. She *craved* the illusion of safety behind her locked door, but she didn't need Alicia picking up any hint of desperation. Tipping back her head, Elly fanned her neck, making herself the picture of relaxation. "As I said, I don't mind waiting. I've been rushing all day. This is pleasant. A breeze. Relatively cool." She waved her hand vaguely. "Relaxing."

Royal's expression was bland as he studied her. She pivoted

slightly, giving him a view of nothing but her profile. He wasn't her problem right now. Alicia was.

Alicia had to believe in the image of working mother with an abusive husband somewhere in the background, and Alicia intimidated her because Alicia was a woman who had her stuff together. Bright, quick, she'd been born having her stuff together. Struggling just to get through each day without a new disaster, Elly couldn't help believing Alicia had judged her early on and found her a failure.

Breaking into her thoughts, Alicia said, "It might be half an hour. Sure you can wait?"

"Absolutely. You're saving me from two weeks' worth of laundry, in fact." It was awkward being around somebody she had to lie to all the time. Especially when the other person knew she was lying, yet kept her questions and thoughts to herself. Hard to develop much of a social circle when you were a liar and a thief. "If I'm lucky, I can avoid that stack for another week." She managed a chuckle and hoped it was more light-hearted than it sounded to her own ears.

"Know what you mean." Alicia grimaced. "Myself, I'm thinking seriously about pitching a mile-high pile of clothes in the trash and buying a couple of weeks' worth of underwear instead. Think I could get away with that?"

Elly nodded politely. "Why not?" Sometimes she thought wearily that, maybe in different circumstances, maybe without all this deception, she and Alicia could have been friends. She could use a friend.

Pulling a red-and-yellow wooden box on wheels out from under a shelf, Alicia rolled her eyes apologetically. "It's too bad we're running late. I know you want to get Tommy Lee home."

"An early supper would have been a change."

"Hey, doodlebugs." Calling to the children on the slides and swings in the side yard, Alicia slapped her hands together and rolled the box toward the children on the porch. "Let's put the equipment away so we can be ready for our story and treat."

Elly was uneasily conscious of Royal Gaines and his motionless stance, his focus on her whether she looked at him or not. He didn't seem like a man with children of his own. He didn't seem like a man who would go out of his way to help at a day-care center with no motive except the goodness of his heart. He struck her as a man who always had a reason for anything he did. Was it possible that this man, Alicia's friend, had stood outside the rental unit without letting her know of his presence?

Of course he could have.

Anything was possible. She'd learned that. She didn't need a remedial course in what people could do when the masks were off.

She took a half step to bring him more clearly into view. When she did, he shifted, the flex of his thigh a smooth ripple under the light gray fabric of his slacks. She cleared her throat and concentrated on Alicia. Headed for the side yard a few feet away, Alicia was intent on rounding up the five or six stragglers. "You don't have to hurry the kids on my account, Ms. Williams. I can stand a few minutes to catch my breath. Do what you have to do. Don't rush them."

"Terrific. I'll have one of the kids bring you a cold drink." Alicia's bright turquoise skirt whipped around her long legs as she turned and lifted a tiny girl toward her, swinging her up in an arc and giving her a hug. "Katie Sue, why don't you run in and bring Ms. Malloy a glass of tea, sugarplum?" Setting the child down, Alicia aimed her for the porch and followed at a slightly more sedate pace.

"'Kay, Leesha." The screen door slammed behind Katie Sue.

Elly wanted to ignore the man lingering patiently among the children, but she was aware of him, aware of his indolent ease and the muscled length of his legs. Aware, too, of her son now slumped casually, familiarly, against the man's side as Alicia continued to speak to her.

"It's been a while since we've talked, Ms. Malloy. You must be relieved Tommy Lee's dye job finally grew out, huh?" Alicia laughed and turned toward Royal Gaines, who hadn't moved, his form a silent, pervasive presence. "Little stinker got into a bottle of hair bleach just before he and Elly moved here."

He hadn't. Elly had lied.

"Oh?" His expression hidden by the flicker of sun and shadows, Royal Gaines tipped his chin in Elly's direction. "What happened?"

"Typical kid story." She regarded him cautiously. Too much detail was bad. Too little made people overly curious. She had to remember, too, what she'd already told Alicia.

The truth was, that to change their appearance after one move, she'd dyed Tommy's hair and her own. He'd been a redhead when they arrived in Palmaflora; she a muddy brunette who'd looked as if she'd been wrung out wet and hung up to dry. And she'd felt worse. She laughed ruefully, maintaining the pretense. "He figured out how to open the locked cabinet. Tommy Lee tends to be—curious."

"I see." Again, as at the beach, his words seemed loaded with portent, with hidden meanings. "I can see him as a redhead. Kind of fits his personality." Royal thumped Tommy Lee lightly on the head, giving him a modified "noogie." "You a curious kind of guy, Tommy Lee?"

"Yep." Impossible, but Tommy Lee edged even closer, his brown head tipping up toward the man who towered above him.

"Ms. Malloy, forgive me for not introducing him sooner, but this scoundrel is Royal Gaines. Royal, Elly—"

"We've met," Elly said, nodding stiffly and avoiding the outstretched hand she glimpsed from the side of her eyes.

"Could even say we're almost old friends."

"Mr. Gaines saved Tommy Lee from a nasty dunking at the beach a few days ago." Elly gripped her shoulder purse.

"Was not nasty."

"Could have been," Royal said with an easy jab against Tommy Lee's back. "You need someone to teach you how to scuba for real. Divers buddy up, you know. You can't go off on your own. You'll scare your mama to death."

Avoiding his gaze, Elly scrutinized the wooden floor. His words were meant for her, not Tommy, and she couldn't tell if they were a warning or a threat. The man was as straightforward as a hairpin mountain road.

"Ms. Malloy, if you want to roam around while we're having our story and snack, feel free. Or join us. Whatever." Alicia waved a slim palm in the direction of the cool interior. "Usually, you're in and out of here so fast."

"Work. You know." Uncomfortable, knowing Royal and Alicia were both watching her far too carefully, Elly nodded tensely.

Alicia swooped down on a boy who'd decided to pry up the screen of the porch. "Sure do."

"Not me," Royal drawled.

"And whose fault is that?" Alicia rounded on him as she handed the boy a sponge ball and directed him away from the door. "Don't expect sympathy from me."

"Didn't ask for any, Leesha."

"True." Alicia scowled at him, and Elly felt the chill of her disapproval even though it was directed at the golden-haired man opposite them. "You're a fool, Royal. That's what I know. And what I'll tell you, as your friend, even though you didn't ask for my opinion."

"Nope, sure didn't. Not asking for it now, either, gorgeous."

With a murmur for adult ears only, Alicia added with an embarrassed lift of one sleek black eyebrow, "Royal's a smart-ass sometimes."

"Really? I'm flattered." His shrug was a flick of movement in the corner of Elly's eye. Leaning forward, his voice as low as Alicia's but with an edge that Elly didn't understand, he said, "And here I thought I was just a dumb fool."

"Hush up, Royal. I'm talking to Tommy Lee's mama. You be good, hear?"

"But being good takes so much effort. And it's so much more fun being bad. You should try it, Leesha."

Elly swallowed. She knew what kind of *bad* he was talking about. And this time, he wasn't talking to Alicia. Once more, Elly knew his words were meant for her. That bourbon-rough drawl was a feather running teasingly over her skin, up close and very personal, and she wasn't in any shape to deal with him today. If ever. He was too complicated, too overwhelming.

"Unlike you, buster, some of us don't have time to be bad." Alicia frowned again at Royal. Picking at a sandspur clinging to her skirt, she addressed Elly. "Truly, I am sorry we're so far behind schedule. It's my fault for not sitting on Royal and keeping him to the straight and narrow."

"Ah, Leesha, don't leave yourself wide open for a comeback." The twitch of Royal's mouth was wickedly mischievous.

Elly blinked. So much devilry in the flash of his eyes from Alicia to her. She blinked again, processing the scene. For that's what it was, she decided slowly. A scene. With Royal Gaines as director, writer and actor. And who was the audience? Elly took a deep, steadying breath, finally understanding. She was.

But that left a bigger question. Why? What was Royal Gaines after?

Opening cautiously, the screen door poked Alicia's hip. Katie Sue poked her head around the door shyly and stuck out a plastic tumbler. "Here."

Alicia took the sweating glass and handed it to Elly. "I think it's lemonade. That okay?"

"Sure." Elly sipped gratefully. "Thanks, Ms. Williams, Katie."

"You're welcome, and Lala says time for cookies. Or else she's goin' to throw them in the garbage. And she said she will, no foolin', so get your patooties in right now." The little girl gave Tommy Lee a limpid peek. "And Lala said you kin lead the line today, Tommy Lee, 'cause you wiped down the counter for her. Even if you did bust open four eggs on purpose."

Elly winced.

"Wanted to see the guts," Tommy said reasonably.

Alicia snickered, and Royal shifted, his polished loafers catching Elly's full attention.

The fallen angel of her memory was nothing like this cleaned-up, spit-shined man standing off to her side.

This was Lucifer on a mission, Lucifer focused and intent and frighteningly powerful. Beautiful in his arrogance and power. A man to take a woman's soul away and leave her spinning, drifting in darkness. In that moment, meeting Royal Gaines's bright green gaze, she was dizzy, the world shrinking suddenly to that narrow space between them, that space that filled with heat and tension and made her bones soften and melt.

From a distance, she heard Alicia. "C'mon, guys." Riding over the noise, Alicia's voice carried authority. "Line up. Right, Tommy Lee. If Lala said you're first, that's the way it is."

And then, breaking the link, releasing her and leaving her limp, drained, Royal spoke to her son. "Go ahead, tiger. I'll wait until you're ready to go. I'll visit with your mom."

Hearing that, Elly almost snatched Tommy Lee out of the line and hustled him home. Instead, she watched her son square his shoulders, step away from Royal and march importantly to the front of the straggly line, throwing a comment over his shoulder to Royal. "Lala likes having me help her. I am *very* helpful, she says."

"Yeah, I'll bet." Royal's face was expressionless. "I can imagine."

Elly could, too. She knew her son.

Led by Tommy and followed by Alicia, the last of the cookie line trailed through the screen door. Her son's voice echoed from the far reaches of the house. Tommy was happier at the Sunshine Center than he'd been in months. How could she uproot him again? How could she not?

"So." Royal folded his arms across his chest.

"Yes. So." Elly couldn't put the contradictory images of him together. His shirt was expensively gorgeous. His shoes cost three hundred dollars a pair at least if she didn't miss her guess. And she didn't think she'd be off by much. She recognized expensive clothes. After all, she'd bought enough of them over the past ten years to know, and Royal Gaines was wearing very expensive clothing.

The scruffy man from the beach didn't mesh with this man with his slicked-back hair and clean-shaved chin. A strong chin, determined. Even with the stubble of his beard, she'd noticed that stubborn jut. If this man ever set a course for himself, she didn't think anything could detour him.

Wishing Tommy would hurry up, she fiddled with the clasp of her purse. "Come here often?"

"Used to. Usually once a week. Alicia talked some of us into reading to the kids, talking with them. Organizing a ragtag soccer team. You see, Alicia is very big on the importance of role models and community input." He straightened from his leaning position, his broad shoulders blocking her view. "But I haven't been here for a few months."

Brushing back her hair, Elly let her hand skim the thin scar, her constant reminder of what was at stake if she let down her guard.

As she caught Royal's gaze following her movement, she let her hand drop to her side, her bangs fluffing over her forehead and sticking to her skin in the humidity.

"Headache, Ms. Malloy? Heat getting to you even here on the porch?" He took her hat and wafted it over her face.

Nothing but courteous concern in his low drawl, but tension shot down Elly's spine, and she wanted to jerk back from him.

She didn't. Instead, she fixed him with a level stare. "Not at all. Why would you think that?"

"Florida summers can be a problem if you're not used to them." Stirring the air, he passed the brim of the hat over her, closer to her arm, her cheek.

"I'm used to them."

"Oh? You're a native, then, or a longtime resident?" Again he moved the air against her, the stiff straw of the brim grazing her neck.

"No." She snatched her hat from his grasp and slapped it on her head irritably, not allowing her gaze to shift from his, even when he stuffed his hands into the pockets of his slacks and the soft fabric tightened across his flat stomach.

"Friends in the area? That why you moved to beautiful Palmaflora, Ms. Malloy?" The intensity in his eyes belied his casual stance, the yawn he barely suppressed.

"No." Elly maintained her steady gaze and didn't elaborate. Friends were a luxury she couldn't afford. Tommy's safety and hers depended on keeping people at a distance. Less chance of a slip. Less possibility of mixing up the lies and half-truths. They'd be safer if she didn't make friends. Going on the attack, she returned a question of her own. "You're very inquisitive, Mr. Gaines, aren't you?"

"I like puzzles." He smiled, a swift, predatory gleam, and she knew she'd made a mistake when he slid in, swift as a fencing thrust. "You interest me, Ms. Malloy. Not easy to do these days, so, yes, I reckon I'm—inquisitive about you. Like Tommy, I'm a curious man."

Alicia stuck her head around the door and suddenly added, "Nosy's what Royal is, Ms. Malloy. He can't help it. Comes with the territory."

"Oh?"

Royal's hand lifted abruptly, the quick gesture saying *Stop* as clearly as if he'd spoken, but Alicia paid him no attention. "Royal's a detective."

"What?" Blood drained in a rush from Elly's brain. Shivers iced the heat flushing over her skin as she managed to whisper, "A policeman?" She felt as if she'd stepped off an out-of-control carousel and everything was whirling under her feet. She gripped the porch railing with all her strength.

"Was." The quiet, one-word hiss raised the hairs along Elly's arms.

"Yes. *Was.*" Alicia whacked her hand against the screen door. "And it doesn't have to be this way. I'm so angry with you, I could spit nails, you know."

For a second or two, Alicia's comment made no sense to Elly, but then, taking a dizzyingly deep breath, Elly understood that she was safe. Whoever he was, whatever he was, Royal Gaines was no longer a policeman.

Alicia's fingers clenched into the mesh of the screen door as she glowered at Royal. "I mean it. I'm furious with you. Beau, though, he's merely confused. And disillusioned because he believed the sun rose and set in your footprints. And he's hurt. A lot of that going around, Royal. You have to understand that I hold you responsible. Every day, I wake up mad all over again, and I don't like it."

"You'll survive, Leesha. And I will, too. One way or another."

"Will you, Royal? That seems to be the question these days. You're paving the road to hell at a mighty fast pace, my friend. And all your intentions are bad."

Royal cleared his throat. "Are we friends, Leesha? Still?"

Elly started, caught by the sound of buried pain in his voice. "I'm not sure."

"Well, I asked, didn't I?"

Her face grave, Alicia nodded. "You did. And I answered you honestly. I'm sorry, Royal, but that's how I feel right now. I can't help it."

"I can't blame you. I don't." He paused, hesitated, and Elly wondered if he were through, but then he tacked on in a tone so low she almost missed it, "If you don't want me to come around here anymore, I won't. It's your decision. Your call."

Watching the creases deepen in Royal's lean cheeks as he waited for Alicia's answer, Elly wondered what that comment had cost him. She didn't know him, didn't trust him, didn't want to feel anything about him, but the glimpse of some hidden pain tugged at her.

Shutting the screen door slowly, Alicia nodded once, brusquely. "Let's talk about this another time, Royal. I have to think."

"Up to you, Leesha." His face was blank.

With a quick change of mood, Alicia turned to Elly. "Little rehashing of old history, Ms. Malloy. You're probably familiar with the situation."

Elly wasn't, but she couldn't speak as she saw Royal's quick flinch. "No, but that's all right," she finally said, turning her wrist so that she could see the face of her watch.

Alicia twisted the handle of the screen door. "Tommy'll be right out. Sullivan's finishing up the story, and then they'll collect their drawings and notes to take home." The turquoise of her skirt blended into the dim interior as she left.

"So." Royal crossed his arms and surveyed Elly's bare legs, the button missing at the top of her shirt. "Interesting uniform."

"Serviceable." Elly took another long drink of the tepid lemonade and rolled the plastic against the side of her neck. With his leisurely survey, Royal had sent a dry heat leaping under her skin. Before he could ask another question, she did. "Police department? You were a policeman?" It took all the strength she had to keep her tone nonchalant. She took another sip of lemonade, tipping her head back and holding on to her hat as she did.

"Detective." Deep grooves appeared along the side of his mouth. "But not anymore." His reckless, brilliant smile stopped short of his eyes. "Now, I'm an overpaid beach bum."

"You get paid?"

"Nope." He plucked a tissue from a stand near the boxes of equipment. "Here. You're dripping."

"Oh." Elly would have slapped his hand away if he'd touched her. He didn't. Clearly, he was a smart man.

Taking the tissue, she dabbed at the darker streaks of pink on her blouse.

"Sure you don't want a helping hand?"

He was teasing, flirting, but he was too self-possessed, too focused, and she recognized that flare of male interest that deepened the green of his eyes.

She couldn't think of what to say to him. There were so many layers of meaning in his comments that he left her off balance, unsure of the rules of whatever game he was playing, and now this current running hot and stinging between them confused her even more. She took a sideways step to the left, another to the right, buying time. "Do you have children here?"

Bare, tanned fingers slipped under the brim of her hat, waggled in front of her startled eyes, skimmed past her nose. "Nope. Never been married, either, if that was your next question." He reached out and snagged her left hand, turning it over, palm up, in his.

"It wasn't." She wanted to hide the calluses and rough skin, but he kept her hand loosely in his even as she tugged against his hold. He was deliberately making her aware of him as a man, and she didn't like it, not at all, because she sensed the purpose and calculation behind his every touch, every comment.

"How about you? Married? Divorced?" His thumb grazed her ring finger, lingered, his touch light, light, but her toes curled with each careless brush of his thumb.

"No." She jerked her hand back, wrapping her fingers in the strap of her purse for safekeeping. His touch disturbed her, distracted her, made her want too much.

"All of the above? None of the above?" He was laughing at her. Not a muscle twitched in his face, but amusement radiated from every line of his body.

"Divorced. A long time ago. Not that it's any of *your* business." Lifting her chin, she threw his words back at him.

He stepped back, giving her room where there'd been room before. His leisurely perusal of her face was enigmatic. "Might be. You never know."

In another man, the comment would have been flirtatious, the first step in that complicated dance of man and woman, of sex, a dance that had always left her moving to the wrong beat. "I don't think we'll be running into each other very much, Mr. Gaines. My marital status isn't significant. You rescued Tommy, and I can't possibly repay you for that. But—" she paused, watching him steadily, seeing the tightening of the lines around his green eyes as she finished, "—that doesn't give you entry into my life. Or into Tommy's."

"Clear enough, Elly Malloy." His gaze was as steady as hers. "But I'm already in your life. Whether you like it or not, I'm here."

The frown that drew her feathery brows together told Royal she didn't like it one damned bit, but he'd been truthful with her. Whether through his actions, her own or Scanlon's, Royal didn't know, but all the threads had drawn together and knotted in the slight figure of Elly Malloy, who made him more curious than he'd been in a very long time, the curiosity swirling slowly, treacherously, through the emptiness.

Chapter 3

Waiting placidly on the old porch in the intimate heat of the summer afternoon, Royal studied Elly Malloy as she considered what he'd said. She didn't frown, pout or grimace as she stared at him, but a subtle shift of muscles pulled the corners of her narrow upper lip. Her sun hat vibrated, a fine, barely perceptible motion.

And the long muscle of her thigh trembled.

She might think she had a poker face, but her emotions moved across the triangle of her face like clouds drifting across a pale sky. Her posture betrayed her.

Ms. Malloy didn't like being pushed. She wanted him as far away from her as she could shove him.

The not-so-fragile blossom was expending a lot of energy trying to hide her feelings.

And yet there was the slight dilation of her pupils when he stepped close, the shallow breaths. She was aware of him.

Whether she liked it or wanted it, her femininity responded to him.

Royal found that the most intriguing fact of all.

"So, Elly Malloy, do you believe fate brought us together, then?"

"I doubt fate was responsible." The swoop of her upper lip thinned even more with cynicism and with what Royal recognized as strain.

"Really?" Idly, he let his gaze follow the shine of perspiration down her neck, down the gleam of soft skin that disappeared into the scoop of her neckline.

"Oh, yes. Really," she said mockingly, smiling all the time. "You're far too—purposeful a man, I think, to be at the whim of fate."

"Maybe you're right." Dewy with heat, her skin had the luster of creamy satin, a glow that captured his attention even when he willed it in another direction. "Maybe I planned to meet you here."

"It's possible." She stared steadily at him, not giving an inch. "I wouldn't be surprised to learn you'd planned this meeting."

"Suspicious lady."

"It's the nineties, Mr. Gaines. The decade doesn't promote easy trust. You're curious. I'm suspicious."

"That's a shame. Seems kind of—unfriendly."

"Does it?" Her breasts lifted the soft fabric of her blouse as she took a deep breath, exhaled slowly. "If so, that's not my problem, is it?"

"Maybe not." Mesmerized by the subtle shift of pink and softness, Royal found his breathing synchronizing itself to hers. Deliberately, he altered his own rhythm, breaking the spell. Heat coiled in his groin as her breathing hitched, followed his.

Powerful, that spiraling heat. Powerful enough to make a man wish he'd done a lot of things differently.

He shook his head, clearing it of that tantalizing hunger, and intensified his effort to find answers to the puzzle of Elly Malloy and her free-with-the-bucks husband. A husband who seemed mighty eager to find her. Excessively so, Royal thought, studying Scanlon's wife. Not that Elly Malloy wasn't worth every nickel Scanlon was offering—

Ruthlessly, Royal ignored the sly nudgings of his subconscious.

He wondered when she'd snap. No matter how hard he worked to provoke an unwary response from her, she managed to control her reactions. Most people, even when they had something to hide, weren't that careful. In spite of the tension vibrating from her, Elly Malloy was very, very careful. "Still, I can't help wondering why you're so suspicious, Ms. Malloy." Angling his shoulder toward her, he blocked her view of the interior of the center.

"I don't like surprises," she said after a long pause.

"I see." He laid his hand against the rough texture of the wall. A splinter gouged his open palm, and he tweezed it out with his thumb and index finger, never letting his gaze move from her. He slipped the splinter into his shirt pocket, adding pensively, "Life's an interesting gamble. If you're open to possibilities. And not too suspicious."

Restlessly, she turned toward the door, peered in past him. "I have responsibilities and no time for possibilities. And very little time for word games. Being suspicious suits me." Her smile was bitter. "If I come across as unfriendly, I can live with that."

"Can you?" He wanted to fold back the brim of her hat and see her face clearly, but he kept his hands safely in the pockets of his slacks. "Everybody needs a friend." The words struck him bleakly. He'd managed to frighten away most of his.

Smoothing her face free of expression, she leaned against the wall, sighing from under the safety of that damned hat brim. "Bluntly, Mr. Gaines, I have a difficult time believing you do much of anything without a purpose. I suspect that you're not here by chance. If you are, fine. If not, that's okay, too, because although I don't have a clue how I fit into your agenda, I have an agenda of my own." Straightening, she plunked her hands on the slight flare of her hips. "You're not on it. And I never gamble."

"No?" He liked Elly Malloy in her aggressive mode. It gave him a glimpse of what she might be with all the walls down, with all the questions answered. "That's pretty direct. Can't misinterpret that message."

She nodded, her hat brim flipping emphatically. "Good."

She walked quickly to the far end of the porch, stooping slightly to peer into the floor-length windows lining the main room of the center. As she bent, twisted, the back of her shorts rode up. Tender, vulnerable, that pale sliver of skin made his breath hitch in his chest.

"We understand each other, then. We'll just pretend that your appearance here was accidental."

"If you say so." He'd known exactly when Elly Malloy was expected.

"Okay. Good. Okay. That's settled." She stood up and, catching his gaze, yanked at her shorts, her gestures uncoordinated and flustered. "Your being here was only coincidence."

"Works for me." Not even hesitating, he'd used his friendship with Alicia. She'd told him about Tommy Lee and his mother. Because of friendship.

Because of old ties.

And so Royal had made sure he would be waiting on the porch when Elly Malloy arrived.

Royal wondered if Alicia would forgive him. Not so long ago, he wouldn't have abused their friendship. Regret knotted his stomach. Her disapproval hurt him more than he could have imagined. And he'd caught the flash of pity on the blossom's face as she listened to Alicia scold him. Pity. Skepticism, distrust.

Well, hell, he couldn't expect anything else. He thought he'd moved beyond caring, but he cared what Alicia thought of him, and, amazingly, he found himself disturbed by Elly Malloy's pity.

"Mr. Gaines—" Regarding him from a distance, the blossom tilted her head. She'd apparently been thinking while she watched the children inside.

"Royal."

"Mr. Gaines," she repeated determinedly, the effort to remain polite evident in her stiff posture, "you seem like a nice man, but—"

"Think so?" A laugh escaped him. Damned if she wasn't doing her best to retreat into social niceties. He was amused. "That's the first time anyone's ever called me 'nice,' I think, in my entire life. I'm honored."

"Don't be. That wasn't my intention." She paced the length of the porch, moving skittishly, her pale legs flashing in the shadows of the porch.

Their smooth curves were a delight to the eyes, the senses, and Royal wanted to run the palm of his hand over her calves, touch the liquid silk of her skin for himself and lose himself in the pleasure of touch.

"I'm not trying to compliment you," she said through

clenched lips, skidding to a stop in front of him as he stepped toward her.

"No? I'm crushed," he said innocently, goading her on purpose. Irritation, after all, was preferable to pity. And if he could scrape away at that careful reserve of hers, he might find out what was really underneath Elly Malloy's caution. "Flattery is the second-best way to a man's heart. If you're interested," he added, pushing harder.

"Not in the least." She glared at him, the splash of color on her neck and cheeks revealing the temper held tightly in rein.

Royal was disappointed. He'd gone fishing and come up with an empty stringer. He hadn't learned diddly. He had, though, found out a lot about Scanlon's runaway wife.

Under the surface of this cautious woman was another woman, a woman of fire and passion with a recklessness to match his own. That was the woman who intrigued him. "Well, you're not interested in winning my heart, you're not trying to flatter me. So what are you trying to do, Ms. Malloy?"

"I'm trying to tell you, Mr. Gaines, as clearly as I can, that I'm not—in the market." Pacing back and forth, she bumped into a child-size stool, tipping it over.

Righting the stool before she could, Royal faced her, crowding her a little on purpose as he asked, "In the market for what? Shoot, sugar, far as I know, I'm not selling anything."

"Aren't you?" Cat face tilted to him, she regarded him wryly, her eyes steady on his. "To the contrary, Mr. Gaines. You're selling *something*. I just haven't figured out what it is."

"A careful shopper, then, are you?"

"I like to know the price of what I'm buying, yes." Exasperation pleated the creamy skin of her forehead, and she threw up her hands. "For heaven's sake—"

"You're not subject to the lure of the forbidden? The impulse purchase?" Pleased that he'd finally gotten under her skin, he needled her again. "Never been tempted, Ms. Malloy?"

"I know what I can afford. More important, I know what's beyond my price. I stay away from things I can't afford, even when they tempt me." She settled her hat firmly on her head, sending tendrils of that fine, cloudy brown hair winging every which way. "And I'm beginning to suspect that you're a man,

Mr. Gaines, who knows the price of everything and the value of nothing.''

''Wise woman.'' He nudged the stool between them. ''But I said you were smart, didn't I? The other day at the beach?''

She nodded grumpily, displeasure in every line of her slight frame.

''So, since you brought it up, tell me, what's my price? Am I a man who can be bought?'' Skating too close, gambling, he was genuinely curious as to her reading of him, interested in what she'd say.

Under the faded rose of her cotton shirt, her breasts rose quickly with her breathing, a tremble of softness beneath the pink. ''Mr. Gaines,'' she said in a deadly calm voice, ''I'm not even going to hazard a guess as to what you mean. You've been playing games with me since the minute I met you, and I don't pretend to know the rules. I don't like you, I don't trust you and I'm telling you now, back off.''

''And if I don't?'' he asked, yielding to a little temptation of his own and touching the damp spot right above her heart. Underneath his finger, her skin was warm, smooth. In that tiny, vulnerable space where her skin met his, where they were joined, her heartbeat pulsed into him, leaving him aching and melancholy. ''What then?'' he whispered. ''What if I don't—back off?'' Touching her, standing so close he could inhale the scent of her breath, he hurt with the need to taste the long swoop of her upper lip.

And despising himself for what he was doing, he still stayed in that space where her breath and scent surrounded him with a promise of something he'd never known.

Red rising fiercely up her neck, she slapped his hand away, a stinging, quick reaction. Under the brim of her hat, her eyes were wide with fear and anger.

With a quick twist of his wrist, Royal extended his hand toward her. A glossy red ladybug crawled along his thumb. Placing the bug carefully along the railing of the porch, he said, '''Ladybug, ladybug, fly away home.''' Glancing at her from under lowered brows as the bug scuttled down the railing, Royal smiled gently. ''Tsk, tsk, Ms. Malloy. *Such* a suspicious nature you have. I was merely being…helpful.''

''Were you?''

"Of course. What else could I have been doing?"

For a long moment, her eyes met his. "You're an extremely clever man, Mr. Gaines," she said finally. Her hand shook as she rubbed her forehead. "And I don't mean that as a compliment, either."

"I didn't think you did," he murmured as the door crashed open in back of him.

Head jerking toward the sound, she jumped.

He'd finally provoked her. He wondered what she would have said next if Tommy Lee hadn't come blasting out the door, Katie Sue trailing dreamily on his heels.

Sticking her thumb in her mouth, Katie gave Elly a solemn look. "Tommy Lee invited me for supper. I like pizza. If you have some."

Stepping back, Royal became a watcher as Elly's shoulders slumped. Then, lifting her son into her arms and holding him close, she spoke to the girl. "Katie, I like pizza, too. You can't come tonight, but I'll talk to your mom. We'll plan our supper. We'll make it a party one night soon. Is that all right? A party?"

Katie's face collapsed into dismay, the pink bow of her mouth turning upside down. "When is 'soon'?"

"Mommy! Now!" Tommy Lee tugged at a wispy curl of Elly's hair. "Katie's my friend. She likes me." Putting his milk-stained lips close to her ear, he whispered woefully, "Nobody else likes me. Just Katie. *Please?*"

Elly dipped her head, and the brim of her hat fell against her cheek, veiling her expression as she pressed her forehead to her son's. "Not tonight, Thomas. You have to check with me first. You know that, honey. I'm sorry."

Like a far-off train whistle, loneliness and exhaustion echoed in her hushed words, stunning Royal with the sudden, unfamiliar need to offer Elly Malloy comfort.

He frowned.

He was the last person Elly Malloy could expect comfort from. Or maybe not, he thought, remembering Blake Scanlon's expression as he'd said pleasantly, affably, his eyes cold as death, "I want my wife back, Detective Gaines. Find her. *Soon*, you hear?"

Unlike Tommy and Katie, Royal was beginning to find the idea of "soon" decidedly unpleasant. He had a mind to let Scanlon wait a little longer, just for that tight-lipped smirk when Scanlon had added "soon."

And maybe for his own reasons, Royal admitted bleakly to himself as he watched sunshine melt over Elly Malloy's face. Highlighting the hollows in her cheeks and shadowy circles under her eyes, the light filtering through her hat turned her mysterious and painfully vulnerable.

Then, even as he started to say something to her, anything to keep her there a minute longer, she left in a blur of pale pink and smooth legs.

He admired the composure that let her sing out a cheerful farewell to Alicia and walk right by him without so much as a word. If he'd been paper, he would have burst into flame with the heat of her anger as she walked away from him, the scent of her a faint richness in the summer afternoon.

Surrounded by shrieking kids imitating a swarm of grasshoppers, Royal didn't think he'd ever felt so alone in his life.

He wondered if she'd guessed that he'd palmed the ladybug from the wall behind her. She was smart enough to consider the idea.

Lifting his still-tingling fingers to his face, he inhaled the lingering fragrance of lemon and Elly Malloy.

No, he wasn't in any hurry to turn her over to Blake Scanlon.

Strolling up behind him with toys thrown into the basket of her skirt, Alicia poked his arm and dumped the blocks and plastic cars into a box. "What's on your mind, Royal?"

"Not much." Weariness swamped him.

One hand still clutching the loop of her skirt, Alicia said slowly, "She's a nice lady, Royal. Every time you looked at her, I thought you were going to have her for dinner. Don't go messing with her."

"Thanks for your concern, Leesha." He pushed away from the wall. "I'll keep it in mind."

Dropping her skirt, she closed her hand over his, holding on to him, her grip firm. "Do that. For the sake of whatever might remain of our friendship."

"You knew I was trying to find out about her?" Of course she had. If he hadn't been spending the past months in a haze, he would have realized Alicia wouldn't have told him anything unless she had a good reason, friendship be damned.

"Even without a shield, you're still a damned good detective. I figured something about Elly Malloy was itching you. Actually, I was pleased to see you interested in something other than a bottle and the four walls of that place you found. I didn't see any harm in letting you know she'd be here to pick up Tommy. In fact, I thought you might be able to help her. I think she needs help, but after seeing how you had to roll up your tongue every time she got within three feet of you, I think I made a mistake. I'm serious about Elly, Royal." She raised one slim, dark hand and gripped his chin, forcing him to face her. "Something's very wrong in her life. You better not make it worse, or so help me, I'll sic Beau on you and I'll be right behind."

"Why did you think I could help? Doesn't she have friends? People around her?"

"She makes a point of keeping folks at arm's length." Alicia's grip tightened. "Tommy was a terror when he started at the center, but he's calmed down considerably. I think he was one frightened child there for a while."

"Yeah?"

"Yeah," she mimicked. "And I think Elly's frightened, too, no matter what she pretends. Especially this last week." Considering him for a minute, she added reflectively, "Elly could probably use a friend, even if you're not the first one I'd choose." She closed his hand in both of hers. "I'm going to tell you something else about her. Something I probably shouldn't, but I'm hoping there's a little left in you of the man I used to be proud to call friend. I don't know."

Royal lowered his head. His eyes stung.

"I didn't hear everything that happened to you, Royal, but for all your wildness, you were the best cop I'd ever met."

"Until Beau," he said through the lump in his throat, holding on to her hands too tightly.

"Well, Beau, sure," Alicia said with a cheeky grin. "Beau's different. He's going to be my man. He just hasn't figured that out yet."

"But he will." Royal wanted to smile and couldn't make the muscles of his face obey.

"Of course." Smugness sparkled in Alicia's caramel eyes. "He's a smart man. He'll catch on."

"But, Leesha?" He squeezed her hands.

"Yes?"

"I can't— Don't count on—" He cleared his throat and couldn't go on. He couldn't let Leesha count on him as Elly Malloy's knight on a white horse. Leesha didn't know. "You shouldn't expect— I can't," he wound down, exhausted by the struggle to put his failure into words.

"Fool." She punched him lightly in the arm. "Don't screw up with Elly, though, hear?"

"Yeah, reckon I do." Royal leaned against the wall, wishing he could sail away on the rising breeze, away from Leesha's determination to find some good in him even now. Sliding down, he hunkered on the floor, his head thrown back, eyes shut so that he wouldn't have to see Leesha's face as he betrayed her trust. "So what were you going to tell me about Ms. Malloy?"

"When she enrolled Tommy, she insisted no one else should be allowed to pick him up."

"Doesn't seem that unusual, for a single mom. Could be all kinds of reasons." Opening his eyes, he stared past her to the front yard and the passing cars.

"Of course. I didn't ask questions. Our job is to keep the kids safe. I didn't even think anything about her request except that she repeated it several times, and then, as she was leaving, almost as if she thought she needed to clarify her insistence, she rushed into an explanation, saying Tommy's father was abusive, he drank, she needed to make sure we understood the seriousness of her situation." Alicia stooped and retrieved a plastic bat that had rolled under the porch swing. "You know."

"She said too much."

"Way too much. So I backed off. But I worry about her, about Tommy. She's wound tighter than a spring. She needs help, and she's made it clear that she won't take any from me. Not that I've offered. At least not outright. Lord, if I did, she'd probably yank the kid out of here faster than she made tracks out of here ten minutes ago. Play detective, Royal. Find out what's wrong."

"You have absolutely no idea, Leesha, what you're asking. If you care about the Malloy woman, you should keep me fifty miles clear of her." He uncoiled and stood up, dusting off the back of his slacks. "I'm already involved in her life. And I don't see anything good happening to her as a result, believe me."

"Don't you, Royal?" Leesha's soft question hung in the air.

"Not one damned thing." He headed toward the screen door.

"Have a little faith, Royal. In me. In yourself."

"That's the funniest line I've heard in months. You doing stand-up comedy in your spare time?" Pausing on the step outside the closed door, he saw her beautiful face, like some ancient Egyptian goddess, through the screen mesh. "You're something else, you are, Alicia Williams. Beau's a lucky man to have you in his life on any terms."

"Of course he is." Her hand rested on the mesh near his face. "And, Royal? Don't give up on yourself just yet, hear?"

Letting his hand linger on the other side of the mesh, he swallowed, unable to speak. He gave a mute tap to the screen and left, feeling her gaze on his back all the way to his car.

Damn her for trusting him. And damn her for making him responsible for Elly Malloy and her tough nut of a kid who looked up at him as if were Batman, Robin and Superman all rolled into one.

Damned kid. He should have more sense, even at four or five, than to give his trust that easily.

With the engine of the Mustang idling and his hand on the turn signal, Royal couldn't decide which street to take away from the day-care center. He didn't know where to go. The car vibrated under him.

He was free as the proverbial bird.

He could go anywhere. Nowhere. Nobody was expecting him. Nobody was depending on him.

Like the singer said, freedom was just another word for nothing left to lose.

Scented with frangipani and gardenia, warm air moved over his face, his skin. Out to the west, pink and purple, the color of Elly Malloy's gauzy sundress, mingled with soft blue.

Leesha was worried about the blossom.

He wasn't. But unanswered questions buzzed in his brain.

He told himself he didn't care about the apprehension flitting through Elly Malloy's brown eyes, the shadows underneath. He told himself she wasn't his business. Eyes narrowed against the blaze of color, he told himself he didn't care that Scanlon was a son of a bitch.

Fingers curling around the gearshift knob, he watched the blue yield to deeper shadows. Then, with sudden decision, he shifted into Drive and took the left turn to the older section of Palma-flora.

He thought he'd continue his personal surveillance of Elly Malloy. That's what he'd do if he were still a cop and she a suspect.

In a way, she was. According to Scanlon, she'd taken the boy and left Tallahassee, avoiding a custody hearing. She was living under an assumed name.

He parked the car under the arching branches of an ancient live oak down the block from her one-story rental.

Pouring coffee from the thermos he'd picked up from a drive-through, he inhaled the scent rising from the jug. Been a while since coffee had tasted so good, he realized, sipping the brew and staring down the block to Elly's house.

He smiled and slumped down into his seat as twilight settled gently around him.

A throng of kids in baggy shorts whipped by on in-line skates. Tommy Lee hadn't left the house as far as Royal could tell. Interesting. Not typical kid behavior.

In a while, when it was dark enough to move without being seen, he'd go closer. He frowned at his light gray slacks. He hadn't dressed for night work. Resting the cup on the dash, he eased open the car door, pressing down the switch that turned on the overhead light. Stooping near the front wheel, he twisted underneath and reached up to the axle, running his hand along the joint over and over, methodically smearing grease onto his pants, streaking the light fabric into a camouflage. Finished, he thumbed out a glob and covered his face. Once upon a time, he'd dressed for this kind of activity. Once upon a time, he'd carried camouflage paint.

Once upon a time, this nighttime world had been his life.

He scuttled back inside the car, spread an old newspaper across the car seat and settled in for the wait.

Adrenaline thumped inside him, and he grinned at his reflection in the car mirror, the whites of his eyes gleaming back at him from the greasy darkness of his face. Damn, he'd missed this. He'd loved being a cop.

Later, locking the car behind him, he glided from tree to tree, closing in on her house.

The front door was shut, but her windows were partially open. No air-conditioning except the evening breeze that carried her light voice to him.

"Tommy, we need to talk." She placed a grilled-cheese sandwich in front of him. She'd tied the ends of her blouse into a bow under her breasts, and the pale skin of her stomach gleamed in the overhead light. "I think it's time to leave Palmaflora."

Royal stiffened. Ms. Malloy's instincts were dead-on.

Tommy shoved the plate away. "No."

Stooping beside Tommy, she put her arm around him. "Honey, I know. I know." Her hair lifted, floated in a baby-cotton cloud around her, settled on her shoulders as she took his face in both her hands. "This is hard."

He shoved her hands away. "You don't know, you don't! I *won't* leave!" Tommy's voice rose hysterically. "I won't leave Katie! You can't make me!" The chair rocked as he stood up. "I will run away all by myself, I will. I am big enough. I can do it."

His arms flailed as she gathered him to her, crooning, "Easy, honey. I know, I know." Above his head, her expression was haunted.

"No, you don't," he wept, burying his face into the crook of her shoulder. "Mr. Royal said he would take me to the Fourth of July rodeo. He *promised* he would. Today. Before you came. And Katie and me are going to have pizza. You *said* so." He plucked at her hair, sobs racking him.

"Honey, don't cry. Please don't."

"Will if I want to," he muttered, hiccuping with the force of his weeping. "But I don't want to move. I like Leesha and Lala and Katie, and Mr. Royal is my friend, too. I know he is," Tommy added earnestly, lifting his tear-wet face and rubbing his nose against Elly's. "And I like story hour and I'm tired of moving and I can't remember what I'm supposed to."

From his vantage point, Royal saw the shine of tears in Elly Malloy's eyes as she stared toward the retreating back of her sobbing son. "Tommy!"

From the interior of the small house, a door slammed. "Go away! I'm very mad at you, Mommy! I don't like you this minute. Not at all."

Sinking to the floor, Elly wrapped her arms around her knees, bending her head forward. "Oh, Tommy," she whispered, "I'm doing the best I can. I can't do any more." Her shoulders shook silently in the harsh light of the empty kitchen.

Congealing cheese oozed and settled in an artificial bright yellow during the long moments that she huddled on the floor. All guards down, thinking herself unobserved, she yielded to the anguish that pinched her small features and bleached them of color.

Royal couldn't watch. Casting his eyes to the tropical darkness, he inhaled, filling his lungs with the melancholy scents of the summer night. Someone's cigarette smoke drifted to him. Overhead, a plane droned faintly in the distance. He leaned with his back against the house, his eyes burning, while beside him, on the other side of the wall, Scanlon's woman rocked back and forth in silent misery, her grief seeping through the walls of her house to Royal.

Closing his eyes, he turned his cheek to the warm wood of the wall separating them. He rubbed his cheek back and forth against the boards.

Elly Malloy was a woman who could break a man's heart.

If he let himself care.

The blow came from behind him, out of nowhere, a hard crack to the back of his head. Falling forward, his face scraping the house, Royal twisted, turned, reached out for the feet thudding into his ribs, his face. Pain, real and fierce, ratcheted through him as a pointed boot toe slammed into his nose and blood gushed forth.

Holding on to the boot, he wrestled his attacker to the ground. Grunting, Royal dragged himself to his knees and, with no room to swing, braced his right elbow with his left fist and whacked a stocking-covered chin. Scrabbling for the slick nylon, he fell into unconsciousness as a second blow bounced off his skull.

Chapter 4

The heavy thud against the side of the house brought Elly scrambling to her feet and screaming, "Tommy!"

Racing down the hallway to the room they shared, she grabbed her purse and slung it over her shoulder and neck, leaving her hands free, ready for anything. "Tommy?" She snatched up the bag she kept packed outside the bedroom and threw open the bedroom door.

Lying across his narrow bed sound asleep, Tommy had curled himself around the stuffed whale she'd bought when he was two. Moving swiftly to the partially open window and staying to one side, she slammed the window down and locked it. Her heart beating with slow dread, she peered out into the darkness.

"Mommy?" Tommy opened one eye sleepily. "Love you." Rooting into the sheet, he rolled over, flinging an arm out. With a metallic whistle, Baby Whale tumbled to the bare floor, his threadbare belly ceilingward.

Picking up the toy, Elly tucked it under Tommy's arm. "But I'm not going to move, Mommy," he murmured in his sleep as she curled his fingers around the scruffy fluke. Leaving the door cracked, she moved back toward the front of the house.

The noise had come from the side, not far from the kitchen,

where she'd been wallowing in self-pity and frustration. "Damn," she groaned under her breath. Racing to check out Tommy, she'd left the window open behind her in the kitchen. Even blocked, as all the windows were when open, any of them could be forced open. All it would take was sufficient determination and strength. Or a crowbar. Furious with herself, she edged toward the cracker box of a living room, her back melting into the wall. She had to check the front of the house.

Ever since she'd seen the cigarette stub in the flowerpot earlier in the day, her subconscious had been preparing for this moment. Her mind was focused, clear. She'd readied herself and Tommy for a fast exit, and now she would deal with whatever was out in the dark.

Then she and Tommy would leave this place they'd made into a home.

First, though, she had a job to do here. The muscles running along the ridge of her shoulders ached with the tension of holding still. She was so tired of running, so tired of forever looking over her shoulder. She couldn't see an end to the constant vigilance. In the past week, she'd finally accepted that Blake would never let her escape.

Despair had filled her when she'd realized that. But a spark deep inside, some instinct of survival, kept her feet moving forward, kept her running from the pursuer nipping at her heels. All she knew how to do anymore was run. Running was all she could do.

Run. Protect Tommy. Stay alive if she could. And pray for a miracle. Pushing her shoulder blades against the wall, Elly forced herself to concentrate.

Hyperalert, she paused. All the sounds of the house were magnified, the smells more intense. The wall at her back seemed to become part of her skin. She wouldn't act hastily. If she didn't have to uproot Tommy, she wouldn't. But she was prepared to dash back for him, grab the suitcase and crawl out the window. She'd had to do that once before, and ever since, she'd made sure she had an escape plan. But she was so tired, so tired of staying alert, keyed up. *Prepared.* Even adrenaline and coffee didn't give her a buzz these days. Every incident drained her resources, leaving her at such a deep level of exhaustion that sleep didn't restore her.

She couldn't keep up this kind of life much longer. She would make a deadly error at the rate she was going. She would trust the wrong person, turn left when she should turn right. Or she would surrender to emotional exhaustion and give up, call Blake and wait for the executioner's blade, yielding to the relief of not having to run anymore.

With her eyes closed, she centered herself on the sounds around her, assessing them. The kitchen noises were familiar, comforting. The chug of the refrigerator motor. The drip of the kitchen faucet. Her whole existence reduced itself to these ordinary sounds.

Opening her eyes, she eased her foot forward.

In the glass of the picture over the sofa, she could see into the kitchen.

Empty.

A faint scratching against the front door stopped her before she turned the corner toward the kitchen. Clearing her throat, she called, "Yes? Who is it?"

The scratching came again. And then a murmur, rough, the sound of her name whispered softly. She turned her head and listened as silence gathered around her house.

Gaze fixed on the door, she opened her purse with one steady hand and pulled out a plastic jar of ammonia. Palming it, she loosened the cap with her thumb and finger. Staying away from the windows, she moved toward the front door.

"Elly?" Through the four-inch window openings, once more came the whispery rasp of her name. Slurred and quiet, the voice was seductive, luring her to open her door.

"Who's there?" She could almost identify that voice. Almost. But she wasn't sure.

A scraping sound. A groan.

"Anybody there?" Earlier today at the rental unit, she'd suppressed that urge to call out. But this was different. This was her *home*. Sending conflicting signals to her, that voice teased her with its hint of familiarity, but she wasn't about to abandon caution. "Be with you in a minute, okay?"

She waited a moment for a response before shouting to the back of the house, "Henry! Someone's at the door. Do you want me to see who it is?"

Not lingering for the nonexistent Henry's answer, she duck-walked under the last window and, from the protection of the door, she yanked it open, muscles tensed and ammonia jar at the ready in case she was wrong.

Curled into a fetal position, the man lay on her front stoop. Blood oozed steadily from the back of his head, his nose, his cheek. The acrid scent of ammonia burned in her nose as the jar fell to the grass and rolled out of sight. Her purse dropped beside the door. "My God," she whispered, appalled, "Royal?"

Out in the darkness, a car started up, squealed around a corner. "Elly." His hand twitched.

Dropping to his side, her knees scraping against the concrete stoop, she reached out to him. Hand hovering over his face, she drew her fist back to her mouth. She was afraid to touch him. What if she made his injuries worse?

Glancing from him to the street in front of her house, she watched for movement in the dark, for signs of an intruder. Tree limbs moved in the rising wind, and telephone lines wavered overhead, a trickery of motion and shapes.

But nothing, no one, came leaping toward them from those uncertain shadows that strained her eyes and nerves.

Turning back to Royal, she bit her lower lip. His shirt was torn, dirt streaked his face and slacks, and along his rib cage, she saw the muddy outlines of a boot. "Can you stand up?"

His long frame shifted, went still, and she heard the jagged intake of breath. "Not just yet."

His voice was so low she could scarcely hear him. Her hair brushed against his bloodied cheek and clung as she leaned forward in distress. She touched his cheek gently. Bristly and grease stained, the lean planes of his face and chin were cold, even in the heat. "How can I help you? What should I do?"

His words came in gasps and pauses. "Get me inside. Can you?"

"All right. This is going to hurt," she said grimly, standing in back of him and working her hands under his arms. His chest was hard against her palms. Clasping her hands together and doubling over him, she pulled. His shoulder muscles rippled against her forearms and breasts in an intimacy of shared effort.

"Hell." His breathing was labored, and she stopped, her face remaining next to him. Warm and coffee scented, his breath stirred the hair along her cheek.

Beaten and battered, he should have seemed harmless, diminished. He didn't. She knew better. The air around him snapped with tension, hummed with the cold anger vibrating from him.

Even so, she held on to him with all her strength, afraid that if she let go of him, she'd never be able to lift him again. He was bigger, more solid, than she'd expected, and she knew each inexpert tug hurt him more than he revealed. "I'm sorry, I'm sorry," she chanted, tugging once more and wincing as he flinched under her hands.

"Me, too." In his blood- and grease-smeared face, Royal's eyes glittered at her. "But I'll live." Edginess surfaced, crackled around them.

"That's encouraging. I'd hate to waste all this effort." Jittery, she made a note to watch her step. Even wounded and vulnerable, Royal Gaines was a threat.

"Smart mouth—" A low groan stopped him.

"Right." Preparing to lift him, she inhaled and tightened her stomach muscles. "Okay, here we go. Ready?"

"Yeah." Left arm clasped tightly around his chest, he raised his head. "Let's get this over and done with before I puke all over your step." He straightened his legs and pushed as she pulled. "Wait," he grunted. Finally, his words coming out in short bursts, he said, "I can stand. Give me a second." He leaned back, resting against her bare legs. Dark with night and grease, stiff with drying blood, his hair scratched the top of her thighs.

"You okay?" Still gripping him under the arms, she wiped her damp face against her shoulder. Her arms were quivering with strain, but she didn't dare let go.

"I'm feeling better by the minute, sugar." The light coming from the kitchen to the front stoop shadowed the angles of his face, lost itself in the dark, oily streaks dulling his bright hair.

"I can tell." Staring at him, she shook her head. "Picture of health, a real poster boy, that's what you are. How silly of me to think otherwise." She took a tremulous breath and gathered her strength. "Don't men ever get tired of pretending to be tough?"

"Part of our charm, sugar." Undaunted, he fixed her with a gleaming green eye. "It's why you women love us."

"Oh, gosh, thanks for clearing that up for me. I never understood it before." Elly tightened her grip ferociously and steeled herself against the feel of his body against hers, the forgotten texture of male skin and muscle. The damned idiot was three breaths away from collapsing in a heap and he couldn't stop joking. She sent a silent prayer that she could haul his battered, foolhardy self safely inside before he passed out.

Bending forward, he coughed. As he leaned against her, sweat popped out along his hairline, and he clenched his mouth. "Hell. Let me catch my breath."

"I can move you. You don't have to stand up. I can do this. I can."

"Doesn't surprise me a bit," he grunted, steadying himself. "I reckon you can do about anything you put your mind to."

Tugging and pulling, she worked him into the living room. Sliding her arms free of him, she was amazed to find them shaking, her muscles quivering. She hadn't been aware at the time that she was straining as hard as she'd been. She shut and bolted the door behind her. "You're heavier than you look."

"Nice bedside manner, Nurse Ratched."

"Who?" she muttered, leaving him there while she circled the room, pulling down the shades.

"A mean nurse. She liked pain."

Distracted by the lights of a passing car, she paused, looked toward the street. She rubbed the goose bumps along her arms as she watched the car pass in front of her house. "What?"

"Never mind," he mumbled. Working himself slowly into a sitting position, he leaned against what passed for her sofa and fought for breath. "Damn," he groaned, and wrapped his arms around his middle. "Nurse Ratched would be very happy if she were here."

"Oh." In the breeze drifting through the small gap of window and sill, the shades flapped fitfully. Bass beat throbbing, the car slowed at the Stop sign, waited and turned the corner. As it did, light from the street lamp winked inside.

Her neighbor's teenage son. Giving her arms one last rub, Elly knelt down beside Royal and gingerly touched the gash over his eye. She grimaced. "Nasty."

"Yeah, 'nasty' covers it." His head dropped forward, and she saw the deep cut at the crown of his scalp.

"You're going to need stitches in that one." In the slash,

drying blood matted strands of hair darkened with sweat and grease. "Let me see your eyes."

The obedient tip of his head mocked her. "Bossy, aren't you?"

"I'm a mom. Bossy comes with *my* territory." One at a time, she lifted his eyelids. "Hold still." She grabbed her purse in one quick step and returned to him. Fishing in its depths, she found her keys and twisted the end of the miniature flashlight dangling from the key ring. Her purse clunked to the floor. Shining the light into his eyes, she watched as his pupils contracted and reacted. "Seems okay."

Underneath the cut over his eye, the skin had swollen, leaving a puffy slit. One eye barely visible, the other a baleful flash of green, he glared at her. "Sympathy's not your strong suit, is it, Ms. Malloy?"

She regarded him irritably. "If you want an ice pack or a ride to the emergency room, I can help you. If you want pity, go scratch on someone else's door."

"Like a junkyard dog, huh?" His laugh was closer to a shaky bark, but he groaned again as she probed his ribs tentatively.

"You or me?"

"Killed anyone with that razor of a tongue?"

"Don't tempt me." She stuffed the flashlight in her shorts pocket and leaned forward, cautiously touching his ribs.

He gasped. "Yeah, sugar, that hurts. Keep it up, and you'll have me out cold." Sweat beaded along his forehead, slid down his face and left pale tracks through the blood and grease.

Despite his wisecracks, she could see the pain shimmering in his good eye. "Do you want me to call an ambulance?"

His eyes were shut, and he passed a darkened hand across his face, mixing sweat and grease and revealing more clearly the ugly scrapes on the left side of his face.

"I can't tell how badly you've been hurt. You don't have a concussion, but you might be bleeding internally. You need to see a doctor." Suddenly drained, Elly sank to her knees beside Royal, her muscles shaking uncontrollably, her arms and legs quivering.

"Give me a sec," he gasped. "Rough neighborhood you live in, Elly Malloy."

"Must be the company you keep," she mumbled, head down

as she tried to think what to do. Should she call an ambulance, whether he wanted one or not? Would he let her drive him to the emergency room? Reports would be filed. If the newspaper got wind of what had happened— If pictures of her— Elly bumped her chin against her knees. She'd done the best she could. "I've never had any problems in this neighborhood. Must be your attitude. What happened?"

"I was careless. But that's no surprise. I've been pretty damned dense lately." Scowling, he palpated the wound at the top of his head. "Malignant stupidity. I wasn't paying attention."

"You fell?" Tilting her head sideways, Elly glanced at him. In her fog of exhaustion, she couldn't follow what he was saying. "You got this banged up from a fall? I don't understand. That doesn't make sense."

"Your neighbors have an interesting way of welcoming a fellow to the neighborhood, sugar."

"What?" She massaged her kneecap anxiously. He'd been attacked. She understood that much. She would have to call the police.

She couldn't.

"A committee decided to shower me with affection." He was motionless, watching her too closely with that brilliant right eye. "A couple of knights of the evening used me for a punching bag."

"I'm sorry," she repeated helplessly. She pressed her fingers against her eyes. It was bad. The police were going to be involved. There seemed to be no way she could keep them out of it. And then Blake could— A thought struck her. Her head shot up. "What were you doing in my neighborhood, Mr. Gaines?"

"Back to 'Mr.', are we? Wondered how long it would take you to realize you'd reached a first-name basis." He edged up straighter against the sofa and took a shaky breath. "I promised Tommy Lee I'd check to see if he could go to the Fourth of July rodeo. You left the center before I got around to suggesting—"

"You were at my front door when you got beaten up?" Elly frowned as she interrupted him. He'd left something out. "I heard the sound against the kitchen wall."

"They dragged me off the walk and bounced me off your house, sugar."

"But the kitchen's nowhere near the walk—"

"Very impetuous gentlemen they were. Never once asked me if I wanted to check out your landscaping." His words were coming more easily even though he still took careful, shallow breaths as he tried to sit upright. Dropping his hand to the sofa, he hoisted himself to his knees. "Can you lend me a shoulder?"

"Don't get up! You probably shouldn't be moving around like this!" Distracted by the sudden pallor appearing under the grime on his face, she rose to her feet. "I think you need to see a doctor. I really do."

His face contorted by pain, he glared at her. "I really, really don't."

"But you may be seriously hurt!" She gripped her hands together to stop their shaking. She hesitated, but she didn't have any other choice, not if she wanted to face herself in the mirror tomorrow morning. "I'll take you to the hospital if you don't want to call the paramedics. Whatever you want."

"What I'd like you to do is help me stand up." Fierce with determination, he stared her down. "If you will. Please," he said through gritted teeth. "I need a shoulder, not a lot of dithering around."

"All right." She squatted next to him and lifted his arm around her shoulder, his lean form unfolding with hers as they rose together. "And I don't dither, you hardheaded, stubborn jack—"

"You're such a sweet-talking woman, Elly Malloy." He grinned at her, his teeth flashing white in the grease-darkened contours of his face. "I might fall in love with you just for your sweet ways."

She wanted to punch him. He wobbled back and forth in front of her, and it wouldn't take more than a whiff of air to knock him on his behind, and he was joking like a fool. "What are you trying to prove?"

"Not a thing. Look, I'm fine." He swayed and then steadied himself with a grip on the end table. "Well, more or less." He lifted his arms out to the side carefully. "At least I don't have any broken bones."

"But you couldn't breathe—"

"I got kicked in the ribs. The gut. And areas south. The 'growin' place', as one of Leesha's kids terms it. I got the wind knocked out of me, but I'm all right. I have bruised ribs, and tomorrow my face and head will look even worse. That's all. Nothing critical, so I reckon I'll take a pass on that hospital trip. If you have some pressure tape and a butterfly bandage or two, I can put Humpty Dumpty back together again."

"B-but—" Raking her hands through her hair, Elly stuttered into speech, stopped.

He'd been beaten in her yard. She was responsible. If he were bleeding, if a broken rib punctured his lungs, if— He could die. She had to take the risk. She couldn't let him die to save herself. "I'm taking you to the emergency room. I'll call the police. This has to be reported."

"No emergency room. No police."

"No police?" She went dizzy with relief, her knees buckled and Royal reached out, grabbing her elbow before she fell.

"What's going on, sugar?" he asked softly, his face not two inches from her own. "Why don't you want the gentlemen in blue here any more than I do? What are you hiding?"

"I don't know what you mean."

"You didn't see your face when Leesha mentioned I'd been a detective. Sugar, sure as the devil whistles 'Dixie' down in Georgia, you're hiding something." He smiled, a tight, small lift of his mouth. "What are you hiding, Elly?"

She jerked, and his hand slid to her waistband, his fingers slipping inside the waistband and holding tightly, cold and rough against her stomach. "I offered to call the police, remember? You're the one who decided not to. I could ask you the same question. What are you hiding?"

"Ah. We're playing I'll-show-you-if-you'll-show-me, are we?" He leaned one inch closer, his breath mingling with hers. "Cards on the table, jokers wild?"

"We're not playing anything. I'm trying to help you." She inhaled the sharp scent of his anger and sweat and pain. And underlying it, something darker, uniquely male. Disturbing. Startled, she rocked back on her heels, her fingers pressing into him as she grabbed his arm to keep from falling.

In his good eye, the pupil darkened and swallowed up the bright green. He stared at her, his brows drawing together in a frown, and almost reflexively, his forefinger moved against her skin, brushing her navel. He glanced down at his lean, grease-smudged finger, and with a quick, clumsy motion, raised his hands, stepped back. ''Right. You're the Good Samaritan saving the wounded traveler. That's the game of the moment.'' He scrubbed his hands down the sides of his slacks.

Following his movement, her breath coming too quickly, Elly said, ''Your pants are ruined.''

''Yeah, well, I can buy new ones—'' He laughed. Amusement mixed with self-mockery as he poked a finger through the rip at his pants pocket. ''Nope. Guess I can't. Not anymore.'' He leaned against the wall for support. ''So, since neither of us, for reasons of our own, wants to invite the police into this little incident, what about those bandages? Does the offer of aid and succor hold?''

Disturbed, she couldn't answer.

''Or are you going to cast me out like the dirty dawg I am into the cold, cruel night?'' His grin was pure provocation.

But she caught the slight tremble of his hand as he touched the abrasions on his face, and said slowly, wondering the whole time what kind of mistake she was making, ''The streets may be mean out there, but it's a warm night. I think you'll survive—''

''Right.'' Flattening his hand against the wall, he tried to turn, but his knuckles went white.

''—but I wouldn't send even a junkyard dog away if he looked as bad as you do,'' she finished in a rush.

''I see.'' His head dropped, and his hand flexed once against the wall.

''Probably not,'' she muttered.

''You said that once before.''

''What?'' She jammed her hands into her pockets. Fastening on to the miniature flashlight as if it were a life raft, she gripped it for all she was worth.

''That I didn't see. That I wouldn't understand. Maybe I understand more than you think I do.'' Shoulders slumped with fatigue and pain, he faced her. His face was cold and hard, but his wary eyes, even half-shut, were filled with sympathy.

For the first time, she saw the man she'd glimpsed behind the teasing mask. This man with his weary eyes and battered body, this man watching her with such understanding that she wanted to weep, this man was far, far more alarming to her than the fallen angel of the beach.

And that was the most disturbing fact of all she realized as she led him down the hall to the bathroom. There was danger. And then there was *danger*. Stripped of his mask, Royal Gaines was terrifying.

Because his understanding weakened her.

Trailing her down the hall, where an overhead fluorescent light dimmed, brightened, dimmed, Royal stayed so close on her heels that she was afraid that if she suddenly stopped, he'd barrel right into her.

"Tommy?" He gestured toward the bedroom.

"Asleep." Elly wasn't about to volunteer any more information about her son, who'd apparently adopted Royal as the next-best thing to Baby Whale. "He didn't wake up."

"Good." Royal waited for her to switch on the bathroom light. "He'd be scared. I worried about that."

Her hand still on the light switch, Elly looked over her shoulder at him. "Did you?" She frowned. "Tommy handles most things in stride," she said uneasily. "Why would you think he'd be frightened?" She wanted to know whether the man was guessing, fishing or— Why was Royal worried about Tommy?

"It's late. I look like I've been run through a mangler. Even though I'm not a stranger, seems like this would be a scary moment for a kid his age," Royal said, shrugging. With his movement, he scowled.

"At any rate, he didn't wake up." Elly opened the cabinet above the sink and took out a basket of first-aid supplies. If Royal Gaines had guessed about Tommy's troubling insecurities, the man had been dead on target, and that unnerved her. She surveyed his face, touched the oil on his shirt. "I don't think soap and water's going to clean you up. What is this stuff?"

"Axle grease."

"From a car?"

"Yeah."

"You didn't say anything about rolling around under a car. What did they do? Drag you from one end of the street to the other before you made it to my door?" She tried to wipe off the grease with a bit of toilet paper. The paper tore and stuck to her finger. "Darn. The blasted stuff's all over you. Your clothes, your hair. You're a mess."

"So I am. It's a long story. Can it wait until I've gotten some tape on my ribs and cleaned up my head?"

"Sure." Elly recognized a wall when she ran headfirst into one. She dropped the subject. He was covered in axle grease? Fine. She couldn't care less. "I have some goopy junk that I keep on hand for Tommy. He's always getting into unidentifiable substances that soap and water won't clean. We'll see if it works on you."

"Whatever you say."

"You're being so docile that you're making me nervous." Her laugh was shakier than she'd intended. "Even Tommy protests."

"Take advantage while you can."

At the back of the cabinet, she found the can of jellylike solvent. Lifting the lid off, she stuck her finger in it and then used another bit of paper to clean the oil from her hand, testing the solvent. "This should do the trick." She filled her fingers with the gooey mixture and stood on her tiptoes, working the substance into his skin and hairline, into the strands of hair near his wound.

As the cleaner melted the grease, she wiped his face with toilet paper. With each stroke across his face, through his hair, she found herself growing silent. The shape of his head was beautifully curved under her hand, sleek, perfect, a temptation to the touch in the way it shaped itself to her palm. His face filled her view, everything centering on its planes and hollows, its shadows and the one green eye watching her intently as she worked her fingers into the stiff clumps of his hair.

He stood too still, his breathing matching hers, his body seeming to lean over her, to encompass her, and in the mirror to her side, she saw herself, him, saw her half-parted lips, the flush of pink in her cheeks. Saw herself, aroused.

"Sit." She motioned to the toilet seat.

"Yes'm." He sat, his long, narrow hands clasped between his legs, his head bent forward. "I'm in your power." Doubled over as he was, his shoulder brushed the top of her thigh.

He was too close to her in the confines of the small room, and she edged closer to the sink. "Really? In my power, huh?"

"Totally."

"Now, why do I doubt that, I wonder?" Ignoring him, she poked through the basket of supplies.

"Because you can't see what a pitiful specimen I am? How weak and vulnerable?" he asked innocently as she reached for a washrag and soap.

"Pitiful?" She snickered. Stooping, she glanced back at him. "Rude? Unpredictable? Wily? Oh, yes, those characteristics come easily to mind. But pitiful? Not in this life, buster."

"Hell, I can't decide if I should be offended or if I should say thanks." He glanced at her, his exhaustion showing clearly in the light's merciless glare.

"Don't worry about it," she told him sweetly, rummaging through her truly pitiful stash for a halfway decent washrag. "No, I don't think anybody in her right mind would ever describe you as pitiful, not even now. Not even in your beach-bum disguise." Her hair slipped forward into her eyes, and she brushed it back, anchoring it behind her ear with a finger as she leaned back on her heels and studied him.

"Disguise? Interesting term." He sighed and rested his head on his hands, his face out of sight.

"No, actually, the more I think about it, the more I'm certain that's exactly the right word." Rising to her feet, Elly paused, replaying the vague picture that had suddenly flashed into her mind. "A disguise. Like an undercover cop." The washcloth dangled from her hand. "Were you? Undercover?" A curl of dismay eddied through her. Heaven help her if he'd been following her, investigating her.

The toilet lid squeaked as he shifted. Angling away from her, his knees skimmed against her. "Nope. I'm not a detective any longer. Remember?"

"Yes," she said hesitantly, sorting out her impressions of that day when he'd saved Tommy. At first, she'd thought he was drunk. Then she'd discovered he wasn't. But he *had* been drinking, and he'd looked like a man on a two-day bender. He'd looked exactly like a man who lived inside a bottle.

On the porch of the day-care center, though, he'd looked as though he'd stepped straight out of *GQ*. Royal Gaines was a man of a thousand faces. Turning on the faucet, she filled the sink with warm water and dropped the soap bar into it, swishing the faded green rag through the water and making bubbles. "Why aren't you a detective anymore?"

He tapped her nose, and Elly felt the cool slide of the grease from his hand to her nose. "There's an old rule. Don't ask questions if you're not ready for the answer. Are you sure you want to know?"

"Yes." She sudsed the rag. Water dripped down her forearm as she turned toward him, the small of her back pressed into the rim of the sink. "I don't like mysteries."

"That's a good one, Elly. Because I do." Suddenly he stood up, his hip bumping her leg, his finger moving from her nose to her throat and to the back of her neck. His thumb tilted her chin up. "And, sugar, you're the biggest mystery I've seen in a month of Sundays." His mouth hovered over hers, and that scent of danger and alert male enveloped her, wrapped around her like a cloak.

One of her legs was between his, and the press of his thigh against her was accidental, purposeful. Arousing. But Royal Gaines never did anything without a purpose. Dimly, she wondered why she wasn't afraid, why she didn't slam the bathroom door in his face and head for the hills.

She should have been terrified.

She wasn't.

Later, much later, she would recall that in the moment when he hesitated, frowning, in that moment it was she who took a step.

Beguiled by that scent, by the sudden heat flaring between them and flushing her skin, she stepped forward into the unknown, welcoming the touch of his mouth against her.

Chapter 5

She could never have guessed that he would kiss her so gently, so delicately, his hands not touching her, simply hovering near her face protectively, and his lips warm, hot, tasting the corner of her mouth.

He kissed her like a sixteen-year-old boy filled with wonder. He kissed her as if the taste of her were a miracle. He kissed her as if she were fragile, priceless.

And he made her feel for the first time in her life as if she were on the verge of a momentous discovery.

The metallic scent of solvent, of oil and blood and Royal Gaines, drifted around her, mixing in a strange and provocative blend that made her hum with pleasure, with need, and she leaned forward, craving his touch.

His tongue slipped over her lower lip, and as she sighed, opening her mouth to tell him she'd kill him if he didn't touch her, he nibbled her lip, tugging at her bottom lip. She tilted her head, and with her movement, as if some chain had snapped, he moved forward, his tongue delving deep inside. With an inarticulate sound, he slid his palm under her hair and cupped her head, tipping it closer to his mouth. His thigh nudged the juncture of her legs, and vibrations rippled through her, internal muscles clenching and coiling. His left leg moved restlessly against her, and she jerked, shaken by hunger, by longing.

"Easy, sugar, easy," he murmured, and she wondered if he even knew he spoke. "We have all the time in the world. There's no hurry. Let me taste you, Elly. Please."

With his words, his breath sifted teasingly across her earlobe, her cheek, and she turned her head toward the source of that exquisite pleasure. Earlier, he'd been so cold, but now the heat of his skin, of his breath, of his touch, burned her. And forgetting everything in the pleasure of the moment, she welcomed that fire, craved it.

It had been so long since she'd *felt,* felt anything except fear and suspicion and terror. And loneliness, so deep and pervasive that it rose now like a snow-buried tulip toward the heat of his touch, betraying her.

She tangled her fingers in his hair, holding his mouth steady against hers while his clever mouth moved with such inventiveness against hers, against her neck and chin, skimming her jawbone, the curve of her ear. Every stroke of his tongue, every slide of his mouth over her skin—*everything.* And still, not enough, not nearly enough.

She could defend herself against him. She had no weapons against herself, against her own, desperate loneliness.

"Ah, Elly, Elly." His mouth slanted against hers, a fierce hunger in the taking, an urgency now in him demanding a matching urgency from her, and still he didn't touch her.

Instead, moving in so close that paper wouldn't have fit between them, he pressed her against the hard rim of the sink. Startled by his sudden aggression, Elly dropped her arms, her hands sliding down his forearms as he lifted them and braced his palms on the wall behind her, one on either side of her head. He leaned over her, his body against hers, and her world filled with him, with the texture and scent and feel of Royal Gaines.

To keep from touching his battered body, his bruised and scraped face, Elly gripped the edges of the sink counter and wondered why it didn't crumble underneath her hands. She couldn't open her eyes. She didn't want to leave this darkness where sound and touch were magnified. In mingled embarrassment and need, she whispered, "Please."

"What, sugar?" His mouth scarcely left hers, but his words curled over her damp lips, leaving them tingling.

"Touch me."

"Where, sugar?" Palms bracing him, he remained looming over her, so close that she felt the warmth of his forearms, his biceps surrounding her, his mouth sliding back and forth against hers teasingly. "Where do you want me to touch you, Elly?"

She hadn't known she'd needed the sound of her name, that proof that she wasn't anonymous, the proof that he knew he was kissing *her.* That need, too, had been more powerful than she could have guessed because, with her name spoken between them, with her *self* acknowledged, embarrassment fled, leaving only need.

"Where, sweetheart? Tell me."

"Anywhere," she whispered, stretching on tiptoe and nipping his bottom lip. Her fingernails ground into the slick surface of the sink, slipped. "Anywhere. Just touch me."

And he did. But not with his hands. With his body moving over hers, gently, so gently that pleasure was pain, he touched her with himself, with the planes and ridges of his long body against hers, his hips moving in a rhythm that called to hers and found her body pressing back, moving forward, retreating, the beat of blood and need thrumming through her until she didn't think about anything except the wildness inside her, the wildness that needed release, needed an end to the aching hunger winding so tight inside her that she thought she'd cry.

"There, Elly? There?" His thigh lifted against her, rubbed slowly, over and over, pushing hard against the seam of her shorts.

"That's a very good idea." She twisted, welcoming that pressure that built into quakes inside her with each push of his thigh. "Yes, *there* is very nice." Her breath caught in her chest.

"Nice?" His chest vibrated against her with his muted chuckle. "Interesting choice of words, sugar. You like *nice,* do you?" His hips stroked against hers, and as he anchored her against him, mouth to hungry mouth, his tongue echoed, repeated that seductive motion of his narrow hips. "I think, Elly Malloy, I like *nice,* too. It's beginning to grow on me. *Nice* has a lot going for it."

She felt the shift of his feet, the rocking of his pelvis against her, heard the scratching slide of his hands down the wall to the sink, where they gripped hers, fingers flexing between fingers. On tiptoe, connected to him only by the tenuous link of their lips and tongues, she trembled from piggy toe to the top of her head, her body caught in the grip of a fever that shuddered through her.

She didn't know whether it was the long day, the stress or the simple need to be with another human being. She didn't care. The moment was enough. After all the long days and weeks and months of standing alone, of burying her feelings and fears, she was stunned by this unexpected pleasure, dizzy with the feel and scent of Royal Gaines. Lost, and not caring.

She whimpered.

When she did, his body stilled its eager movement against hers, and her fingers convulsed against the sink in protest, in acceptance.

Royal heard her small, wounded cry, its sound unbearably poignant in its need and longing, and he clamped down on the fierceness of his hunger. Primitive, that need thundered in his veins, pulsed in his groin. Struggling for control, he lowered his forehead to hers, breaking contact with her soft, tremulous mouth. Lungs and ribs hurting, he labored to breathe. Dropping his hands to the sink, he gripped her narrow ones.

The tremor of her fingers sabotaged his better self, urged him to forget caution, reason, enticed him to forget everything except his body's demand to plunge deep into the slight, warm body of Elly Malloy and find forgetfulness there. And behind his eyelids, battling with his will, the color of his need beat dark red and primal.

He wouldn't have bet a plugged nickel on his conscience. No one else would have, either. Dazed, he found himself stepping away from her, stepping back, and in that moment he felt a kinship with Lucifer of old, plunging bright into that darkness, falling, falling swift and fast into everlasting emptiness, cast out of heaven, its shining gates clanging shut, forever closed to him.

Bemused, Royal looked down at his hand still clasping Elly's. His, stained with grease. Hers, dwarfed by his, pale and shaking in his grip. A streak of axle grease showed dark against her neck. Reluctantly, he straightened his fingers, releasing her, releasing himself.

In the mirror behind her, he saw his reflection. The man in the mirror, that lost, bleak soul, was not one he'd relish meeting in a dark alley. He could almost smell the hell-scent of sulphur and despair rising from that man. He rubbed his face, buying time, erasing the hopelessness in his face with a shaking hand. "Well, sugar, you've got the old kiss-and-make-it-better medicine down pat, I'll give you that."

He couldn't think straight, couldn't decide what to do next. He couldn't meet her eyes, not just yet.

The back of her head quivered, a barely perceptible motion in the mirror, and he lifted his hand to brush her hair back from her face, to tell her that he was sorry for everything, that he was sorry he'd kissed her—

It would have been a lie.

Kissing Elly Malloy reminded him of everything he'd thrown away, willfully, deliberately.

Her head lifted, and her voice was steady, husky. "I shouldn't have kissed you."

Royal blinked. "What?"

As she pushed her shoulders back, the material of her blouse shimmered in the mirror. "You shouldn't have kissed me, either."

"No." He already knew that. He couldn't begin to calculate the cost of that mistake. "I shouldn't have." For the first time, he became aware of the stifling heat in the box of a room. Oppressive, still, the air lay heavy on his skin, weighing him down. "But I did."

"I could have stopped you. I didn't." She sighed. Her mouth was swollen and pink, and he wanted to smooth away the imprint of his kiss. "I made a mistake. That kiss had nothing to do with you. It wasn't personal. It didn't mean anything."

"Golly gee. And here I was picking out china patterns," he drawled, sinking languidly onto the toilet seat. He suppressed the grunt of pain. "I think I've just been shot down."

"I wasn't trying to hurt you."

"Heaven help me if you ever really put your mind to humiliating me, then, sugar," he muttered, stretching out his legs on either side of hers. Her words stung. "A guy kind of prides himself on believing that when he kisses a woman, it means *something*."

Elly, though—well, hell, cool as ice water—was dismissing those moments that had turned him inside out and left him hungrier than he'd ever been in his life. Aside from her still-puffy pink lips, she didn't seem affected in the least.

"I'm only trying to explain—"

"Sugar, do us both a favor?"

Her hair floated around her cat face as she turned toward him. Her expression remote, she lifted her chin. "Yes?"

"Quit explaining."

"Oh."

He eyed her testily, trying to convince himself that what he was feeling was frustrated desire. He knew better. Even when he'd been fifteen, he'd cheerfully accepted that a girl might not be ready to dance when he was. He'd never taken rejection personally. Or seriously. Rejection had never meant all that much. So he couldn't figure out what was making him feel now as though he was ready to butt heads with a bull in the pasture.

All in all, ribs, ego and aching growin' place, he felt downright cranky. "Let's just drop the subject, okay?"

"I don't want you to misunderstand, okay?" Holding his gaze, she frowned. "That's all. I don't want you to think—"

Irritation flared inside him. "Sugar," he said, drawing the words out slowly, "I didn't misunderstand one damned thing. But, darlin', I'd sure like to be around when you decide to dole out a kiss that does mean something. Give me a call if that notion ever strikes you in the middle of the night. Or day. Any time. I'd be dee-lighted to oblige." He shot her a blinding smile, a smile designed to befuddle her brain and leave her senseless. A smile he hoped would leave her as disturbed and aroused as he was.

It didn't.

She remained in full possession of all her faculties.

He didn't like that, either.

The overhead light cast a halo around the feathery lightness of her hair. He hadn't wound his fingers in those feathery strands, hadn't breathed in their scent. But he'd wanted to. He took a deep breath and looked away from that cloudy mass of her hair because it wasn't likely in this life that he was going to have another chance to gather it in his hands and stroke its softness. The regret was an actual pain kinking inside his gut.

She frowned again. "You're angry."

"Hell, sugar, I'm not angry, annoyed or, bless your sweet, luscious self, all that disappointed," he lied, confusion and melancholy stirring in a perverse mix that left him bristly and defensive. "Like you said, it wasn't a big deal."

"Your ribs are hurting, aren't they?" She reached out toward him, her hand hovering near his face, not touching him. With a puzzled look, as if she hadn't realized what she was doing, she let her hand fall to her side. "I haven't wrapped them. I— Your ribs hurt," she repeated, gesturing vaguely in the direction of his abdomen.

He surrendered. "Yeah, I reckon they do. In spite of your special brand of medicine."

"Can we forget this happened?" Again, with the same vagueness, she gestured, her hand floating past his eyes as if disconnected from her arm.

"I can. Can you?" Narrowing his eyes, he smiled gently at her. Maybe she wasn't as composed as she seemed. That would be…nice.

"Of course." Her smile was all lady-of-the-manor prissiness. "Why shouldn't I? It's not the first time I've ever kissed anybody. And you could make me believe the earth was flat sooner than you could convince me it was your first kiss. We're both consenting adults. Good heavens, it was *only* a kiss." Her laugh was amused, sophisticated, inviting him to see the silliness of it all.

But he didn't want to. He wanted to see her flustered, dazed, vulnerable, the way she'd been—the way he'd *thought* she was—when they were kissing. He wanted her to admit that she'd been lost and gone in the moment, too.

"Nothing happened. Only a kiss. Nothing more." In control, serene, she continued to smile at him.

"Yeah. Not like we went at each other hot and heavy on the sink, huh?" He'd thought about that, too. He wondered if she had. He squinted at her, trying to see Elly Malloy going at it with him, hot and heavy, and so careless of where she was that she wouldn't even realize she was bumped up against a sink. Or a wall. Or—

Deep red flowed up her neck into her cheeks, and she looked away. "No, not like that."

"We don't have a problem, then, do we, sugar?" With every wisecrack, he felt like a bigger bastard, but he couldn't stop badgering her. He wanted to shake her up, make her admit that she'd been swept away, too.

Solitary sex had never been his choice.

But cool, ice-water-in-her-veins Elly was making him feel that he'd been all alone there in that honeyed darkness of sighs and touches. For all her reaction now, he might as well have been alone in his own bedroom.

She made him feel as if she didn't give a damn.

But he did. And he didn't want to. It wasn't in his plans. The sting of desire, of needing something from her, left him confused and irritable. "Everything's peachy keen, no problems, right?" No, hell, not *a* problem. About a hundred and ten problems, that's all.

She shifted, her slim legs shining smooth in the light. Black against her skin, a streak of grease from his slacks ran down her inner thigh to her knee. "I don't see a problem."

"Good. I didn't think you would." Smiling back at her, his expression as serene as hers had been, Royal leaned back against the tank and snapped his fingers. "There. Forgotten. In the past."

"Right. Forgotten." Imitating him, she snapped her fingers. Her breasts lifted beneath her blouse, their shape as round and soft as her mouth had been under his.

He'd wanted to kiss her breasts, too. He hadn't, but he still wanted to, still wanted to see if the soft, pebbled tips were the same rose-plum color of her mouth. He swallowed, the strangled gulp audible in the silence.

Her gaze met his.

The red flush that had stained her neck and cheeks rushed upward again in splotches and hectic color. "Well. I'll find the pressure wrap. The butterfly bandages. I might have to shave some of your hair where it's matted down. I'll soap it first, though, to make sure. I'm sure you don't want to walk around like a medieval friar. I'm sure all that stuff's here somewhere." She turned away, bending down to a cabinet clumsily, awkwardly, her shoe heel slipping on the floor with the quickness of her motions, betraying her. She was as aware of him as he was of her.

And then Royal finally got it. What was really pissing him off was the realization that the simple kiss hadn't been simple at all. Not in the least. Not for him.

He didn't want that careless kiss to matter. It shouldn't have meant anything to him.

But it had.

The kiss had disturbed Elly, too.

He didn't want to think about this woman, couldn't afford to *want* her with this aching need that made him feel like a kid with his nose pressed up against the candy-store window.

But he wanted her. Even now, even in spite of everything he'd said, in spite of everything he'd pretended, he wanted her.

He didn't like this tenderness growing inside him, this urge to protect her. Tenderness was a complication he didn't want, not with Elly Malloy.

Tenderness was dangerous.

And danger was all around them. He couldn't let himself forget that again, not for a second. Ignoring the twinges and stiffening muscles, he leaned forward, asking the question that had bothered him from the beginning. "Why did you open your front door, Elly?"

Arms still crossed, breasts lifting with her quick inhalation, she shrugged. "You called my name."

"I could have been—" he started to say *your husband,* but he caught himself "—anybody. You took a risk."

"I thought I recognized your voice."

"You could have been wrong."

Tinged with sadness, her smile changed the contours of her face and showed him yet another Elly Malloy as she said, "I knew what could happen if I were wrong. I try not to take unnecessary chances. I don't like surprises."

"You said the same thing earlier today."

"Did I?" She rubbed the thin line under the fluff of bangs. "I don't remember."

"I do. I pay attention to what you say. Even ex-cops have a tendency to focus on details. You said you didn't like surprises. I listen to you. I remember trivial things. Specifics."

Her laugh was shaky. "That's a scary thought. A man who listens when a woman says something. I don't think I've ever met a man like that."

"Maybe you've been hanging around the wrong kind of man."

Royal caught the way her mouth tightened, the way she deliberately kept her face blank.

"Could be. But I don't date." She rummaged through a shoe box filled with bandages and tubes of ointment.

"Difficult to date, I'd think. Being a single mom. Divorced. On your own. Must be hard. Raising Tommy Lee all by yourself. Without his father."

A tube slipped from her grasp into the sink bowl. "Sometimes. But I don't miss dating."

"Don't you?" Royal remembered the loneliness he'd tasted in her kiss, the hunger. "Now, that surprises *me*."

She whirled on him, the shoe box held like a shield in front of her. "Look, I don't date, I didn't open my door impulsively or naively. And I take care of my son and myself. I was prepared. For surprises. For unwelcome visitors."

"The ammonia."

"The ammonia," she agreed, her hand bending the edge of the cardboard box.

"In the eyes?"

She looked down at the floor, back up at him, put the shoe box back on the sink. "If necessary." Her hands shaking so slightly that Royal almost missed their flutters, she laid out a box of elastic wrap and another flat package containing butterfly bandages. "If I had to. Yes."

"You're tougher than you look, aren't you?"

"I've learned to be." She picked up the solvent container. Put it down. Picked it up again. "I can do what I have to."

His gaze moving over her fine-boned frame, Royal regarded her. Under the smooth skin of her calves and thighs, supple muscles moved easily. He noted the muscle definition in her slim arms, remembered their strength as she'd maneuvered his weight into her house. "I believe you."

"Good." Steely determination glinted in the brown eyes meeting his. "Now, Detective, unbutton your shirt—"

"Gosh, I like a woman who knows her own mind—"

"So I can tape your ribs."

"Damn. Just my luck."

"You never quit, do you?" Pulling the elastic tape out of the box, she flicked the metal tabs on the wrap, a tiny clicking sound.

"Not while I can breathe." He slipped the last button free and grinned, liking the way she gave him an exasperated glance.

"Breathing may be a problem once you're taped tighter than a two-thousand-year-old mummy." She stepped forward, hesitating as she looked at his shirt, his chest. Pink tipped her cheeks again. She brushed her hair back from her face with one hand and took his filthy shirt with the other.

He heard the sound of dismay when she saw his ribs. He glanced down at the purpling welts and bruises, shrugged and then regretted his nonchalance at the pull of tendons and ligaments.

"This is bad, Royal." She touched his side, her fingers light and cool on his skin. Dangling from her hand, the end of the wrap brushed against him, its metal tabs cold as they swung across his belly. "Your stomach and side look as though someone used you for a floor mat." She wrinkled her face in concern and looked at him, her eyes wide with distress. "I hope taping you isn't a mistake."

"It isn't."

But he'd made a big mistake. Because Elly Malloy wasn't the woman Scanlon had sketched to him.

Observing her quick, competent motions as she readied the sink with clean, soapy water and unrolled the tape, he went over the puzzle pieces again.

In Scanlon's version, Elly had faked her own death in order to kidnap Scanlon's son. That woman would have been very devious. Or very, very desperate. Royal wondered which woman would turn out to be the real Elly, regardless of whatever name she was calling herself.

If she'd faked her death out of desperation, she was going to need every bit of toughness she could find in her five feet three inches. Gritty and gutsy, she'd spun a web of lies to hide behind, but the daily pressure had to be enormous. She had to know that Scanlon wanted her back, but she'd constructed this life for herself and her son, this life that was nothing more than a flimsy house of cards. Even so, even knowing the risk she was taking, she'd opened her door at his call for help when he could have been Scanlon himself.

The woman who'd done that had enough courage for five men.

Royal wondered if she realized quite how vulnerable she was. Her ammonia wouldn't have been worth squat if he'd been one of the goons that had surprised him in the bushes near her kitchen. As she stepped between his legs, passed the bandage around his waist and anchored it, he sighed.

He didn't want to like her, he didn't want to be responsible for her or her equally tough son in any way, but here he was, and he'd brought violence into her house. Maybe he did owe her an apology of some sort. "Elly?" Bending forward and sucking in the gasp that almost came whistling out, he touched her wrist. "Look, I'm sorry."

"For kissing me?" She threw up her hands in annoyance, and the tape unrolled across his knees to the floor. She stooped to pick it up, and her hair floated across his thigh. Looking up at him with the tape in her hands, she said, "We both agreed. The subject is closed—"

"No. For coming here tonight. I shouldn't have done that."

She was quick. "You think those men followed you? That they knew who you were?"

"I believe it's highly probable."

"I thought—" She closed her mouth tightly, stopping the flood of words. Unconsciously, she placed her hand on his knee for support and leaned toward him. "Why would thugs beat up on you?"

"I'm not a good man, Elly. I know a lot of bad people. Bad people make a game out of hurting people sometimes."

"I don't understand." She edged closer, her pointed chin tilting up toward him. Elastic tape wedged between her fingers, she curved her hand over his thigh in unspoken entreaty. "I need to know why you were attacked, Royal. For my own sake. You see, I thought—" Again, she tightened her lips, stopping whatever she'd been about to say.

He knew what she thought. She thought the men had attacked him because of her, that they'd been waiting for her, so he answered her in the best way he could. "I've made enemies. Some of them are crooks. And some are cops."

"Explain it to me. Please." Her fingers tightened, and an arrow of exquisite pain shot straight to his groin. "Were those men who beat you up cops? Does what happened tonight have anything to do with why you quit being a detective?"

He chose to answer her last question. "No. I managed that all on my own. I screwed up." With that admission, desolation filled him. Too many memories. Too many regrets. But what could he have changed? He was what he was. A strand of her hair drifted across his fist in a tickling, teasing slide and he turned his palm toward it, letting the tendril wrap around his thumb. He wanted to bury his face in the mass of that light, soft brown and forget all the reasons why he found himself in Elly Malloy's bathroom with her on her knees in front on him. He shrugged, and the effort hurt now that his muscles were stiffening and tightening up. Or maybe it was the deeper hurt, the loss he hadn't admitted, not even to himself until this moment. "I threw away everything in my life."

"Why? What did you do?" With slow movements, she untangled the bandage and moved in to his chest, passing the bandage around his waist and back, pulling the tape tightly around his aching ribs, smoothing it with easy, gentle strokes while she waited, silent, for him to say whatever he was going to.

Royal had a hard time shaping his thoughts into words. He hadn't talked about what had happened with anyone, not even Maggie. "I like to walk on the razor's edge. It's my drug of choice. The danger. The adrenaline. The buzz of figuring out what a crook will do before he's even decided himself. I like crawling inside their minds and living there, thinking like them, walking the same streets they do, and then, just when they think they're safe, I walk up and tap them on the shoulder. And they look like they're going to sh— Well. I love being there, waiting, when they think they've made it home free."

"Sounds like you were doing a good job."

"It's more than a job. It's who I am."

"How so?" Her tongue was caught between her teeth as she kept working the bandage into place, her hair tickling his bare skin with her every dip and twist around him. "Are you saying you had no life outside catching crooks?"

"Not much. It's where I'm alive, you understand?" He trapped a handful of her hair and tugged lightly until she paused and looked up at him. "I live it, breathe it. I love the expression on their faces when they see me." Excitement crackled through his blood as he remembered. "They always think they've figured all the angles, but somewhere along the way, they forget something, and there I am."

"Lift your arm as high as you can."

Feeling his muscles protest, Royal lifted his arm. He definitely wasn't in the condition he'd been when he was a detective. "That okay?"

"Sure." She ducked under his arm. Her head was under his arm as she reached to his back to catch the roll of tape, her breath damply warm against his nipples, and he felt them harden to that whisper of air. She'd worked the tape almost to its end and she passed it once more around his chest with the hand that had been on his thigh. Her expression as she leaned forward to catch the roll was so endearingly earnest and sweet that he almost told her to shag him out of her house as fast as she could. Stretching the tape as tight as she could, she fastened the end tab in place and leaned back on her heels. "Do you realize you talk about being a cop in the present tense?"

"Do I?" Excitement trickled away, and he leaned back wearily, shutting his eyes, letting himself drift away. "I didn't know that. But it doesn't matter."

"No?" She stood up, and he thought she brushed her hand across his cheek. "Maybe you still care."

"I used to say that there was a thin line between us and crooks. One or the other. I think I probably have more in common with the weasels. One thing is for sure, though. I don't think of myself in any way as a cop. I gave up that right when I surrendered my pistol."

"And why, exactly, did you do that, Royal?" Her voice was soft, lulling him to sleep, hypnotizing him as she soaped his scalp, working the hair free of his wound and then blotting the wet strands. "What did you do that was so terrible? Did you start selling drugs? Did you kill someone? Did you take bribes? How did you screw up, Royal?"

The bite of ointment on his scalp jerked him back to alertness. He opened his eyes and found himself nose to nose with her, the warm brown of her eyes compassionate and, for the first time since he'd known her, unguarded.

Of all the things he wanted least from Elly, compassion and pity topped the list.

Capturing her wrist, he tugged her closer. The tube of Neosporin tumbled to the floor. "That's what Palmaflora thinks. That I was involved in murders, in a police protection ring that allowed toxic dumping, that I betrayed my partner, my best friend. That I sold out. Because I was the department's fair-haired wonder. Because I was corrupt and liked the easy life."

"Did you?" Her whisper was soft.

"What if I did?" With his free hand, he captured her other wrist. "You're in my power now, Elly. You've let me in your house. No one knows I'm here. I told you, cop or crook. What do you think? Which am I, Elly? Tell me."

Chapter 6

In some remote corner of his soul, in the darkness filling him, Royal yearned for Elly to tell him she trusted him with her life, with herself, with everything she had. He yearned for her to take a leap of faith and see past the disillusionment and emptiness killing him.

With the narrow bones of her wrists clasped in his hands and exhaustion blanketing him, he thought he must have been hit over the head harder than he'd realized to hope for that from her. From anyone.

For months, for a lifetime, he'd pretended that he didn't care about anything, didn't care about the destruction of his reputation, of his life. Now, too late, Elly made him care, made him regret the waste of his life. He'd made his choices, lousy though they were. He shook his head, clearing it of the fatigue muddying his reactions. "Cop or crook? Saint or sinner, Elly?"

"I think you've cleverly managed to avoid telling me why you think those men attacked you." Elly watched him as he blinked stupidly at her with his good eye, trying to keep up with her. "And I think you're testing me for some reason. So quit trying to intimidate me. Every time you want to distract me, you play games of one kind or another with me. I don't like it one

damned bit. And I'd like some straightforward answers, buster."
She didn't move, didn't make an attempt to free herself.

"You're too damned smart," he said, staring at her but not releasing her wrists. "But I underestimated you, Elly. You're quick out of the starting gate. Nothing escapes you, does it?"

"I could say the same about you."

"Compared to you, sugar, I'm the last horse in the race." He'd tried to make her think the attack was random, but she hadn't bought that for a minute. He'd thought he could blow it past her. He'd deliberately avoided identifying his attackers. In fact, his muggers could have been anybody's goons trying to force him to pay up any number of gambling debts. They could have been—

She jiggled her wrists and stuck her face close to his insistently. "Spell what's happening out very clearly for me, will you? Because I need to know if you recognized these men. You act as if you're keeping some bit of information from me, but I need to know why they attacked you. Were they cops? Is that what you've been hinting? Because I don't care if you screwed up, I don't care why you quit being a detective, but I have to know if those men attacked you because of something in your past. Tell me." She shoved his shoulder. "*Were those men cops?* Is that why you didn't want me to call the police?"

"They could have been."

Indignation bloomed in her face. "If you were attacked by cops, that's lousy. Even if you screwed up somehow, they shouldn't be allowed to get away with assaulting you. Because that's what it was, even if they were former colleagues. And no matter what, the attack should be reported, especially if you have the slightest idea who those jerks were."

"Some people hold grudges."

"Do they have a right to?" Her steady gaze met his as she finally came out and asked him the sixty-four-thousand dollar question.

"They think so."

"Why?"

"If they're good cops, they're pissed at me because they think I sold them out."

"Did you?"

"Do you think I did?"

"Why do you keep answering questions with a question? It's damned annoying, let me tell you."

"Is it?"

In the mirror to her side, her annoyed movement shimmered and flashed. Her shrug was a nonanswer, a tiny lift of one shoulder. "Did you betray your colleagues, your friends? I haven't the slightest idea. You'd be capable of it, I think. But if you did, I think you'd have a darned good reason."

In the twilight zone where pain and tiredness had taken him, he discovered that her offhanded observation left him speechless. He cleared his throat. "Thank you."

"Even if it didn't wash with anyone except yourself. You're like an onion, Royal, layer after layer, all translucent and deceptively clear." Resignation replaced the irritation.

"You sure cut a guy down to size, sugar." He focused on the wary depth of her eyes. "My body's not the only thing that's taken a beating tonight."

"I'm so sorry," she said, not the least apologetically, a faint smile glowing in the warm brown of her eyes. "Anyway, the way you read the situation is that the attackers could have been good guys who had personal reasons for interacting violently—"

"Such fancy talk. I'm stupefied with awe."

"Stupefied, I believe." Her smile melted into a genuine one.

"Remind me to check for extra wounds before I leave, will you, sugar?" He scowled at her. "I must have lost an extra quart of blood since I've known you. I'm goin' to need a transfusion if I hang around you much longer."

"Poor baby." She wrinkled her nose at him before continuing. "But enough sympathy. Back to business—"

"Tough lady, keeping that elegant little nose to the grindstone. And such a lovely nose it is." He lifted their joined hands and skimmed the back of his down the bridge of her nose.

"I said 'business,' Royal. Not monkey business." She shook her head, bouncing his hand away. "I'm clear about the motivation if they're good cops. But if they're bad cops?"

"Same thing. Kind of a lose-lose situation, huh?" He yawned and his ears popped.

"But if they're not cops? What about that possibility?"

"I have a whole bunch of gambling debts. They could have been making me aware of their feelings on the subject. They're not patient men." And if those men had showed up to collect gambling debts, they had come from Scanlon. A wisp of an idea teased him, vanished like smoke.

She frowned. "Gambling debts. That doesn't sound like you. You're not that kind of personality. To gamble to the point you'd owe some slime-bag money."

In his lassitude and sadness, her absolute certainty moved him. "But I am. I did. I truly did lose almost every dime to my name." He laughed. This truth was so easy, but she wasn't buying it. "You don't believe me, do you?"

She was so sure of herself, she didn't miss a beat. "You're a man who likes to play games."

"It's simple," he said patiently, bewildered by her unwillingness to accept what was, in fact, the truth. "I like walking the edge. I like taking risks. I like all kinds of games. Poker's one of them."

"Oh, I don't doubt for a second that you might gamble. Play the dogs. Whatever. I can see that. The excitement would appeal to you. It would jump-start your engine."

"Lot of things jump-start my engine, sugar," he drawled, tiredness slurring his words again, everything blurring and fading in and out, but he didn't want her following the thread of her thoughts any further. "Interested in a drive?"

She rolled her eyes, amusement clear in the shake of her head. "Sheesh, give it up, Gaines. Take a rest."

"But resting is boring, sugar. Leastwise, that's what I've always found." His eyes drifted closed, and he forced them open with an effort that for a second seemed beyond him.

Scratching the back of one calf with her foot, she stood on one leg, assessing him in much the same way he'd evaluated her earlier. "You do like being in control. And you wouldn't like losing that control. Losing control to anyone or anything would kill you."

"But gambling's an addiction, sugar." He didn't know why he was trying to convince her of the worst about himself. The more she understood, the harder he pushed her away. Weariness made him feel as if he were moving through molasses, and he closed his eyes for a moment. Lord help her, if she didn't already know he was bad news, he didn't have to work overtime dotting the *i*'s and crossing the *t*'s for her. He opened his eyes grittily.

"See, with addictions, a person can't help himself. Control doesn't enter the equation."

"That's the point. If you started to lose money, you'd stop gambling. You'd stop before you became addicted. To anything. Drugs, habits, people." She shook her head slowly, reaching her conclusion. "No. I don't believe that you're in debt to hoodlums." And then she amazed him, left him staring at her witlessly. "Unless—" she scrunched her face in thought, her pink mouth pursed "—unless you meant to be. Because you didn't care one way or another. Because you'd given up on everything important to you."

"All you need is a couch and you could hang out a shingle, Elly. All this analysis is putting me to sleep. You're boring me, sugar, let me tell you." This time, his yawn was deliberately rude. Only Maggie had fought him so hard, had believed him despite all the evidence to the contrary. Maggie, of course, had known him better than anyone. They'd been partners, in sync. Even Leesha had reservations about him.

But skinny, mouthy, fragile blossom Elly Malloy, who didn't know beans about him, who had no facts to base her statement on, she'd pinned down the perverse pride that had driven him down the road to his own personal hell. "Do I owe you ninety bucks, sweetheart? For the fifty-five-minute hour?"

Tilting her face thoughtfully, she frowned. "Did you, ex-Detective Gaines, set yourself up for a fall?"

"You'd make a hell of an interrogator, Elly. You don't give up, either, do you?"

"Never."

Under his thumb, her pulse beat rapidly and he loosened his grasp, circling her wrists with his thumb and forefinger, the inner skin of her wrist so silky he wanted to bring it to his mouth and run his lips over it, just to test that smoothness for himself, to breathe in the scent of her skin that came to him like a promise of redemption.

One thought stirred in the fog of his brain. He released her wrists, and she stepped back. "And you're not afraid of me, are you?"

"Should I be?" Reaching behind her and gripping the washrag she'd cleaned his scalp with, she waited for his answer.

"Yes." He nodded sluggishly. "People get hurt around me, sugar."

"I won't. I told you. I can take care of myself and my son. You're not responsible for me."

Hearing her echo his own thoughts, Royal almost smiled. "But you saved my life. So that makes you responsible for me."

Bemused, he peered up at her.

"Not likely." She narrowed her eyes. "You saved Tommy. Do you consider yourself responsible for him?"

Thinking of the sturdy little boy with the streak of stubborn curiosity and the unwarranted trust Tommy had given him, Royal felt his breath catch in his throat. He remembered Scanlon's thin-lipped smile, the curiously self-satisfied smile as he'd talked of his wife's kidnapping of his son. The kid had a sweetness to him that was pure Elly and none of Scanlon, a sweetness that looked through Royal and saw something of value.

Goofy little squirt. And for all his chunky weight, the kid had been so small, so fragile, when Royal had plucked him from the water. A moment more— Reluctantly, he nodded. "Yeah, I reckon I do. Damn. Guess that makes Tommy and me linked for life, huh?"

"Linked for life? Again, not likely. Besides, you don't strike me as a man who'd get all gooey and sentimental about kids."

He looked up at her, suddenly disturbed by the idea of his empty days stretching down the years. "How do I strike you, Elly?"

"Oh, the lone-gunslinger type, that's you," she said mockingly. "Fast out of town and not one for long-term commitments." Bending over him, she lifted the strands of his hair at the crown and smoothed down the edges near the wound. "This is your lucky day, Detective, I'm not going to have to shave you." She dropped the washrag into the sink. Water splashed onto her leg, glossing it with shine and light. Holding the edge of the package between her teeth, she ripped it open and pulled out a bandage. "Once the swelling goes down and the bruises disappear, you'll be as beautiful as ever."

"But will I be able to play the violin?" he asked mournfully, trying to tease her, provoke her, trying to do anything he could to erase that image of himself alone for the rest of his life.

"Could you before?" Her grin was cheeky.

"Nope."

"Well, there you are, then." She patted his shoulder companionably, her other hand lingering against his scalp.

The feel of her fingers running over his scalp was soothing, restful. He liked very much the feel of her hand on him. He could sleep for days like this, with her touching him, smoothing his hair, brushing his forehead gently. Lethargy and pain made his bones feel too heavy for his muscles to move, and he turned his face, brushing his mouth across her knuckles. "You have the smoothest skin, Elly Malloy. And you smell like an old-fashioned flower garden." He kissed the streak of grease running across her hand, nudging her palm to his mouth.

Elly felt her womb clench. His touch against her open palm turned her insides to melting chocolate.

And then he looked up at her. "Did you know that you smell of flowers and hope?"

"No." Elly swallowed. His words made her want to weep. Such tenderness in his exhausted, shadowed eyes. Such despair. She stroked his head. "You need sleep, Royal. And you're in pain. Let me get you something."

"An elixir for what really ails me?" His eyelids drifted shut, opened. "Can your medicine cure a malaise of the soul, Elly?" Lifting his hand slowly, he captured her hand. "Do you have something like that in your medicine cabinet?"

Heat flooded her, liquid and luxurious. "Probably not. But I can help you sleep, Royal. Sleep is what you need right now." She slipped her hand free and turned away from the torment in his sea bright eyes. Fumbling in the cabinet, she found the bottle of painkillers her veterinarian friend had given her six months ago. She shook out two of the small white tablets. "Here." She opened Royal's hand and dropped the tablets into it.

Turning them over and over with his thumb, he studied them. "I know these," he said finally. "These are prescription pills. I've had them before. After surgery. What are you doing with this kind of painkiller, Elly?"

Unplugging the sink and turning on the cold water, she let it run for a second before filling the tumbler. "Drink." She held the tumbler to his mouth. "Take the pills. We'll discuss my medications another time."

He drank. He gulped down the pills, then stood up, wavering

back and forth in front of her. "Call me a cab, Elly. So I can go home."

"All right. You're a cab, Royal. Here." She slid her arm around his waist, avoiding his taped rib cage. "Come with me."

"Smart aleck." He rested his chin on top of her hair. His breath ruffled her bangs. "The best-smelling smart mouth I've ever known. I'll dream about the way your hair smells, Elly, the scent of your skin."

"Fine. Sweet dreams," she muttered, guiding him into her living room and the lumpy couch. "Sorry for the condition of the couch, but it's either that or the floor. I'll get you a pillow." Holding him, she followed his frame as he folded down onto the couch.

"Sure." He let his head fall to the back of the sofa. "This is nice." He lifted his head and fastened his gaze on hers, stopping her retreat. The bandage on his head gleamed whitely in the room. "I won't forget *nice,* Elly. I'll remember that, too." And then his head fell back again, and his eyes closed. That fast, he was asleep, the strands of his hair gleams of sunlight against the drab couch, his face drained and bruised and completely vulnerable in sleep. A strand of gold hair curled over the edge of the beige tape wrapping his chest and ribs.

In the hot room with the summer scent of night-blooming jasmine drifting in, the sweetness pulsing through her was unbearable. The summer night and its smells reminded her of other times, other places, of a time past when the whole world was filled with promise, a time she didn't think would ever come again for her. Royal had spoken of hope. She didn't see much of that ahead, either.

But Tommy was alive, and so was she. They went to the beach, they let ice cream drip down their chins, they roasted marshmallows on twigs over a small campfire in the backyard. She had what was most important to her in the world—her son. Comparatively speaking, she had nothing to complain about.

But Royal Gaines made the boundaries she'd established for her life seem like prison bars.

The glint of gold hair across the top of his chest shone in the light. Wistfully, she touched her lips to his forehead, and went to get the pillow and a sheet to cover him. Without his shirt, he'd be chilled before morning, even in the heat of her house.

When she returned, he hadn't moved. Sliding him sideways, she lifted his long legs up onto her couch and settled his head on the pillow. When she adjusted the pillow to make it more comfortable, he murmured, "Elly?"

"Me," she answered, flipping the sheet open. "Go to sleep."

He didn't stir when she slid off his shoes. Inside was embossed the name of the Italian manufacturer she'd expected. Whatever Royal had done with his money, he'd had enough at one point to buy himself exorbitantly expensive footwear, footwear that would shine up as gorgeous as ever. Expensive goods wore well. While she didn't miss them, she couldn't help the "Ah" of appreciation that escaped her as the supple leather caressed her palm. A woman could be forgiven the occasional craving.

The craving for Royal Gaines and his touch, for the teasing shimmer in his eyes that stirred her—that was another issue, and one she was in no shape to deal with at the moment. Her fingers lingering against the pliant leather, she placed the shoes on the floor.

Hesitating, she decided to leave his socks on, curiously reticent to strip them from his long, narrow feet.

Irrational, illogical, and she couldn't begin to explain it, even to herself, but taking off his socks struck her at that moment as somehow an invasion of his privacy. With him already sleeping half-naked in front of her, she felt the balance of power had shifted entirely to her. She unbuckled his belt and slipped it through the loops, the long hiss of the whisper of leather over fabric companionable in the quiet house. Coiling the belt, she placed it carefully inside his shoes and lined them up beside the couch where he'd see them when he opened his eyes.

As she stood over his sleeping form, a wave of longing filled her. She wanted normalcy. She had a complicated script of lies and evasions. She craved ordinary, and she had Royal Gaines in her life, asleep on her couch. Royal Gaines, the least ordinary man she'd ever met, a complex man with his own evasions and half-truths.

A man with his own demons to fight.

And what he touched in her went beyond sexual hunger.

Elly sighed and turned away. She could think more clearly in the morning.

As she did every night, she checked the windows, making sure that the restraints were secure so that none of the windows could be opened easily or without alerting her. She closed and locked all the windows except for the ones in the living room and in the bedroom. Leaving a light on in the kitchen in case Royal woke up disoriented, she turned on the attic fan that would draw the cooler night air in and vent out the heat of the day.

Lying in bed with her own sheet drawn over her, she listened to the faint sounds of the night. She didn't expect to sleep. She had too much to think about. Turning on her side, she heard Tommy's whuffling breaths, a tiny whimper, and she reached across the gap between their beds to take his hand in hers.

If Royal were correct, she and Tommy wouldn't have to uproot themselves.

Moonlight slanted in past the sides of the roll-down shades.

But did she trust Royal enough to accept his explanation? An explanation that had enough holes in it for a manatee to swim through? If she went along with him, she could buy herself and Tommy time to make better plans than her present slash-and-burn mode of disappearance.

She didn't believe for a second that he'd allowed himself to fall into a gambling addiction. She could, though, accept that the attack had been personal.

Because Royal Gaines was definitely a man who could make enemies if he decided to.

Turning over, tangling herself in the sheet, Elly switched her grip so that she could continue to touch her son while she let her thoughts drift and eddy with the pass of moonlight and shadows across her ceiling.

Royal was more than the careless beach bum he pretended to be. He'd treated her to the charm of the sun-bright, teasing, flirting man, and she'd glimpsed in unguarded moments the dark melancholy of his despair, a despair she didn't understand, a despair she was certain he didn't want her to see.

Six months' worth of paranoia had sharpened her survival instincts. She'd heard his evasions and not been fooled by the accidental meetings. She rubbed the scar on her forehead anxiously. Royal was involved in *something*. Whether or not that something affected her and Tommy was what was keeping her awake.

That, and the knowledge that someone had been watching her, following her. Regardless of who had attacked Royal, the person who'd left the cigarette stub in the flowerpot was connected with her, not him. If she hadn't been alert and careful, she would have missed that minute bit of evidence that someone, for reasons of his or her own, had watched her.

She didn't believe in coincidences. Somehow, despite his charm and his despair, Royal Gaines was, as he'd said, involved in her life. The question for her, the ultimate life-or-death question, was why?

Caught in a draft of air from the reopened window, the shade popped against the window frame.

"Mommy?" Breaking her hold, Tommy sat bolt upright. "Mommy!"

"Shh, honey, Mommy's here. Right beside you. Don't worry, sugarplum," she crooned, climbing into the bed with him and pulling his rigid body close to her. "We're hunky-dory. You're safe. Go to sleep, honey."

His eyes, wide and terrified and unseeing, met hers. "Mommy!"

Gathering him as close as she could, Elly sang quietly into his soft, baby cheek, letting her voice reach him in the night terror that held him captive. Over and over, she whispered and sang, lulling, soothing, until her voice cracked.

When his shivering stopped and the regular pattern of his breathing told her he was once again sleeping deeply and not in that nightmare world from which he couldn't be woken, she bit her lip to keep from crying. She knew what had brought on this episode.

She couldn't rip Tommy from the friends and security he'd grown comfortable in. She'd take the risk that the attack in her yard had been aimed at Royal.

She could believe that, too, if she could forget that unsettling sense that someone had been watching her. Those unseen eyes had been watching *her*, not Royal.

Like her son, Elly shivered in the sultry summer night.

No matter what, she reminded herself, she wouldn't let down her guard with Royal Gaines. She'd weigh everything he said and did, stay prepared and keep an eye on him.

If the idea of keeping watch on his tarnished gold self sent a different kind of shiver up her spine, well, she'd deal with that, too. For Tommy's sake, she was prepared to take what was, after all, a small risk.

Considering the possibilities and the risks, she thought of the man sleeping yards away from her and her son. He said he'd come to talk with Tommy about the rodeo. Maybe he had.

With Tommy's sweaty, infinitely sweet body curled into hers, she plummeted into sleep.

And awoke, screaming at the sound of gunshots outside her house. Awoke to the sight of Royal Gaines, bruised, bandaged and frighteningly fierce, standing over her.

"What the hell is it, Elly?" His weight balanced on the balls of his feet, he scanned the room. "What's the matter?"

"I heard gunshots," she whispered, sweat drenching her nightgown. "Gunshots. Outside." Wadded in the sheet, her fists shook as if she had a fever.

Later she would recall how the coiled tension of his body loosened at her words. He sank onto the edge of the bed and covered her flailing hands with his, holding them still. "Firecrackers, Elly. It's the Fourth of July. Firecrackers."

"Firecrackers," she said dully, not comprehending. She'd heard gunshots.

"That's all. Take a deep breath." He urged her head down toward her knees, his fingers rough and callused against the back of her neck. Water spilled across the bed, splashing onto her knees as he grabbed the glass of water on the nightstand and held the rim of the glass to her mouth.

Elly wanted to cling to his hand for all she was worth.

She didn't.

Even now, even thrown back into that Christmas terror, she tried to free her hands from the unbearable comfort Royal offered her. He grounded her when her heart fluttered and banged against her rib cage like a trapped bird, grounded her when she was ready to flee, to scream, to take that final slide into panic.

"Hey, Mr. Royal!" Tommy butted his head between them, jarring the glass of water in Royal's hand.

Steadying the glass, Royal replaced it on the stand, drops of water following his motion. "Hey, yourself, water boy."

"You came for me!" Tommy poked a finger in Elly's face and threw himself at her. "I told you he wouldn't forget."

"No, he didn't." Elly's voice was strangled. She hoped both Tommy and Royal would pass off her smothered words as the result of Tommy's energetic hugs.

In the storm-cloud bruises of his face, Royal's clear gaze held hers as she raised her head. "You okay, Elly?"

"Sure." With trembling fingers, she lifted the damp sheet away from her body. In that instant of waking, she'd forgotten where she was. Pleating the sheet over and over, she avoided looking at Royal. She hadn't fooled him. "I was startled, that's all. I forgot today is a holiday."

"Did you, Elly?" he asked softly, leaning forward until the purples and blues of his face and body filled her vision. "That must have been a hell of a...surprise." His warm palm remained at her nape, a connection of flesh and bone between them that calmed her.

"Yes." Concentrating on the fanfold she was making of her damp sheet, she slowed her breathing, fought back the memories. "I was dreaming."

Royal stroked the line of her chin with his thumb, casually, just letting her know he was there, nothing sexual in the comforting motion that reminded Elly of the way she'd soothed her son during his night terrors.

"Tommy Lee, why don't you and I go into the kitchen and see what we can find for breakfast?" Royal's thumb continued that slow, lingering stroke along her neck even while he spoke to Tommy.

As much as her will told her to push Royal's hand away, to fight her battle one more time, the touch of his hand was such comfort, such a relief, that Elly found she couldn't summon the energy to reject that reassuring stroke of his hand.

"Your face is funny looking." Tommy stuck his finger into the corner of Royal's eye. "And you got a white thing stuck up on your head and over your eyeball."

"You can make fun of my funny face while we dig up something for breakfast. That work for you?"

"Yep. But I'm not making fun. That's mean. The kids made fun of me when I started at Leesha's. But Leesha made them stop. So I would not make fun of you. Even if you do look funny." Tommy gazed at Royal's face, the bandage around his ribs. "Big Band-Aid. I want one." He slid a stubby finger inside one of the overlaps. "Cool."

"Maybe your mom'll find an extra one for you after we bring her breakfast in bed."

Touched by Royal's attempts to let her pull herself together, Elly nodded. "Sure."

"Mommy don't let me eat in bed. No place except at the kitchen table. Or in the car. Only sometimes," Tommy added conscientiously. "But never in bed."

"Well, we'll be gentlemen and give your mom a chance to wake up and meet the day. Sometimes, a man needs to take care of a lady, especially when that lady's his mom, you know?"

Elly couldn't remember the last time anyone had taken care of her.

Tommy wiggled closer to Royal, speaking in a confidential tone. "I'm a gentleman. I take real good care of my mom. I ran all the way through the woods when—"

"That's enough, Tommy. I'm getting up." Elly couldn't let him finish his story. Five years old, and he had to be as close-mouthed as a spy. "We'll talk about the rodeo while we eat."

"Sure." Scrambling over Royal's knees, Tommy slid onto the floor, his bottom bouncing on Royal's bare foot. "Sorry," he said, his glance apprehensive.

"No problem," Royal answered easily, hauling the kid off the floor. "I have five other toes."

Tommy Lee darted a look at Royal's foot.

"On the other foot. Not this one." Royal wiggled his toes obligingly.

"Okay. But I didn't mean to—"

Cupping his hand around Tommy Lee's neck, Royal stemmed the flood of words. "It's all right, Thomas Lee. Really." Royal thought Elly flinched, but he couldn't check, not with the boy's enormous eyes drinking in everything he was saying. "I don't say things I don't mean, hear? I'm not angry. Squashed toes are a *very* small deal in the grand scheme of things."

"Squashed toes." Tommy giggled and squatted down to check Royal's feet, poking at each one. "Nope. Not smashed." He gave Royal a grin of pure mischief. And relief.

The boy's too-quick apology disturbed Royal. The mother's haunted eyes and drawn face disturbed him. Everything about

Elly Malloy Scanlon whoever-the-hell-she-was disturbed him, and he wasn't going to be able to walk away from her and her kid, who decided to drape himself companionably across Royal's thighs, balancing on one leg and swaying from side to side.

Elly had done the same thing. Last night. One palm cupped around her neck, one around her son's, Royal shot her a glance.

Her face was pale and tired and, in the morning light, plain, stripped of its sparkle and sass. He could see now more clearly than ever the strain in her features, the depth of her exhaustion, and if he'd had Blake Scanlon in front of him, he would have smashed the man's thin-lipped face to pulp.

Maybe Elly had faked her death. Maybe she had kidnapped Scanlon's son. *Her* son.

And maybe she hadn't.

Reaching down, Royal swung Tommy up to his shoulders, managing to stifle an unmanly whimper of pain. "Let's give your mom some privacy. I'll bet I can find some eggs in that kitchen. Or cereal." He'd be double-damned if he'd let the kid know how much his muscles and ribs screamed at the effort. Not this kid.

And with Elly's son on his shoulders, Royal rose awkwardly from her bed, where the rumpled sheets smelled of her sweetness, and he turned to look at her, to say only that he'd see her in a few moments. In response, she lifted her pointed chin and regarded him steadily with lost, brave eyes.

Chapter 7

Wearing that bright flag of her bravery and courage, Elly Malloy was the most beautiful woman he'd ever seen in his life. He'd tried not to care about her. He told himself he didn't. He couldn't. But if he'd had a heart left, it would have broken in that instant.

He couldn't face her, not knowing what he knew, not suspecting what he suspected. He'd done the unthinkable, and he couldn't change anything, not about himself, not about the decisions he'd made. If she knew, she would despise him.

He retreated into the ordinary events of the day. Life had, after all, a rhythm that carried people forward even when they couldn't find the strength to paddle on their own. "Eggs or cereal, Elly?"

"Neither, thank you. I'm not hungry." Her hair fluttered and sifted around her wan face as she shook her head.

How he could have thought her plain for an instant, Royal couldn't imagine. Scrutinizing the colorless delicacy of her face, the curve of her spine, he decided that *plain* had never been the right word. Short on vitality and energy, she had the spare loveliness of a seashell lying silver on the sand in the moonlight: a muted curve of shape and sleekness veiled in darkness.

"You need to eat." He resisted the impulse that urged him to smooth her hair back, tuck her head against his chest and let her rest in his arms. "I know you didn't eat last night." The words slipped out, and he hoped she didn't pick up on them. If she did, he'd have to lie again so that she wouldn't know he'd been watching outside her window, and he didn't want to lie to her this morning. He was becoming increasingly reluctant to play cat and mouse with Elly Malloy. And that, more than anything, threw him off balance and made him feel as if he were losing control. "Tommy and I are reasonably competent males. We can manage to pull breakfast together without you. Guys can function in a kitchen, you know. Right, squirt?"

"Yep." Tommy patted Royal's head, carefully avoiding the butterfly bandage he'd spotted. "See? I did not hurt you."

"See, Elly?" Royal smiled at her. "We can manage. Your son's not going to destroy me in fifteen minutes. Stay here. We'll bring you food."

"In bed!" Tommy half bounced, then closed his eyes blissfully. "Like a party! All of us. And Baby Whale."

Elly gathered the sheet up close around her. "No, please. It would be a waste of food. I couldn't eat a bite. I'll fix breakfast for you two. And you shouldn't be carrying Tommy, Royal. He's too heavy for you right now—"

"Am not." Tommy bounced on Royal's shoulders, and Royal saw Elly wince in sympathy. "Am not, am not, am not," Tommy chanted. "Giddap, horsey." He thumped his heels against Royal's chest.

If he could have, Royal would most definitely have giddapped.

"Tommy! Stop that this instant." Elly's voice had a level of command that made Royal recall the voices of any number of military-school martinets he'd been subjected to during his early years. With a stern look at both Royal and Tommy, she said, "Royal's...sore this morning. Remember his bandages? His bruises?"

"Yep." Tommy toppled forward to peer into Royal's face. With one finger, he lifted the swollen area near Royal's eye. "Pretty colors," he said admiringly as he traced the outline of the scrapes and bruises.

Royal figured the terror would request his own set of multi-colored bruises.

"You can't roughhouse with Royal, Tommy. I mean it."

"'Kay." Perched on Royal's shoulders, Tommy went so still that Royal was afraid the kid wasn't breathing.

"You can move, Tommy. I'll let you know if I'm hurting. I'm not half as bad as I look." Royal directed his comment to Elly. He didn't want her protecting him. Last night, he'd needed her tenderness. He'd had fuzzy, pill-induced dreams of her hair floating over his face, of her hands drifting down his body like cool snowflakes easing a burning fever.

Last night, he'd let her take care of him. Last night, she'd been in control, not him. She'd been in control of his body, of his dreams, of some core part of him that he wasn't ready to relinquish.

But not today. Today would be different.

He stood up, Tommy wobbling on his shoulders.

"Wait!" The sheet bunched around her shoulders, Elly hesitated.

Swinging Tommy off his shoulders and to the floor, Royal hustled Tommy into the kitchen before Elly could marshal her objections. Opening cabinets, Royal searched until he found everything he needed. Tommy climbed up and down a metal two-step ladder, fetching and carrying and bumping into Royal's legs every time he turned.

"Thanks, squirt." Royal took the box of high-fiber cereal and ripped open the opaque wax wrapping.

"No problem." Tommy scooted the ladder over to a tall, two-doored cupboard. "The sugar's way up here. I can get it." On the top step, he turned too fast.

Stretching out an arm, Royal caught him as the ladder skidded east and Tommy flew west.

"Whoa, kid. This isn't a launching pad." Deciding it was safer all around for both of them, Royal settled Tommy back on his shoulders and went about the business of finding food. Puttering around Elly's kitchen with her son using his shoulders as a drum, Royal filled a kettle with water, found cups and bowls and found himself whistling even when an enthusiastic thump of Tommy's left heel landed against a deep bruise. "Easy with the feet, guy," he cautioned.

"Sorry." Tommy grabbed Royal's ears for security and peered into his face. "I hurted you again?"

"Nah. I'm a wuss. Whine, whine and complain. That's me. Wuss of the week."

"Are not."

"Am, too." Royal reached up and tapped Tommy's nose. "Don't argue with your elders, brat."

"What's a brat?" *Thump, thump, thumpety-thump* went his heels against Royal's collarbone.

"You, if you don't quit using me for a kickboard." Royal captured a bare toe and suppressed a groan. "These are lethal weapons, kid."

Tommy giggled. "Yep. I can scuba and karate and I used to play the piano and I helped Mommy when— Oops." Letting go of Royal's ears, Tommy clapped his hands over his mouth.

"Yeah, well, we've all 'oopsed' once or twice in our lives, kid." Marveling at his discretion, Royal fired up the old gas stove and put the kettle to boil. He'd shamelessly used Leesha's friendship, yet he was drawing the line at pumping the kid for information, ignoring a golden opportunity to fill in the blanks in what he already knew about Ms. Elly with her lost, brave eyes.

Hell's bells. He was developing a conscience in his old age. That explained the pinching and pain in the region of his heart. Passing up a chance for information? Hell.

Obviously, Armageddon was right around the corner.

Banged up, beat up and with a five-year-old whomping away at his aching chest, he should have felt meaner than a snake. He didn't. The swamp-nasty ugliness that had been living in him for months had vanished overnight, and he felt freer than he had in months. Amused? He didn't know. There was just this *lightness* sliding slow and easy through him. It took him a few minutes to identify the feeling, and when he did, he stopped short, sending Tommy bobbing up against him.

He was happy.

"Well, I'll be a son of bitch," Royal whispered, amazed. *Happy.*

"You sweared." Tommy tilted forward and put his hand over Royal's mouth. "I do, too. But I get sent to my room. I won't tell Mommy you said a dirty swear. 'Cause we're going to the rodeo, right?''

"Thanks," Royal muttered, "but I'm pretty sure you shouldn't keep secrets from your mom." He felt as if the kid was pulling a fast one, trading silence on the dirty swears in return for a guaranteed trip to the rodeo. Tommy Lee clearly had a future as a businessman. Or a scam artist.

And he liked the goofy little squirt, damned if he didn't. Like his mom, the kid was worming his way under Royal's skin. Not a good sign. Royal knew he was going to have to do something about that.

But not just yet.

"Come on, Tommy. Grab that tray." Royal pointed to a heavy plastic pizza castle souvenir. In the short time he'd been in her house, he'd noticed Elly was real short on accessories. Real short on permanent kinds of belongings. "Throw a couple of pieces of toast on that saucer, and we're all set." Royal stooped to Tommy's eye level. "I'll carry the tea. You can haul the tray. Okay?''

"Works for me." Tommy took the tray with both hands and, tray tipping dangerously from side to side, led the way to the bedroom.

Sighing, Royal recognized the echo of his own words. Kids. They didn't have a lick of sense. They'd imitate anybody, no judgment at all. Good thing God made kids so cute. To survive, they needed every advantage they could get. He was beginning to reach the conclusion that Tommy Lee especially needed a helping hand if he was going to survive in the world around him. Damned little coot.

Royal frowned as they headed in a procession of two back down the hall to the bedroom. Elly was supposed to protect the kid all on her own? Not likely. She thought she was on top of everything. She wasn't. She didn't have a clue.

It wasn't his concern, Royal reminded himself grimly. Not his problem. His job was to do what he had to do. The die had been cast, wheels set in motion—it was a done deal. Whatever happened afterward was none of his business. He'd told himself that originally, and *nothing* had changed that fact. If he had to remind himself every hour that the status was still quo, he would.

Nothing had changed the facts. Not Elly's kiss, and certainly not the sight of her in a spring-pink dress that looked like spun sugar. Nope. He was on guard, ready, prepared to resist the lure of her in that dress that buttoned to the neck and cupped the curves of her slight breasts. Above the short line of pink hem, her kneecaps gleamed in the sunlight like satin.

She wasn't wearing stockings.

"Here." Royal handed her a cup of heavily sugared hot tea. He'd half expected to trip over her on the way back to the bedroom, but she was sitting on the stripped bed, hands clasped between her knees. He placed the cup in her hands. In spite of the heat, her hands were cold. "It's not poison. Drink it, Elly."

Her head jerked up. She nodded slowly and took a sip. "Thanks." Holding the cup clasped in both hands, she drank steadily and silently, as though finishing the sticky-sweet tea were a chore she'd assigned herself, and by God, she would drink every last drop.

Setting the tray on the stained, lumpy mattress, Tommy climbed up beside her. Picking at a piece of toast, he rubbed his head against her arm until she raised it, draping it across his shoulders while she proceeded resolutely to finish the tea.

Royal began to wish he'd brought a smaller cup, but he'd seen only four cups in her cabinet, not much choice there. The house was clearly a furnished rental. He gave Tommy a glass half-filled with juice.

"Nice crystal, Elly." Royal pointed to the cartoon characters cavorting around the glass that had come from a local fast-food emporium.

"The best." She swallowed. A drop of tea glimmered on her chin, and she absentmindedly rubbed it away with the back of her hand.

Her chin would be sticky. Sweet to the taste.

"Yeah, I noticed you had a complete set." Royal leaned against the wall and folded his arms across his chest. He needed a shirt. Walking around Elly's bedroom wearing nothing but his worse-for-the-wear slacks and a pressure bandage felt kinky.

Probably because she was so buttoned up, so *dressed.* Except for her bare legs.

He figured she'd covered up to send him a message...and he got the message, loud and clear.

But all those shiny little buttons, like some kind of fake pearl, one after the other, marching all the way from her throat to her knees. He couldn't seem to stop thinking of the tiny button at the base of her throat. She couldn't have realized how that little sucker drew his gaze again and again to that indentation of her throat, to the swell of her breasts. He searched desperately for a topic of conversation. "All four glasses, huh? I'm impressed. Set you back much?"

"All my life's savings." She drained the last of the tea, looked around for someplace to set the cup. "Tommy wanted them. And I like them. So don't be a snob." She lifted her chin challengingly, the first sign of vitality she'd shown since waking up.

"Hey, they're swell." He lifted his hands in surrender.

"And don't be snippy."

"Whoa, there, little lady. Guys are never snippy. *Snippy*'s a girly-girl word. It's got no macho, Elly." Royal smiled at her, intrigued with the way Tommy's eyes shifted from Elly to him and back again, taking everything in as they teased. The kid wasn't used to teasing. "A guy's got to have a testosterone kind of word. Like *snotty* or—"

"Boogers," Tommy offered helpfully, sneaking a glance at Royal.

"Yeah, that's a good one." From the corner of his eye, Royal caught the faint movement of Elly's lips. She'd almost smiled.

"Okay. Enough's enough. Both of you. *Boogers,* for pete's sake." Her smile wavered on her lips, and finally blossomed into a mischievous grin that transformed her. She stood up, cup still in hand and gestured to Royal. "You're a terrible influence."

"I know." He took the cup and turned toward the door. Looking around the room with its stripped bed, he bent and scooped out the suitcase shoved behind the door. "Going on a trip, Elly?"

It was the first time he'd seen her speechless.

She fumbled, hemmed, hawed. Her feet even twitched. "I use it for storage. This place is short on closet space. I keep extra clothes in it. Winter stuff. Sweaters. You know. Storage."

Tommy's squeak would have given her away if her own hesitations hadn't.

"Interesting decorating technique." Casually surveying the

room, noting the absence of personal touches, the lack of a dresser or chest with the usual feminine arsenal of perfumes and lipsticks, Royal could see how she could be out of the house in a matter of minutes if she had to. The woman was prepared; that was for sure. "Find the minimalist look to your taste, do you?"

"Some of us have to watch our money more carefully than others." She stared pointedly at the leather belt he'd found neatly rolled this morning in his shoes. "*Some* of us can't throw money around like confetti."

"Low blow, Elly. Told you, sweetheart, I'm broke these days. Lucky if I can scrape two pennies together."

"I know what you said." She crossed her arms. "And I believe you. Sort of. But, ex-Detective, you look like old money, and you dress like a man who's never watched a penny in his life."

"That's what I like about you, Elly." He shook his head in admiration. "You don't let anyone walk over you."

She blanched.

Royal could have kicked himself. He hadn't meant anything with his comment. He truly did admire her grittiness. But hers was a history he could only guess at, and he'd been careless, sculling along on the smooth surface of teasing. "Like you said last night, you're a tough cookie." Deliberately, he looked her up and down, letting his gaze roam from button to button and back up again, before letting it settle on that top button that was driving him crazy. Putting all the sizzle he could into the lift of his eyebrow, he gave her a slow smile that hinted of other things they'd both said and done last night. "Nice outfit, cookie."

Her face flushed as pink as her dress. "Devil."

"Royal's not a devil. He's my friend." Tommy bounced off the bed and threw his arms around Royal's leg, squeezing hard.

"And Beau told Leesha Royal was the best damned cop—"

"Tommy Lee!" Elly's appalled gasp almost made Royal laugh, but he squelched it fast and quick.

Tommy stopped and buried his face into Royal's pants leg. "Oops."

"'Oops' isn't the half of it." Elly swooped down on him and detached him from Royal's leg. "No swears. You know better. You're grounded. No rodeo."

Tommy's piteous glance met Royal's.

Hell. Royal raked a hand through his hair. He couldn't resist those woeful eyes. "My fault," Royal said easily. "I slipped this morning and let out a dirty swear, and you're right, I'm a lousy role model, but shoot, Elly, I promised the kid, and, you know, a promise is a promise. And a swear doesn't seem serious enough to cancel out the rodeo." He set the suitcase noisily on the floor. "Whew. Feels like more than sweaters in there, Elly."

Her glance followed the suitcase. She bit her lip.

"I know, I know. I'm a skunk and a devil and an all-round son of a gun, but the Fourth of July comes only once a year and Tommy said he'd never been to one, and…" Royal was running out of diversions. He felt like throwing up his hands and telling Tommy he'd done his best, but it hadn't been good enough.

"Please, Mommy?" Tommy's voice was small and unsteady. His bottom lip quivered pitifully.

No question, Royal would have given in. He wasn't that tough.

Elly was. She didn't yield. She looked from the suitcase to Tommy and then back to Royal.

"I'm sorry, Mommy. I *tried* not to do no more swears. And Leesha said I was doing real good. *Please,*" he said, and even Royal could see the little squirt was trying not to cry, "*please* let me go. 'Specially if we're going to mo—" He buried his face in Elly's neck. "Please, Mommy." This time he sobbed, a tiny, smothered sound.

Royal kept silent. Elly wouldn't welcome his suggestions. Tommy wasn't his kid. He was Elly's. And Scanlon's. Royal took a step back. He had no right to interfere.

"Oh, honey, please don't cry." Elly smoothed Tommy's hair back from his face, the curve of her body protecting him and signaling her distress.

"I'm trying not to," he sobbed, his whole body shaking. "I am, but I cannot help myself."

Royal backed out the door, reaching down for the suitcase and taking it with him. Moving swiftly in spite of his sore body, he took it into the kitchen and out of sight. From the bedroom, he heard Tommy's sobs subside, Elly's murmurs, the creak of springs as she sank onto the bed with Tommy.

Royal wouldn't take advantage of her son's innocence, but he had no compunctions about investigating the mother, not when an opportunity was practically slapping him in the face. In his mind, he saw a distinction. No one else might, but he did, and operating on that distinction, he placed the suitcase on the kitchen table.

Reaching into his pocket, he retrieved his keys. Using a slim metal pick dangling from the ring, he popped the lock and opened the lid.

No sweaters.

But he hadn't expected any.

Senses alert, he didn't touch the neatly stacked clothes. Several sets of shorts and tops for Tommy. A pair of jeans, slacks and a dress for Elly. Sneakers. Underwear for both of them.

Elly's current taste seemed to run to plain white, cheap cotton. Except for a lacy, skin-colored bra of French lace that was more expensive than his leather belt that she'd mocked. He liked her taste in French lace. He'd give a year's salary in a hummingbird's heartbeat to see her in that bit-of-nothing bra. But, of course, he didn't have a year's salary.

With one finger, he carefully lifted the stack of underwear, not disturbing its arrangement in case she'd made provisions for snoopers like him. Although he didn't see an obvious arrangement that would reveal her stuff had been tampered with, he wouldn't put it past her to have taken care of that detail, too.

He was learning that Elly Malloy was a very careful woman.

He continued his quick inventory. A clear makeup case filled with toothbrushes, lipstick, a vial of perfume. A wallet.

Carefully flipping it open, he saw the wad of bills…a stash of one thousand dollars in fifties and twenties. She also had a new driver's license. Elena Malone would be spending that money.

But not in Palmaflora.

She didn't kid around when she said she didn't like surprises, that she planned ahead. In spite of her fragile appearance, Elly clearly had no intention of being caught like a mouse in a trap. Not by him. Not by anybody. She'd stripped her bed. She had no ties to Palmaflora, to the rental house. She was ready to run.

Well, too bad for her, but he had no intention of letting her vanish into the night. The second he'd checked the contents of her beat-up suitcase, he'd made up his mind. He'd do whatever he had to in order to keep her in sight.

He had to.

He was beginning to see that the stakes were higher than he'd dreamed, and he was in the middle of the biggest gamble he'd ever taken in his entire life.

As the sobs diminished in the room down the hall, he snapped the suitcase shut and moved swiftly and silently to Elly's bedroom door. She'd shifted toward Tommy, and her back was toward Royal, the softness of her hair moving like cobwebs in a summer breeze as she nuzzled her chin into the boy's belly.

"Tickles," he giggled, his tear-damp face wrinkled in glee.

"Want me to stop?" She blew a raspberry in the vicinity of his navel.

"Want to go to the rodeo." He opened his eyes and looked up at her pleadingly. "And Royal wants me to go with him, too."

With one foot, Royal eased the suitcase back into position a tick-tock before Elly turned her head.

"Royal," she said, exasperation clear in her voice, but something else there, too, something that let him think she wasn't altogether disappointed to see he'd stuck around.

"Yeah, sugar, it's me."

"For some silly reason, I thought you'd gone home."

"Now, why would you think something like that, Elly?"

"Gosh, I don't know. Wishful thinking?" Ironically amused, her eyes met his.

"Isn't there a caution about being careful what you wish for? Confess. You'd miss me if I disappeared, wouldn't you?"

"Absolutely," she said, nodding amiably. "About the way I'd miss a nail poking up in my shoe." And then she turned brilliant red.

Royal took pity on her. "Anyway, how could I leave? Young Thomas—" Royal caught the way the muscles at the corners of her eyelids tightened in a reaction similar to the one she'd had last night "—and I made breakfast, and no one's eaten anything except toast. Be a shame to toss all that food. Wasteful."

"And you've never wasted food, right?"

"Nope. I'm a bona fide member of the clean-plate club."

"Me, too." Tommy lizard-slid off the bed and onto the floor.

"We made eggs and cheese, Mommy. And we cooked 'em dry so no salmon bugs would swim in our gizzards."

"Wonderful." Elly's sigh of resignation could have been for the salmon bugs or for the eggs and cheese.

They ate. They drank juice from the matched set of cartoon glasses. Royal made Tommy laugh until he snorted orange juice through his nose.

And he made Elly smile until the shadows that had been in her eyes vanished and she laid her head on the table, weak with laughter, her eyes sparkling like sunlit bayous.

They were going to go to the rodeo.

Elly had no chance to stick to her guns, not with Royal working overtime to persuade her that a Palmaflora Fourth of July rodeo was an event no one should miss, a once-in-a-lifetime experience. "It's an educational opportunity, Elly," Royal said with a perfectly straight face. "You know. Horses. Cows. Creatures with horns and hooves. Men in boots and hats."

"Been to the rodeo often, have you?"

"Once or twice. Cow country isn't my territory. But every kid needs to see the parade and hear the bands. It's almost a religious moment, Elly."

She hooted, her fork sprayed scrambled eggs onto the table and she clamped her lips together.

Royal thought she'd changed her mind when orange juice dribbled down Tommy's face, but he wasn't sure. Yet every time Tommy giggled, Elly's face softened and warmed.

She was a pushover for the kid.

And Royal used that against her. He wanted her to go to the rodeo. There were things he had to do, and he wanted her within reach, within sight.

After they finished eating, Royal and Tommy cleaned up. Tommy chattered nonstop. "I'm not a lot of trouble and underfoot all the time, and you like me, don't you, Royal?"

"Yeah." Royal handed him a plastic bowl to dry. Elly was back in the bare bedroom rummaging through her closet for a hat and sunscreen lotion. "You kind of grow on a man, squirt."

"Huh?" Tommy spun the purple bowl on his finger like a Frisbee. "Whatcha mean, Royal?"

"I mean you're the kind of guy another guy could get used to being around."

"Oh." Tommy climbed on the stepladder and shoved the plastic bowl and plates inside a cupboard.

Royal hoped it was the right one.

Climbing down the top step with the dish towel dangling from his hand, Tommy stopped, the toe of one battered sneaker hanging in midair. Royal prepared himself for another Tommy launch.

"You know something, Royal? You kind of grow on me, too." Tommy's jug ears almost waggled with pleasure. "Isn't that great?"

"Yeah." It wasn't great at all. No way, no how. Not for Royal, and most assuredly not for Tommy. The kid couldn't get used to having him around. This was a temporary deal. "Go tell your mom we're ready to rock and roll." Royal flipped soapsuds at him, and Tommy ducked, running shrieking out of the room.

"MommyMommyMommy! Come on!"

He galloped out of the room like a normal kid. Not in the least like a kid who'd been on the run for six months. Not like a kid with a mother who woke up screaming at the harmless sound of firecrackers on the Fourth of July.

Watching him screech into the bedroom like a fire engine, Royal slapped his hand against the sink. Hell, he'd known Elly Malloy was going to be trouble, but he sure hadn't expected her kid to tie his insides into knots.

He was going to keep his distance from the kid. That's all there was to it. Simple. Easy as pie. No problem.

When Elly returned to the kitchen wearing her floppy hat, Tommy trotted by her side, shirtless, a bandage wrapped sloppily around his chest, over his shoulder and back again. With each step he took, the bandage unraveled, leaving a beige elastic tail behind him.

"Rodeo attire?" Royal picked up the end and tucked it back into the elaborate loops and dangles. How could a man resist a kid who kept looking up at him like he was wearing Superman's cape?

Draping a faded kid's T-shirt over Tommy's shoulders, Elly smiled. "He likes the no-shirt look." Her gaze skimmed over Royal like the feathery brush of her hair, and a trail of warmth followed her slow perusal until she lifted her eyes and met his. "He's adopted you. Monkey see, monkey do."

Taking a breath, Royal glanced down at his own naked chest. He'd forgotten his shirt. "Uh, we're going to have to make a detour. I'm underdressed."

"*Un*dressed," Elly snickered, tossing him his ripped and grungy shirt. "But, hey, who's complaining?"

Shrugging gingerly into the tattered shirt, Royal risked a grin. "Turnabout's fair play."

Her face was all pink innocence as she looked at him, her eyes as wide as her son's. "I have no idea what you mean." Mischief gleamed in their warm depths as she grinned back at him. "Anyway, I don't play games. So don't get your hopes up, Detective."

"Spoilsport." Royal shoved the tail of his shirt into his pants.

Sashaying past him, she tugged a button hanging by a thread to his shirt. "And button up, buster. If I'm going to the rodeo with you, I don't want to fight off all the two-legged female creatures."

"Growing fond of me, are you, sweetheart? Because that's an honest-to-God compliment." Royal laid his hand on her forehead and leaned forward solicitously. "Are you running a fever, Elly?"

Elly thought maybe she was. Royal's rough palm sent shock waves of heat right down to her toes in their hand-painted sneakers. "Probably nothing more than indigestion. From the eggs."

"I cooked the eggs." Tommy looked up at her with apprehension.

"Couldn't have been the eggs, then," Elly added hastily. "Must have been all that sweet tea on an empty stomach." She'd slipped. She hadn't meant to let Royal know how the sight of his bare chest affected her senses. There was something primitive and overwhelmingly male about the tight wrap around his chest, the curls of hair edging the top with gold and rising to the base of his neck, a column of corded muscles that denied the life of dissipation he proclaimed.

Before leaving the house, she ran through her mental checklist. Everything she needed was in her purse. The suitcase was in her car. Shutting the door behind her, she wondered, as she did every time she left, whether or not she and Tommy would return to this place.

"Do you mind if we take my car?" Keys in hand, she turned

blithely to Royal, as though he couldn't possibly mind. "I have to drop off some cleaning supplies on the way to the fairgrounds." No matter what his answer was, she was determined to have access to her car, even if doing so meant creating a fake errand. "If I can make the stop now, it would save me time tomorrow. We can meet at the fairgrounds. That would work better for me. Okay?"

"No," he said slowly, watching her jiggle the keys. "How about swinging by my house and letting me change? I'd say I'd meet you there, but the parking area's going to be a madhouse. We'd have a hard time linking up. It's really easier if we stick together."

Elly nodded. That suited her. She wanted to see where he lived, too. She needed some answers to her questions about Royal Gaines, ex-detective. His house would give her clues about the man. "Sure. Give me directions, and we're off."

She still hadn't figured out how the rascal had led her down the garden path until she'd found herself agreeing to the rodeo. But he'd made her laugh until her sides hurt, and for that, she'd even trek to the rodeo with him and Tommy.

And for the way he treated her son, for that alone, she'd forgive Royal Gaines any number of sins.

For that casual male affection he showed Tommy, she'd even forgive Royal for making her body sing with need and hunger and longing.

She would leave Palmaflora. And she'd take with her this aching hunger he'd stirred.

Unsatisfied, the hunger would linger. Eventually it would vanish. It had to. She had no future here. She had no future with Royal Gaines. The hunger would die.

But in the meantime, she had to stay alive.

Chapter 8

Backing up her lie, Elly stopped briefly at the rental unit she planned to clean the next day and then headed toward the beach.

If Royal hadn't directed her to pull off the main road onto the weed-covered side road right before the bridge to the island beaches, she wouldn't have realized anyone lived back in the pine woods. He motioned for her to drive into the shell driveway leading to the house.

Away from the main road and its continuous whine of tires, the clearing was curiously quiet in the heat, the only sound the laboring rattle of her car engine.

A small frame house with a wooden staircase that stretched upstairs to the living area, the house wasn't what Elly had expected. The weathered wood was silvery in the shaded thicket of trees and bushes. Sandspurs mixed with the tough grass yard. The house sang to her of permanence, of sanctuary.

Contrasting with the cool gray of the house, hibiscus and flame vines mixed in a riot of red and yellow and pink. Close to the house, the bright green leaves of a scarlet morning glory vine crawled up the side of the staircase and sent tendrils around the handrail. The golden-throated flame of the flowers drew her eye up, up to the porch with its sagging screen and unpainted door.

No, it wasn't what she'd anticipated, but Royal's house had an odd appeal. There was a wild beauty in its shabbiness that captured her fancy, and the more she stared at the clearing and the house, the more easily she could see Royal living there.

She'd been prepared for run-down, for shabby. She'd even prepared herself for one of the old Florida mansions, cool and arrogant with high ceilings. She'd prepared herself for a sleek and contemporary house, a single man's castle, but not for this house that was rooted in its surroundings. She wasn't prepared at all for the spell it cast over her.

"So?" Holding the passenger door of her car open, Royal sent her an enigmatic glance. "Coming in?"

"Why does that question sound like one on a pass-fail test?"

"It's not." He leaned into the car interior.

"Really?" The brilliant sunlight streaming around him changed him into a dark silhouette, and she couldn't read his expression, couldn't identify the intensity she sensed.

"I'm not trying to trick you, Elly," he murmured. "And I'm not playing any games. I'm offering shade from the sun, that's all. Nothing else. You don't have to feel uncomfortable. Or… afraid."

"I'm not." But she left the engine running. The engine heat and late-morning humidity had already sent her hair into a fine frizz. The wind whipping in the open window during the drive down Flora Avenue to the unit she was to clean and then on to Royal's house had given an illusion of coolness. Now, though, perspiration collected along her hairline, and the cotton dress clung to her back and legs. "I'm fine out here. You won't be long, will you?"

"No, but I'd like to shower before I change."

She closed her eyes against the sudden, unwanted image of Royal in his shower, drops of water beading in the gold of his chest hair free of bandages, water sluicing down the lean muscles of his back, muscles the shape of which she'd learned by braille the night before. His red-gold hair would darken, turn seal sleek with water. Opening her eyes, she discovered that he seemed to have moved even closer to her in the confines of the car, all his bright power focused on her face. She should have kept her eyes shut. "All right. Take your time. Tommy and I'll wait here."

Stretching toward her, he lifted the brim of her hat and traced the damp line of her forehead, his fingertips skimming the line of her scar. "It's cooler inside, Elly."

A tiny quiver rolled from her toes to her forehead, to the spot where his hand lingered.

"I have colas, maybe some iced tea in the fridge." Backing out of the car, he swung the door back and forth, giving her time, space.

He'd noted her reaction, damn him. But she couldn't have stopped it if her life had depended on it. "I'm not thirsty."

"I am. Tommy probably is."

"Yep," Tommy muttered. "*Real* thirsty. I want to see inside. I *don't* want to sit in the car. It's hot."

Royal's expression didn't change, but amusement deepened the green of his eyes.

Well, why not? She almost had to laugh at her own contrariness. Her throat was parched with heat and thirst, but mulish obstinacy rooted her in her car. And she'd taunted him about *his* need for control. She wanted to go inside. But, obscurely, she felt she *had* to stay *outside*.

He'd overwhelmed her in her own space. Inside, on his turf, she'd be even more at a disadvantage. Because everything about this house and its location pulled at her in some indefinable way. "We're fine," she repeated stubbornly.

"Up to you. And Tommy." Royal smiled. "It's not the wicked witch's cottage, Elly." He shifted, and the sun glinted like polished brass along the fine hairs of his arm where it rested on the door.

To keep from ruffling her hand along that shine of hair and skin, she tightened her grip on the steering wheel. "Funny. It has that kind of air. As though it's under a spell." Turning off the engine, she rested her arms on the steering wheel. "This is...peaceful."

"It is." Royal pulled the tail of his shirt free of his waistband and wiped his face. He inhaled, and a gap between his waistband and skin flickered. "Awful hot out here, Elly. And you could admire the scenery from the porch, you know. With a cold drink."

"Yep." Before she could grab Tommy to stop him, her son climbed over the seat and scooted out next to Royal. "And I can play and visit while you put on your rodeo clothes." Tagging after Royal, Tommy caught up to him. "Right?"

"If your mom says you can." Royal glanced over his shoulder. "You don't want to stay out here in the heat, Elly."

But she did. She was charmed into near-somnolence by the humming quiet and peace. She couldn't imagine resisting the inside of the house. She would end up begging him to let her stay here in this enchanted place if she didn't keep her wits about her.

Somewhere in the distance, a merry, rollicking bird song broke the silence. A flash of russet and a line of white sailed into view, then disappeared. Enthralled by the clear music of its song, Elly tracked the quick flight of the small bird. The outside of Royal's house delighted her, and she couldn't tell why.

Like Royal, the house was deceptive.

"You'll roast. Come on inside."

"Mommy!" Tommy danced around Royal in the sunlight. "Come *on*."

"Oh, fiddle, why not? You're right. It's too hot to sit in the car, I guess." Curiosity more than the ninety-eight-degree heat and Royal's coaxing finally pulled her out of the car. Following Royal and her son up the worn stairs, Elly turned and looked over her shoulder at the clearing. The world outside had disappeared in the branches of the tall pines and the soughing of their limbs. Somewhere out there, beyond her view, the real world waited.

But here, here was peace.

And safety, she thought, dazed. A refuge.

Unlike the doors and windows at her house, Royal's door was unlocked, open to anyone who chose to walk in. But she didn't feel threatened or uneasy.

Royal shucked his shirt and shoes the minute he stepped inside and ambled through an arch to the kitchen. Reaching up, he pulled the chain to a wooden paddle fan. With air circulating over them, he stuck his head into the interior of an ancient refrigerator. White vapor misted in the warmth of the room. "No tea," he said finally, withdrawing his head, "Sorry."

"Soda. Iced water. Anything you have."

"Soda! Soda!" trumpeted Tommy, butting Royal's leg. "Soda!"

She answered the questioning lift of Royal's eyebrow with a nod. "Why not? It's a holiday."

Dropping ice cubes into a plastic cup and a tall, fragile glass, Royal handed the plastic one to Tommy, who took it carefully with both hands and walked with short steps back out onto the porch, banging the screen door open with his behind. "Goin' to swing." He gestured with his head toward the rope hammock slung across the far corner of the porch.

"Sure, squirt. But stay on the porch, where your mom can keep an eye on you."

Startled, Elly turned to him. For a man with no children, Royal had an uncanny idea of how she felt about hers. As if he understood her fear.

Catching her baffled look, he shrugged a bit self-consciously before heading toward the back of the house. He stopped and came back. Tucking the flat of his hands into his waistband, he stared at her for a minute, almost as if he were ill at ease. Then, abruptly, he spun on his bare heel and headed for the bedroom with long strides, saying only, "Look around. Make yourself at home."

She could, too. "I will. I have to warn you, though, I'm nosy, too."

"Good luck," he called back dryly.

"Oh, wonderful. Permission to snoop." She surveyed the room. The house had a charm of wood and wide windows and space. Lots of space, she realized, seeing no furniture. She called to him, "And you had the nerve to call my decorating minimalist."

"Reckon we have a lot more in common than you thought, huh?" His voice came from behind a partially closed door where the edge of a navy futon on the floor showed.

"Probably not." Glancing toward the bedroom door, Elly strolled to the refrigerator. Opening it, she scanned its bare interior. No food, no leftovers from carryouts. "I'm quite sure we have nothing in common."

His voice came over the sound of the shower. "You mean we're not soul mates, Elly?"

"Nah." Clinking the ice cubes against the lovely crystal he'd given her, she strolled around the living-room space with its deep windowsills and wide-plank floor. No television. No stereo.

Other than the table and chair in the kitchen and the futon in his bedroom, the place was empty. But not barren or sterile. It had a sense of purposeful emptiness, like a Japanese garden, or—

And then it hit her.

Royal's house reminded her of a monk's cell. Ascetic. Stripped of extraneous distractions, of luxury, of everything except the most basic of necessities. As if he were punishing himself, voluntarily donning a hair shirt.

She couldn't move.

Royal's house went a long way toward explaining the contradictions she'd sensed in him, the aura of control conflicting with the don't-give-a-damn attitude, the ascetic with the wastrel. Angel and devil. A soul-deep conflict.

Steam from the shower drifted to her, heavy with the scent of his soap and shampoo. And outside, oh, outside, the fragrance of flowers turned the warm air silky with perfume, rich and seductive.

As if lightning had scratched the words across the sky, she understood the message of his house. This was not the house of a man who would have a gambling addiction, or any addiction. Intuitively, she'd known that, but his house clarified the point for her. Royal might deliberately choose to race full speed down the road to self-destruction, but it would be *his* choice.

Complex, complicated, he was far more dangerous than she'd dreamed.

Walking around the living room, Elly trailed her hand over the polished pine shelves of a bookcase. Empty. But the wood was satin smooth, a lure to the senses.

Circling the room and watching Tommy swing belly down on the hammock on the front porch, she decided that the most interesting fact was that Royal might be wrestling with his demons, but he'd selected a living space that charmed with its proportions and lines. He'd chosen a house that would give pleasure to anyone with an eye for beauty.

And to anyone with a need for peace.

Her heart turned over in pity for him, in compassion that he could torment himself so. What had he done to himself, to deny himself even the smallest pleasures of life? She could handle, barely, the way he appealed to her senses. She had no chance against this subversive appeal to her heart. "Hey, slowpoke, are you drowning in there?" she called.

Pipes clanked and gurgled as he turned off the shower. "Give me a sec. I'm clean, but I look like hell. Going out in public with me may offend your delicate nature, sugar, or destroy your reputation, so feel free to pretend you've never seen me before in your life. I won't hold it against you because, quite frankly, I don't know if I'd claim acquaintance with me right now."

"Because of the way you look? I didn't think you were so vain, Detective."

"Neither did I. But I hadn't really taken a good look at myself until now. Soap and shampoo can only do so much." There was a long pause, and then he poked his head and shoulder around the door. Dark as molasses, his wet hair dripped onto the floor. Water beaded thickly on his naked shoulder. "And, Elly?" Sending droplets flying, he raked a hand through his hair. He'd taken off the butterfly bandage.

"Yes?" She wished the man would learn to wear a shirt. Or warn her.

He braced his arm against the door, keeping it open while he ran a towel over his hair. "I don't have friends in Palmaflora right now."

"I know. Because they think you're a bent cop." Fascinated, she watched a drop trail down his forearm to his elbow, his biceps, and into the deep curve of his armpit, where gold gleamed briefly before he lowered his arm.

"Yeah." He stared at the floor. "They might be rude. Unpleasant. Some of the good citizens might decide to say anything."

"Oh, swell. More excitement." Elly wanted to tease him, to erase the somber expression. In his house, he shouldn't look as if the weight of the world crushed him. "Am I going to have to defend you? Should I be prepared?" She smiled gently as he stared at her. "Don't worry, Royal. I'm not going to fall in a swoon if someone gets snarly with you. I can take care of myself. And based on what happened last night, I may have to take care of you, too. But that's okay, big guy. I'm up to the challenge. I've been taking karate classes at the gym. You're safe with me.'' Pushing back her sleeve, she made a muscle. ''See?''

He shook his head. ''You're a mean woman, Elly Malloy.''

''And don't you forget it.'' She smoothed her sleeve flat and settled her hat more firmly on her head.

''Should I get you a T-shirt labeled Bodyguard? A really cool one in hot pink. You'd look great in hot pink, sugar.''

''What you should do, Royal, is hurry up.''

''Your slightest wish, et cetera, et cetera.'' He disappeared behind the door, and she heard the squeak of a drawer being opened.

Leaving the bare rooms behind her, she joined her son on the porch, collapsing awkwardly on the hammock with a swirl of skirt and groans to Tommy's chortles.

''I like Royal's house. It makes me happy.''

''Me, too, Tommy.'' In fact, she was jealous of Royal, that he could come home every night to this place where the very floorboards sang of serenity. Of safety. Placing her empty glass carefully on the floor and laying her head on the pillow near her, Elly swung her feet up beside Tommy. A faint, clean scent of Royal drifted to her from the pillow cover, and she suspected that more nights than not, he slept here, on the hammock under the high ceilings of his porch, which looked down on the woods and wild, extravagantly colored flowers.

If she lived here, she would, too.

And she would bring in huge armfuls of those flowers and stick them in every corner and place candles all around the porch railing so that the glow of candlelight and sparkle of stars would fill the darkness all through the night.

She closed her eyes. Lots of candles and flowers, their scent perfuming the air, her skin, his, enclosing them in perfume and candlelit darkness—

''Ready?''

Woozy with sleep and peacefulness, she smiled up at him, marveling at the fact that he could be so bruised and beautiful at the same time. Like his shabby house, he needed some up-keep. They both needed someone to care for them. ''Hey,'' she said without thinking, just reacting as she lifted her hand to him, wanting to touch him.

"Hey, yourself," he said, and the rasp in his voice sent shivers all over her, chasing away the lovely torpor.

"I'm ready." Setting the hammock rocking wildly, Tommy dived to the floor. "Rodeo. And I'm going to ride a horse, right? Right?"

"Pony," Royal said, not looking away from Elly but calling after Tommy, who took the steps two at a time, heading like a bullet toward the car.

Elly couldn't move, not with Royal's gaze warming every inch of her body.

"You're dangerous, Elly."

"I was thinking the same thing about you," she said. "You're a very dangerous man, Royal Gaines."

"Guess that makes us two of a kind after all."

"Let me up," she whispered, breathless as his gaze lingered at her throat.

"I'm not touching you, Elly."

Her toes curled as he opened his hand and, not touching her, let his palm shape the slide of her neck into her blouse, her breasts. "You must be," she said in a voice she didn't recognize as her own.

"I want to." He bent over her and brushed her hair back from her face. He slid his palm lightly over her cheek, down her throat, his palm resting on the button at the top of her dress. "I want to do more than touch, Elly. But you know that, don't you?" He slipped his thumb under the edge of her neckline, flicked open the button.

"Yes."

"Do you know, too, that your eyes telegraph everything you're thinking?"

"I'd make a lousy poker player." She turned her head, welcoming the lazy stroke of his hand along her collarbone.

"You're no card shark," he agreed. He ran his fingers slowly down her arm. Goose bumps followed that slow skim. "You shouldn't look at me like that, Elly." Working his fingers through hers, he clasped her hand.

"Why not?" Lost in lassitude, Elly flexed her fingers in his. "I like looking at you, Royal. I'm sure I'm not the first woman to tell you that."

"No." He tugged on her hand. "But no one's ever looked at me quite the way you do."

"And how is that?" Half-sitting, she raised her other hand and trailed it over his chest, down the ridged muscles of his arm to his right hand. He wasn't wearing the pressure bandage around his ribs, and she could feel the heat of his skin through his shirt. "How do I look at you, Royal? Tell me," she whispered recklessly.

He moved so fast that she was on her feet before she realized that he'd grasped her under her arms and set her on the floor. "You look at me like you'd like to tie me up and drive me crazy with touching and stroking. And you could, too, Elly." He slipped his hand under the ruff of her hair and enclosed her hands in his free one. His kiss against her wrist was swift, hot. "You could make me howl for the pleasure of having you run these hands over me."

She smiled, pleased. "Could I?"

"Sweetheart, you have no idea what you could make me do." His grip on the back of her neck tightened. "And fortunately for both of us, I have enough of a sense of survival left to keep my mouth shut."

"That's sweet," she said, and smiled again. "Such an ego booster, Gaines. You must not be thinking clearly."

"Oh, yeah, I'm thinking *real* clearly. Otherwise, I'd forget you have a five-year-old within shouting distance and I'd let you do your worst with me. Or your best." His grin was pure devilment. "And I'd show you what I could do to you. The prospects have kept me awake since I've met you. So, believe me, Elly, I'm thinking clearly. And with my brain, not with some other neglected body organ."

Without her volition, her gaze dropped to the neglected but seriously interested organ making its presence known under the worn zipper placket of his clean Levi's. She blushed furiously. Delightedly.

"Hmm." She could feel her blush deepening as she tried to look everywhere except below his belt. "Um." If he'd back up, she'd have something besides faded denim and aroused male in her view. "Uh." In her sneakers, her toes curled with pleasure. "Well…"

"Yes?" he encouraged, not moving an inch. "Anything else

you want to say? Maybe try something with two syllables, just for fun?"

"Hmm. Don't think so." She took a deep breath. "Nope."

"Mommy! Royal! Come on! The ponies will be all gone by the time we get to the rodeo." Tommy ran back to the top of the steps and jumped to the bottom. "Whoa!" His feet skidded in the sand, and he tumbled into sand. Grinning up at them, he dusted himself off and headed for the top step, prepared to take a second flying leap.

"Car, Tommy. I'm on my way." Elly slid her hands free of Royal's. Like lazy bubbles rising slowly to the surface, pleasure trickled through her. With her hand on the screen door, she faced Royal. "Thanks for letting me see your house. I think it's extraordinary. Beautiful."

"What?" Puzzled, he turned to look behind him. "Beautiful? This?"

"I love it. You're lucky you have this place."

"Sugar, after I gambled all my money away, this was the cheapest joint I could find to rent. Extraordinarily *cheap* is what this is." He shook his head, reinforcing her guess that he hadn't consciously chosen the house, that his subconscious had saved him in spite of himself. "These days, cheap suits me very well."

"I doubt that." She preceded him down the steps, picking one of the orange-red morning glories that curled around the banister. "Whether you know it or not, Detective, you also walk like old money." Dancing in back of him and circling around to the front, she laughed. "Absolutely a world-class walk. And a really terrific tush." She relished the dark red that slashed his cheekbones above the bruises. Served him right for all those innuendos he pitched to her. Coming in like soft lobs, they took a tricky spin at the last second. Walking backward toward the car, she tilted her head teasingly, staying just out of reach as she eyed his behind. "That butt's pretty darned close to a ten, I'd say."

With a quick side step that left him laughing and her skirt sliding through his fingers, she whipped open the car door and ducked inside. Trying to avoid frying her fanny, she inched under the steering wheel, making sure her skirt and not her skin made contact with the hot vinyl. As she stuck the keys in the slot, Royal stopped her.

"Explain, please, the 'old money' crack." The smile lingered, but the lines around his eyes indicated that she'd touched a nerve.

"It's nothing. A joke."

"Tell me. I'm curious why you made that particular joke. Your brain fascinates me, Elly, if you want to know. I'm never sure what you're going to come up with next."

"Sometimes, I speak before my brain is linked up with my mouth." She closed her hand around the keys. "I'm sorry if I made you uncomfortable, Royal. If I said something I shouldn't have." She switched the key on, and the engine vibrated the car body.

"You didn't. You made an observation. I'm interested in why you made that crack. That's all. No big deal."

"All right, I'll tell you. People who've grown up with money, who've never had to scrabble from one paycheck to the next, they have a certain confidence in their stride, a kind of arrogance, I think. Not everyone. I know I'm generalizing. But I notice things like that. And—" she sent him a quick grin "—you have a way of walking that's hard to ignore."

"Ah." He snapped his seat belt into place. "You're flirting with me."

"A little." She did a bootlegger's turn and headed back toward the main road. "Seemed like the thing to do. Payback time. I didn't think you'd object."

"Not in the least." He angled in the passenger seat and faced her. "Flirt away. I was curious, that's all."

"I know. You're insatiably curious." She checked both ways before pulling onto the road. Curiosity of her own prompted her question. "Your folks had money, didn't they, Royal?"

"Yes." He leaned back in his seat, shutting off further questions.

Apparently, she had touched a nerve. "Do you know," she began, "that for all your teasing and approachability, you keep people at a distance?"

"Do I? Fascinating," he said with a drawl, and didn't speak again until she pulled into the parking lot of the country fairgrounds.

The parade route ended at the fairgrounds, and it looked as if people had been lining up with folding chairs and stools since early morning.

Music blared from the midway carny rides, raucous and shrill. Blending into a pulse-pounding, foot-stomping wall of sound, country music, rock and roll and reggae music thumped and reverberated from the various music tents spread around the grounds. Stepping out of her car, Elly felt the ground vibrate with noise and rhythm. Pounding through her sneakers to her stomach, the insistent, unrelenting beat and noise almost made her ill.

Too much noise. Too much color and confusion. Too much—everything. She wanted Tommy to enjoy himself, but she saw only a thousand and one ways for him to get lost, a hundred chances for him to slip free of her hand.

"This isn't—"

Forestalling her, Royal swooped up Tommy in one hand and settled him on his shoulders. "The view's better up here, squirt. Hang on. Come on, Elly. Into the fray. Your son's safe with me."

"What about your ribs?" Elly raised her arms to let Tommy return to her. "You can't cart him around all day."

"I'm a fast healer." Grinning impudently, Royal backed away, holding Tommy in place around his crossed ankles.

"That's the biggest fairy wheel I ever saw." Tommy pointed toward the midway. "I like riding on Royal's shoulders." Inside out, Tommy's shirt rode above his belly button. Smiling blissfully at her, he hugged Royal around the neck.

"Fine. Stay. You're a grown man, Royal. If you're letting yourself be a martyr, it's your own fault. I'm not going to feel sorry for you."

"Good. I like lugging the little squirt around, Elly, and he doesn't hurt my ribs. And he's safe in sight. And hand."

He'd known what she was going to say and solved the problem before she spoke.

He'd reacted similarly before, as though he understood how anxious she was in crowds and unfamiliar places with Tommy, as if he were inside her head listening to her terrors.

Either he was psychic or she'd given herself away somehow. She didn't believe he was psychic.

The more time she spent with him, the more she was convinced that he knew more about her than he should.

She might have to make a decision sooner than she'd planned.

"Watch it, fella," Royal said evenly to a teenage boy with red-and-blue-dyed hair who lurched into their path, his drink cup swinging perilously close to Elly's dress.

"What you say, man." Snapping his fingers, the boy ambled off.

"Stay close, sugar. It's a jungle out here."

Tommy tipped forward, his shoulders blocking Elly's view of Royal's reaction. "It's a rodeo, not a jungle. You're being silly, aren't you?"

"Absolutely." Royal patted Tommy's knee.

Royal's hip bumped Elly companionably as he threw his arm around her and led the way through the crowd. In all the red, white and blue, his green shirt was easy to spot, its silky cotton lustrous. His bright hair gleamed in the sunshine like liquid honey as he scanned the crowd.

"Expecting someone?"

"Checking, that's all."

"For…?"

"Anybody who looks familiar. Or angry." He grinned down at her. "In case we have to make use of those karate lessons."

Reaching up, she pinched his hand where it dangled far too close to her breast. "Don't make fun. You never know when a good karate kick or two could come in handy."

"I don't want to insult you, Elly, but how many lessons have you had? Just out of curiosity, you understand?"

Dipping forward, Tommy stuck his head between theirs. "Me and Mommy had three lessons. And I can jump better. But Mommy kicks higher."

"There's a scary thought," Royal muttered, carefully moving his hand to a discreet position on her shoulder.

"See how well it works?" She smirked at him. "And I didn't even have to do anything." Patting his hand, she commiserated, "Poor baby."

"Poor baby? Is that how you see me, Elly?" The impudent grin he gave her was all grown-up male, testosterone charged and cocky.

"Maybe not," she said hastily, speeding up her steps. Sufficiently provoked, Royal was apt to pull any stunt. "Definitely not," she added as he let his arm drop casually to the flare of her hip and his smoky green gaze fastened on the unbuttoned neckline of her dress.

Chapter 9

Royal thought the designer of those buttons on Elly's dress should be shot. Hanged. Tortured. Because that's what the damned dinky things were doing to him. Torturing him. Slowly and exquisitely. And the more Elly flirted with him, the stronger his temptation grew to nudge aside one or two more of those tantalizing buttons and work his way right down to the last.

For a whole bunch of reasons, he was grateful they were out in public and that Tommy Lee was perched on his shoulders like some pint-size Jiminy Cricket.

Off to the side, scarcely visible, a stillness caught his attention. Engrossed in the way Elly's button moved with each breath she took, he would have missed that telltale sign if the attack on him the previous night hadn't made him wary, alert in a way he hadn't been since he'd taken a metaphorical hike into the sunset from police work. He let his gaze widen to include that figure that just missed blending into the hurrying crowd.

Five kids burst from behind a tent a hundred yards away, and a firecracker exploded. Royal felt Elly's flinch, admired the control that kept her from screaming. She'd been jittery since they'd gotten out of the car, and she was working hard to conceal her fears from Tommy. But Royal noted each one. Even as he focused on that figure across the way from them, he touched her elbow and said softly, "Easy, Elly. Only another firecracker."

Howling with laughter, the kids fled.

Elly laid her arm on his, and he could feel the tension whipping through her. "What's going on?"

"Nothing."

"You're lying. Don't patronize me by keeping the truth from me. I don't like it. I can handle whatever's happening."

A nervous edge crept into her voice, but he didn't make the mistake of underestimating his tough cookie. No. Not *his*. Just…Elly. Elly, who thought she could handle anything the wicked world threw her way. And damned near did.

"Tell me what you see."

"You got it." He angled his body close to hers, and her scent rose to him, subtle, heated by her fear. He could get drunk on the sweetness. "Over by the beer booth." He didn't have to warn her not to turn around. Elly wouldn't make that kind of error.

"Right." Slipping her arm through his and drawing it close, she stood on tiptoe, laughing, and kissed him lightly on the mouth, her lips meeting his, her head turning naturally in the direction of the booth.

"Very good," he murmured into the corner of her ear. His breath puffed the fine strands of her hair.

"I'd make a good detective, huh?" Her lips vibrated against his with her words, sending tingles down to his toes.

"I meant the kiss." He tipped his head so that he could see the man more clearly.

"Of course you did," she said sweetly, and nipped sharply at his bottom lip.

"Witch." Royal looked down into her laughing eyes, back at the man who'd alerted his antennae.

"You deserved it." The vibrations deepened as she snickered, and he decided that talking to Elly and kissing her at the same time was one hell of a foreplay technique.

"Of course I did. I'm a beast. And you have my complete understanding and permission to keep punishing me." Two could play this kind of game, he decided, letting his *s*-words linger against her pink mouth.

"Brute, fiend."

He figured it was inexperience that made her miss the vocabulary possibilities. "Yes. A sneaking, slinking skunk." He let his hand rest in the curve of her waist. "All those. Keep going, sugar."

"*Uncle,*" she whispered, letting her heels sink to the ground. Her mouth slid to the corner of his, lingered. Almost shyly, the tip of her tongue touched his bottom lip, making him catch his breath.

The woman caught on quick.

"*Uncle* here, too," he agreed. "Do you recognize that man, Elly?"

"No. Should I?" She spoke into the bend of his neck.

"He's been near us ever since we arrived in the parking lot. I wouldn't have paid any attention to him except that since we've been standing here, he hasn't moved. I'm—"

"Curious." Her lips moved against his skin in a smile. "I know. Me, too. So, buster, satisfy my curiosity, will you?"

"That's difficult. I can think of lots of other ways I'd like to satisfy you, satisfy myself." He dropped his hand a half inch lower, flattening his palm against the swell of her rear.

"You don't miss a beat, do you?"

"Can't afford to," he said ruefully. "Lots of competition."

"Somehow, I suspect you don't have much trouble." Her chuckle lifted the side of her breast against his arm, warm and yielding. Unlike the woman herself, who promptly stuck her tongue out at him and leaned away as he let his arm rest against that slight curve.

The teasing was becoming serious. His aching body was finding new ways to ache and hurt. If he didn't watch out, the laugh would be on him.

Surrounded by dust and noise and the distant whine of music and machinery, breathing in the smells of cotton candy and straw and horses, Royal felt more alone than ever. Holding Elly Malloy, he had a glimpse of the emptiness that had always filled him, the brutal emptiness that had driven him to be a cop until he'd let it become his obsession, his whole identity.

Such an obsession that, short of that identity, he couldn't get a handle on who he really was.

Not cop, he was nobody. Nothing.

Until recently, he hadn't cared.

Elly was making him care.

And briefly, he wondered if that would be the killing blow. Because she would leave. One way or another, Elly Malloy was going to walk out of his life.

But in the meantime, while she was there, filling his senses, making him smile, warming the cold edges of that emptiness, he couldn't seem to defend himself against her. He no longer wanted to. He'd thought he had some sense of self-preservation left, but he was wrong. Where Elly was concerned, he had no armor.

Except the tinfoil shield of his wisecracks.

Elly stirred against him. "Our friend hasn't moved."

"Neither have we. Let's try an experiment, sugar. Okay?"

"Maybe. Depends on what you have in mind." She clasped his hand safely in hers, swinging them well clear of interesting territory.

"Let Tommy and me disappear for a few minutes—"

"No." There was no equivocation in her guarded stance or her voice, and he understood the roots of her fear.

"I want to see if Tall, Dark and Ugly follows me or stays with you. I won't go far, and I'll be within calling distance."

"Where Tommy goes, I go. Period."

"You leave him with Leesha at the center."

"That's different. You're not Alicia."

Her quick comment stung. He understood, but the tiny, unexpected pain that followed her words surprised him.

Seeing his reaction, she paused, and concern, or something he wanted to believe resembled concern, flickered through her whiskey brown eyes. "And the center isn't in the middle of a crowded fairgrounds." She reached up for her son. "Tommy, you need to hold my hand now. Royal's going for a walk."

Tommy clasped Royal tightly around the neck, choking him. "Want to stay with Royal. Me and Royal growed on each other. We got to stick together, see, Mommy," he explained reasonably.

The chubby hands grabbing him so tightly moved Royal. He'd been an outcast for so long. The feel of Tommy's small, sweaty hands choking him with affection comforted him. Where Elly guarded her trust, her son gave it away freely. Royal swallowed the lump in his throat.

"Your mom's right, Tommy Lee. I'm going to be busy. I can't take you with me." Lifting Tommy Lee clear of his shoulders, Royal swung the boy to the ground and added, knowing it would erase the hero worship in the boy's eyes, "You'd be in the way."

"Oh." A world of hurt shimmered in Tommy's face, in his unaccustomed silence and acceptance. "But I wouldn't get in your way, Royal. I wouldn't. I promise."

"Yeah, you would, kid. Sorry. But that's the way it has to be. I don't have time right now to fool around with you."

"'Kay." His bottom lip was clamped between his teeth, but Royal saw the tremble of the childish mouth. "No problem."

Royal wished he could snatch the spoken words out of the clammy air, wished he could turn the world back on its axis long enough to change the moment.

He couldn't. He'd done the right thing. He knew he had. For Tommy. The boy would be better off not trusting him, not building up impossible hopes and affection.

Elly hoisted her son onto her hip, and Royal almost grabbed Tommy right out of her arms, almost told the truth and said he hadn't meant a word of what he'd said, he was only being silly, didn't Tommy know that?

Royal didn't. What would be the point? What he'd done was the right thing, the fairest thing, in the long run. He was stunned to find out how much the short run could still hurt.

He shoved his hands into his pockets and looked at Elly, stretching his lips in what he hoped would pass for a smile. "I'll be in shouting distance. Go down to the pavilion and wait."

"Right— But, Royal, Tommy didn't—" Compassion softened her face, deepened the brown of her eyes.

With the press of his finger against her lips, Royal stopped her. "It's all right, Elly. I understand." He did. He knew Elly understood. But Tommy didn't. He was a kid caught in the middle of a very grown-up mess.

Spinning on his heel, Royal lengthened his strides easily, showing no hurry, acting like a man with nothing on his mind except finding the closest bathroom. Then, with a quick movement, he melted into a group of eight teenagers, bending his knees so that his head didn't stand above theirs. Bumping and shoving at each other like a litter of puppies scrambling and climbing over each other, they moved away from Elly, their chaos and color safely concealing him.

Staying with them until they passed a corn dog booth smelling richly of grease and cornmeal, Royal ducked behind its walls and circled back, trotting down the crowded pathway on the other side until he approached from the rear and now followed Elly, Tommy Lee and the man casually stalking them.

He was right.

The attack last night had been aimed at Elly, not him. That meant her ex-husband was connected with it. Scanlon was covering all the bases. Apparently deciding it wasn't enough that he'd set Royal in motion, Scanlon had sent in at least two reinforcements.

Clamping down on his urge to collar the man and demand answers, Royal sorted out his impressions. Since he wasn't the target, Scanlon's thugs should have ignored him until he left Elly's house. But they hadn't. And, even after beating him up, they could have gone after Elly if they'd wanted. They hadn't done that, either.

Royal dodged a tall, bushy-bearded man pushing a baby stroller one-handed through the throngs. Why had the reinforcements abandoned the job halfway through? Peculiar behavior on their part, no matter how he rationalized it.

And why had they run away when they could have finished him off? No one had come up. Nothing had distracted them. They'd beaten the billy blue blazes out of him, and then abandoned the obvious target of their evening.

No matter how he torqued the events of the past two days, he couldn't make sense of the pattern.

Beating him up and taking a pass on the acknowledged target struck him as unnecessarily subtle.

He'd never figured he was important enough to Scanlon's plans to warrant a stomping. Scanlon viewed him as an errand boy, a man who'd stepped over the line once too often and was in no position to have a delicate stomach. To Elly's ex-husband, he was nothing more than a gofer whose job was to find her and return her like a lost package. So they could talk. A simple request. Hell, anybody could feel sorry for a man whose child had been stolen from him. A real simple, sympathetic role.

But Scanlon was subtle.

Royal's instincts as a cop, as a man, told him that Scanlon was capable of Byzantine twists and turns. For revenge, for pleasure. For the sheer hell of it.

Like an animal sniffing the air, checking for danger, Elly's shadow lifted his head. Royal stooped and fiddled with the laces of his shoes. The crowd parted around him and flowed back together, obscuring his view of Elly until he caught a flash of pink fabric and two gaily painted sneakers. He let out a sigh of relief and waited.

For the longest time, the dark-haired man stayed utterly still. Finally, with an impatient gesture, he resumed his pursuit, closing the gap that had opened up when he stopped.

As the man strode off, Royal dodged the crowd that suddenly formed between him and his quarry, cutting off access. Taking a shortcut through the back of a North Carolina barbecue booth, he sped past the woman stacking paper plates and bottles of vinegar. A bottle wobbled as his elbow jiggled it, and not stopping, he righted it with a flip of his hand and wrist. Elly was no longer in sight. "Damn." His movements jerky and uncoordinated, he scanned the crowd until he spotted the brim of her hat and its pink-gauze bow.

"Great hat, sugar," he muttered, keeping track of Elly's bobbing hat and bow.

"Hey, watch who you call 'sugar,'" the heavily sweating cook in the white paper hat warned as Royal hurried past the grill, where heat shimmered up from slabs of ribs and roasts. "Or you'll be dinner." He waved a long-pronged fork under Royal's nose. "Crowded enough back here. Customers stay out front."

"Sorry." Royal shrugged and sent him an easy smile. "Smells great."

"The best, dude. Come back the front way and buy a plate."

"Later. Got to go." Ducking under the door panel, Royal exited at a quick step, refraining from running. He wouldn't get to Elly and Tommy at all if he drew attention to himself. Narrowing the gap between them, he slowed and took in the details swirling around him.

Scanlon was wiping out Royal's gambling debts to the tune of three hundred thousand dollars. Scanlon said it was because he wanted Elly back, to talk to her, to convince her to make fair child-custody arrangements. On the surface, Royal thought, it made sense, still did. But from the beginning, the money had tweaked him. Granted, a loving father would give anything—everything—for his child, but something about the offer reeked of other motives.

Scanlon believed he was desperate enough to do anything for that much money, and Royal hadn't contradicted him. Royal hadn't cared enough to exert that much effort. And most of all, he didn't give a damn about what Scanlon believed.

During that long weekend of gambling, Scanlon had concluded that he needed the money, wanted it.

But what did Scanlon want?

Tommy, of course. No matter which way Royal ran the options through his mind, that fact remained constant: Scanlon wanted his son.

Question was, did he want Elly? Or was Elly expendable? And if she was, how did Scanlon fit Royal into his plans?

Moving invisibly behind Scanlon's man, Royal smiled nastily.

Scanlon saw him as a pawn to be moved around the chessboard until the queen was captured.

Blake Scanlon had made a bad mistake.

Down the dirt pathway of the main aisle, Elly made her slow, painstaking way, and wherever Elly went, her pursuer followed. A stop at the portable potty. A wait in line for lemonade.

Shortly before she and Tommy arrived at the pavilion, her mystery man was joined by a second man, the two moving sharklike through the waters of the crowd.

That cinched it for Royal. These two were definitely his assailants.

Stepping sideways into the shadows of a banyan tree, he waited to see what they would do. He expected them to close in on either side of Elly and waltz her away unobtrusively.

They didn't do that, either. Instead, after what looked to be a jovial conversation, they separated, merging into the masses of people and taking up look-out stations at opposite ends of the pavilion. Leaning against a live oak tree, Tall, Dark and Ugly shook out a cigarette, stuffed the pack into his shirt pocket and lit up. Yawning, he stretched his thick arms overhead and then folded them across his chest and waited.

Stunned into immobility, Royal frowned. Why would they

follow her but not grab her? Like last night's attack, their behavior seemed purposeless.

But it couldn't be. He knew he was missing some important
point, the key to the whole mess. Whatever was going on was
calculated. Scanlon would never invest the kind of money and
time he had in a project that had no purpose.

T.D. and U. looked as though he'd settled in for the duration.
Royal sighed. A knot tightened in his stomach. He was getting
a real bad feeling about this setup. The men weren't making a
move on Elly and her son. So that meant they were waiting for
someone else.

And it looked like he was that someone.

Pawns were meant to be sacrificed, he reminded himself as
he strolled toward Elly and Tommy Lee. Might be interesting
to see what Scanlon had planned.

But he thought he'd rattle T.D. and U.'s cage first. For fun.

Stooping slightly and rounding his shoulders, Royal held one
hand protectively against his ribs as he approached Elly's stalker.
He couldn't overdo it. After all, he'd been carting Tommy Lee
around all morning in full view of this outlaw. "Hey, my friend,
can I bum a smoke?" Royal coughed, let his hands shake, not
much, just a fine, alcoholic tremor. "Rough night."

The man regarded him impassively, his blue eyes cold and
empty. Slicked back from his face, his hair separated into greasy
clumps. "Get your own."

"Yeah, man. Would if I could. But I'm tapped out, and my
lady friend doesn't like me to smoke around her and the kid,
you know?" Royal's chuckle was self-mocking, shading into
desperation.

Something flickered in the blue eyes. "So?"

Royal shrugged. "Sorry, man. Thought I'd ask. Thanks, anyway." Figuring he'd better follow through on his act if he
wanted to make it believable, he ambled away. After a few steps,
he stopped at a bench where a seated woman alternated leisurely
sips from a paper cup with long pulls on her cigarette.

She was more easily charmed than Scanlon's man.

Giving her a farewell smile, Royal took a deep drag and
waited until he was out of sight before he coughed and pitched
the cigarette.

"Miss me, sugar?" He made certain Elly saw him before he

slid his arm around her shoulder. "Make it good," he whispered, leaning in and giving her a kiss. "People are watching. You may not know it yet, but you're my girlfriend."

Tension still stringing her tight as a rubber band, she chuckled. "Really? Oh, good. That means I get to wear your letter jacket and high-school ring. I can't wait to tell all the girls at the soda shop."

"You are such a pest," he murmured, tugging her lower lip gently.

"And you smell like smoke." She drew her head back. Her spine was rigid. "You don't smoke."

"Not anymore." He let his gaze drift to the side, toward T.D. and U. The man's attention was totally focused on Royal and Elly. "Used to, sugar. Quit when I burned a hole in the seat of my Mustang. I truly do love that car," he said as she shot him a quizzical look. "Do anything for that beauty. We've been together for ten years."

"A man who's not afraid of commitment. I congratulate you." Game to the core, she managed a smile in spite of the shudder that rippled over her as another firecracker popped in the distance. "What did you find out?"

"I made the acquaintance of our friend." Royal shifted his body in the direction of the tree so that she could see the man more clearly. Dropping his voice so that only she could hear and not Tommy, he said, "You real sure you don't know him, Elly? Think about it," he cautioned when she looked away too quickly.

Like him, she lowered her voice. "I'm positive." She gripped his forearm while Tommy twined himself into her skirt, wrapping it tightly around him and staying clear of Royal. "I don't think I'd choose him as my Humanitarian of the Week. Who is he?"

"He's a stone-cold killer, that's who."

Her whole body shook, her teeth clicking together. "You can't know that. How could you?"

"I know. Believe me on this, Elly."

The effort she made to control her shaking was admirable and ineffectual. "Are you sure?"

"As sure as fifteen years of cop work can make me. And, no, I don't know him, either. But I know his type," he said grimly.

"My wicked ways haven't caught up with me. He's following you, Elly, not me."

"Damn," she whispered, stricken, turning her head toward their stalker. "I thought there was time." She hit his arm. "I need more time!"

Royal caught her shoulders, stopping her. Her gasp was a whistle of sound, barely audible. "Want to tell me about it?"

"I don't know what you mean." She was sickly pale, and Royal was afraid she was going to throw up any second. She pulled Tommy even closer to her, lifted her chin and looked Royal straight in the eyes, a sure sign she was lying. "I can't imagine why that man's following me."

"Of course you can, sweetheart. Try. Because, in fact, there are two of them. And we have to talk."

"About what?" The white line running around her mouth betrayed her as she pulled against his hold.

"Oh, about why two killers are tracking you like hyenas on the scent of blood. That would be a good place to start, don't you think?"

"I tell you, I don't know!"

"Then let's try another topic. These same guys were at your house last night. But all they did was whale on me until their arms and feet got tired. Why did they choose me for their personal punching bag, do you reckon?"

"Quit badgering me!"

"Fine. I will. Answer one last question, though." He lifted his hand and gently traced the spider line of her scar, his heart aching for her, for her son. For her foolish courage that would wind up getting her killed. Because she didn't have a chance on her own. "Is this why you have all those high-powered pain pills you shared with me? This scar came from a gun, didn't it? This is a gunshot wound, sweetheart. Do I win the gold ring?"

She jerked her head away. "It doesn't matter. You're not involved. Leave. Go away."

"I can't. That might have been an option a week ago. To tell you the truth, though, I'm beginning to wonder if that was ever a possibility. At any rate, it isn't anymore. You and I, Elly, we're the eye of the hurricane. And the worst of the storm's still ahead."

"You're wrong. You *can* walk away. Turn around, Royal. Walk away. It *is* still possible for you."

"And you, sweet Elly? What will you do? Run away again?"

She blanched. But she was silent.

"Nothing to say, Elly?"

Staring at him like a deer caught in the crosshairs, she was nothing but bleached-out face and enormous brown eyes. Over and over, helplessly, she shook her head.

As impossible as it was to expect, Royal still hoped she would trust him. He didn't think she would. But with or without her trust, they were going to have to work together. She would have to accept that.

Their lives depended on it.

He'd seen their deaths in those dead blue eyes, the eyes of a killer who could squash them as easily as a fly and with as much emotion. In those eyes, Royal was already a dead man. *When* was all that had to be worked out.

"Here's the deal, Elly. I checked your suitcase this morning."

Her eyelids fluttered, opened, and although he hadn't thought it was possible, she went even paler under the protection of her froufrou hat, and he was swamped with pity. But pity wouldn't save them.

"I know Elena Malone will be looking for another job sometime soon, a new place to live. Even so, in about ten hours, I could find Elena. And her son. And if I can, other people can, too. Not that fast, but they'd find her. One way or another. And then they'd come after her." A series of poppers exploded around them like gunshots.

Elly's knees buckled, and she sagged against him, her slight form a deadweight as he supported her with his hands under her arms, her hand still gripping her son's.

"Mommy?" Tommy's voice quavered, and the glance he sent Royal was terrified. "Mommy!"

Her eyelashes fluttered shut once more and stayed closed, delicate brown fans against her colorless skin.

Holding Elly upright with his arm around her waist, Royal tried to take Tommy's hand, but even unconscious, Elly hung on, or Tommy's grip was too strong to break, Royal wasn't sure. But the boy was a problem, and they didn't need to attract more of the killer's attention than he was already giving their small band. Not risking a giveaway glance, Royal spoke calmly. "Come on, Tommy."

"No. Don't want to." The boy shook his head and buried his face against Elly's side, taking her hand in both of his. "I can't leave my mommy." Defiance and fear pinched his chubby face. "You can't make me. I'll scream like bloody murder if you touch me."

"Good idea. Make sure you do that," Royal encouraged. "But in the meantime, will you help your mom?"

"How?" Pitifully young, Tommy's treble wobbled.

"You hold her hand. Yes, like you're doing, that's good. Now take the hem of her skirt and hold on to it with your other hand."

"I don't understand." Tommy looked like he was about to squall. "I don't know what to do!"

"Sure, you do. You're kind of scared, that's all. Take a deep breath, okay?"

Tommy almost nodded. The inclination was there. At least he was listening.

"Good man. Now take your right hand. The one your mom's not holding," Royal added quickly as Tommy scowled at his hands and seemed about to turn loose of Elly.

"This one?" Tommy raised a grubby fist toward Royal.

"Yeah, that's the ticket, kiddo. Know your right from your left, do you?"

"I'm five. I learned a long time ago."

"Well, that's swell. There's hope for our educational system after all."

"Huh?"

"Nothing. I'm proud of you, that's all. Hang on, Tommy, while I settle your mom."

Anchoring Elly's hat under her cheek, Royal tucked her face into his shoulder. It hid her face and the shadows that too much stress had colored in with a heavy hand. Thanks to the protection of her hat and his shoulder, anyone watching would think she was snuggling up to him.

"Is she okay?"

Royal almost missed Tommy's whisper, but the kid's frantic tug on his arm alerted him.

"She's terrific, kiddo, and we're almost done with what we have to do. Take that good ol' right hand and catch the end of your mom's skirt. Good, good. Now drape it over your shoulder like a cape and hold on for dear life because we're going to make like Superman and fly. Got it?''

Tommy nodded. Two days ago, he would have giggled. Now, though, he didn't. Royal missed that innocent response. He missed that face looking up at him as though Royal could fix the world if necessary. Nobody, not even Maggie, had ever looked at him like that.

In all his life, nobody had ever given him that kind of innocent adoration. Royal wanted that look back on Tommy's face. Its loss hurt more than he'd imagined.

''Here we go. Easy, like playing a game at the Sunshine Center. We're sailing through enemy waters and their lasers are trained on us. We're invisible unless we move too fast. Got that?''

Tommy nodded.

''Move like a cat. Slow and smooth. Because if we go too fast, we set off all kinds of bells and whistles. If we're caught, we lose the game. Got it?''

Tommy nodded again, not friendly, but more natural, and a spark of interest stirred in his eyes.

As they eased their way forward, Elly shifted against Royal, consciousness returning. Confusion filled her eyes as she looked up at him.

''Hey, sugar. Welcome home.'' The word startled him, but it fit. He felt at home with her and her son.

''Mommy?'' Wrapped in her skirt, Tommy clung to Elly's leg.

''I'm fine, honey. A bit dizzy. That's all.''

''You scared me. Bad. I was *really* scared,'' he insisted in a small voice.

''Don't be. I'll take care of you. Always. No matter what. You know that.'' She drew Tommy even closer, and a slim thigh gleamed briefly in the folds of pink material.

'''Kay,'' he said. Lack of conviction showed in every line of his slumped shoulders. ''I know. But—'' And then he was silent, plastering himself against Elly's leg.

Keeping a tight grip on Tommy, Elly tipped her face to Royal wearily. ''Firecrackers again, right?'' Her smile was embarrassed. ''And I wimped out.''

"Firecrackers, yeah. Wimping out?" Powerless in the face of her courage and determination to ask no quarter, he bent down and kissed her fiercely, letting his kiss tell her what he couldn't put in words, what he didn't understand himself. With her wan face and shadowed eyes, she was infinitely precious to him in that moment, and he wanted her to know—to know *something*.

Thought escaped him as her mouth softened under his and she leaned into him, yielding to the strength he offered her as though she had no more will than he to sacrifice that tiny luxury of touch. Damp, her mouth clung to his, and the hunger her lips created had everything to do with regret and despair. And of a longing so strong that sex was too simple a word for what moved in him at the touch of this woman.

Desire, lust. Muted, they were there, too, but they were only the faint light on the horizon next to the blaze of need that grew stronger with each moment he spent with her.

Lifting his head finally, he muttered, "We're not done, Elly. You and I have unfinished business. This—" he kissed her again quickly, tasting the softness of her mouth "—and the answers to those questions I asked earlier."

"I know." Resignation drained her of the color that had touched her cheeks briefly. "You're right. We're the eye of the storm. I'll tell you whatever you want to know. But later." Her glance at Tommy was significant.

"Yeah, later. For the next fifteen minutes, then, pretend I'm the love of your life and stick to me like shine on a mirror."

"Tough job," she retorted with a return to her usual mock-insults and an adoring tilt of her head. Her skin still looked skimmed milk pale. "Why are you the love of my life, O Wondrous One?"

"Because our job at the moment is to lose Mr. Tall, Dark and Ugly. Well, maybe not lose him and his buddy. Basically, we need to pretend nothing has changed, that we haven't spotted them. We have to lull them into believing we're as stupid as they think we are. Just until we can make plans and figure out what we're—"

"What's this *we, Kemo Sabe?*" she asked with a faint smile, dredging up the punch line of an old, stupid joke about the Lone Ranger and Tonto under attack by hostile warriors.

"*We,*" he underscored. "The three of us."

"Maybe." Nevertheless, she let her weight rest against him and slid her arm around his waist.

"Let's go." Trying to watch both thugs, Tommy and Elly, and slip through openings in the increasingly thick crowd all at the same time, Royal hustled Elly and Tommy away from the pavilion and down a packed-sawdust aisle. He hadn't decided whether they should leave or wait for the cover darkness and the commotion the fireworks would provide.

Tommy tagged along at Elly's side like a forlorn tugboat, and she curved into Royal so trustingly that Royal could almost believe her act was real.

Without Royal at Elly's side, what would Tommy have done? He would have been terrified. Royal didn't even want to consider what Elly's stalkers would have done with her helpless and her son confused and frightened.

She needed him.

Tommy Lee needed him.

He'd never been anyone's knight in shining armor before. That wasn't his style.

But he found he wanted to be theirs, at least for a while.

For today, if not for tomorrow.

He wasn't hero material. He'd already made mistakes, made decisions that affected Elly and her son, decisions that would make her despise him when she knew. And he would tell her. He had to.

The day of reckoning drew nearer with each passing hour, but for now, he was their only hope.

And that realization made him pity the woman in his arms. She deserved more than the husk that he was.

But he was all she had. Without him, she would be at the mercy of a cold-blooded killer.

And her ex-husband.

Chapter 10

Dust blew around her, into her nose, stung her eyes.

"We're not going for the pony ride?" Tommy plucked at her skirt, and she looked at Royal, indecisive.

"Can we? Do we need to leave? Or stay?" She covered her face. "I can't think. I can't think!"

"Easy, sugar." Royal's palm slid under her hair, bumping against her hat. "Nothing's going to happen here. For the time being, we're safe unless we give ourselves away by letting our friends know we've spotted them." He kneaded her nape, working down her shoulder, massaging out the knots in her muscles.

"Then what?" She let her head fall back against his palm, indulged herself and pretended for the moment that she wasn't alone. Sometimes, pretending was all a woman had. "What happens when we leave this sanctuary?"

"Then we'll use darkness to cover our behinds and give us some options."

"We have options?" she asked, hoping she didn't sound as forlorn as Tommy. Royal's touch drained her of resolution, weakened her because she wanted to believe in its solace. "We actually have some choices of what we're going to do?"

His grin was daredevil brilliant, and the energy coming from him buzzed against her, exhausting. "Always, sugar. Until darkness, I don't see any reason Tommy can't ride the ponies. We can even go over to the ring and watch the bull rides. We'll talk. We'll figure out plans as we go. We'll take it a step at a time now that you're no longer in your elegant swoon. That suit you, Elly? Or do you have a better idea? I'm flexible."

"I'm out of ideas." Elly took a breath and tried to think. "I have my car. If I can get to it, I'm prepared." With her car, she could go anywhere, become anyone within hours. He was right. She did have options. "I'll go get the car."

"I don't think they're going to let you do that, sugar." His voice was terribly gentle.

"You're right. They're not going to let me run away again." She was alone. That much she understood very clearly. Royal's arm around her waist was an illusion. She couldn't forget that fact. No matter how tempting it was to think she could depend on him, she couldn't.

She couldn't let herself trust the treacherous sweetness of his kisses, of his touch. She couldn't let herself trust him.

She couldn't trust anyone. Blake's tentacles stretched far. His influence was too pervasive. Anyone could be an enemy. And those who weren't, those who tried to help her, would be caught in the cross fire. Like Royal. Either way, she would be responsible.

She curled her fingers around his hand for an instant before lifting his arm. "Okay. I understand."

"No, sweetheart, you don't." He cupped his hand over hers and drew her closer. "Smile, Elly. Remember, everything we do is being watched."

She smiled with dry lips.

"Elly," he said, turning her toward him and keeping Tommy between them, "I'm not going to walk away from you. I have a score to settle with these guys." His smile glittered with menace.

"Because they beat you up." She couldn't swallow. All the danger she'd sensed behind his bright charm was there in full force, no longer hidden. She'd known he was dangerous. She'd had only a hint of the darkness in Royal Gaines. She was glad she wasn't the object of that glittering smile. She was mortified to realize how grateful she was that his energies were directed against her enemies and not her.

"Take a breath, sweetheart. We'll make plans." He leaned forward and whispered into her ear, his breath raising the hairs along her arms and curling her toes. "We'll make the bastards wish they'd never tangled with us."

Again, that *we*. But there was no *we*. She couldn't drag innocent people into the danger zone of her life. That would be unconscionable. She poked him in the ribs and wanted to grab him around the waist and beg. She didn't. She'd learned the hard way: ask no quarter. She would handle whatever was coming. By herself. "This isn't your problem, Royal."

Ignoring her, he kept walking, shortening his long stride to match hers. "Now let's stroll on toward the ponies and let Tommy forget what happened here a few minutes ago."

"All right," she said dully, defeated by his insistence on including himself in her disaster. She would answer Royal's questions, and then he'd be gone. Risk taking might be part of his life's blood, but even he wouldn't think the odds were worth his life. But she was more grateful than she wanted to admit even to herself for his strength, for his knowledge today. He'd given her a chance. His skills had discovered their pursuer. Even as cautious as she was, she would have missed the men Blake had sent after her.

They would kill her when they were ready. And take Tommy back to Blake. She was now beginning to understand that she would never escape.

A scrap of Popsicle wrapper blew across her foot, stuck to the tongue of her shoe, and she stooped to pick the sticky scrap off. The temptation to sit there and never move again was so enormous that it frightened her. If she lost that stubborn, one-foot-in-front-of-the-other desire to keep moving, Blake would find her. If it weren't for Tommy, she'd give up. She was so tired of running, of thinking and planning and never having a chance to let down her guard.

No matter what she did, Blake kept closing in on her, boxing her in, herding her into an increasingly narrow tunnel. How much longer could she keep going on like this? Her resources were dwindling.

And Tommy wasn't a baby who could be carted around willy-nilly. He needed stability. Roots. He needed a home that would be there, not only from morning to night, but from month to month. Like Royal's house, which melted into its environment as if it had always been there, peaceful. She couldn't give Tommy that kind of security. That kind of peace. Not now.

Not while they were living on the run, changing homes every couple of months in the middle of the night, picking up and abandoning their few belongings in a moment of suspicion—that was no life for him, for anyone. Even if she survived another year, Tommy had to start school. And each time she sent down roots, she established a paper trail that Blake could follow.

She almost welcomed a confrontation with her ex-husband. A confrontation would bring an end to this limbo of her existence.

And Tommy? Blake would have Tommy.

She would do anything to prevent that.

Straightening, she dropped the scrap into a trash barrel and kept walking, Royal beside her, keeping her aware of him, bumping his hip against hers. There, beside her, brushing her skin, her hair, with quick, skimming touches.

Pretending, creating an illusion for Tommy, she and Royal bought cotton candy. They bought hot dogs. Elly couldn't eat hers. Her bottomless pit of a son gobbled his and begged for french fries. The three of them waited in line for the enormous Ferris wheel, which gave them a view over the whole fairgrounds and parking lot.

"I see the car. As far as I can tell, no one's there right now." Royal smiled. "Having fun, sweetheart?"

"Buckets." Her knuckles were white on the bar holding them in. "I hate this."

"I love it." Royal's grin was as brilliant as the fierce blue sky burning down on them.

"Me, too. I love it. Me and Royal love fairy wheels." Tommy tried to lean over the metal bar.

Royal's hand moved even faster than hers. "Sit."

Tommy sat, his face glazed with mustard and happiness.

He rode the ponies. Five times, Elly and Royal circling the rink with him.

The three of them watched the grand finale of the parade,

Tommy whooping and shrieking with all the other kids as the clowns pitched bags of red-and-blue candies toward them.

They were the image of a normal family in all the red, white and blue of the Fourth of July. Watching the spray of candies flying around them, Elly wished for one heart-filled moment that the illusion of normalcy was real. Candies sparkled in the air.

"I caught one, Royal," Tommy screamed, clutching a white mesh bag in one fist while Royal kept a firm grip on the seat of Tommy's shorts. "This is my very best day of my whole life." The tag end of Tommy's rib wrap hung below his shirt, and Elly refastened it as Tommy rattled the bag of candies in her face.

"Good hands, kid."

"I was going to play Tee-ball—" When Elly didn't stop him, Tommy continued. "But...we moved. Right, Mommy?"

"Right, honey. We moved." She hugged him and kissed the tip of his nose, her heart splintering for her child.

As the evening shadows filtered over the fairgrounds through the tree branches, Elly noticed that Royal's calculated route took them closer and closer to the parking lot, to the area where she'd left her car. Along the posts of the fence separating the parking area from the fairgrounds, strings of red, white and blue flags fluttered in the breeze, signaling an elusive coolness. The ripple and snap of the flags punctuated the increasing chaos and noise around her.

She would have preferred quiet.

Crowds were safer. She was pathetically relieved by the mass of people and their cheerful pandemonium.

Near the entrance to the ring where the bull riders and bronco-busters would perform, Royal stopped near a Sno-Kone stand and lifted Tommy back onto his shoulders. "I'm going to page Beau, Elly."

"Beau?"

"Beau Bienvenue. A friend of mine from the old days in the department."

Anxiety whipped through her. "Why are you going to call him?"

Increasing her apprehension, Royal didn't answer immediately.

She hadn't anticipated he would make a hundred-and-eighty-degree turn and decide to involve the police in her affairs after all. Foolishly, she'd thought she'd escaped that trap last night. She'd miscalculated. "Are you calling him because of me and Tommy? If that's the reason, forget—"

"Hold on, Elly. Keep our audience in mind. Don't let them see you're upset. Beau's on duty today at the parade, not playing desk jockey, so I have to page him and wait for him to call me back. We need his help."

"No. Absolutely not." She started to walk away from him and came up short, stopped by his arm around her waist. "It's too dangerous. You don't know what's going on. Who's involved."

His eyes narrowed. "I know these men are hired killers. I know we need Beau's help if we're going to get past them."

"And you trust him?" She wrinkled her face in dismay. She hadn't counted on having even more people involved.

"Completely."

"I don't know him. How can *I* trust him? Don't bring him into this, Royal. I won't let you." She tried to pry his hand loose, but he'd wound his fingers into the fabric at her waist. Short of ripping off the skirt of her dress, she was effectively chained to him.

Studying her, his gaze lingering where her pulse beat furiously at her neck, he waited a long moment. "You trust Leesha, don't you? Like I said earlier, you leave Tommy with her every day. As far as I can tell, you don't leave him alone with anyone else. You consider her a safe person."

"Of course I do. Otherwise, I'd never leave him at the center. What does that have to do with your policeman friend? Anyway, I thought you didn't have any friends left on the force and that was why you didn't want me to call the police last night." Her words tumbled out as she felt the net closing around her. Blake had connections to the police. If the police knew where she was, Blake could, within hours. And she couldn't get to her car. Her hands clenched, she covered her mouth to keep from screaming at Royal, to keep from terrifying her son still riding on Royal's shoulders.

"Elly, listen to me." Pulling her hands free, Royal covered them with his. Then, his voice empty of emotion, he spoke so calmly that he caught her frantic attention. "Leesha trusts Beau.

She's going to marry him once he figures out that Leesha is a long-term lady and not a weekend woman.''

"Terrific. I'm happy for both of them. But it doesn't make any difference to me. In fact, that's an even better reason for keeping them out of this mess.''

"I have three friends in my life, Elly. Leesha and Beau are two of them. Maggie Webster Barnett, my ex-fiancée and former partner, is the other. I trust them with my life.''

"That's your decision. Not mine." The thought of Royal with a fiancée gave her a pang, a small, unexpected hurt. "But I can't trust them. I don't want them involved in what's happening.''

He reached down and brushed her hair away from her face, his warm palm cupping her cheek and soothing her alarm. "Elly, whether these men following us make their move against us tonight or tomorrow isn't the issue. They're coming after us, sooner or later. We have a better chance if we set the time and place. We can't do that without help. I don't like asking for help, either. But we have to. Without some help, we're going to be real big newspaper headlines real fast. Because these men will find us. Or someone like them will. Someone we're not prepared for until he rises up out of the dark to ambush us. I don't want Tommy there when that happens. You don't, either.''

"No," she whispered, defeated. "I wouldn't want Tommy to see that. It would— But asking for help? Involving all these people I don't know? Who don't know me?" She was losing control. Royal was forcing her to trust him and his friends. To keep Tommy from being caught in the middle of a firestorm, she had to reach out to these strangers. Frustration raged through her. All her decisions were being removed, one by one. Anger pitching her voice higher than she wanted, she said, "Call your friend, Royal. Do what you have to do.''

He brushed his hand lightly along her cheek. "I'm not trying to force you into anything. But we have a problem. To me, this is the best way to deal with it for both of us. But it's your decision.''

It wasn't, and they both knew it. Events were propelling them past the boundaries of choices and decisions.

"You're hustling me." She pushed his hand away. "And I don't like it. Everything's being taken away from me, and I'm this puppet *thing* controlled by an unseen hand.''

As if they had all the time in the world to debate the issue, he smiled. "Okay. I get the picture." He shrugged, but she knew him well enough now to read the lines of tension at the corners of his mouth. "What do you want to do?"

There was an enormous impulse to walk away from him, walk past the men who'd been following her for God only knew how long, and walk to her car as if her life were normal. By pricking the balloon of her anger, Royal had given her the illusion that she had to make some of the decisions, that she was more than that puppet she felt like. "At least you have a plan. I don't. Make the call."

"We'll get a Sno-Kone first. We're in no hurry, right, Tommy?" Royal glanced up at Tommy. "It's the Fourth of July. We're celebrating." His warning gaze was for her as he lowered Tommy to the ground.

Silently, they stood in line for the icy treats. The excitement and heat were wearing out even Tommy, who leaned drowsily between them while Royal handed over money for three neon-colored cones in a corrugated carrier.

As she walked in a stupor with Royal toward the phone mounted on a pole near the Sno-Kone stand, he nodded toward the ticket booth on the far side of the refreshment stand. "Look, I'd like to keep our shadows in as much confusion as we can. It probably doesn't matter, but I'd rather they didn't wonder why I'm making a phone call or who I'm getting in touch with. Let's throw them a curveball and split up for a moment. Instead of going with me to make the call, will you buy the tickets so our comrades will figure we're planning on staying for the rodeo events for a while?"

"I can do that." Gripping Tommy's hand, Elly weighed her options. Despite what Royal had said, maybe she *should* slip away. If she could get to her car, she could be Elena Malone for a day or two and then, well, then Elena could disappear, too. Other people vanished into the underbelly of the country for years. She could, too. She'd just have to make better plans than she had so far—that was all, no matter what Royal had said.

The prospect of constructing another new identity daunted her. She was lucky she could remember her name. Lucky Tommy could keep as many facts straight as he did.

Royal had brought her safely to the vicinity of her car. It

might be best for all three of them if she used this chance to disappear.

"Elly, you will wait here for me?" His expression as he held out a red Sno-Kone to her and a smaller purple one to Tommy was grim. He dropped the carrier into a trash can. "Or are you going to split and run the minute my back's to you?"

"I told you to call your friend," she countered wearily, checked. She'd been stupid to think she could keep a step ahead of Royal. "Why would I run now?"

"Because you're used to taking care of things on your own. Because you don't trust me to see this through. Because you're afraid I'll let you down. Sugar, I could give you a hundred reasons why you'd slip away. Don't leave, Elly." His face was as serious as she'd ever seen it, an intensity in the lean planes that tightened the skin and darkened his eyes and almost made her believe in him. He handed her a twenty-dollar bill. "Please stay."

She lifted Tommy to her hip. She wouldn't get as far as her car. Either Royal or Blake's men would be there to intercept her. She was safer sticking with Royal, no matter how uncomfortable it made her to depend on him. "Go make your phone call, Royal. I'll wait. You don't have to worry about me." Feeling trapped, she smiled for their audience and walked to the ticket booth.

But she stuffed the money Royal had given her into her pocket and used her own, a useless rebellion that made her feel better. With the tickets in her hand, she lingered at the edge of the ring. Letting Tommy peek through the slats in the fence while they waited, she kept Royal in clear view.

Sauntering toward the phone, Royal looked neither left nor right. In his green shirt and jeans, he was the picture of a man out for a good time, not a worry in the world. He punched out a number, his shoulders hunched so that no one could see the numbers, and then he seemed to speak into the phone, laughing once as though in conversation.

All pretense, all illusion.

He would be holding down the receiver button while he waited for Beau to return the call. The phone would ring, but it would look as if he'd been talking on it, not waiting for a return call. His game would be to make it seem casual, giving no indication that he was making a call for reinforcements.

When he returned, she said, "You really were a good detective, weren't you? It must have killed you to quit."

"I'm alive." He didn't look at her.

His simple answer revealed more pain than she guessed he'd want her to see. Maybe he was forcing her to trust him. Maybe she was only seeing the man he kept hidden from everyone else except for his three friends, but she could see how giving up his profession, a profession he was uniquely suited for, could have destroyed him.

Elly tried to generate enthusiasm for the bull riding. She couldn't. She was in overload. So was Tommy. After ten minutes of stupified observation, he fell asleep in her lap.

"Want me to hold him?" Royal's denimed knees scraped along her thigh as he shifted toward her.

"No. He's comfortable. He'll wake up if we move him."

"And you're not sure I won't take off with him, are you, Elly?"

She glanced down at the ring as cheers erupted from a packed section off to their left. Royal had taken them to the top row so that he could see anyone coming up toward them. "That's not the problem. Not anymore. I don't think you're going to steal him from me." She rested Tommy's head against her breast and avoided looking at Royal. "What did Beau say?"

"We're going to give our shadows the slip after the first series of fireworks. I told Beau where your car is. He's coming in the patrol car, and we're going to crawl in the back and drive right out of here, chauffeured by Palmaflora's best."

"But my car?" A cry escaped her. She couldn't leave her car. It held everything she needed for her next move.

"They'll be expecting us to go to your car. In fact, I'll bet they've already put a tracking device on it now they know where you are, what you drive."

She buried her face against her son's soft hair. "You're taking everything away from me. You're leaving me nothing, nothing!"

"Aw, Elly, hang on, sugar. Think about what I'm saying. Your car is a giveaway. Where it is, you are. All they have to do is go in and pluck you like a ripe peach. You know I'm right.

We can't take the chance. If we leave the car here, we'll have a window of opportunity. Because, Elly—'' he slipped his hand under her hair and cupped her head ''—they'll be waiting for us near the car.''

Down below her, the rider circled one hand in the air and held on for dear life with the other. She knew how he felt. A groan went up as the bull convulsed in a mighty bend of muscle and power and sent him flying.

Royal was right. She'd cut her losses again and again. What was one more time? ''We're going to camp out in Beau's squad car?''

''The first step is to get away from here for a few hours and think things through without having to keep up the playacting. We're going to Beau's. Leesha will be there, too. Maggie and Sullivan are coming in the morning. Can you hang on until then, Elly?'' He stroked down the length of her hair, down her back, working the heel of his hand against her vertebrae. ''You're not in this alone anymore, sweetheart.'' With his arm around her hip, he hitched her closer to him, her thigh resting along the length of his, side by side. ''Put your head on my shoulder, Elly. Rest for a few minutes. You can shut your eyes. Nobody's going to sneak up on you while I'm here.''

In the brilliant night-lights of the ring, his hair shone so golden that it hurt her eyes, and obediently, she shut them, surrendering to the promise in his eyes. He would keep her and Tommy safe. She could sleep for a few minutes, sleep until the fireworks. She was safe. Royal was there.

Royal didn't think he could bear that last, confused glance Elly gave him as she yielded to sleep. Running on empty, she'd looked at him with such wariness and despair—and trust. He took a deep, toe-curling breath. Beneath the wariness, there had been that faint, ambivalent trust.

She made him think of a starving, tiny cat he'd found in a drainage tunnel the spring he was ten. Leaving deep, bloody gouges in his arms, the cat had clawed him, her eyes wild with fear and distrust as he tried to pet her. Not much more than a kitten herself, she was pregnant, her ribs showing above her distended belly. All gold eyes and scrawny body, she hissed and spit, her tail spiky with fear and terror. He'd backed out of the tunnel, but every day he took food to her, coaxing her closer, letting her grow accustomed to him.

Her distrust stronger than her hunger, she never let him touch her. But the food was always gone the next day. On his last day home from military school, he found her with her three kittens. Two were dead. The third, a minute scrap of black fur, looked up at him blindly, its head bobbing and weaving on the thin stem of its neck.

Reaching out for the small cat he'd named Goldie, he touched her for the first time. The tip of her nose was burning hot, and he must have spoken or cried out. Something. Snarling and yowling, she'd thrown herself at him, scratching and clawing his face and neck as she jumped over him to the entrance of the tunnel and freedom.

Not knowing better, only desperate to save her, he grabbed at her. In her frenzy, she shot straight out of the edge of the creek bed into the path of an oncoming car.

Sobbing, he'd carried Goldie's kitten home, hugging it close to his chest. The rapid patter of its tiny heart terrified him. He was all Goldie's kitten had left in the world. The responsibility was so enormous his own heart beat in syncopation to the kitten's as the tiny creature nuzzled at his chest.

His parents had taken the kitten to the animal shelter. He'd overheard his mother's shocked question, "Who knows what kind of diseases the thing has?"

His father had said, impatience in every syllable, "You're not going to be home to take care of him, Royal. You can't take him with you to school. And you certainly can't expect the maids to feed him and clean out his litter. What in heaven's name were you thinking?"

Weak and malnourished, Goldie's kitten died before they took it to the shelter, its tiny claws tickling the palm of his hand in one final movement that broke Royal's heart for the last time.

Now, even twenty-eight years later, Royal felt the prickle of anger and an old grief in his eyes. Like Goldie, Elly was wary, taking what he offered only on her terms.

He was all she had, whether she knew it or not. And, like the ten-year-old boy he'd been, he was doing everything he could to coax her close enough to save her. But he wasn't a boy, and she wasn't a feral kitten. The situation was complicated by adult issues, adult needs.

Anything could happen.

Royal wanted to run from the rodeo ring as fast as he could. What had he done, taking on the responsibility for their lives? Who was he to play God?

He'd had the gall to meddle in Elly's life. She might have done better on her own. Without his interference, she might have managed the same way Goldie would have. Through determination and raw instinct.

He glanced down at Tommy. Mouth open, the boy gave a soft snore, turned and wiggled his head against her breast. And still asleep, Elly tightened her arms around her son, her body shifting to accommodate him. "Shh, honey," she said, turning her own face into Royal's chest.

"Oh, God," he groaned, doubt squeezing him. "Why didn't I leave well enough alone? Did I do the right thing for you, Elly? For your son?"

No one answered him. Not God. Not Elly.

In the ring below him, thousand-pound hooves thundered on the ground, men grunted and buzzers raucously signaled the end of each trial. In minutes, the lights would be turned off, and the fireworks display would begin.

Royal tried not to think about the repercussions of what he'd set in motion, tried not to think about the moment when he'd have to tell Elly. When he did, she'd never look at him again with that faint glimmer of trust. He hoped she wouldn't panic and run straight into the path of danger.

He bent down and kissed her forehead. The sweet scent of her hair rose to him. "Elly, wake up. It's almost time to make our exit, sweetheart."

She came awake instantly and silently. "I'm ready." Her gaze clung to his, waiting.

The lights dimmed, flickered. "Ladies and gentlemen, in three minutes, prepare yourselves for the greatest display of pyrotechnical wonder in the whole Sunshine State! But first, a round of applause for our winners in tonight's rodeo events. In first place with the highest overall score is Buck Tyler out of Okeechobee! First place in broncobusting goes to Hank Tyler, Buck's baby brother! And finally, making it a clean sweep for the Tyler family, T.J., from right down the road in Tarpon City, will be cartin' home that big ol' bull-riding trophy. Let's give it up for those rough, tough riders, folks!'' The metallic voice let out a yell that reverberated through the air.

Under the roar of applause, Royal told her what they were going to do.

"Jump from the seats?'' She swallowed and lifted her chin with determination. "Okay.''

Royal scrutinized her. "I know you don't like heights. And this will be a long drop, but I'll be there to catch you. It's safe. I won't drop you. Can you do this, Elly?''

"I'll do it.'' Her mouth was grim. "I can.''

"Good.'' He smiled. "When I tap your arm, that means I'm out of here. You slide out of your seat and head to the last seat on the end of our row. I'll go first. When I'm on the ground, you drop Tommy to me. You'll have to trust me with him, Elly. You can't swing down the tiers carrying him.''

She nodded. "Go on.''

"When I have Tommy, then it's your turn. Slide over the edge and drop straight into my arms. Doesn't that sound romantic, sugar? Falling into my arms?''

"Sure.'' Scarcely paying attention to his teasing, she was gathering her reserves.

Royal grinned. Anybody who'd bet against Elly Malloy would be taking a sucker bet. She would be ready. Adrenaline pumped hard through him as he waited the final minutes. They would make it. Their pursuers hadn't left the stations they'd taken near the entrance and exit gates. They'd remain there. They had no reason to expect Elly and him to take a more unconventional exit.

The second explosion of red and green burst above them. Elly flinched, Tommy sighed, "Cool,'' and Royal nudged her.

"Now, Elly. Move!''

The woman could move. In the darkness following the dying sparks, she was right on his tail.

Ducking under the metal rail, Royal dropped over the edge of the top seat. Hanging from the top tier, he swung himself down the seats. Bending his knees, he let go and landed in a crouching position on the ground and straightened, looking up.

Lit by the flashing colors of the next series of fireworks, Elly's face peered at him. He nodded and, that fast, she held Tommy over the edge and let go.

The kid fell like a sack of potatoes into his arms. "You got good hands, too, Royal. That was fun. Let's do it again."

Royal set him on the ground. "It's your mom's turn now, Tommy Lee. You hang on to my leg and don't let go, no matter what I do, hear?"

"Yep." Chubby arms grabbed and held on to him.

A flutter of pink caught Royal's eye in the darkness as Elly sat on the edge of the wooden seats. And then she was in his arms. He caught her around the shoulders and rear, her body plummeting straight to him, magnet to magnet. "Good woman. I knew you wouldn't chicken out." Turning her to him, he slid her down the length of his body, her stomach pressing against his chest, his belly, her thighs against his, and the touch of her body on his left a trail of fire and need.

She stood before him, her forehead resting on his chest, her breathing shaky as she brought herself under control.

Her breasts trembled into him, a sweet motion that shot heat right to his groin, and there in the brilliant blues and greens of a Fourth of July fireworks, he kissed her with all the despairing and useless passion in his aching heart.

And wanted more. Needed *everything*.

Her mouth yielded, returned his kiss, alchemized it into a kiss of hope and redemption, her lips moving against his eagerly.

Lifting his mouth, he stared at her.

"I'm sorry, Elly." He didn't even know what he was apologizing for. Not for kissing her, for touching her. No, never that. Maybe for all that she'd been through, for the ordeal yet to come. A flood of feeling left him inarticulate, stole all his easy teasing and left him only those meaningless words "Forgive me."

Chapter 11

"Everybody set?" Beau Bienvenue's smooth voice came from the driver's seat.

"Take off. We're in." Royal spoke into her ear, and she shivered at his rough tone. "Glad you remembered to short out the interior lights."

"Naturally." Amusement rippled in that honey-soft voice, and Elly decided that Leesha was a lucky woman indeed if she got to listen to that deep voice whispering sweet nothings to her all night long. "I'm careful, Royal. I don't take chances."

"Yeah. It's a wonder we're friends…you so boring and all." Royal's chest vibrated at her back as he squeezed himself in behind her.

Squashed together on the floor in the back of Beau's squad car, Elly felt the shift of Royal's thigh against her fanny. He worked his long legs to either side of hers and clasped his arms around her waist. In front of her, Tommy hummed tunelessly to himself, his back braced against her knees.

She decided to accept the humming as a good sign. He could have been screaming, or, worse, silent and clinging. But somehow, he'd picked up on Royal's devil-may-care attitude and decided they were playing a game. During their race to the tem-

porary fence separating the fairgrounds from the parking lot,
he'd giggled as Royal shoved him under one arm and called him
a football. Giving Tommy back to her, Royal jumped up and
caught the top of the fence, bending it down and holding it by
force.

Stepping into his outstretched hand for leverage, she scrambled over in an undignified heap and waited. Still holding the
top edge of the pliable fence down, Royal handed Tommy to
her and then vaulted over himself.

And then in a mad race of firecrackers and explosions, they
dashed to Beau's car, Tommy giggling and laughing all the way.
For those brief seconds, Elly had wanted to laugh, too.

Royal's kiss had sent her body into another world where exhaustion and fear seemed the illusion, and his touch the only
reality, his energy pulsing through her like a glittering stream.
Pulling away, he'd laughed. "Race time, folks."

And off they'd gone, exhilaration bolting through her with
each duck and dodge across the parking lot, with each booming
explosion of color and sound. The colors splashing across
Royal's shirt in the darkness were carnival mad. He held her
around the waist, lifting her clear of the ground with each of his
long, running strides. Cradled in his other arm, he carried
Tommy. Eyes wide with excitement, Tommy clung to Royal's
neck.

Now, hunched in the back of a police car, she was astounded
by how *alive* she felt. "Thank you, Detective Bienvenue," she
offered to the back of the seat. "For helping me." She wished
he weren't involved, but he was, and truly, some part of her was
relieved in spite of herself. She'd done the best she could. What
would be, would be. *Que sera* and all that. She smiled. She felt
as if she were on the verge of a momentous adventure, of an
incredible discovery. She hadn't felt this way in— Had she ever
felt this intoxicating mix of energy and excitement? "You're
taking us to your house, Detective?"

"Just call me Beau, ma'am. I'd be more comfortable. Since
this isn't really an official outing, you understand?"

She did. "I never saw you tonight, Beau." Laughing, she
added, "As far as I'm concerned, this car is on automatic pilot."

Tommy snickered.

Tickling her ribs, Royal edged his palm across her abdomen.

She gasped with pleasure. Grabbing at those exploring, teasing fingers, she covered them with the flat of her hand, stopping their provoking journey.

"Spoilsport," he whispered. With a tiny pull, he teased the lobe of her ear with his teeth, and shivers of delight rippled over her skin.

Leaning back against him, she murmured, "I know what you're doing."

"Yeah?" His lips moved against her neck in a smile. "And what's that, sugar?"

"Distracting me."

"That's what I'm doing?" He turned his hand palm up and curled his fingers through hers, his fingers sliding along her palm in a secret, toe-curling caress. "Gosh, I'm so glad to have it explained."

Holding her hand in his, he blew softly at the nape of her neck. Strands of hair lifted, moved, left a vulnerable spot there, and all the while shivers ran over her, puckering and tightening her skin, her nipples. As her head fell forward helplessly, Royal dipped his mouth to that spot just above the neckline of her dress and nipped sharply. Hot shivers spurted down her spine, pooled underneath their joined hands.

In another life, another place, she would have been uncomfortable, embarrassed to be so easily aroused, so oblivious to place and situation, but she'd traveled to the end of her world and stepped off, falling into this dazzling freedom of sensation.

What was happening had nothing to do with *her.*

In a few hours, everything would come roaring in on her once more. She understood that. This was a temporary freedom. Like everything else, an illusion.

But illusion was all she was going to have.

And illusions were better than loneliness, infinitely preferable to terror.

Royal bent his knees, scooted forward and enclosed her in the cradle of his thighs and pelvis, his hard chest supporting her weight easily. Sighing, she let her head rest on his chest. Pressed against him, she heard the strong beat of his heart, its powerful rhythm drumming into her, through her, filling her, a steady, reassuring cadence in the darkness.

The car bumped over a curb, slowed to a stop. "Okay, folks.

I'm goin' on inside. I'll open the door on Elly's side. Give me a few minutes to close the blinds. Then go on around to the back door. It'll be unlocked. The interior lights of the car are still off. Far as I can tell, we weren't followed. No reason to expect we would be, but I checked the whole way. Took a few extra turns on the way here to make sure. You're safe. See you inside." The driver's-side door opened. There was a quiet click at the door near Elly. "And, Royal?"

Royal's "Hmm?" buzzed along the side of her neck.

"Leesha said she'll kill you if you don't behave yourself." Beau paused and then said slyly, "Are you behaving yourself, Royal?"

"Always." Royal pulled his hand free and gave Elly's hip a friendly pat. His hand slipped under the hem of her dress, his fingers stroking the top of her thigh in slow, tantalizing movements that moved higher and higher. "I'm behaving. Right, Elly?" His index finger nudged under the plain band of her panties, circling, touching. Teasing.

She couldn't answer. Jerking forward, she inched her hips away from the muscled cradle of his legs. "Wicked, wicked," she scolded.

"What's wicked?" Waking up, Tommy tried to turn toward her, but wedged in between legs and door and seats, he couldn't.

"Royal's a wicked man, honey, that's what." She tugged at her dress and slapped away his helpful hand.

"Why is he wicked? What did he do?" Squirming energetically, Tommy finally scrabbled to his knees and around to face her.

"Nothing important." Elly shook her hair back and freed her neck from the exquisite torture of Royal's mouth over her skin. She'd lost her hat somewhere in the wild run to Beau's car, and she missed it. But like almost everything else in her life now, she could survive without it. "He's being a pest."

"Am I?" His whisper into her ear started the shivers all over again. "A pest?"

"Definitely." She scrambled forward and pushed open the door, scooping Tommy along with her, Royal right behind them. "Come on, honey. We're going in."

They moved silently and swiftly through the pitch-blackness, stumbling against an edging around what Elly imagined to be a flower bed. The back door opened easily on oiled hinges.

With his hand on the small of her back, Royal directed her to the living room at the front of the house. She liked that unconscious intimacy, the sense of connectedness.

She would miss that most of all.

"Hi, Ms. Malloy, Tommy." Alicia Williams stood up and came toward her.

"Call me Elly, please."

"Of course. And I'm Leesha. Or Alicia. Whichever you're more comfortable with."

Elly steeled herself for a barrage of questions and explanations. She'd been so careful about not revealing any personal information to Alicia Williams that the woman had to have a hundred questions. She would want explanations. Royal had involved these people, but they were his friends, not hers. They owed her nothing. She straightened and took a deep breath, preparing for the ordeal.

Giving her space, Alicia stopped a few feet away. "You must hate this, Elly. If I were in your shoes, I would. I'm not going to pry. It's none of my business, none of theirs. But we'll help you, no matter what's happening." She didn't touch Elly, didn't offer an arm around the shoulders, didn't make any of the obvious, easy gestures of reassurance. Instead, her face serene and accepting, her dark eyes rich with understanding, Alicia Williams waited calmly for Elly to take the initiative.

"Thank you." Elly sank onto the couch. She couldn't believe the generosity of this woman she'd admired for so long. How could Alicia offer help without wanting to know the consequences? It was too much. Elly bowed her head, overwhelmed.

"Beau, why don't you get Elly a cold drink? I'll show Tommy where y'all are goin' to sleep, okay?" Alicia's voice rolled over Elly soothingly. "You sit there and catch your breath. Everything's going to be all right. Beau and Royal could handle an army if they had to."

"That's my woman," Beau said with a wide smile.

"Think so?" Alicia stared him down with a lift of one sculpted eyebrow. "Don't go counting your chickens, Beauregard Bienvenue. Those eggs might not ever hatch if you don't take care."

"I take care, Leesha." Something more than teasing moved across the dark planes of his face as he came to her side.

"Do you?" Alicia cast Beau a challenging glance as he laid his arm across her shoulders. Her scarlet, thigh-high skirt shimmered as she bumped him with her hip. Side by side, they were almost the same height and extraordinarily striking in their sleek, long-limbed grace. "Don't take anything for granted, Beau. You know I mean that." Smoothly, she extricated herself from his light grasp. "I'm not an easy woman—"

"Lord, *no*body ever accused you of being easy, woman," he groaned. "Least of all me. Leesha, you are the most complicated, stubborn, exasperating—"

Alicia waved an elegant hand languidly. "The man adores me, Elly. He can't help himself." She stooped and faced Tommy, eye to eye. "Isn't that right?"

"Uh-huh." Tommy rubbed his eyes. "Beau should marry Leesha."

"Exactly, my man. That's what I've been telling her." Beau's teeth flashed in a blinding smile. "But the woman won't give me the time of day."

"It's not the time of day you're after, Beauregard Bienvenue." Alicia's grin was knowing. "Is it?"

"Huh?" Tommy yawned.

Alicia gave her attention to Tommy. "Come on, Tommy. Let me show you where you can sleep. Your mom will be in with you in a little while. Okay?"

"Yep." He nodded and followed Alicia's long-legged stride in a daze, turning his head and yawning "G'night" as Alicia led him through a door and down a long hall where a nightlight gleamed in a welcoming glow.

Beau handed Elly a clear glass filled with amber liquid.

She looked up at him questioningly. Alcohol would knock her out at this point.

"Drink it, sugar. It's only sweet tea. Leesha keeps Beau stocked in it. Told him to think of her every time he takes a sip. You do that, too, don't you, Beau?" Royal sank onto the sofa close to Elly and threw his arms along the back.

"You kidding? Of course. I'm wooing the woman. I have to. She's giving me enough trouble as it is."

"Can't be a bee buzzing around all the flowers and expect the orchid to take you seriously."

"You got that right."

"What has Beau finally gotten right?" Alicia strolled up to him, and took the glass he handed her.

"Not you," he murmured, looking at her with a hunger that made Elly ache. "But I'm trying, Leesha. Give me credit for that."

"I give you all the credit you deserve." But Alicia softened her words with a tantalizing smile. "Now, Elly, Royal, what's the plan? What do you need?"

Elly lifted her glass in Royal's direction. "He hasn't told me all the details. I imagine he's saved a few—"

"Not surprises, sugar. Because you don't like them. A few...refinements, maybe." He stood up abruptly. "We need a safe place for a few days, Beau, while we sort things out. And we need a place for Tommy to stay. He can't go with us."

Stricken, Elly stood up. "I didn't understand. You didn't make that clear. I thought we were—" She rubbed her forehead fretfully. "How did I miss what you were suggesting? I never thought for a second you meant for me to leave him! You know I won't agree to that, don't you?"

"We can't maneuver like we'll have to if he's along. And hiding out for a few days will be too confining for a five-year-old. Too dangerous. Elly, you said you didn't want Tommy to be caught in the middle. I assumed that settled the question."

"But I thought you meant we had to find out about these men, get away from them at the rodeo and then Tommy and I would go on our way."

"That's not a...permanent solution, sugar. If you think about it, you know I'm right. That's what I meant when I said you didn't want Tommy around when those torpedoes came after us. We have to have a safe spot for him. Somewhere no one will find him. With people who will guard him with their lives. Leesha. Beau. Maggie and Sullivan. Then you and I will have room to maneuver. I think."

She clung to his arm. "Royal. I don't think I can do this. The situation...I have to...I can't."

"Elly, you have to. It's the best way to protect him from— from whatever you're afraid of. You know Leesha. I've been watching you. You like Beau. And when you meet Maggie and her husband, you'll trust them with your son. You wouldn't be able not to.'' He pulled her to him and enclosed her tightly in the circle of his arms, his body, and she knew he was right and was furious with him because he was.

"Let me go.'' She struggled against the comfort he offered so freely, effortlessly, in this hour when he was asking her to do the impossible. To go into hiding without Tommy.

"I can't, Elly. These are determined men. And they have more experience at killing than you do of running.'' Royal's hand swept down her spine, back up. "They won't give up. And one time, they'll find you. And Tommy will be with you.''

Behind her, she heard a low cough. "Excuse me, Elly, I know I'm intruding, but let me tell you what I've found out in the couple of hours Royal gave me.''

Bewildered, she whirled out of Royal's arms to face Beau. "What do you mean, 'found out'?''

"He means, sugar, that I asked him to locate whatever information he could about you.''

"You had me investigated?'' Disbelief crackled through her. "You checked me out?''

Royal nodded.

Foreboding shook her from head to toe. What was going on? Was she being arrested? Was all Royal's sympathy and concern an elaborate con game? "You sent Beau snooping into my business because you didn't have the decency to ask me what you wanted to know?''

"I'm a cop—''

"You *were* a cop. I thought you were my friend. I trusted you, and you went behind my back. Why would you do that? You owe me an explanation.''

He went very still. There was a long pause, and she had the impression he was choosing his words too carefully. "Answer one question first, will you, Elly? Would you have given me the answers to all my questions?''

She wouldn't have, and the expression in his eyes dared her to admit the truth. "What does it matter now?'' she asked tiredly. "I hate what you did. It was…deceitful.''

"Do we want to talk about deception and deceit, sugar?'' His voice sharpened.

"No," she admitted. How much had he been able to find out? And did it matter anymore if he knew the whole of it? She was too tired to make the decision, but the habits of the past months kept her lips sealed. She'd done as much as she was capable of doing when she'd gone along with his decision to ask his friends for help.

But even now, even in Beau's house, she couldn't rid herself of these faint tremors of uneasiness, couldn't quiet that small voice that said Royal was holding a hidden card. With his talk of card games and gambling, he had her thinking in his terms. "Maybe you did what you had to do, I don't know. But your actions were despicable."

"You're the linchpin, Elly. These men are connected to you." His tone was frighteningly reasonable as he added, "How else was I to find out anything about them? I have no vehicle license number, no name, only a description. You're the thread that connects them. Be fair, Elly."

"Why should I? I don't want to be fair! This isn't a game, with rules and points and a score sheet. There are no winners, only losers. So you can see fairness has no meaning to me right now. It's only a *word*. This is my son's future we're talking about." She glared at him. "I can't take *any* chances, and you're playing fast and loose with our lives. You think this a game of cops and robbers. Well, it isn't."

"I know it's not a game, Elly."

"No. You say you understand. Maybe you do. Here." She tapped his forehead. "But not *here*." She placed her hand over her heart. "Here where it counts, you don't understand. You have nothing at stake."

"Like you, my life," he reminded her mildly. "Whether either of us likes it, the cards have been dealt to both of us in this *game*." He emphasized the word, as if she'd touched a sore spot. "I don't have a pat hand, and I'd like to change the odds. If we can. I stand to lose, too."

"But not someone you love." Wondering if he could begin to see the situation the way it was for her, she lifted one shoulder helplessly. "That's what's at stake for me. Tommy. And he means more to me than my own life, than anything else *in* my life. Sure, I care what happens to me. I like living. But I'd give my life that fast—" she snapped her fingers "—for him. And as for you, Royal? I'm not sure how high a value you place on your life. So what kind of bet is that for a *game* of this magnitude? Tell me, will you? Can you ante up that stake?''

He couldn't. What he felt for her and Tommy was too formless for words, too vague. The impulse to shield her and her son ran through him so strongly that he couldn't check it, couldn't name it. That impulse forced him to protect her from Scanlon and whatever he had planned.

Royal knew he couldn't protect her if he told her everything about his involvement. She'd take off in fear and anger at this point. One way or another, he had to make her see that she had only one choice if they were to find their way through the maze they were in.

"Nothing to say, *Detective?*" Under the sarcasm, he heard her fear, her need. Like Goldie, she was scratching and clawing and spitting in terror.

Royal veered off in another direction. "While you're deciding what we're going to do about Tommy, would you like to know what Beau found out?" he said gently, staying out of her personal space, wanting her to *think*, to realize what he was saying was the truth. "Tell her, Beau."

"Ms. Malloy?" Taking sides, Beau waited for her permission to speak.

Staring at both of them, Elly wavered. Plucking at her skirt, she looked at Royal with a lost expression.

"That okay with you, Royal? If Ms. Malloy gives me her okay to reveal private stuff? You got any problems with that, Royal?" Withholding his support of what Royal had done, Beau sent him a measured look.

Royal felt the chill of separation from his friend. They'd teased and joked, but he'd made the phone call, the phone call he'd sworn he would never make. He'd asked for help. He'd jeopardized Beau's career. But without a single question, Beau had shown up at the rodeo. He'd been there, solid as a rock. A friend. A colleague. He deserved explanations, details. Under the circumstances, Beau had a right to be prickly.

"Well, do you, Royal?"

"Your call, Beau." Royal let his answer send a silent message that he'd fill in the gaps, that he understood the risks Beau had taken. Out of friendship? Loyalty? For the sake of old bonds?

He didn't know. He did know that he owed the man for what he'd done this night. "You handle it."

Beau gave a decisive nod. Message received. "Right." He took Elly by the elbow and led her back to the couch. "What do you say, Ms. Malloy?"

Elly's dress was a narrow stripe of pink against the smooth gray linen, and she seemed so overwhelmed by the three of them, so alone that Royal wanted to shove Beau out of the way, grab her and the kid and find a fast plane to anywhere else. But he couldn't. He couldn't protect her without Beau's help.

"You're 'mizzing' me to death, Detective. What happened to Beau and Elly? You're sounding so official I don't know whether to confess or hold out my hands for the cuffs." Her laugh was shaky, but she'd found a remnant of humor somehow.

Royal felt like giving her a big "Atta girl," but he was half-afraid she'd knock him out of his socks if he did.

"Right. Elly." Pulling the black-and-white-striped ottoman closer to her, Beau sat down and leaned against the edge of the couch. Like Royal, he was careful not to crowd her. "Leesha, any chance you could find something to eat? I think we'd all feel a whole lot better with some food. If you don't mind?"

"Sure thing, honey."

Catching Leesha's amused smile and raised eyebrow as she answered, Royal figured Beau would be paying for that delayed "if you don't mind."

Elly didn't speak until Alicia returned, almost as if she needed the presence of another woman in the room. Finally, picking apart the strands of a piece of string cheese Elly finally said, "Go ahead, Beau. Royal's right. These men are connected to me. Alicia deserves to know. You do, too."

Templing his fingers, Beau crisply enumerated what Royal had suspected and had guessed at. "Elly Malloy has no past. The paper trail stops a few months back."

Elly started, and then clasped her hands together, watching Beau with fascinated attention.

"You applied for a driver's license using the most basic identification. A library card as proof of residence. A certificate of completion from a driver's-training class of dubious reputation. No history of social-security payments, a couple of easy-access credit cards that popped up in your credit report. But far as I can figure, Elly Malloy sprang full-grown in Palmaflora. A woman without a past.''

"You found all that out in a couple of hours?" Elly leaned back against the sofa and shut her eyes. "That was fast."

"In a few more hours, Elly, I would have found out what your real name is."

"Oh."

Easing near her, Royal said, "Beau likes computers. He has *sources.* Of all kinds." He gently touched her scar. "Tell us about this, Elly. How it happened. Tell us who you are." He knew. Beau and Leesha didn't. The information had to come from Elly, not him.

Jerking forward, she bent her head between her knees, taking deep, raspy breaths. She didn't look at them. "My ex-husband hired two men to kill me."

Scanlon had said Elly faked her death. Royal hadn't believed that lie since first meeting her. Now, in this serene room as Elly's low voice recited the horror of that night, Scanlon's lie became obscene.

"Yes?" Beau didn't move, didn't distract her from her recitation by so much as a gesture. "Go ahead, Elly," he encouraged, and Royal remembered again how much he'd enjoyed working with Beau. The man was a natural-born interrogator, better than Maggie had ever been.

Before the shooting changed her into the stranger who married Sullivan Barnett, Maggie had been direct, too blunt for the kind of circuitous questioning that worked best. The kind of head games Beau and Royal grooved to.

"Your ex-husband tried to kill you." Beau restated the information as Elly's mouth worked silently, the words not coming out. "And when was that, Elly? While you were still married?" He handed her the glass of tea.

"No." She shook her head, kept shaking it.

Beau set the glass on an ebony-and-brass end table. "They tried to kill you—" he said again, priming the pump of confession, of revelation, and Royal smiled grimly. Nobody was better than Beau at getting people to spill their secrets. "When did you say that was, Elly?" Like honey, his words flowed into the silence.

"After our divorce was finalized," she began, speech finally coming. "This past December. They shot—" she swallowed "—they shot me. In the garage of the house. Tommy and I had…we'd gone to Naples to visit my parents. I…I had to come back to the house. I'd left behind…something…a package I needed. The men were waiting for me. In the garage. When I drove in. The garage light was out. I thought the opener was broken. They must have taken out the bulb. I don't know, but the door opener didn't work right, I drove in and then there they were."

Royal closed his hand over the fluffy cloud of her hair, the fragile shape of her head. He touched her scar, that narrow white line of pain and terror. He'd guessed that Scanlon had lied, but this was evil. Scanlon had sent those men after her in the dark, in her own home where she would be most defenseless. "And then what did you do?"

"Nothing. I can't remember what happened after…" Her rocking continued, slow, steady. "After." Her face wiped clean of emotion, she rubbed her forehead in a monotonous, almost robotic fashion. "Tommy ran for help." She rocked back and forth, over and over, her voice so calm it frightened Royal.

Scanlon was a dead man. And Royal was going to make sure he suffered, one way or another. "He ran to—?"

She paused in her unconscious rocking. "A friend's." Hunched over, she didn't move, not even her clasped hands. In that dreadful blankness, it was clear she was reliving those final moments.

"A friend who helped you go into hiding." He curved his hands over her shoulders and worked at the tight muscles. "Who helped you establish a second identity."

"No." She sighed and doubled over, resting her face in her hands. "I wouldn't ask her for that kind of help. Blake would have made her life a hell on earth if he knew she'd helped me the way she did."

"Blake?" Royal slipped his question in. The identification had to come from her.

"My husband." Like Royal, she was still keeping her own secrets. She didn't name Scanlon.

"What did your friend do?"

Elly raised her head. "She came back to the car. I was unconscious, but somehow she got me out of the car." Her hands fluttered in the air, conjuring the scene, the coppery smell of her blood. The terrified child who'd run for help. Drawing in her breath, Elly finished. "Then Meggie cleaned me up and stitched the wound. Tommy and I vanished. At least I tried to."

"Doctors have to report gunshot wounds." Beau sent Royal a significant look.

Royal knew that expression and gave Beau a faint nod. Something about Elly's story was making Beau uneasy. Like him, Beau had picked up on the omission, the two details Elly had skirted over. The attack came after the divorce. Why had she gone back to the house? And perhaps most important, why had Scanlon ordered her killed if they were already divorced? Where was the advantage, the profit, to Scanlon? Elly had said the attack came afterward. So what was Scanlon's motivation? And why would Elly lie about when the attack occurred? Even now, she wouldn't give Scanlon's full name.

From long experience working with Beau, Royal knew he would check every detail.

"Did your friend take you to the emergency room of a hospital?"

A faint smile flickered over Elly's pale face. "She's a veterinarian. And my friend. She didn't report anything. Nobody knew she was involved. I don't like to involve my friends." She shot Royal a faintly hostile glance. "It's not fair to them. They can get hurt. Killed."

"How did you and Tommy get away?"

"Meggie drove us downtown. We walked to the Trailwinds Bus Station. I wouldn't let her take us all the way. I didn't want anybody connecting her with that night. She wouldn't be safe. I don't know what Blake would have done to make her talk. Something. Anything." Her head dropped wearily. "I married Blake. And he became a monster." Tears slipped silently down her cheeks. "I loved him, *made* love with him. And all along, behind the smiles, this other man waited. What did I *do?*" she whispered. "How could I have been so naive? So *trusting?*" She scrubbed her wet face. "What kind of fool was I? What did I miss?"

Chapter 12

"Not one damned thing." Speaking for the first time, her voice husky with emotion, Leesha broke the hush that fell over the three of them with Elly's words. "People are what they are. Some of them are like icebergs. You see only a fraction of what's hidden. *You* weren't the problem. *You* didn't make a mistake. *You* didn't turn him into a monster. He did that himself." Leesha stuck her hands on her hips and rounded on Beau and Royal. "Y'all stop this right now. Elly's going to bed. Talk all you want to, hash over whatever you need to, but can't you see she's exhausted?"

Royal shifted uncomfortably, looked at Beau and then started to explain. "We were—"

"Hush. I know what you were doing. She's had enough of your questions. I know we need answers and explanations, and all that stuff, but here's the deal, folks. Elly's going to bed." With irritation, her husky voice dropped into an exaggerated drawl. "I'm goin' to bed. We're callin' it a night. Tomorrow, we'll work out the details and decide how we're going to finesse this caper." She stooped and took Elly's hands. "Come on, Elly. You can go to sleep. Nothing's going to happen until tomorrow. Men. Cops. Get an idea in their head and don't have enough sense to quit. Just like a dumb chicken that'll stand out in the rain and stare up at the sky until it drowns. You and Tommy are plumb tuckered out. You're asleep on your feet, and Beau and Royal can't see what's going on in front of their faces. Let's go, Elly.''

Obediently, Elly stood up. She stumbled. Royal started forward, to go with her, and she looked back at him, dazed, as though momentarily she didn't recognize him. Leesha's frown stopped him in his tracks. "Leave her alone. You men have done enough. I'm calling it a night. And I'm going to bed, too." She gave Beau a level, unfriendly stare. "In the guest room, Detective Beauregard Bienvenue." In a flash of scarlet and caramel, her sleek legs took her out of the room. Grumbling with every step, she directed Elly in front of her.

"Whew." Beau grinned. "When she's on my side, she'll defend me like a tiger, won't she? Can't you see how one of these days she'll make sure I'm not passed over for chief of police?"

"What I think is that you'll be lucky to get her to walk down the aisle with you. I'm telling you, Beau, she wasn't looking at you like the future father of her children."

"Leesha's a passionate woman." Beau's gaze lingered on the hall somberly, his expression at odds with his words.

"And she's feeling passionate right now about the way Elly's husband treated her?"

"Leesha's got a soft spot for women who have to deal with bad guys. Bad-guy husbands. Boyfriends." Beau circled the room restlessly. "She ever tell you about her first husband?"

His own gaze drifting to the hall and his ears tuned to the sound of Elly's murmuring voice, Royal shook his head. Elly was talking to Leesha. That was good. Elly would be easier with the decision to leave Tommy in Leesha's care. Absently, he answered Beau. "Only that the marriage lasted two years. Leesha's never talked to me about him."

Collecting the plates and glasses, Beau stood irresolutely, the plates held in front of him. "What the hell. Maggie knows. You might as well. Leesha was married at nineteen. She quit college to marry the jerk. Huh." Beau shook his head in disgust. "That smart woman quit because Clyde Moody didn't want a wife who was busy with anything except filling his needs. He said she didn't have time for him if she was going to school. To make the proverbial long story short, he almost killed her before she was able to walk away from him. She can't have children because of him. So, no, she damned well wasn't looking at me like the future father of her children. For Leesha and me, there won't be any children except the ones at the day-care center.''

"I see.'' Royal pivoted. He'd been surprised by that look of uncertainty on Beau's face. "That's the reason you're both dancing back and forth about marriage? Not because of your flower-buzzing ways?''

"Seems to be. I don't care.'' Beau shrugged. "Sure, I like kids. My brothers' kids are cute. But I get to play with them and then walk away. I get to go home to a good night's sleep, too.'' His grin was mischievous. "Andy and Michael now, they don't.''

"They still in Tampa?''

"Yeah. Andy made lieutenant. Michael wants to stay on the street. But he's young. Four kids may make him change his mind. Michael and Rhea are...busy folks, let me tell you.'' Beau chuckled. "Between cop work, croup and chicken pox, both of my baby brothers are busy.'' He rinsed the plates and stacked them in the dishwasher.

"You like your nieces and nephews. You're good with them. They swarm all over you. I always reckoned you'd have a big family.''

"Yeah, well, they don't have a lick of sense. Kids are okay. But I can see being happy in my life without them. I can sure as hell see myself happy with Leesha. And not missing a little clone of myself.'' He leaned back on the sink counter and braced his arms on the rim. "Now, I might regret not having a clone of Leesha, though.'' His smile was tinged with sadness. "I'm nuts about her. Nothing I can do about it, either. I've tried. Got any love potions, Royal?''

"Nary a one, friend.'' Royal opened the refrigerator door and held it. Reaching in for a beer, he confronted the issue between them. "Want one? Or maybe we aren't refrigerator-opening friends anymore?'' With the beer in hand, he waited.

"Seems to me that decision's in your hand.'' Beau pointed to the beer. "Not mine.''

"You want a beer?'' Royal waited. This was the test. If Beau knew him as well as Royal hoped, if any remnant of friendship remained… If Beau trusted him at all—

Narrowing his eyes, Beau took the bottle. "We're going to talk about the past, are we? We're finally going to bring everything out into the open?"

"Let's talk on your porch." Royal unlocked the French doors and stepped out onto the screened-in porch Beau had built. Baskets of flowers, their colors pale in the darkness, swung from the ceiling rafters, their scents soft in the heat.

"You can't help taking over, can you? Even in somebody else's house." Beau stretched out on a chaise longue that had been added since the last time Royal had visited. "Okay. The doctor's in." He watched as Royal took a deliberately long swallow of beer. "Damn you. You're testing me, aren't you?"

"I suppose so." Royal sat down in a chair opposite the chaise and rolled the bottle between his hands. "This kills me to ask for help, Beau, but I'm out on a limb and there's a man with a chain saw down at the bottom of the tree. I don't mind so much for myself—"

"But Elly and Tommy have hooked you," Beau finished, tipping his bottle and drinking. "I thought so. You look at her like a man who hasn't had a meal in three weeks. What's the deal with them?"

At Beau's deliberate change of subject, Royal almost dropped his bottle. Gripping it more securely, he asked, astonished, "You don't want me to confess about my wicked ways? You don't want the tell-all about why I quit the force?"

"A week ago, yes, I'd have taken those answers. I thought you owed me explanations. We were partners for a long time before you and Maggie were paired up. But tonight, seeing you with Elly, all my doubts are settled. You never turned. You didn't sell out to the politicians and then try to cover yourself by lying about the corruption in the department."

Royal swallowed. After all this time, Beau's simple statement of faith had such enormous power. He looked away from his friend, unable to hold his gaze. On the other side of the closed French doors, Leesha walked through the kitchen. She stared at them impassively and then poured a glass of water and walked back to the hall and out of sight.

Following Royal's gaze, Beau said, "You couldn't have

known Chief Jackson was hand in glove with Charlie Callahan on that toxic-dumping scheme. You wouldn't have helped Jackson cover up a murder. I should have been clearer about that all along no matter what everybody was saying about you getting off scot-free. I should have had more faith in you, in what I knew about you. All that drinking and screwing up was just you thumbing your nose at everybody, wasn't it?"

Royal muttered. He couldn't speak. Back and forth, he rolled the bottle until it was warm, all the cold sweat dried by the friction of his palms.

"Probably ticked you off that folks were so quick to think the worst, and you got all puckered up and decided you might as well rub their faces in it. That's how I see it now, anyway. You, going your own way, and to hell with what everybody thought." Leaning forward, Beau stuck out his hand. "I owe you an apology. Because I didn't give you the benefit of the doubt. Because I didn't see through the act. I should have been a better cop. A better friend. I should have understood. I didn't. I judged the book by the cover. I was wrong."

Royal's throat closed. His voice was raspy. "Thanks." He clasped the hand held out to him, the hand that welcomed him back. "Thanks. This, uh, well, you know—"

"Damn. You're a slick-talking dude when you put your mind to it, Royal. Shut up and drink your beer." Beau's teeth flashed in a grin. "No, on second thought, fill me in on Elly. Because I'm a mite confused about some of the details."

Royal did. Like trailing moss, clouds moved dreamily across the sky as he told Beau everything. Royal told him about the debts, about throwing away his inheritance, about betting on a low pair and winding up in Blake Scanlon's debt.

Beau sat upright in one fluid movement. "Hell. That's big-time trouble, Royal. When you set out to destroy yourself, you don't do it halfway, man. You blew all the money your folks left you?"

Royal laughed. "Yeah. Except for what I gave Maggie to use for the day-care center. Leesha wasn't supposed to know about it, though. All the money's finally gone. And I'm relieved, if you want to know the truth. It felt like a chain dragging me down, Mama and Daddy's way of controlling me from the grave."

"Blake Scanlon, though. That man's got a finger in everything that happens in Florida. Judges. Police departments. His influence runs all the way up to the governor's office and back down to the smallest county in the state. Damn. And he's the ex Elly's running from?"

Nodding, Royal told Beau about Scanlon's request to bring Elly back to him. For a talk. And he told Scanlon's version of Elly's Christmas story.

"Oh, boy, this is really bad." Beau whistled, a soft, disturbed warble. "You're in debt to Blake Scanlon. And this is what I've let myself in for. Whew. Nasty situation, Royal. Ugly."

Royal kept his expression blank. He didn't want to pressure Beau. Having asked Elly to be fair, Royal couldn't now do less. "You can still back out. There's time. By tomorrow, though, you won't have a choice, either. In or out, Beau? And whichever way you call it, we're still friends." Picking up the half-full bottle by his side, Royal poured it into the flowerpot on the table. It had gone flat. Or he'd lost his taste for it.

"Shame to waste my good beer like that." Beau stood up. "I'm in. I'm sure Leesha will be, too, but I can't speak for her." He laughed. "Hell, I wouldn't *dare*. I'll fill her in on the details in the morning. But right now, I damned sure need another beer." The kitchen door slammed behind him.

Leaning back in his chair, Royal stared at the stars shining faintly in the lightening sky. All these people were depending on him not to blow this. They were staking their lives on his skill, his judgment. Beau. Leesha. Elly. Tommy. And Maggie. Maybe Sullivan. They were giving him a second chance.

And he cared.

Oh, God, he hadn't realized how much he cared. He'd tried so hard not to.

When Beau returned, Royal told him the rest, falling into the old rhythm of reporting. His sentences clipped, his words short, succinct, he recited the details of the attack at Elly's house after he'd followed her, narrated what he'd found in Elly's suitcase with its alternate identity.

"No wonder Elly didn't want to call the police after the attack on you. She knows how much leverage Scanlon has. Anybody could betray her. In her place, I wouldn't have called the cops, either. She would have expected word of her location would have gotten back to her ex-husband within minutes. I'm impressed she offered. And I think it's real interesting she had the suitcase ready for a speedy getaway.''

"Right by the bedroom door. She plans, Beau, well and thoroughly. This isn't her first foray into disappearing. She's jumpy, she's sharp and she's prepared to cut her losses. Most people are trapped because they can't walk away from the environment they've worked so hard to create. Elly's only weakness is Tommy.'' He turned his head to one side, then the other, listening to the cheerful creaks of mortality. "And her own limitations, I guess. She's wearing down. She's tired, and she's not thinking clearly because she's so tired.''

"Yeah, I saw. But I thought that was because of the attack and the goons. Whew. For such a peanut, she's tough.''

"But she needs help. I'm it.''

"We're it,'' Beau corrected. He made an impatient motion. "But I don't understand. Scanlon already knew she and his son were in Palmaflora, right?'' Beau paced the porch. "And all he wanted you to do was bring *her* to him? To talk? Not the boy?''

"That's it. Said he wanted to be civilized about custody arrangements even though she'd faked her death and kidnapped his son and heir. His words, Beau. Not mine.'' Stretching out his arms, Royal twisted his neck. Damn, he was stiff and sore. At eighteen, he could have taken that beating and stayed up for two nights in a row without noticing it. Well, he might have noticed it a little.

"I'll check the records out of Tallahassee, talk to some folks. See what I can find. I'll pull the reports from that night.'' Perplexed, Beau shook his head. "Crazy. He wanted you to leave Tommy *behind* when you brought Elly to him?''

"Yeah.'' Royal grinned, the thrill of the chase sparkling like champagne through him. "He thinks I'm stupid. A drunk.''

"Well, be reasonable, man. Three hundred thousand dollars would buy a lot of bottles of oblivion. For that kind of money, he should have asked you to snatch the kid. Forget the mother.''

"My thoughts exactly.''

"And Elly doesn't know you're involved?''

"Nope.''

Again Beau gave a tuneless whistle. "Oh boy, oh boy-o. But you're going to tell her?''

"When she's in a safe place. So that she won't run straight into Scanlon's trap. Because there's a trap out there, Beau. I can *smell* it. I just can't see it."

"She doesn't know you know who her ex is?"

"Not that, either, and she's being careful to keep it from us. But that part has to come out. She has to know we're going to look for ways to catch him."

"Do you know why she went back to her house? Or how she managed to disappear so damned easily? Had she planned to bolt all along?"

"No, no, and my guess is she had. Elly doesn't like surprises, Beau," Royal said quietly. "Getting shot in your garage tends to take away the fun of surprise parties."

"Well, buddy, you're going to hand her a giant-sized surprise when you tell her you're in debt to her husband."

"I know. I'll handle it. When the time's right." Royal would have to figure out how. And when. But not until she and Tommy were safe.

"Good luck. I wouldn't want to be in your shoes."

Royal laughed. "I'm not real happy to be standing in these babies myself." He stuck his beat-up shoes in front of him. "You ever think I'd let myself go like this?"

"Nope. Hell, I never saw you with *dust* on your shoes, much less cow crap."

Howling with laughter, they flung their heads back and thumped each other, their feet drumming loudly on the porch floor. Choking, Beau gasped, "All that tobacco-farming money? Gone? Every last dime?"

Royal roared, the situation striking him as enormously funny. "Every last penny. I'm a free man. Nothing tying me down, nothing left except the Mustang and the old house I live in. And it's about to fall down."

Gasping for air, Beau doubled over. "You've got nothing, man."

"Hell you say. I've got termites."

Whooping, Beau said, "Think you could hock that fine wardrobe of yours?"

"I may have to do that. To pay the exterminator." Royal slapped his knee, everything seeming crystal bright. "It's a hoot, isn't it?" He laughed, a belly-deep roar, and threw his arms wide open, exhilaration pumping through him. "Free and with Blake Scanlon drawing a bead on me. God, ain't life fun!"

When Elly woke up the next morning, her decision was made.

Last night, she'd kept Blake's identity from Royal and his friends. That was foolish. They were more vulnerable if they were in the dark. She had to give them his name. Did she want to fill in the gaps and explain why she'd gone back to the house? Did they need to know why she'd been ready to run away even before the divorce was final? Out of habit, she'd even lied about when the divorce took place.

For their safety, she would tell them everything except the details of her insurance, because knowledge of it would only endanger the rest of them. That was why she hadn't even entrusted it to her parents.

Blake could exert unbelievable pressure.

And as she'd learned, he could kill.

No, she hadn't risked her family. She wouldn't risk these new friends.

Ignorance might be bliss. In this case, ignorance of that package definitely offered safety. She hoped. Because Blake would kill anyone who knew its contents.

Cradling a cup of coffee in her hands, she faced Royal and his friends. Sullivan Barnett, a journalist, according to Royal, and his wife, Maggie Webster, Royal's former fiancée and partner, were seated with Alicia and Beau at the dining-room table, their matching cups of coffee scarlet against the clean pine table, the brew satiny brown and shiny in the cups.

Even if she hadn't already decided to leave Tommy in the care of these people, one look in Maggie Webster's eyes would have convinced her. Her dark eyes were serene with an otherworldly peace that said Maggie had been places none of the rest of them ever had, that she'd seen things no one would believe. But then Maggie had died and come back to life when no one expected her to. Maybe that explained it; Elly couldn't decide, but she knew Tommy would be safe with this woman.

And he'd be safe with Alicia, who'd talked to her during the long night hours and told her about her ex-husband. Alicia's arm around her shoulders as they both wept hot tears had been a message of hope, of survival. That hug of sisterhood, of shared terror had let her believe that there would be life...*after*.

Elly lifted her cup and drank. They were all watching her, including Maggie's husband with the bright blue eyes in a face carved by pain. Like Maggie, he, too, had an air of having touched some far shore unknown to the rest of them.

Elly placed her cup carefully on the table and folded her hands in front of her. Next to her, Royal slid his leg along hers, a warm, solid strength. "I'm astonished that you all, strangers to me and Tommy, are willing to risk your lives for us. You have to believe me when I say that's a possibility. Blake wants me dead." She would keep to herself the reason. It was a small protection she could give them, the only one. "I'm not sure why. I wanted the divorce. I didn't ask for alimony or for anything except child support. I wanted out. That's all. He agreed. But he tried to kill me. He'll kill any of you who stand in his way. And he'll get away with it."

"We won't let anything happen to your son," Maggie said in a low, husky voice thick with sunshine and honey. The others murmured agreement, their shared glances telling Elly they'd already discussed everything that had been said the night before.

"You can trust us." Sullivan nodded, his movements echoing his wife's, as if they were two parts of the same being. "I believe you. He won't get to Tommy through us."

Alicia and Beau nodded.

Elly bowed her head. She wasn't alone. Not since she'd married Blake had she felt this kind of closeness to other people, this kind of support. If anything happened to her, Maggie and Alicia would care for Tommy. They wouldn't let Blake have him.

"As far as I know, the Tallahassee police didn't investigate the attempt on my life. I don't know how Blake covered up my disappearance, the blood in the car. Tommy's absence. But he would have made up a convincing story. People will believe him. Because he's Blake Scanlon, if for no other reason."

At the mention of her ex-husband's name, there was a small silence, and then Royal spoke. A tiny smile tugged at the corner of his mouth, as if she'd pleased him somehow. "I know."

Sullivan's extraordinary blue eyes shone with interest. "Blake Scanlon. Interesting man. I've heard rumors. No facts. He covers his tracks well. His reputation is solid. But there are these rumors, quiet and persistent. In fact, I've met him. I interviewed him about a year ago about the water-reclamation bill that was coming up for a vote. He's—"

"A bastard." Royal's brilliant green gaze met Sullivan's. "And he's not going to get away with what he's done. Not any longer."

Sullivan's mouth twitched, and Elly figured it was his version of a smile. "We're in this together, Royal. We're on the same side, you know."

Maggie's hand covered Sullivan's, and then she touched Royal's wrist. "Sullivan agrees, Royal. You don't have to prickle up like a big old porcupine."

Royal blinked. "Was I bristling?" He blinked once more. "Old habits die hard. Sorry, Sullivan." He grinned, and a flash of sunlight blazed in his hair, sidetracking Elly.

His hand brushed over her bare thigh, cupping it, his touch turning her into liquid sunshine.

Impossible, unbelievable, but joy filled her to the brim.

The sunshine and coffee, the presence of people who believed her, who would help her, filled Elly like a blessing. She trusted them.

Believing, hoping, when she'd never expected to feel either of those emotions again, she told them so, haltingly, awkwardly, because it had been a long time since she'd opened up herself to others, since she'd dared to be honest with anyone except her son. And even from him, she'd hidden so much. Tommy didn't deserve her burdens. He was only a baby.

So, hesitant and tentative, she surrendered him to their care.

She told them about her escape, about the plans she'd made for months. "I got on the bus with the stuff I'd been hiding for a few months in the spare-tire space in the trunk of my car, and we left. I stole another woman's identity to save my son's life and mine."

"What about your family?" Beau asked. "Couldn't they help you hide? Help you financially?"

"Blake owned the bank where they had their mortgage. If I'd told them *anything,* given them any clue, he would have destroyed them one way or another. He can do that, you see," she said, trying to make them understand how powerful her ex-husband was. "He's so smooth that people would never believe what's underneath the surface." She shivered and rubbed her arms. "Someone's walking over my grave." Her laugh was half-hearted. "Stupid saying, isn't it?"

Stepping in back of her, Royal crossed his arms around her, enclosing her in the warmth of his body, his strength. "Yeah, sugar. But no one's walking over your grave." His chest vibrated against her in an illusion of security.

She told them about saving up cash for her escape, about working part-time as a waitress in a small café right outside Tallahassee, where no one knew her. She told them everything except why she'd taken the terrible risk of returning to the house in Tallahassee.

And with her words, plans were made.

As the day wore on, slowly and agonizingly, they discussed everything they had to do.

Beau's brother Michael had a cabin near Lake Okeechobee. Tommy would stay with Maggie and Sullivan at their beach house for three days, not going to the Sunshine Center. If anyone came checking, Alicia would say that Tommy had been absent since the holiday, and that she hadn't heard from Ms. Malloy. Beau would drive Elly and Royal to Okeechobee in his personal car when twilight fell. Royal would have Sullivan's cellular phone with its safety lock. That would be their link with each other.

Here in Palmaflora, Beau would investigate the men who'd been following Elly and try to link them to Scanlon. Sullivan's job was to search public-access records and query his sources to discover anything concrete about Scanlon's activities and plans. The purpose was to put Elly's ex out of commission. Behind bars.

Elly thought she heard Royal growl something that sounded like "six feet under."

That easily, the deed was done.

It was time to leave.

Elly prayed she wouldn't regret giving her trust this last time. Her track record so far had been lousy.

"Want to go, too," Tommy complained, clinging to her leg. "Don't leave me, Mommy. You need me."

Stooping to Beau's highly polished floor, Elly wrapped

Tommy in her arms. "Honey, I've left you overnight before. You'll have Leesha, Beau, Maggie and Sullivan. You'll go to the beach every day. You're going to be all right." She knew his fear was that she wouldn't return. She wanted to promise him she would, that nothing on earth could keep her away from him.

She didn't.

Promises weren't meant to be broken.

In surrendering him, she had surrendered control. Surrendered, because Royal was right. Tommy was safer away from her. Surrendered him because she couldn't flee anymore. The time had come to turn and fight, to face her enemy. To save this child whom she loved more than anything or anyone she'd ever loved in her life.

For Tommy's sake, she would leave him.

For her own sake, she sent a silent, desperate prayer upward.

"Tommy, listen to me, kiddo." Next to her, Royal squatted and went eye to eye with her son.

"Nope." Tommy squirmed in her arms.

"I know I hurt your feelings yesterday when I said I didn't want you to go with me. That you'd be in the way. That was true yesterday because I had a job to do to protect you and your mom. Now, today, it's your turn. You have a job to do for your mom. You have to take care of her by staying here and being a decoy."

The heat of Royal's body flowed to her, enveloped her and made her feel safe. With her son, Elly turned to face Royal, taking Tommy onto her lap as she folded into a sitting position on the floor. Royal was in front of them, his knees angled on either side of her shoulder, his face inches from hers. Stripped of charm, stripped of everything except a blazing intensity focused on Tommy, Royal's face was resolute, hard.

"You remember the time you saved your mom when she was shot?"

"Oops." Covering his mouth, Tommy twisted his head toward her.

"I told them, honey. You don't have to keep secrets anymore." Elly felt the enormous weight she'd borne lifting from her. If everything went as planned, Tommy could start to live a normal life. She wouldn't have to worry about him every second she couldn't actually see him. "We're not going to move, Tommy. We're staying in Palmaflora."

"With Katie?" From within, a light bloomed in his face, and Elly remembered the lighthearted, happy infant and child he'd been. *Before.* Before his world and hers had exploded in a flash of gunfire and pain and terror.

Fiercely, she made a promise to herself. Tommy would be that child again. Blake wouldn't get his way this time.

"With Katie, honey. And everybody. We're not moving and hiding anymore. Not after this week."

"Tommy—" Royal held out his hand "—you do your job. I'll do mine. I promise on my honor to take care of your mom. Will you trust me?" His eyes were dark green with pain, but he kept his gaze on Tommy. "If you will trust me, Tommy, I *promise* you, I'll keep your mom safe. I'll bring her back to you. Will you trust me?"

Elly knew how painful that question was for Royal. Alicia had divulged what had happened in Palmaflora, why Royal had cultivated his don't-give-a-damn attitude, his pretense that he was more dissolute than he actually was.

"Can I see Katie?" Tommy wiped his hand along his shorts. "'Cause I want to see her."

"As soon as this is over, you can see Katie every day," Elly promised. "You can go to her house. She can come to ours."

"Katie can come to my house?" Tommy whispered. "Really?"

"Really."

"'Kay." Tommy stuck his hand into Royal's. "I can be a decoy like in my soldier games. But I will be lonesome." His bottom lip stuck out.

"I know, honey, I know. But I'll be *back*, sweetie-pie." She buried her face in his flyaway hair and swallowed the lump in her throat. He'd been such a sturdy, good-natured baby, all the promise of the man he'd become in his energy and curiosity.

She wanted to be around to see her son become a man.

Standing up, she carried him with her, her arms wrapped around his chubby body. "I have to go now, sweetie-pie," she murmured. "You be good for Leesha and everybody. Don't go wandering or exploring unless someone's with you. Just for these three days, honey, please." She handed him to Alicia.

"Take care of him. *Please*." Elly controlled the wobble in her voice. She was not going to cry. That wasn't the memory she wanted Tommy to have of her if the worst happened.

"Elly, nothing's going to harm him. I make that promise personally." Alicia took Tommy and slid him onto her hip. "And, Tommy?"

"What, Leesha?" Tommy looked as if he couldn't decide whether to be intrigued or to squall, and Elly wanted to squall herself.

"We're going to teach you how to scuba before your mom and Royal return. And then we'll have a picnic with soda and pizza, and you can show everybody what you've learned. But we'll have to work hard because they're not going to be gone very long. Can you handle swimming *every* day? And wearing a mask?"

Tommy chewed his lip. "Yeah." He nodded more eagerly as he thought through what she'd said. "No problem. I can do decoys and scubas, Mommy." Tilting toward Elly from Alicia's hip, he patted her face. "Don't worry, Mommy."

"Of course not, honey. You're in good hands. Bye, sweetie. Bye." Elly had to hurry toward the front door. Her insides were twisting and turning and deep sobs were shaking her apart. At the door, she turned. "Love you, Thomas Lee. You remember that, hear?"

As she and Royal crawled into the back of Beau's shiny gray car, she looked back at her son. Through the screen door, she saw Tommy's bottom lip tremble, and she started, shoving Royal's restraining hand aside. "No, Elly. You can't," he murmured regretfully, and she stayed crouched in the back, peering above the rim of the car window.

Beau turned the ignition key. With the throbbing sound of the car's powerful engine, Tommy's face crumpled into tears. But he kept waving his hand, over and over, his nose mashed and flattened against the screen door. His small hand waving to her from the door was the last thing she saw as the car pulled away.

Chapter 13

They arrived at Michael's cabin late in the evening. Leaving the roads slick and black, clouds and fitful rain showers slowed them down. Unable to see anything except the intermittent flicker of passing cars and the beat of rain against the back window, Elly tried to sleep, leaning back against Royal's chest, his knees, but the back of the car was cramped. "Pretend you're on a really cheap airline," he advised halfway into the trip as she wiggled and shifted and scooted forward on the gray floor carpet.

"What?" She tried to turn and look at him over her shoulder.

"No legroom. Long flight. Ten-inch-wide seats. You know. Economy section."

"Sure." And she tried to empty her brain of the pictures and sounds filling it. But that last sight of Tommy brought tears to her eyes whenever she let herself see him in her mind's eye.

Finally, though, lulled by the whisper of the tires under her and the drizzle of rain on the windows, Elly dozed on and off. Cramped, miserable and afraid she'd regret her recent decisions, she preferred the unconsciousness sleep gave her.

Once, as a flash of neon orange aroused her, she heard Beau telling Royal that he'd put himself between a rock and a hard place, but the vibration of Royal's chest against her back pitched her back into that warm oblivion of sleep, a place where thinking and planning were impossible.

By the time the three-hour drive ended, she was afraid she'd been permanently pretzeled from riding in the back of Beau's sports car, what with Royal crammed in behind her so close she couldn't shift position without embarrassing herself and him.

As they drove up, Beau slowed the car and unrolled the car windows. The rain had let up, but the ground was pocky with puddles and dripping bushes. In the darkness, frogs sang a mad chorus of desire and pleasure.

The cabin was set way back in the scrub near an inlet from the river. Isolated, almost invisible except from the air, it was two rooms and a kitchen. A basic hunting-and-fishing cabin, it was stark, the Everglades thick around it.

"You'll be able to see anyone coming up the road. Unless it's me or Sullivan, no one should be driving up here, Royal. We don't get mail deliveries here, nothing like that. The cabin has electricity, occasional hot and cold running water. You'll have to light the water heater. The place is bare bones, nothing fancy. But at least nobody knows about it."

Royal pushed the driver's seat forward so she could climb out. "If one person knows, anyone can find out that information," he said grimly, his breath ruffling the hair at the back of her neck as he followed in back of her. "You know that, Beau. First rule of police work."

"True." Surveying the territory, Beau frowned. "Michael, Andy. Me. We're the only ones who come out here."

Elly shivered. Royal had spoken her own thoughts. As safe as it seemed, the cabin was still vulnerable. They all knew that. They knew how far-reaching Blake's tentacles were.

But the cabin was what they had. It would have to do while they figured out what was going on.

The three of them walked around the cabin in the dark, Beau's powerful flashlight pointing to shapes in the underbrush, under the house. When they returned to the front of the cabin, he handed them Sullivan's cellular phone.

"Don't call unless there's a problem. You could be tapped or traced. I'll check in with you at four-thirty each afternoon, but from different phones. If you get a phone call any other time, don't answer. If I have a message, I'll leave a number on the voice mail. The signal for an emergency will be Tommy's name, meaning your cover's blown and you're on your own until we can reestablish communication. That about it?"

"Yeah." Royal nodded. "Elly? Anything you want to add? This is the time."

She shook her head. As far as she could tell, they'd covered their bases. Her nerves were jumping. But she'd made her choice. For better or for worse, she'd committed them all. Put them in harm's way. Let them step in front of Blake's power. None of them could turn back now.

And she'd kept one vital piece of information from them. Was that a mistake? She strained to see through the darkness on either side of the tunnel of light from Beau's flashlight.

Beau clicked off the light, and Royal moved next to her, his body a solid presence that made the heavy, thick night less frightening. The car door slammed, echoed in the silence of the backwoods country. Down the overgrown lane, Beau's taillights winked red and vanished, leaving them behind.

"Stars would help," she said, rubbing her arms as goose bumps skipped up and down her arms. Hot and humid, and she was shivering as if she were in a snowstorm.

Royal covered her arms with his as he looked up at the sky. "Clouds. Another storm's headed our way according to the weather reports on the radio. We'd better get inside before we get soaked. Beau's going to have a crummy ride back to Palma-flora." He grinned at her, his teeth gleaming quickly in the darkness. As her eyes became accustomed to the night, she could make out the shape of his face, could see the shine of his eyes as he looked around them. "Well, sugar, let's go make ourselves at home and check out the accommodations at Club Bienvenue. What do you say?" He pushed open the screen door and then the rough cypress front door.

"Is it safe to turn on the lights in the cabin?"

"We're probably safe using them tonight. We'll have to see what happens. Play it day by day. See what Beau and Sullivan find out."

"Hmm." She shivered again. Royal was as uneasy as she was. His abrupt manner, the clipped words, his constant scanning of the darkness outside the cabin's windows revealed his tension more clearly than anything he could have said.

Inside the door, he pulled a chain, and light washed over his face. Lines of strain showed at the corners of his eyes, and he moved lightly, balancing on the balls of his feet in smooth, ready-for-anything strides, his gaze sweeping the room and back to her. "Hungry, sugar?"

She shuddered. "You're kidding, right? I think I'd throw up if I tried to eat." Standing in the center of the room, she tried to decide what, in fact, she *did* want to do. She couldn't eat, she was too wired to sleep, she didn't see any books. And all she could think of was Tommy, alone, his face pressed against the screen door as she left. She made a tiny sound of dismay. She'd never get through the three days at this rate.

A silvery blue fish mounted on the wall stared down at her unsympathetically.

Royal ran his hands over his face, scrubbing hard at his chin. His bruises were changing color, the scrapes healing, and the dark shadows under his eyes made her lift her hand up and touch his face gently. He was putting everything on the line, too. He turned his chin to her palm, scratching it with the bristles gilding his face. Reaching out, he lifted a strand of her hair, let it slip through his fingers. "Such pretty hair, Elly." He carried the strand to his face and breathed in its scent, his expression somber. "God, I love the smell of your hair." Winding the strand around his finger, he drew her even closer. Her shoes bumped his.

"Just the two of us, Elly. You, me and the creatures of the night, whoever they are. And I don't want you to be afraid of me. You don't have to worry I'm going to throw you down on the floor and have my wicked way with you." He flashed a rueful grin. "I'd like to, of course. But I have, as you remarked, an affinity for control. And I can control myself. You've been through enough—"

"Shh," she said, touching her fingers to his mouth. Damn the man. He was trying to distract her, to make her think of anything except the long hours of anxiety ahead for her, for them both. "I'm not afraid of you. I would never have left Tommy behind if I didn't trust you."

He winced.

"I'm a grown woman. I make my own choices. Some time ago, I swore, no one would ever make them for me. They may not be great, but they're mine. So, buster—" she smiled "—maybe you should worry about me jumping your bones." She gave him a push in the abdomen. "Don't sweat the small stuff, Detective."

"Bad word to use around a man, sugar," he drawled, some of the tension leaving his face with the return of his teasing manner. "That's a word to make a man break out in a cold sweat."

"*Detective?*" she asked innocently, and sashayed ahead of him into what looked like the cabin's kitchen.

"Witch," he murmured, following her.

"Beast," she said cheerfully, some of the chill leaving her as she glanced at him over her shoulder.

They hadn't been able to salvage the jeans he'd worn to the rodeo. They'd both changed. As her gaze lingered on the long curve of his buttocks and thighs, Elly decided she liked the look of Royal's rear in Beau's too-tight jeans.

Both of them had borrowed liberally from Beau and Alicia. Sullivan's shirts had been too tight for Royal's slightly wider shoulders. Fitting Alicia's more elongated shape, her shorts hung around Elly's knees. Laughing at Elly in Leesha's shorts, Beau had volunteered a couple of his T-shirts as dresses. Saying "that was a good idea," Alicia had raided Beau's closets until she found some rope belts that Elly could use with the T-shirts, turning them into a semblance of casual summer dresses. Maggie contributed the yellow shorts Elly now wore, Alicia the gauzy cotton tops in brilliant colors that Elly secretly delighted in after the no-color clothes she'd worn for months.

Tearing her gaze away from Royal's rear, Elly focused her thoughts elsewhere and realized she was hungry after all. "I think I could eat some soup if there's any in the cupboard." She started at one end of the kitchen cupboards, Royal at the other, his cheerful whistling punctuating the *rat-a-tat* slamming of doors.

They could get through this. She just wouldn't think about Tommy and the men following her and Royal. And she wouldn't let herself think of her ex-husband and the webs he would be spinning after her disappearance.

"You miss Tommy, don't you?" Royal handed her an opened can of tomato soup.

"He's only five." Unable to move, she held the can, fighting off memories. "Remember how you were at that age?" She raised her face to his, tears collecting in her eyes. "How frightened you would have been all alone."

Taking the can from her, he plopped the column of red stuff into a pan. "No, actually, I don't. My parents shipped me out to boarding schools, military schools, prep schools. They weren't interested in four-year-old kids who cried and made messes and interrupted dinner parties with chicken pox."

"What?" Stunned, Elly looked at him. The man was tough, resourceful. But he'd been a child like Tommy, frightened and alone. On his own. Abandoned. "Oh, Royal. How awful for you."

"Hey, sugar—" his eyes glittered with self-mockery "—don't shed any tears for me. I had *everything*. I was the golden boy. Anything I wanted, I had."

"Except love." Her heart hurt for the child Royal had been, the boy who'd had so much. The boy who'd had nothing of value and had grown into a man who joked and teased and kept real emotion out of his life. "I'm so—"

"No big deal, sugar," he interrupted. "What do you say we drop ancient history and get this meal on the table?"

"All right." She was shaky inside, the impulse to comfort him making her drop knives. What he'd told her about the child explained so much about the man. "You're right. And besides, I'm starving."

Tomato soup and crackers in chipped mugs. Grilled-cheese sandwiches made from frozen bread in the freezer and processed cheese that had an expiration date somewhere in the next century. Baby sweet pickles Royal found in the refrigerator. Elly discovered she was more than hungry—she was ravenous, the buttery smell of the bread and cheese tantalizing her until her stomach rumbled.

"Whoa. What was that?" Royal pulled his head out from a cupboard. "For such a tiny mite, you make a big noise, sugar. I thought you said you weren't hungry?" He tilted his head and lifted one golden eyebrow.

She blushed and flipped the sandwiches with the spatula he

handed her as he banged the drawer shut with his denimed rear. "That's all right, Elly. I like a woman with…an appetite." His glance teased her, invited her to play, to forget what he'd told her about himself. To forget for a few minutes where they were and why.

With that thought, anxiety drifted back over her. "I know what you're doing, you know."

"Well, I should hope and pray you do." Slouching on the counter, Royal regarded her with mock concern. Beau's purple T-shirt tightened across his chest as he folded his arms. He'd tucked the shirt into a pair of Beau's faded jeans, and the pull of the light cotton fabric across his chest outlined the contours of his stomach and rib muscles, the muscled shape of his belly. "A woman of your advanced age and experience should be able to figure out how to flirt. To…tease."

"Right. All that experience." She glowered at him.

"There hasn't been all that much experience, has there, Elly, not really?" His tone was gentle.

"No."

"Blake." Royal shifted, and Beau's jeans cupped him, drawing her attention to the zipper placket that was washed and worn thin.

"Blake," she agreed, looking away.

"Why, sugar?" Royal didn't move, and his expression was so tender that he made her want to weep for all the spoiled years. "Why him? And only him? He's not worth a strand of your hair."

She couldn't remember now, not after so long, why there had been only Blake. "I thought I was in love with him. I *was*. My brain went soft, I guess. Now I can see all those warning signs I missed." She sighed. "I was too adoring, too ready to believe anything he said. And I didn't understand that he didn't love me. I was 'suitable.' Quiet—"

"Pshaw. Not you, sugar." Royal's smile made her blink. "Never meek and quiet. The man can't be all that bright if he misjudged you like that."

"And he thought I was stupid," she finished, the bitterness and resentment still pinching. "It took me a long time to figure out that was what he thought of me. That I was too stupid to make a fuss, too stupid to understand what was happening around me—'' She slapped her hand on the counter.

"For that alone, I could kill him,'' he said, smiling, and his smile was that of the stalking tiger.

"Let's hope you don't get the chance. I'd really, really rather not ever see him again." Shivers skipped down her back again. "He scares me, Royal. He's…changed. He used to look at me the way you'd look at…an ant on the floor." She slid the sandwich onto the chipped plastic plate he held out. "How long do you think it will take Beau to get back to Palmaflora?" Picking up the spatula, she tapped it restlessly against the counter.

"Ordinarily, much less time than it took us to get here. But he's not going to speed. He doesn't want anybody else to know he was in this area. A fellow officer wouldn't give him a ticket, but anonymity and invisibility are the order of the day." He took the spatula from her, bent his knees and nudged her nose with his. "Come and eat, Elly. There are only two or three ways we can pass the time until we hear from Beau. Eating, sleeping, and foolin' around, sugar. Personally, I'm hoping you give in to your temptation and jump my bones. Foolin' around's a great way to pass the time. Just about my favorite game in the whole wide world."

Heat prickled through her at the expression in his eyes. Looking away from him, she picked at her sandwich. "Trust me, you'd be disappointed."

"Would I, sugar?" His eyes sparkled and deepened.

She nodded. "Definitely." They were only joking, doing a verbal form of what he called "foolin' around," in order to keep their minds off what was happening; she understood that, but the more he teased, the more her skin flushed and tightened.

He stepped away and put both their plates on the rickety wooden table. The table rocked as he pulled up a chair and motioned her into it. "Because of that lack of experience you mentioned?"

"It wouldn't be worth your while." She felt the beginnings of a smile pull at her lips as he stretched out his legs and tapped her foot with the tip of his shoe. Primly, she drew her legs together under the table.

"Shame, though." He shook his head regretfully as he said, hopefully, his drawl so broad she could have crossed the ocean on it, "Of course, sugar, you understand I'd be willing to sacrifice myself?"

"I couldn't ask you to do that." She shifted in her seat, and his eyes followed the movement of her legs and arms, making her so conscious of her body that she forgot what she was going to say next.

"Sugar, you wouldn't have to ask." He bit into the sandwich, and rivulets of cheese dangled from the bread.

Scooping them around his thumb, he popped the strings into his mouth. Propping his elbows on the table, he shot her a narrow-eyed glance that made her wonder exactly how much teasing they'd both been doing. "Experience isn't all it's cracked up to be, you know, Elly," he said gently. "Sex is pretty basic. You know, even birds and bees do it, sugar. It's mostly buttons and body parts. Turn this, push that. That's what most folks mean when they talk about experience. But it's kinda mechanical when you get right down to it." He laughed as she blushed and her gaze flickered away. "Pun not really intended."

"Hah. I doubt that. With you, nothing is accidental." She tugged the edge of Maggie's yellow shorts.

"My control's not that good." He just sat watching her. "Not all the time. Not in every situation, Elly."

That edgy, prickling heat flared and raced through her, scorching her nerve endings. "Um, well…" She plucked at the loose neck of Alicia's blouse.

"Sex is easy. But everybody's a beginner when it comes to lovemaking, sweetheart. Because that comes from here." He touched his heart, and his eyes were such a deep, brilliant green that she felt she was drowning in their sea depths. "Elly, the best lovemaking combines heart and mind. And that has nothing to do with how many people you've done the deed with, or how often, or anything except what's going on between you and the person you're with, the person you care about."

Clearing her throat, she picked off a piece of cheese, rolled it between her fingers, mashed it flat. "You were engaged to Maggie. You cared about her. You loved her." She wanted to clamp her hand over her mouth, take back the words. Made incautious by their isolation and exhaustion, she'd strayed into private areas she wouldn't have normally invaded. She dropped the mangled bit of cheese onto her plate. "I'm sorry. That was inexcusably rude—"

"I *love* Maggie," he corrected. "I always will. I'd crawl across hot coals for her."

Elly picked up her sandwich. Put it down. No one had ever loved her that way. And she? Well, she'd only felt that kind of powerful emotion for Tommy. Not looking at Royal, Elly envied Maggie Webster with every cell of her being. "She's lucky. You, Sullivan, both of you loving her." She made herself pick her sandwich again and take a bite. She made herself smile while cold loneliness seeped through her, numbing her very bones. "But I'm sorry, Royal. It must be difficult for you, seeing them together all the time. Still loving her."

Royal pushed her mug of soup toward her. "Drink it before it gets cold, Elly." He tipped his chair back. "I love Maggie in a special way. When she was shot the first time and died on the table, it was the worst moment of my life. But something happened to her. She...came back...*different*. Not the same person. The woman who came back from the dead was meant for Sullivan, not me."

"I'm sorry. I don't understand." Elly wanted to weep for the sadness in his lean face, for the loneliness in his eyes that spoke to her own.

"It's simple, really, but it took me a while to sort it out. The way I love her now is not the way Sullivan loves her. She's a part of my life, my heart. She always will be. But she's not the keystone of my life. I would be devastated if something happened to her. But I'd survive. And I know that. That's the difference, Elly. Sullivan wouldn't. Maggie wouldn't if something happened to him."

"But that's sad. Like swans that mate for life." She wanted to cry at the idea of Maggie and Sullivan, separated by disaster, death.

"Oh, I don't mean they'd literally curl up and die, not that." Musing, he frowned slightly. "Although, with them, I'm not too sure. I don't think Sullivan would want to live without Maggie. But they *complete* each other. I've never had that with anyone, not even with Maggie when we were engaged. You?" He tipped his own mug up, but his gaze was steady on her as he waited for her answer.

"No. Never." The wind rattled the window, and Elly jumped, sloshing tomato soup onto the table.

"Is that what love is to you, that kind of completion?"

"I don't know what love is. I thought I did. But I made an enormous mistake. And I'm not that naive twenty-two-year-old anymore. Love's an illusion, that's all." She sighed and glanced toward the darkness beyond the windowpanes. "I don't ever want to trust anyone like that ever again. It's too dangerous."

"Life is dangerous, Elly. You can't hide behind the walled gates forever." He pushed his chair away from the table. "Tommy will grow up, leave you. You'll have nothing left, not even memories to warm you in the cold nights. That's no way to live. When this is over, you're going to have to take a chance."

"Oh? And you're the expert? You're giving *me* advice?" Jerking away from the table, she faced him. She couldn't bear to think about the emptiness of her life as he described it. "You? My God, Royal, you've buried yourself because you can't be a cop anymore. You've shoved away all your friends and become a walking dead man."

"What do you know about it?" he growled, his face dark with anger.

"I know what Alicia and Beau told me, I know what you've said. No one made you quit the police force. You made that choice. Well, gambling man, maybe you should have taken the biggest risk of your life." She jabbed his chest.

Capturing her hand, he said, his voice as cold as death, "I didn't have a choice."

"Of course you did. We always have some choice. Maybe you should have gambled that people would believe in you. Instead, you handed them a silver platter filled with reasons to believe every rumor they heard. That was your choice, Royal. Nobody made you quit being a policeman. You were the one who pushed people away. You didn't give them a chance to believe in you because you were afraid."

"I've never been afraid in my life."

"Bull," she said succinctly. "You were shaking in your battle-scarred boots, Gaines. Because if you took a risk on them and they let you down, well, where would you be? So you didn't. You preempted them. Hey, it's easier, safer, not to take that kind of risk. I understand, but don't you talk to me about taking chances. Because when push came to shove, buster, you made your own walled castle. *You* didn't take a chance. Why, Royal? Why didn't you give people a reason to believe in you?''

He flung her hand away, spun on his heel. ''Because.''

Approaching him, she touched his shoulder. ''Because you wanted them to believe in you in spite of everything.'' Leaning her face against his hard back, she whispered, ''Why was that so important, Royal?''

''Pride.'' His voice was muffled. ''They should have known I wouldn't take bribes. They should have known me well enough to understand I'd never be a part of a cover-up.''

''You left the department because of your pride?'' Pride was a stern taskmaster for a lonely child who'd rather be left out of a game than ask to play. ''This is all about pride, then?''

''Sometimes, that's all a man has.''

For a long moment, she held him in the silence broken by the whine of wind, the rattle of windows. She understood now. The lonely child he'd been, the boy who'd been shoved out of his own home, that child had yearned for acceptance, for a place of his own where he would be believed in, trusted, no matter what. Where he would be loved for himself alone.

And he hadn't found it.

He didn't turn around to face her. His back was rigid under her hands, and she wanted to find those cold, autocratic parents who'd sent him off to school and shut him out of their lives and explain to them what they'd done, what harm they'd done to that child.

His spine stiff under her cheek, he stepped away, his back still to her. ''I think we should call it a night, Elly. We've said too much.''

''Have we?''

He nodded, an abrupt, artificial jerk of his head. ''We have three days to get through. This isn't the way.''

''Perhaps you're right.'' She let her hands fall, empty, to her sides in the face of his pride, that pride that refused to accept compassion and tenderness. He'd let her ease the pain of those bruises on his body, but not those on his heart. She wondered if anyone could, or if that emptiness in him went too deep for healing.

She wanted to comfort the man. And she wept for the child he'd been, that child touching a part of her heart the man hadn't.

Chapter 14

Following Royal down the space that wasn't really a hall but connected the bedroom to the kitchen, Elly realized the next two days were going to change her, change her life in more ways that she could foresee. When she came out the other end of this tunnel of days, if she did, everything in her life would be altered, transformed. Like a caterpillar emerging from its cocoon, she would be newborn, her whole life ahead of her. If she survived.

If Royal survived.

He'd stumbled into her life and made himself responsible for her, for Tommy, and now this man with the smile that hid his pain was sacrificing himself for her. Trying to make her believe he was there only for the fun of the game, for the rush of adrenaline, he dazzled her with smiles and touches that left her aching. And with every effort, he convinced her otherwise.

Royal Gaines was a beat-up knight in borrowed clothes. She knew one when she saw one.

He shoved aside the curtain that served as a door. The bedroom was sparsely furnished. Two single beds and a chest of drawers, a bed stand between the beds. A yellowed pull-down shade covered the window that faced the creek.

"This is it. You'd probably prefer it if I slept on the pullout in the living room, but I think we should stick together. I'm sorry you won't have privacy, but that's the way it has to be." Arms folded across his chest, his face closed, he faced her. Shadows angled across his face. He was only doing the best he could with what he had to work with, a man who had put his life on the line for her.

"It's okay, Royal. Privacy isn't a priority right now. The arrangement is fine." Elly walked to the window, lifted the shade and looked out at the rain, those silvery streaks slanting across the blackness between the two of them and the rest of the world. "Anyway, how's it different from two people sitting next to each other on a trans-Atlantic flight and sleeping the whole way? Unless you snore?" she inquired politely, playing the game, trying to chase the shadows from his face.

"Haven't had any complaints." He sat down on the bed. Stood up. Sat down and leaned back against the iron headboard. Shucked off his shoes. Watching her too carefully, working too hard to maintain his role as the sinner of the century, he was showing the strain. "Nope, not one little ol' complaint about my sleeping habits, sugar." Placing his arms in back of his head, he crossed one ankle over the other and gave her one of his patented killer smiles, all casual nonchalance.

She smiled back. She had to. She couldn't help her response to that combination of rakish grin and golden hair. It was a nice effect. The man could have a future as an actor if he never went back to being a policeman. "Good. I'm happy for you." Elly strolled to the stand and switched on the lamp. Looking over her shoulder, she paused and then added teasingly, "For your information, I don't snore, either."

"Yeah? Should be a quiet night, then." One foot beat a tattoo against the other. He sat straighter. "Anything to read in that bedside stand?"

"Let me see." As Elly pulled on the drawer, it stuck.

Freeing it with a sharp yank, she fell back on her fanny. The shallow drawer flew upward, and silver packets rained down on her, landed in her lap, her hair, bounced across the floor and formed a shining stream of foil between her and Royal. Open-mouthed, she stared at the regulation handcuffs that clattered to the floor beside the river of condoms. "My goodness." Feebly, she shuffled the packets in her lap. "I've heard of being prepared, but—'' She glanced at the handcuffs and felt her face burn. ''Good grief.''

''Michael.'' Royal sat up abruptly. His face was stern, but his shoulders were shaking. ''Michael and Rhea,'' he said in a strangled voice.

''What?'' Elly scooped up a handful of packets and stared around the room, not quite sure what to do. The drawer had been stuffed with the little squares.

''They're—'' his face crumpled, straightened ''—they're busy people. It's Michael's fishing cabin. But Rhea comes here sometimes with Michael. They don't fish.'' Guffaws ripped through him as he gasped, ''Oh, Lord, Elly, if you could see your face.'' He slid to the floor beside her. ''Michael's going to hear about this.'' Picking up the handcuffs, Royal dangled them in front of her face. ''Cute touch, don't you think?'' Catching the gleams of light, the metal handcuffs swung back and forth in front of her.

She couldn't answer. Wild visions popped into her head.

Handcuffs in one fist, Royal scrabbled through the packets, searched under the beds. ''So where's the key?''

''Here.'' Elly fumbled in her lap and handed him the key. Stuffing the packets in her other hand back into the drawer as Royal righted it and dropped the cuffs inside, she scooped up another handful from the floor, flinging it into the drawer. She slid the drawer onto its wooden runners. ''No books,'' she said, bending forward and letting her hair hide her flaming face as images continued to flash in her mind. ''No magazines.''

''Guess Michael and Rhea didn't have time to read,'' Royal drawled, looking at her and dropping a fistful of packets into the drawer. ''Just a couple of crazy kids, huh?''

''Sure. Whatever.'' Elly scrambled to her feet. ''Do you want some water? I'm thirsty. I'll bring you a glass. A pitcher.'' Her whole body burned and tingled with embarrassment.

Darting out of the room, she heard Royal's chuckles, heard the decided clunk as he shoved the drawer closed. No, she thought, rummaging in the cabinets for glasses and a container, not embarrassment. Something much, much worse. Because in all those pictures flashing and blazing behind her eyes, not one contained Michael or Rhea, those two busy people she'd never met.

But Royal was in the pictures.

She was, too.

Heat sparked through the tips of her fingers, her toes, her eyelashes, flared to the ends of her hair.

When she returned with a glass pitcher of cold water and glasses, he was already under the sheets, the bedspread pulled to his waist, the overhead light and bedside lamp turned off. Only the gleam of his hair and his skin shone in the dim light from the kitchen.

"You want to leave that light on, Elly?" Bedsprings creaked as he faced her.

"Yes. No." She sped into the kitchen and pulled the chain. Damn that drawer full of condoms and cuffs.

Back in the bedroom, she slid under the covers of her bed and skimmed out of her bra and Maggie's shorts, dropping them on the floor. She kept on the T-shirt and her underpants.

Pulling the sheet to her chin, she scooted as far down under the covers as she could.

"Good night, Elly." Perfectly calm, only that glimmer of amusement rippling in it, Royal's voice bridged the silence.

"Good night." She turned onto her side, away from that silent shape an arm's length away. Fluffing the lumpy pillow, she burrowed her face into its sunshine smell and tried to go to sleep.

Royal had checked the bars on the windows, bars similar to the arrangement she'd set up for air in the Palmaflora house. He'd locked the doors. Through the partially opened windows in the bedroom came the sound of a steady rain. Pinging on the tin roof, slashing against the wooden sides of the house in sudden bursts, the sound of rain filled the room.

And in the quiet between the rain, she heard Royal's breathing, slow and steady, reassuring, lulling her to sleep.

She couldn't sleep, though. Every time she shut her eyes, she thought of Tommy and came alert with the rush of panic. She made herself think of that spill of foil, tried to let her mind drift where it had gone so effortlessly as Michael and Rhea's stash fell to the floor. Better to think of that than the other images striding into her mind and terrifying her.

But sleep eluded her, leaving her alone with her melancholy thoughts. She remembered the wasted years with Blake. All those years when she'd had nothing.

No, not wasted. She had Tommy. Tommy was worth those years in the sterile prison of Blake's house.

She turned, easing the sheet over her so that she wouldn't wake Royal. Turning again, restless, she thought of all she'd missed in life. She'd made her choices. But she'd never imagined the cost.

Rain whipped on the windowpanes.

And what would she change? She stuffed the edge of her pillow into her mouth to keep from crying out with loneliness and fear, with regret. What would she change? Everything, everything except Tommy. For him, she'd endure those loveless, lonely years again.

The sheet scratched against her thighs like the caress of a lover's hand. She went still. She didn't have to be lonely. Unless she chose to be. That part of her life was ended. Blake didn't control her life any longer. Startled by the realization, she opened her eyes. She'd walked away from that life into a new one, one with different choices.

She might have only days, hours, left of this new life. But she could *choose* how she spent the rest of it. Was she going to let the past with all its ugliness, its sadness, keep her bound to it? She pleated the sheet between her fingers, thinking.

In a sudden, fierce gust, rain rattled the window, and she turned toward it, toward Royal. With her dark-adjusted eyes, she watched the rise and fall of his chest. He was sleeping.

"I'm awake, Elly." He rolled on his side to face her. "I haven't slept, either." The rich roughness of his voice brushed over her skin in the darkness, tightening it.

If the light had been on, she would never have had the courage.

Sitting up, the sheet clutched in one hand, she slid her feet to the floor, indecisive still, her heart pounding under the T-shirt. The strap of her bra, pale in the dark, lay across the wooden floor. "Royal?" She cleared her throat, reaching inside her for the second time in her life for the courage to take an enormous, unbelievable step forward.

Days ago, a lifetime ago, teasing, he'd told her the choice would be hers. But he wouldn't ask. She would have to take the risk of going to him, of trusting him. She hesitated. She couldn't do it. She'd been crazy even to think she could. She lifted her foot, ready to slide back into her own bed in humiliation.

If she did, would she regret this act of cowardice for the rest of her life, however long that might be?

"Royal?" she whispered again, trying to frame the words.

"What do you want, Elly?" Something guarded in his voice kept her foot hovering over the floor.

"Will you sleep with me?" Asking him was harder than she'd guessed.

"Why?" he said bluntly. "To thank me for my help?"

"You think I'm offering myself to you out of some convoluted sense of gratitude for your help?" she asked in amazement. "That I'm offering myself up like some sacrificial lamb?"

"Are you? Isn't that what's going on?"

"No."

"Then what is?"

Rain thrummed hard against the roof, echoing the beat of her heart.

"Why, Elly?"

Like her son, she retreated, unable to spell out what she needed from him. "Because."

"Because of that lack of experience?"

"No," she said in a small voice. "Not that." She put her foot on the warm wood of the floor. "Well, maybe, a little," she admitted, trying to be as honest as she knew how.

"I see." The sheet rustled with his movement.

"I doubt it," she muttered, embarrassed and uncomfortable.

"Because you want to forget what's happening?"

"Yes. I'm so scared. And worried. I can't sleep." She twisted the sheet in her fist.

"And I'm the analgesic of choice?" In the gap between window and shade, a shaft of watery moonlight gleamed gold in his hair, disappeared behind clouds, leaving the room dark again. Private. "You want me to be your sleeping pill, Elly?" he inquired politely.

"No." Her answer was so quiet she didn't think he heard. She cleared her throat awkwardly. "Just…because."

"Because." There was a long silence, a silence filled with possibilities, with the sound of rain and hesitancy. "A one-night stand, Elly? Is that all you want? Will that be enough for you?"

"I don't know what I want." Wishing she could see his expression, decipher what he was asking, she stared at him through the darkness. "I'm so tired, Royal, so tired of being alone. I want...to forget. For a while."

"Sounds impersonal, Elly, whether you realize it or not. Kind of...mechanical. I'd like to have the sense that you knew who was making love to you. When you shut your eyes, when I touch you, I'd like to be sure you knew it was *me* touching you, nobody else. But to be blunt about it, the way you put it, anybody would do. Where's the heart in that, Elly?"

"I don't know. But it's not mechanical. I'm scared, Royal. I want to be held, to hold. To *feel* something besides this numbing terror. Is that enough for you? Two lonely people comforting each other?"

"Comfort." His disembodied voice was flat.

She waited, her heart drumming sickeningly. Yes. No. But she couldn't cross that expanse of floor between them, couldn't take the step that would take her to his side. She wasn't that sophisticated. She wasn't that confident. Afraid he would accept, half-sick with regret that he wouldn't, she was paralyzed. She couldn't make herself move.

The space between the two beds seemed to shimmer in the darkness, seemed to grow impossibly wide.

And then he spoke, his voice so husky and low that she shivered.

"It's not the Grand Canyon, Elly." Propped on his elbow, he was leaning up in bed. "There's a bridge across." Still half reclining, half sitting up, he reached across the gap. "It's only two baby steps and you're home, home free, Elly."

Underneath the careful invitation, she heard his longing, heard the urgency and something else she couldn't name in the slow, terse words, and that made all the difference. She flew across the distance, the longest distance she'd ever crossed, flew into his waiting arms, breathless with longing and apprehension and anticipation.

"Brave woman," he whispered into her ear, pulling back the sheet and wrapping her in his arms. His legs tangled with hers in a private dance. "But I always knew you were. You're the bravest person I've ever had the privilege of knowing, Elly Malloy."

"I'm not Elly Malloy," she muttered, her heart fluttering and drumming inside her so fast she couldn't think. "That's not me." Amazed at what she'd done, she was incoherent. Restlessly, she shifted her legs, and his thigh slipped between hers, bumping intimately against her and sending sharp convulsions rippling over her. "That's not who I am. You don't know me."

"Oh, yes, I do. You're the woman who walked away from a nightmare and into my life. You're the woman who took care of her son and protected him at the risk of her own life." He touched her scar with his finger, with his mouth, trailing his lips down her neck. "You're the woman who makes my heart shake me apart when I'm within sight of you. I know you, sweetheart, no matter what name you're using."

As close as they were in the narrow bed, she moved closer and took his lean face between her palms. "I'm Abigail Eleanor MacGuire, Royal."

"Pleased to meet you, Abby," he said, and took her mouth with his in a fierce kiss that shuddered through her with urgency and passion. "I'd be honored to make love with you." He ran his hand down her back to her rear, familiarly, as if he'd known her before, as if they'd joined this way a hundred times, and her fear ebbed, leaving only sparkles of anticipation behind. "Aw, Elly, you have no idea how sweet you are." He took the kiss deeper, his hands cupping her buttocks and lifting her on top of him as he rolled onto his back. "You're a miracle, you are, sweetheart. You make me tremble like a sixteen-year-old boy, learning about love for the first time."

"Shh," she whispered against his mouth, cherishing his words that soothed her fears, eased her spirit like a balm. But she couldn't let him think she needed promises, false words. She wouldn't let him talk of love when that was the cruelest illusion of all. Between them tonight, she wanted only a kind of honesty they could live with on the morning after. "It's all right, Royal."

Still on his back he chuckled and slid his palms up along her sides, tickling lightly along her rib cage and making her move fitfully against him. "Only all right? Elly, *feel* what you do to me." He placed her hand over his heart. "Believe me, this is better than all right."

Under her open palm, his heart thundered, shuddered. She looked at him in amazement. Such power, such strength, and it was in her control. "So strong," she murmured, stroking his hot skin, twining her fingers in the thick nest of his hair. "I can do that to you?"

"Sugar, that's not the half of what you do to me." He covered her hand with his and moved her hand downward over the silky fabric of his boxers. "See?" he murmured into her ear.

And under that silk, the hard column of flesh that trembled, moved, to the sheath of her hand, responsive to the curl of her fingers. Power there, too, under her control, enchanting her. "I might have known you'd wear silk," she whispered, stroking that living barometer of his response to her.

"And you wear cotton." He slid his hands down to the elastic waistband, edged one finger under the narrow band. "I never knew cotton could be so sexy. May I?"

She buried her face in his neck. His question forced her to participate, to admit she burned in the same way, needed the same touches she gave him. She didn't think she could speak the words out loud. She didn't have the courage, the experience, to tell him she ached to have him touch her, too. She nodded once into the crook of his neck.

"What's that, Elly? I didn't hear you." He circled his finger around the rim of her navel, not moving lower, teasing now in a different way. "Was there something you wanted, sweetheart? Speak up, sugar." Laughter, warm and affectionate, bubbled up from his chest, bouncing her where she lay against him.

"Devil," she gasped, surging against him as the tip of his finger teased the dip of her belly button. Her pelvis rocked into him, and the lift of his hips moved in response.

"Come on, sweetheart," he urged. "Say the words. Tell me you want me, too. I can't hide the way I feel. You have me at a disadvantage, you know." He twisted, and the proof of his words nudged hard against her belly, pulsed at the V of her thighs. "Let me hear you say you're burning to ashes with me, Elly. Play fair." He rocked gently at the entrance, and her body followed that one-step, two-step rhythm he set.

"Is this a game, then?" she asked forlornly, the delicious rocking sending electrical sparks all over her. She hadn't wanted anything more, but she couldn't bear the thought that to him what they were doing was no more than a game.

"Not a game, Elly." He went still. "Whatever we're doing,

it's not a game. I don't know what to call this—'' he took her mouth in a hard, fierce kiss that left her trembling ''—but it's the most real moment of my life, believe me. I don't want to hurt you, sweetheart. I want to give you pleasure. I want to make you forget everything except what I can make you feel, what we can feel together.'' Gripping her chin, he made her look at him. ''But, Elly, you have to make a decision. I don't want a passive lover in my bed tonight. Lovemaking should be mutual. I want you to take a risk, too.''

''I did.'' Resentment stirred in her. He was complicating what should have been so simple. ''I asked *you* to make love with me.''

''No, sweetheart, you didn't,'' he clarified. ''You said you wanted to be held. To hold. To be comforted. Well, Elly, that's what we're doing. I'm holding you. You're holding me. Nothing more. You have to decide.''

She thought she had. He was asking for something else, and she couldn't decipher what he meant. She'd admitted she wanted him, she'd taken that huge leap, and yet he wanted still more, and she was confused. ''I don't understand.''

''Because if this is all you want, Elly, just to be held and comforted, I can stop now. I can stop any time you want me to. But stopping wouldn't be my choice. I want to turn you inside out with ecstasy. I want you shaking and trembling and calling my name.'' He stopped and slid his hands down her neck, over her collarbone. ''But I can hold you like this all night. If that's what you want. I need to know, though, exactly what you want. I don't want to misunderstand. Tomorrow, I don't want you to say I overwhelmed you or took the choice out of your hands. I want much more. But it's your choice. So, Elly-Abby, tell me what you want, sweetheart. Give me that, at least.''

She didn't understand his last words, but she thought she'd figured out the rest of it. That child who'd been left on his own all his life needed to know he was more than a boy-toy. Because of his own loneliness and pain, the man wanted her to commit something more than her body. He needed more from her than an easing of his male impulses.

She needed him tonight, but she had something she could give him, too. The encounter wouldn't be one-sided, him giving, her taking. That realization worked through her, easing her doubts, her insecurity, and gave her confidence where she'd had none.

"Is this—" he ran his palms down her sides, and her skin prickled in the wake of that touch "—all you want?" His hands stopped again just under the edge of her panties.

"No." One hand braced carefully on his shoulder, she lifted her head and faced him. "I want you to make love with me, Royal." Her voice was steady, clear. Determined. "Whatever we call it, whatever it means, I want to be with you tonight. Not with just anybody, and not just to make me forget." She took his hand and slipped it under the elastic band and down to the curve of her hip. "I want to make love with *you*, Royal."

"Thank you, Elly."

She smiled against the slick skin where his neck ended and his chest began. "You're welcome, Royal." Delicately, tentatively, she touched her tongue to the dip under his Adam's apple. "Salty," she whispered, and then shivered as his warm palm moved over her bare skin, the edge of his fingernails scraping lightly, lightly against her.

"Sweet," he murmured. Clasping her hips, he held her securely, his thumbs at the edge of her navel, his fingers curving to her back, to the swell of her fanny, where they moved in a mesmerizing tracery of arcs and circles. "You feel like satin, Elly. Did you know that?"

"No," she said, captivated by his image. She'd been Tommy's mother for so long that she'd lost all sense of this side of her nature. And then Blake had never— Royal's thumb swooped into her navel, stroked the bead there in slow, tantalizing circles.

"Oh!" Startled, she jerked up as his thumb slid downward. With one quick movement, Royal flicked her panties off with one hand, all the while moving his thumb beguilingly closer.

Stopping, his thumb caressing the edge of her nest of cloudy curls, Royal watched her eyes widen, grow dazed. Even in the fitful light, he could see her face soften with astonishment as he stroked her. "It's been a long time for you, hasn't it, Elly?"

"Yes," she sighed, her head falling back, the cloud of her hair spilling in a nimbus around her face.

In the too-big neck of Beau's T-shirt, her throat was a long, lovely invitation to kisses, and he nibbled leisurely, sucking gently and tasting her.

"Ah, that's—"

"Nice?" he teased.

Her breasts lifted with her movement, and bending at the waist, he lifted to take one peaked nipple into his mouth. Her shivers under his hands, his mouth, spread to him and made him clumsy where he'd never been clumsy before. His hands shook as he traced the delicate ridges of her ribs, her spine, his fingers reading the language of her body, her skin, *her.*

The tiny murmurs of surprise she gave thrilled him. Moved him because they told him she'd never been touched like this. "How long has it been, Elly?" He trailed kisses down the center of her body, from her neck to her belly button, lingering there.

"Forever," she sighed. "Years. Not since Tommy was born."

"Oh, sweetheart, what a waste." His heart broke for her, for what she'd admitted. For Elly to have lived untouched, unloved, during those long years tore him apart. "You're a treasure, Elly. You should have been cherished."

"You make me feel cherished, Royal." She slipped her arms around his neck, curling her hands into his hair. "You make me feel alive for the first time in years. You make my body sing and hum, and I never knew it could be like this between two people."

"It's only beginning, sweetheart." Cupping her rear, he lifted her, bringing her to his mouth. And then, because he delighted in her, because he wanted her to remember these moments later, he opened her to the touch of his lips and tongue and kissed her intimately.

"Royal, don't— Ah, yes, yes." She stiffened against him, shudders moving under her skin, in the deep muscles of her thighs and belly. She reached out to hold him, push him away— he didn't know.

With a quick, rolling motion, keeping her in his arms, he turned them until she was on her back looking up at him with wide, stunned eyes. Easing himself up her body, he parted her and entered in one smooth stroke on the last of her shudders.

The kernel remaining of his conscience made him ask in that last moment, compelled him to ask, because he could still stop if she said no, "Are you sure about this, Elly? Please be sure." He withdrew, aching and tight with control. "You may regret this."

"I may," she said, and her breath shivered over his chin. "But this is what I want. I trust you, Royal."

"Sweetheart, don't, don't," he muttered, moving up to kiss her mouth, wanting to stop the words she would hate herself for saying in the morning. "You shouldn't trust me."

"But I do, damn you, I do," she wailed, and surged upward, toward him, breaking the thin thread of his control.

He'd done everything he could so far to protect her. He had one more thing to take care of.

"Wait," he muttered. "Wait, sweetheart," he said, and reached over to the drawer, pulled hard. He barely heard the smack of the handcuffs on the floor. The pitter-patter of the falling condoms blended with the sound of the rain on the roof.

"Bless Michael and Rhea," she said with a sigh that feathered over him, tickling the hairs of his chest. "There's a lot to be said for being prepared." Her bare foot slid along his calf.

"A lot," he agreed, and reached down to lift her leg higher, fitting them together more tightly.

She was smooth and warm and welcoming. She was heaven on earth after eons in hell, and he wanted to lose himself in her, remain linked with her in that sweetest of joinings, but she moved against him and his body answered her unspoken question.

Yes, Elly, yes, you're beautiful, and this is more than a game to me, and yes, you should have been treasured and loved, not left alone. Let me show you what you've missed, what I feel, and love me back a little, share all this warmth with me, give me everything inside you, your courage, your sass. Your love. Yes, yes, Elly.

He plunged his hands into the mass of her hair and opened her mouth as he had her body and kissed her with all the passion and grief and remorse that filled him.

Kissed her because her touch chased away the emptiness and made him hope, made him believe in happily-ever-after when he knew there was no such thing. He kissed her because he had to.

He knew he should stop, knew he would regret this indulgence in the morning.

Her hesitancy as she sat on the edge of her bed had speared through him like a streak of fire, and he'd wanted her so fiercely that it had been all he could do not to leap out of his bed and grab her before she could take her words back.

He'd tried to resist.

He'd tried to give her every chance he could to back out, to change her mind, because he couldn't. The sight of her with the sheet clutched in her hands had torn him apart with longing, and he'd trembled even as he waited, even as he forced her to admit that she wanted him.

He'd needed to know that, needed to make sure she was clear about her decision.

Because she would hate him when he told her about his involvement with Scanlon. She would never forgive him.

And he would be in hell again, this time forever.

Hell was endless loneliness.

There was no hope in hell, no redemption.

Chapter 15

To the sound of raindrops and the smell of loamy earth blowing through the window, Royal loved her. Her murmurs and hesitant moves filled him with tenderness, a tenderness that made him awkward and diffident in the face of the emotions swelling through him. He'd told her sex was buttons and bodies, but this...this *tenderness* was new to him. It left him unsure of himself and as clumsy as a boy. Rocked to the core by the need to show her that these moments with her were more than sex, he was awkward and unpolished when he most wanted polish and skill.

He was as inexperienced in this new loving as if it were the first time for him.

With every kiss and touch, he yearned to give her everything he knew how, to make her see what a wonder she was. And slowly, as she touched him shyly but with eagerness, he came to understand the truth of what he'd said. What they were doing had nothing to do with experience, but everything to do with the heart.

He told her so in low, husky words that praised her, cherished her. "What a wonder you are, sweetheart. I wanted to turn you inside out with pleasure, but you make me tremble with every touch.''

"Do I?" She blew gently into the line of hair on his abdomen.

"Unlike you, I can't hide what I feel." Shuddering, he struggled to slow his responses, to ease the pace. It was too early.

She smiled against his belly as long, rolling vibrations moved through him. "I like making you tremble. Do you know how powerful that makes me feel?" Reaching down, she touched him.

He jerked. "Be my guest, Elly. I've always liked a woman who knew what she wanted," he gasped. Deep tremors ran over him, down to his toes, as her fingers closed around him.

"I remember."

Treasuring her, he used every ounce of his discipline, everything he'd learned about lovemaking, to take her into a place where she'd never been.

And in taking her there, he found himself.

With her in those moments of exquisite pleasure as he rocked inside her, filling her and reaching higher, in those moments when her sighs and surprised cries rippled over him, he felt the emptiness in his soul dissolving and disappearing. With Elly, he was not alone. Her hands sliding along his thighs and his buttocks spoke of her desire.

She was not a passive lover.

She touched him as he touched her, learning the language of his body as he learned hers. Where she touched, he burned ice-hot. Where he touched her, her body flushed with heat under his fingertips.

He edged Beau's shirt up her stomach, over her breasts, using the soft fabric and sliding it against her in a new kind of teasing that left her breathless and laughing.

"Ah, I said you were a wicked man, didn't I?" Her soft laughter ended on a gasp. "I had no idea, none at all. Oh, Royal," she whispered. "Please don't stop. I love your wicked ways."

Wet from his kisses, her nipples shone in the dim light, and he skimmed the hem of the shirt over them, lightly. As they puckered and grew hard, he kissed them again, raking his teeth gently over them until she was twisting in agitation beneath him, and she gave a sharp, bewildered cry. Her shivers deepened, and he felt the clench of her inner muscles on him and he shuddered with her, their bodies moving slickly together toward some far shore he'd never seen, never known.

"Yes," she whispered, wrapping her legs around his hips as he reached between them, "yes." She lifted her hips against his, curved up toward him, shaking. "I thought that was a myth."

"Do you like that, sweetheart?" He reached higher.

She jolted, and the internal quakes of her response drew him deeper into her, deeper into loving that merged his self with hers until he couldn't tell which trembles and shivers were hers, which his.

And suddenly there was nothing except the furious pounding of his heart, hers, and her voice crying out his name. In time with that ancient rhythm of their hearts, their bodies merged, beat against each other until time and space and boundaries shattered and he no longer knew who he was.

When he lay facing her, their bodies still joined, he swept her hair back from her face and kissed that line of courage that marked her forehead. A faint shine of perspiration dewed her body, and he tasted the sweet saltiness of her breasts.

Her hair spread across the pillow, him, she was already asleep.

He would tell her in the morning, he promised himself. But not tonight, not while she was wrapped in his arms and happy, not while the aching emptiness in him was filled with her.

There would be time in the morning.

But in the morning, she was sleepy eyed and rumpled and plastered against him, laughing drowsily as he stroked the narrow length of her back, and it was still raining, that gray, cool downpour that veiled the world outside the window in mystery and left them inside in a world where nothing mattered except the pleasure of touching.

Of loving.

"Good morning, Elly." He shifted, bringing her on top of him, where she sprawled in delectable abandon.

"Morning." She stifled a tiny yawn. Creased and unruly, her hair fizzed and foamed around her sleepy cat face. Marked with his kisses, her breasts and belly showed pale blue spots. Gently, he brushed his fingers over those signs, the imprint of his passion. She stretched like a cat, too, unwinding. Her face scrunched and wrinkled with an enormous yawn, and then she opened her eyes and looked down at him.

Her face burned with brilliant color that swept over her neck and breasts. "Mm-hmm."

Rising, he cradled her fanny in his hands and kissed her breasts, her mouth, in long, deep kisses that sent heat and hunger rocketing through him. "Say 'hello,' Elly."

"Hello, Elly," she repeated obediently on another yawn that lifted her breasts and made them tremble in fine, distracting quavers.

"Not much good at morning conversation without your coffee, sweetheart?" He concentrated on one pink, delicate nipple as she sighed and collapsed bonelessly over him.

She was all languid, warm woman. Elly, sweet and yielding and so soft that he silenced the warning voices in his head. Tamping down the fierce hunger that whipped him, he took her slowly, carefully, in a gentle loving as they turned and murmured softly in the rain-drenched gray light.

His last thought as he plummeted into sleep was that he would tell her in the afternoon. He slept, her arms loose around his neck, her legs entangled with his.

Looking down at Royal as he lay sleeping beneath her, Elly brushed her fingers lightly over his golden head, down the strong column of his neck and into the springy gold of his chest hair. Wonder filled her. She'd taken a risk. She'd stepped off the edge of the world into this richness she'd never understood.

Words were words, after all, pale ghosts to the reality. His chest hair prickled against her fingertips.

From the first, she'd been attracted to him, drawn to him, in spite of every reason not to. But he'd stayed at her side, protecting her stubbornly every time she tried to send him away. What she felt for him now filled her to the brim, overwhelmed her.

She was afraid she'd let herself fall in love with this difficult, complicated man.

And if she had? What then?

Skimming the bruises along his ribs, she decided she didn't care. She'd never imagined that she could be such a sensual, wanton female, and the discovery delighted her. No matter what happened to her during the rest of her life, she couldn't regret these moments.

She'd known her life would change when she made the decision to trust Royal and his friends, and now she trembled on the brink of a life she'd never imagined.

She wanted all the richness, all the complexity of the coming years. She wanted *everything,* and she wasn't going to allow Blake to cheat her of even one of those days. Never again.

Sliding quietly out of the bed, she picked up her clothes, dressed in one of Beau's T-shirts and belts and headed toward the kitchen.

She was starving. All her senses were hyperalert, more intense. The smell of the rain and damp earth coiled through her, the smell of cooking bacon made her mouth water and, as she turned the bacon, the cool metal fork was as sleek and smooth as Royal—

She flushed and flipped the bacon.

When the scents of coffee and bacon woke Royal, she heard his grunt as his feet hit the floor. "Elly?" Alarm crackled in his voice. In two strides, he was up and loping down the hall. "Elly!"

"In here."

Naked, he stood in the doorway, his golden hair rumpled, his face beard bristled, every inch of him fierce and ready for battle.

"Hey," she said, shyness leaving her speechless.

He took a deep breath and blew it out. The aura of danger vanished as he smiled at her and left her quivering inside. "I thought you'd left."

Tipping her head to the side, she waggled the bacon fork in his direction. "Now, why would I do that? You weren't that bad, Royal. Really," she consoled him, dodging his outstretched arms.

"Golly, I know," he said pitifully. "It's a shame, isn't it, sugar? But I think practice might help." He hauled her up against him, and the fork skittered across the floor as she dropped it. "Want to practice, sweetheart?" His mouth swooped over hers. "I'm ready, willing and—"

"I can tell," she murmured, standing on tiptoe and curling her fingers into his hair. "You do a lot for the concept of advertising, buster, let me tell you." She wiggled experimentally against him. "Oh, yes. That's a great idea. I think practice would do us both a world of good."

The belt around her T-shirt clattered to the floor, slithered along the wooden planks to rest near the bacon fork.

She welcomed Royal's roughness, his wild hunger as he backed her up against the kitchen table and lifted her onto it. That she could leave him shaking and out of breath astonished her. For so long she'd known only Blake's domination, and now to have power over Royal, over this man's body and heart, moved her to tears.

Letting her see the feminine power she had over him, Royal gave her a gift beyond price. He restored to her the self she'd lost.

All during the long, rainy day and into the early afternoon when the sun finally broke through the bank of low clouds, they practiced.

In those final moments, Elly felt despair in Royal's urgent touches, in his intense control that shattered only when he'd wrung a final, keening cry from her.

"Elly, forgive me," he said, and then, not leaving her there in the backwash of her climax, he drove her up again, taking her with his hands and mouth until she was incoherent with pleasure, the touch and scent of him burned permanently into her skin, her heart.

They waited for Beau's call in the bedroom to the sound of the dripping oaks and pines outside the window.

And then Royal told her.

"What?" Unbelieving, she faced him, waiting for the punch line. She saw the tiredness, heard his words, and none of it made sense, not now. "My ex-husband hired you to find me?"

Crossing his arms, he nodded abruptly, his face closed and forbidding. "He offered three hundred thousand dollars if I would bring you to him. Not Tommy, you. To talk. About the custody arrangements."

"What are you saying?" she asked stupidly. "I don't understand."

"I met Blake Scanlon at a private, high-stakes poker game. I lost everything I owned. He offered to pay my debts if I would make arrangements to get you to a neutral place where he could talk to you. He said you'd kidnapped Tommy, faked your death so you could run away with him. Scanlon said all he wanted was to discuss custody."

"That's why you were at the beach? You'd followed me?"

He nodded. His face was scoured of emotion. The lines around his mouth and eyes stood out in stark relief. The yellowing bruises and scrapes were ugly in the stern contours of his face.

Elly could feel the blood draining from her head as she swayed in front of him. "I'm sorry, I can't make sense of what you're saying." She shook her head. "You're not making sense."

"I called him and told him I'd made contact with you. That I'd talked with you."

"You called him?" Her mouth was dry. "You told Blake where I was?"

He hesitated, and she yearned for him to tell her she was misunderstanding, that she'd gotten the wrong message. But again he nodded, a silent executioner who held her life, her son's life, in his hands.

"You betrayed me." Staring at him, she struggled to find the sanity in all the craziness. "You wouldn't have agreed to what he asked." She didn't know whether she was begging him to deny what he'd told her or trying to convince herself. "I know you, Royal, you *couldn't* have done that!"

"I did."

"No," she moaned, shaking her head back and forth. "No!"

"Yes." He shifted, moving away from her, and his back was to the window and the blaze of sunlight that washed the world outside the cabin. "I warned you not to trust me, Elly."

"There must be an explanation. Please! Tell me." She grabbed his shirt.

"I agreed to Scanlon's terms." All the angles and planes of his face were carved in pain. "I called him when I found you."

"Won't you defend yourself?" she whispered, stricken with pain and loss.

"I called Scanlon," he repeated.

She pounded his chest. "You betrayed my child! How could you do that? How?" Sobbing and screaming in terror and bewilderment, she beat against the hard muscles of his chest.

"What am I going to do? You've set me up, haven't you?

You've made it easy for Blake to kill me this time, haven't you? And what will you do? Watch? Oh, God,'' she cried, drumming her fists into him. "Damn you, Royal, damn you.''

Not once did he lift a hand to stop her. Not once. Solid, silent, he took every blow, every word she screamed at him. She longed for him to defend himself, to explain.

He didn't.

On the nightstand with its spill of condoms, the cellular phone rang.

Royal snared her wrist, held tight as he reached for the phone and punched the Send button. "Yeah, me. What the hell? How'd they disappear?'' Narrowed and fierce, his eyes met hers. "Elly and I should leave here. Now.'' He waited, his grip tight against her as she tugged against him, wanting to flee. "All right. Until tomorrow. No longer. I swear, Beau, heads will roll.'' Royal tapped the End key and laid the phone down, studying her intently.

"What happened?'' She plucked at his fingers. Tears of fear and rage streaked her cheeks.

"The goons vanished.''

"What?'' Frantically, she tugged against him, ready to bolt into the wilderness, prepared to hitchhike back to her son if she had to. "Turn me loose!''

"I can't.'' Royal stooped and rummaged amid the clumps of wrappers and clothes. The click of the handcuff around her wrist was loud in the silence that fell between them. "I can't do that, Elly. I can't let you leave.''

"You can't stop me.'' She yanked at the links he still held.

"I have to.'' He looked around the room, at the stand, the chest of drawers, the beds. "If you leave, Scanlon will pick you off like a sitting duck.''

"That's what you want, isn't it?'' Appalled, she dug her heels against the floor, her sneakers scraping the wood as he half lifted, half pulled her toward the bed she'd slept in. "And then you'll get your thirty pieces of silver.''

"Is that what I want, Elly?'' He closed the second bracelet around the iron post of the bed, below the heavy knob that topped it. "If you say so.'' Hunkered down, he searched for the key. Finding it, he stuffed it into his pocket and swiveled to look at her.

He looked like a man caught on the rack, tortured to the breaking point, she thought vaguely. "Don't do this to me, Royal, please."

"Elly, if you run from here, you'll run straight into Scanlon. You'll have no protection at all." He reached to touch her knee, and she jerked away.

"Don't touch me. Just...don't. I couldn't bear it."

His eyes were remote and distant. "Whatever you say." He stood up and strode to the window.

Later, she would remember his expression in that moment as he turned away. Now, though, she fought to sort through the mess she was in. Tugging at the restraint, Elly sank onto the bed. her sneakers sliding off with her abrupt movement. "You have to unlock these. Don't you see what you're doing?"

His bark of laughter was harsh, self-directed. "No, damned if I do. Not anymore." His shoulders slumped forward, and he raised his arm, resting his forehead on it.

"Why are you doing this to me, Royal?" She rattled the links against the bed pole. "It's unforgivable."

"I'm trying to save your life." He whirled to face her, and his expression was dreadful in its pain and torment. "I'll do whatever I have to do to keep you safe."

"You're taking away my choices, Royal. You're making yourself responsible for me. You're not. I have the right to make my own decisions about my life, make my own mistakes." She jerked angrily against the cuff. "I'm *not* your responsibility."

"You are. I created this mess. I have to make it right."

"At my expense?" She rattled the chain again. "I'll never forgive you for this, Royal. I couldn't." Meeting his gaze, she willed him to understand. "You know about pride, Royal. I have mine, too. Don't steal it from me."

"Will you promise to stay here? Where I can protect you?" Harsh with control, his expression was bleak.

"I won't promise anything. But if you keep me chained here, you're killing me as surely as Blake tried to."

Royal winced.

"This is wrong. Can't you see that?" She held her wrist out to him.

"You're right." He reached down into his pocket. The key flashed between them as he looked down at it. "Elly—"

"Don't ask, Royal."

He inserted the key, twisted and took off the handcuff. "I have to ask. Please don't leave. I'm begging you."

"You can't make me stay here with force." Rubbing her wrist, she never took her eyes off him.

"No." Kneeling before her, he touched her wrist gently, and grimaced as she flinched. "I can't use force against you, Elly, even for your own good. I'm not asking you to trust me, but will you stay because I'm telling you it's the safest thing for you?"

Anger and sadness commingled. "I don't know. That's the best I can give you. It'll have to do."

"Elly, I don't want anything to happen to you."

"Listen to me. I don't need rescuing. I don't need a knight on a white horse using me as a decorative accessory while he proves his manhood. Blake did that do me. I swore I'd never let it happen again. *Don't try to rescue me, Royal.*"

They never heard him come in.

He was just there suddenly, framed in the doorway. "Isn't this touching?"

Lunging to his feet, Royal turned around, stepping in front of her and the shiny blue-steel gun her ex-husband pointed at her. "Scanlon."

"Blake!" Elly stepped out from behind Royal and to the side, separating herself from Royal, giving Blake two targets, giving one of them a chance.

"Very noble, Abigail, or would you prefer your *nom du jour,* Elly?" He turned the gun on Royal. "But your gesture is wasted. If you make a run for it, I'll shoot your...lover. He is, isn't he, Abby? By now?"

She didn't answer. Her foot poised to run toward him, she placed it firmly on the floor.

"Much better. Smart, even for you. I know you won't leave him. And if he tries to rush me, why, Abby, the detective knows I'll put a bullet right through your pretty little head. I don't remember you being this pretty, by the way. Congratulations, Detective."

"Good-looking Smith & Wesson, Scanlon. Big .357, long barrel. Not overcompensating by any chance, are you?" Royal edged toward Elly, a movement she felt rather than saw.

She didn't let her gaze drift toward him.

"Excellent, Gaines, that psychological dig of yours. But pointless."

"Where are your muscle men? Why are you doing the dirty work this time?" Elly spit out the words, loathing this man she'd let rule her life for so long.

"Hard to find good help these days." Blake Scanlon frowned. "They made too many mistakes. I can't afford any more errors."

"And why is that?" Royal's foot edged infinitesimally her way.

Blake tapped one finger against his chin. "Didn't Elly tell you why she went back to our home?" He smiled, and chills ran over her. "Ah, I see she didn't. Such a shame you're so predictable, Abby. Not wanting to involve other people. But that's your fatal flaw." His gaze flicked to the floor, back to them. "Now, Detective—are you enjoying my irony, Gaines, my references to the career you sent down the toilet?"

"Can't quit laughing," Royal drawled.

"Go pick up the handcuffs and sit on the bed. Put one cuff around your wrist. *Now*, Gaines. Or I'll switch my rather beautiful scenario for one more immediate, one that involves Abby's blood and brains spattered around the room. Do you like that plan better?"

Elly didn't breathe as Royal stared at her ex-husband and then moved across the room. "Okay. I'm sitting, I'm putting on the cuff. See?" Royal swung the metal in front his face. "Now what, Scanlon?"

"All right. Very good. Abby, go over and pull the cuff around the metal rod of the bed. Put the other cuff on your wrist."

"No."

"Elly!" Royal's voice was scratchy, and she didn't dare look at him as he threw her words back at her. "I don't need rescuing, thank you very much. Do what he says."

"No." Gripping her hands together, she shook from head to toe. "He's going to kill us both, Royal. I'm not going to make it easy for him. Don't you get it?"

"I *get it*, Elly. But do what he says. Please, sweetheart."

"Very good advice, Detective, and I'm touched by your concern for my former wife. But Abby's right. Make no mistake. I am going to kill you both. It's merely a question of how."

"Blake, you don't have to kill Royal. He doesn't know anything. He was only helping me."

"He hasn't told you he was working for me, has he?" Blake stepped farther into the room, staying well clear of her and Royal.

She nodded stiffly. "He told me."

"Foolish, but, Abby, he was going to die anyway. With you. In a car accident, as he supposedly brought you to me to discuss our custody of Tommy. I hoped it would look as if you'd run off with your lover and kidnapped our son. But Gaines kept delaying. He wasn't doing what he was supposed to. So I sent Harold and Markey to give him a little encouragement."

"They were very encouraging," Royal said, his voice filled with menace. The handcuff rattled against the bedpost.

"You knew where I was? All along?" Elly tried to follow the slippery trail of her former husband's thinking.

"Of course. I told Gaines where you were. Actually, Abby, you deserve congratulations. You weren't easy to find. You were very cautious. Now go do what I told you," he said with silky humor, "or I'll shoot your detective friend. Can you live with that?"

She couldn't. She sat. She worked the links under the iron top of the bedpost, clicked the smooth metal around her own wrist.

"Splendid." Blake walked completely into the room. "One more point, Abby. You have something I want. The tapes. And my son. First, where's Thomas?"

She clamped her trembling lips together.

"You're being stupid, Elly. I'll find him eventually. When you don't return, whoever has him will get in touch with the authorities or your parents, and I'll have my son back where he belongs. I expected you'd leave him with the Williams woman, but you didn't."

"What else were you expecting, Scanlon? I'm curious." Royal's knee nudged hers.

In one quick blink, she glanced where his foot pointed under his bed.

Scanlon pivoted toward him. "Incidentally, Detective, if you're wondering, I found you through property records." Laughing, he sat down on the bed opposite them, out of reach.

"Well, *I* didn't. My source traced you through your former partner and his brothers. Not a difficult task, I hear. A fisherman last night spotted the lights in the cabin. That was that. And here I am."

"Blake, if you kill us, it doesn't matter. No one knows where I left the tapes."

Next to her, Royal started.

"So, she really didn't tell you, Detective? Shame. Noble Abby. You wanted to protect him, didn't you? You might have saved yourself if you'd told him. But probably not. No one would have believed you, and my plan was already set in motion."

"The plan to kill both of us and make it look as though we were lovers running off together?" The metal links rattled again with Royal's words.

Blake nodded. "Yes, Detective. That one, the plan that leaves me a grieving father whose wife abandoned him when he'd given her everything. But I want those tapes, Abby. They're not at the house. I've torn it apart. Even disemboweled Thomas's toys. That was a mess." He waggled the gun between them as he mused, "You wouldn't have sent them to your parents. You're too noble to endanger them. Your veterinarian friend Meggie knows nothing—"

"What did you do to her?" Elly pulled against the cuff.

"Nothing. We talked. I could tell you kept her in the dark, too. The tapes weren't in your tacky house or your car. So you've locked them away somewhere, some place you can get to any time you want. You've really impressed me, Abby. I didn't think you could." He pointed the gun at Royal. "But I'm bored with all this discussion. Where are those tapes?"

"What's on the tapes, Scanlon? Satisfy my curiosity, will you? Since you're going to shoot us anyway."

"Oh, I'm not going to shoot you, Detective. And I know you think you're buying time. You're not. You and *Elly* are going to die in a rather kinky scene, handcuffed there, together, candles blazing romantically."

Royal yanked forward, and Elly's arm scraped along the horizontal bar of the metal frame. "Sorry, sweetheart." The glance he shot her was frighteningly fierce. "Hang in there."

"Not much else she can do, is there?" Blake asked reasonably. "Unfortunately for you both, those candles are going to start a fire. Tragic, really."

"Elly, what's on the tapes?" Royal reached up with his free hand and cupped her chin. "Tell me. You don't need to keep any more secrets."

"All right." It was a relief to tell him. "There were five tapes. I'd hidden the first three. I went back for the other two, and Blake's friends ambushed me. You'll never find the tapes, Blake. None of them." She smiled. "Never. But others will. Sooner or later. And then you'll be destroyed, no matter what you do to me."

"You underestimated her, Scanlon." Royal's smile was terrifying.

"Apparently I did." Blake scowled.

She shifted awkwardly towards Royal. "Blake knew I'd found the tapes. That was why he tried to kill me the first time. I found messages on the answering machine. There were electrical outages, and the machine had to be reset, and I heard these old messages to Blake. He thought I was too stupid to understand, or he would have made sure they were completely erased. There was a message from Mike Gannon. I knew who he was. I bought miniature, voice-activated tape recorders and hid them in Blake's office. So that I could buy mine and Tommy's freedom."

"My God, Elly." Royal reached to her hand and held it. "Mike Gannon's behind the biggest land deal in the state's history. The one that's going to turn ten thousand acres of timber into concrete city. If it's crooked, nasty or illegal, Gannon's got a finger in it. Drugs, smuggling in illegal immigrants. Zoning laws. Bribery. He's on every cop's list. But he pays his taxes, he's discreet and no one's pinned anything on him. Too much money behind him. Too many politicians in his pocket. You must have been terrified." His grip on her hand was warm and gave her strength.

"I've been frightened ever since I found the first tape, but I thought I could use the tapes as insurance. I thought I'd be safe if Blake knew I'd release the tapes tying him to Gannon.

"But then Blake tried to have me killed, and I knew I'd never be safe again. All I wanted," she said brokenly, "was to live my life and take care of my child. I knew Blake wouldn't hurt

Tommy—oh, Blake would use Tommy against me to make me surrender the tapes, I knew that. I couldn't leave my son. But I shouldn't have gone back for the last tapes. I didn't think you knew I had them, Blake, so I took the risk. For extra insurance.''

Blake stood up impatiently. ''I found one by accident at the office. That was when I knew you had others. Gannon and I agreed. You had to be eliminated, the other tapes found. I have to have those tapes, Abby. Or Gannon will kill me, too.''

''I don't care.'' She wouldn't cry in front of him, she wouldn't, but, oh, for everything to end like this—

''But I do.'' Blake reached into the satchel and pulled out several candles, placing them strategically around the room. When they were all lit, their flames dancing in the windowpane, he turned to her once again. ''You believe you won't tell me about the tapes, but you will. Oh, not to save yourself pain. I won't underestimate you again. You'll talk to save him.'' He leveled the gun at Royal and pulled the trigger.

The explosion was deafening, and the shock of Royal's arm and body jerking back against the bed had her screaming. Blood from his right shoulder soaked into the pillows and sheets as he slumped white-faced against the bed frame.

''That's a warning, Abby. The next bullet goes to his knee, then his belly. That's a lot of pain. Death is one thing, pain another. Are you going to tell me about the tapes?''

Sick with fear, she tugged at Royal's slumping body. ''They're in separate lockers at the Tampa airport. The numbers and combinations are on my sneakers. Over there,'' she said frantically as he pointed the gun at Royal again. ''The ones I painted. The numbers of the lockers are on the sneakers, Blake!''

He pulled out the shoes. ''So they are. I have what I need, then, don't I? Except for the locker keys. Where are they kept, Abby?''

''At my tacky house! Taped to the bottom of the bedroom door!'' She pulled at Royal's cuffed arm.

''Thank you, Abby. Markey missed them. But he's paid for his mistake. Now it's your turn.''

Pulling the sheet off the bed, he draped it over the mound of clothes and placed its edge near one of the sputtering candles on the floor. Emptying the gun, he kept the silver cylinders in his hand, tossing one of them up and down and finally scattering all of them into the hall. Wiping the gun, he went toward Elly and forced her hand around the grip before letting the gun fall to the floor. Spotting the glitter of metal on the floor, he bent down and retrieved the handcuff key.

Behind him, smoke rose in a lazy spiral from the sheet.

"I think that finishes everything here. The tabloids will have a field day with this scandal, but I'll bear it bravely." He waved tauntingly. "Ciao, Abby. I'll take good care of my son."

Smoke puffed up from the sheet as it glowed red.

Chapter 16

Choking on smoke, Elly coughed and pushed at Royal. Sparks were flying to the floor, the bedding. "Royal, help me."

He grunted. "The phone. Under the bed. I kicked it there when the bastard came in. Call Beau—" He coughed.

"There's no time," she wailed, stretching her leg as far as she could. The distance last night had seemed so narrow when she'd finally crossed to him, when she'd risked herself to reach out for what she wanted and needed. Last night, the distance had seemed like the distance between life and death. Now, in fact, that small space was impossibly far and death unbearably near.

Royal pulled himself as close as he could to the frame that imprisoned them. His eyes blazed at her hotter and more brilliant than the flames licking up the far wall. Encouraging her, sending her a message of faith and hope. And something else. "You can do it, sweetheart."

She couldn't. The distance was too far. She was too short. Her glance swept the room. There had to be another way. The lamp on the stand was tall and skinny, its shade out of proportion. Shoving the lamp onto the floor, she worked it and its shade forward with her feet, directing it toward the head of the bed as Royal nodded.

"That's it, sweetheart. See if you can hook the phone and drag it closer."

If the phone had been at the foot of the bed, she couldn't have reached it.

The exhilaration that swept over her was crazy, insane, wonderful. They were still chained to the metal bed frame that was now hot to the touch. Hanging off the edge of the bed, she swept the phone toward them and picked it up. She tapped out the emergency number Royal gave her and handed it to him.

"Where are the other tapes, Elly? The ones in the house?"

"Taped inside the wall behind the phone jacks."

"Good woman. You may not think you trust me, but we make a swell team, sugar. That means *something*." With a bullet in his blood-smeared shoulder and bruises still marking him, coughing with smoke-filled lungs, he was incandescent with energy, an energy that carried over to her and made her believe they would survive in spite of the crackling and spitting of the fire as it swooshed up the walls to the ceiling. He coughed into the phone. "We're about ninety seconds from being crispy critters here, Beau. ASAP, buddy."

Sweat drenched, Elly regarded Royal solemnly. "Okay. We've called in the cavalry. But I'd like to leave, if you don't mind."

"Hell, sugar, I don't mind at all. But damned if I see how we're going to."

She didn't, either. Suffocating with smoke, she doubled over. "It's getting hard to breathe." Her eyes rolled back, and she sagged onto the bed.

Royal leaned forward and kissed her, breathing his air into her again and again, giving her time. Sparks rained down on him as he scrambled to pull out the sheet underneath them and cover her with it. It looked like the fates were going to cheat them out of the time they needed. And he wanted time with Elly. With Tommy. He wanted *time*.

Beau couldn't get anyone to them soon enough, not even with helicopters. Scanlon would be stopped, but he and Elly would be ashes.

Looking at Elly's sooty, unconscious form, Royal roared, a

raw, animal sound of pain and fury. He'd be damned if he was going to let her die like this. Not his Elly, and by God, she was his, whether she'd admit it or not. She'd been right with him while he played Scanlon for time. Smooth as the Texas two-step, she'd followed his lead and given them the small chance they had.

Working the cuff around his left wrist furiously against the horizontal bar, he studied the post. The bulbous top was welded onto the post. It couldn't be lifted off. The horizontal bar was solid and too thick. Roaring, he jerked up against it, again and again, willing it with all his adrenaline-fueled energy to break.

Coughing, Elly stirred against him. "Wait," she said, straining to speak. "I can get my hand out."

He didn't see how she possibly could without cutting it off.

Standing upright, she pulled against the cuff and folded her thumb under her palm. Coughing and fighting for breath, she jerked against the cuff, trying to slide her small hand free.

He could see the red, bloody streaks where the metal scraped into her skin, and rage exploded inside him. She'd never be able to get her hand free. She was going to die here in this smoke-filled cabin, and there wasn't anything he could do to save her. "Damn you, Scanlon," he roared, and lifted upward with all his strength against the frame, shoving and pulling and lunging against the bar that was going to kill them.

Banging and smacking against the wall, the narrow headboard flew free of the mattress supports and hung from the chain between Elly and him.

Soot and ashes smeared her face as she looked at him, uncomprehending.

"Did you ever enter the potato-sack race, sugar, when you were a kid?"

She nodded, and looked at the heavy rectangle. "Okay. Lead the way."

He did. Holding the sheet over them, he shoved her in front of him, lifting her over the floorboards that burst into flames underneath them. He scooped up one of the cartridges and the gun, loading it one-handed and ignoring the shrieking pain in his shoulder.

Scanlon was a shadow under the tree at the edge of Michael's property. Royal took aim, pointing the gun at the man who'd almost destroyed Elly, who'd terrified her and never given her credit for courage and heart. Sweat poured into Royal's eyes. Staring at that figure, the figure of the man who'd fathered Tommy, Royal hesitated, only an instant. Maybe it was his sweat-blurred vision. Maybe it was pain and exhaustion. Maybe it was the reluctance to face Tommy with the blood of his father on his hands. Whatever, that hesitation gave Scanlon the time he hadn't given Elly and Royal.

Growling with frustration, Royal dropped the gun and ran with Elly toward the creek and safety.

In that mad dash, the head frame dragging between them, Royal threw his head back and shouted with laughter. "Sweetheart, by God, we're going to make it. I love you, Elly Malloy."

At the creek, he bathed her feet and his in the tepid water while the cabin burned behind them. Blisters were already forming on her feet, and scarcely aware of the sharp pain in his shoulder, he dragged her into his lap to keep her from trying to walk down the rough shore. "Wait, Elly. Beau will be here soon. You're going to be all right. And then you'll see Tommy."

Holding her like that while Michael's cabin crackled and blazed against the sky, Royal realized how close they'd come to death. He'd almost lost her.

Instead, against all understanding, he'd saved her. And that was enough. Watching the sparks fly against the dark sky, he smiled. Elly was alive. Anything was possible. Even forgiveness.

When Beau finally arrived, the cabin was smoldering ashes, the wood glowing red in the darkness. "Remind me not to lend you anything again, Royal." Beau contemplated the ruins. "They caught Scanlon. Fortunately, it was after he ran his car into a tree."

"Dead?" Royal coughed. "Better this way. On Elly. On Tommy."

"Yep." Beau glanced over where paramedics had strapped Elly to a cart and clamped an oxygen mask over her face. "She's going to be okay."

"Yeah." Inhaling smoke-tinged fresh air, Royal couldn't stop the grin from spreading across his face. "She sure is."

Impatient to go to Elly, Royal let the emergency-room surgeon stitch him up. The wound was mostly a flesh wound that looked worse than it was, and he fidgeted, trying to hurry the doctor who was putting in careful, neat stitches that seemed to take forever.

But Elly wouldn't let him see her. She told Beau and Leesha to keep him away. Grimacing in sympathy, they did. The police retrieved the tapes. Scanlon's will, unchanged since before the divorce, left everything to Tommy. Elly was appointed executor of the estate, or whatever would be left after the legal tangle was straightened out.

And during the long, lonely days without her, Royal kept busy. He nursed his bruises, his sore shoulder, and felt the tenderness move through him stronger with each day, changing him as if he'd been reborn in that creek in the Everglades.

He played solitaire and thought about the past year of his life, the turns and twists it had taken. Thought about pride. And consequences. And loneliness. He thought a lot about that state of being. And about Elly, alone, raising Tommy.

He thought a lot about Elly and how she'd made love with him, to him. A woman like her didn't give herself easily. Those moments had been important to her.

He thought about Maggie, too, and how he'd thought he was in love with her.

He knew what he wanted now, what he needed as much as the air he breathed. Elly. And Tommy. Tommy, who looked at him as if Royal held all the answers to all the unasked questions the kid would ever have. Tommy, who needed a father. Elly, who needed... Well. Royal hoped she needed him. Wanted him. Shuffling the cards, he watched their smooth surfaces blend one into the other, the bright, gay designs shifting back and forth. He'd gambled everything away once. Why couldn't he win everything of importance back? Riffling the cards in a lightning-quick movement, he looked around his house. Elly liked his house. Tommy liked him. And he was nuts about the silly kid. And Elly? Well, she'd do anything for her kid.

Royal flicked the cards down. Hell's bells. Every gambling man ought to have an ace up his sleeve.

He found her alone in her ticky-tacky house, a house he'd grown quite attached to, despite Scanlon's quite accurate assessment of its architecture. He rang the doorbell politely and waited. When she opened the door, he said, "Still don't check to see who's at your door?"

"I knew." Her hair was shorter, the burned ends trimmed. Her feet and wrist were bandaged, and she was wearing baggy shorts and a ratty shirt tied under her breasts, and she was beautiful.

He stuck out the glossy bouquet of pink roses and baby's breath. "Here."

Her mouth twitched, and hope leapt in him. Painful, invigorating, that sense of caring, of love.

"Aren't you going to ask me in?"

"That's not a good idea." She took the flowers and buried her face in them. "These are so...sweet," she whispered.

"Yeah." He shifted uncomfortably. "Let me in, Elly. I have to talk with you. And when we're through, if you don't want to see me ever again, you won't."

Startled, she lifted her eyes to his, hesitated and then swung the door open. "All right. Come in. We'll have to sit in the kitchen, though. My landlady decided she wanted her couch back."

"A decorating steal."

Leading the way to the kitchen, she looked back over her shoulder at him. In the gloomy hall, he thought she almost smiled. Or maybe it was wishful thinking.

"Sit."

"Yes, ma'am." He folded himself into her uncomfortable chair.

She did smile then. "What did you want to talk about, Detective? Yes, Beau told me. I'm happy for you, Royal, that you're back doing what you love." She shrugged. "Really, I mean that."

"I know." He leaned over the table and fanned out the cards he'd brought with him. Their gaudy faces gleamed against the scratched and gouged table. "Where's Tommy?"

"He's spending the night at Katie's. They're having pizza."

"Oh." He smoothed the cards back and forth into elaborate, intricate designs. "Why wouldn't you let me see you, Elly? At the hospital? Why did you make my friends keep me away from you? I was worried about you. Tell me why, Elly." He stacked the cards in front of him.

"I had to figure out what I wanted out of life, what I wanted the rest of my life to be like. What I felt about…*things.*" Her cheeks went pink.

"And what do you think…about *things,* Elly?"

She shrugged.

Eyeing her intently, recognizing the sturdy pride so like his own, Royal said, "Play one last game with me, Elly."

"What?" She sank into the chair opposite him and folded her legs beneath her so that her feet weren't resting on the floor. "You want me to play cards with you? You came over here for that?"

"Yeah. One hand. That's all. And then I'm out of your life."

"I see." She fanned the cards across the table. "And what are the stakes?"

"If I win, you have to spend one month with me, you and Tommy, getting to know me, letting me have a second chance, a chance to make up for what I did."

"And if I win?" she asked slowly, flipping the cards back and forth between her slim fingers.

"Then I'm out of your life for good. If that's what you want."

She leaned back and studied him. "One hand? A high-stakes poker game?"

"That's it."

"Deal, buster," she said, and leaned forward with a small smile.

Elly kept her eyes down as she picked up the cards. She couldn't believe what she was seeing. Finally, the cards sorted, she looked up. Royal's expression was as bland as custard pudding. He'd already sorted his cards and had laid them facedown, waiting for her.

"Want another card?"

"No, I…I think I'll stay." Darned right she would. Even she knew a royal flush was a pat hand, an impossibly lucky winning hand. Looking at the cards, she tried to figure out what Royal was up to.

"Forgiveness, Elly," he murmured, tapping his cards against the table. "Can you forgive me?"

She frowned. And then, in a flash so bright she wondered it didn't set the house to shaking, she understood. "You knew

Blake was up to something when you accepted his offer, didn't you, Royal?"

He nodded and tapped the cards.

"Why didn't you tell me? Why didn't you defend yourself? Why didn't you explain? Why did you let me believe you betrayed Tommy and me to him?"

"Because." He tapped the cards again and looked out the window.

"Pride."

He lined the edges of his cards up and didn't answer, but the pulse at the side of his forehead beat too quickly.

"You wanted me to have faith in you, no matter what."

Sighing, she laid her own cards faceup. "That's a dangerous habit, Royal. Testing people. Trust is a two-way street. You have to…you have to give them a bridge to cross." She felt heat rise wickedly up her neck, and she picked up her cards again. "Let me understand the bet here. If you win, you'll compel me and Tommy to spend time with you?"

"Yeah. That's about it." His expression never changed.

"You know you can't make me do that, don't you?"

"Honor. Fair play. You can't back out of a debt, Elly."

"So I hear. And if I win, I never have to see you or talk to you again? You'll disappear from my life? You promise?"

He nodded slowly, the light in his eyes dimming. "Yes."

"And you'll disappear from Tommy's life, too?"

He nodded. His mouth was clamped tight.

Elly shook her head. "I don't know if I believe that. See, I know you've read the story every day this week at the day-care center. You've taken the kids for ice cream, and you donated a wading pool to the center. Alicia keeps me informed." She picked up her cards again and studied them. There was no way she could lose with the hand he'd dealt her.

He had dealt the cards. She knew him. He'd deliberately lost once before. And now, the cheat, the scoundrel, was going to lose again, because he'd stacked the deck against himself. Lifting her eyes, she glared at him.

"Bad cards, sweetheart?" he asked sympathetically.

"Lousy." Hiding the excitement flooding her, she continued to glare at him. She finally understood his message. He was telling her the *choice* was up to her. He was giving her the control over what happened next. Well, she knew what she wanted, what she'd wanted since the night at the cabin. Slapping the cards down on the table, she said, "Sometimes a woman's got to know when to hold 'em, when to fold 'em. I fold. You win."

He knocked the table over getting to her, and cards sprayed across the dingy floor. "Do you know what you're agreeing to, sweetheart? Do you know what I want?"

"Want? An interesting term. A puny, paltry, halfhearted word, I think. What does it mean to you?"

"It means, witch—" he lifted her up against him and locked her legs in back of his waist "—that I want to live the rest of my life with you. And with Tommy the Curious. It means I want to be there at night when you go to sleep and in the morning when you wake up all drowsy and messy haired."

"Not a smooth talker, are you?" She rested her head on his chest.

"And it means I *want*—oh, Elly, I *want* like you've never imagined. If you want me even a tenth as much, you'd have to forgive me. I was trying to protect you, and I was arrogant and pushy, and—"

"Shut up, Detective. And kiss me. We'll work out the terms of payment in the morning."

"Whatever you say. I'm yours to command." He kissed her, his mouth slanting over hers.

"I like that. Commanding you," she whispered.

"I love you, Elly-Abby, whoever." He bumped into the door frame. "I could live without you if I had to. I thought it would be enough just to know you're in the world, alive. But don't send me away, Elly. Don't leave me out in the cold, alone. Without you. Without Tommy. Let me come home."

"And I thought you weren't a sweet-talking man," she said on a tiny sob. "Come home, Royal. And let me go there with you."

And in the dim afternoon that blended into night, he took them home.

She came to him across sands rosy gold with the late-afternoon sun, down a pathway lit with torches plunged into the sand dunes. Her pale pink dress was some gauzy, floaty thing that swirled around her like the clouds pink with the sunset. Her floppy, pale straw hat was trimmed with a long pink bow and pale roses. And if he'd thought he loved her before, that love was only a shadow of the love filling him now with each step she walked barefoot toward him, Tommy Lee by her side, her soft gaze never wavering from his.

Walking in front of her in a gaudy, glorious sarong, Leesha sent Beau an enigmatic glance. At Royal's side, Beau shifted, and a smile blazed across his face.

"I love you, Royal," Elly murmured as she reached him and curled her small hand into his. "I *choose* you, to spend my life with, to love, for all my days. And I trust you, Royal, with my heart, with my son, with my*self.*" Her smile was lit with sunshine and happiness.

"You gonna be my daddy?" Squinting up at him, Tommy dug a bare toe in the sand. "Forever?"

Royal squatted to face him. "Forever, Tommy Lee. That okay with you?"

Tommy nodded slowly, thoughtfully. "And you won't make my mommy cry? Ever?"

"I might. But she'll forgive me. And I'll love both of you with everything in my heart." Royal waited, watching Tommy's face. "Okay?"

Tommy slipped his hand into Royal's. "No problem."

Leaning over Tommy's head, Royal slanted his mouth over Elly's. "Let me love you, Elly. Please?"

"No problem," she murmured, opening her mouth to his and softening against him. "I wish you would."

Sinking into the glossy-smooth gulf, the sun flared around them, a message of hope, of redemption. Of forgiveness.

A pledge. A promise that darkness would yield to the light, that blaze of sunlight gilded Royal's hair, shone in his eyes as Elly kissed him back and felt the steady beat of his heart against hers, a promise of its own.

*   *   *   *   *

SILHOUETTE *Romance*

Escape to a place where a kiss is still a kiss...
Feel the breathless connection...
Fall in love as though it were
the very first time...
Experience the power of love!

Come to where favorite authors——such as
Diana Palmer, Stella Bagwell,
Marie Ferrarella and many more——
deliver heart-warming romance and genuine
emotion, time after time after time....

Silhouette Romance——
stories straight from the heart!

Silhouette®

TM

Where love comes alive™

Where love comes alive™

From first love to forever, these love stories are
for today's woman with traditional values.

 Desire

A highly passionate, emotionally powerful
and always provocative read.

V *Silhouette*

SPECIAL EDITION™

Emotional, compelling stories that capture the
intensity of living, loving and creating a family in
today's world.

V *Silhouette*

INTIMATE MOMENTS™

A roller-coaster read that delivers romantic thrills
in a world of suspense, adventure and more.

Visit Silhouette at www.eHarlequin.com

SDIR2